THE GHOST IN THE MACHINE

a novel

By dhtreichler

THE GHOST IN THE MACHINE

Chapter One: Thirty Days

Why is it so hard for me to open my eyes? Oh, it's bright. The light. Can't see yet. I keep blinking, hoping it won't be so bright. Why do I want to see? I don't know. I should be able to, but the images don't mean anything. That bright light is slowly giving way to what? A small room. Light colored walls. One is a monitor wall. One a window to the outside. As I stare for a moment, the images outside start to come into focus. No, it isn't that they're coming into focus. It's taking a moment to recognize them. What are they? Oh yes, live oak trees and blue sky beyond. It's sunny outside. Am I surprised at this? I don't know.

Where am I? I'm lying down. Is this a bed? No. No covers. Is it a table? Why would I be lying on a table? A massage maybe? No. I don't remember anything about a massage. I look around and see the equipment I'd normally see in a hospital. Did I have surgery? I don't know. I don't feel anything. No bandages. I'm not wearing a hospital gown. Seems to be a loose fitting running outfit. Do I run? I think so. Why don't I know what's going on or why I'm here?

Then the incredibly blonde and ever smiling Windy comes to my bedside, or tableside or whatever it is I'm lying on. "Hi. How you feelin'?" she says with her strong Texas drawl. Windy's my best friend from college. She's here with me so everything's alright.

"I don't know, fine I guess." I respond as I move my shoulders and try to understand why I was unconscious and why am I here. I don't remember how I got here or what's happened or happening to me.

The door opens and a tall, thin, good looking man comes in wearing a white coat over his street clothes. I know him. What's his name? Why am I having trouble remembering things? I shut my eyes for a long moment and it comes. Dr. Woodall. He's Dr. Bart Woodall. My doctor. I'm in a hospital. But I don't remember why.

The doctor nods to Windy, touches her arm as he approaches me. "How are you feeling, Sage?" Dr. Woodall greets me.

Sage? Is that my name? Sage what? "Confused. Why can't I remember?"

"You can sit up." He hasn't answered my question.

I sit up. No problem. No tender spots. I scooch to the edge of the table and let my feet dangle. They don't touch the floor. Should they have? I don't know. "Why am I here?"

Dr. Woodall holds out his hand to me. "Can you get up?"

I take his hand and step down onto the floor. I wobble for a moment and then everything seems fine. "Yes." I glance at Windy who is studying me with a look of concern, but I don't know why.

Dr. Woodall studies me, lets me hold his hand as he leads me to a chair, where I turn around and sit.

"Good. Can you retrace your steps? You should be able to." Dr. Woodall watches me carefully as I follow his instructions. When I reach the table I don't sit, just turn to face him. I'm curious as to why he's starting me out with baby steps.

"What's this all about? I don't remember an injury or accident or anything."

"Can you stand on one foot?" Still the doctor, checking out my reactions.

I comply with his request. I sway at first but instantly come back to straight up. "Now the other?"

This time I don't sway. No problem. "What are you looking for?" I'd like an answer to at least one of my questions.

"Connections." At least I know he's hearing me. "Come on over and sit down."

Again I comply with his request. Do I always comply with such requests? Am I intimidated by authority? Why am I asking this question? He pulls a chair over so he can look at me, not in the way a doctor normally examines you, but as someone has a quiet conversation. "How are you feeling?"

"Fine. So why am I here?" I answer to let him know I'm not happy about the lack of answers.

"I want to make sure you're ready to go home." His response is almost casual, as if it isn't a big deal. For some reason there's an underlying tension in his voice I'm reacting to. Why? Why am I reacting this way? I've known Dr. Woodall for a long time, haven't I? He is my doctor. He must have my best interests at heart. After all isn't that part of his oath or something?

"Am I?" I decide to play the game, since he isn't giving what I'm asking for.

"Soon." Non-committal. What's going on?

"Soon like today or soon like this year?" Guess I need to be a little pushier.

"Today, tomorrow. We'll see how the rest of the day goes."

Not what I want to hear. "Damn it Dr. Woodall. Tell me what's going on?"

He brightens. "So you recognize me. That's good. Tell me what else you remember."

"About what?" I don't know where to start.

"You apparently haven't remembered what's happened to you. So tell me what you do remember."

"AppleCore. Something about AppleCore. Does my husband work there? No, that's not right." I search my memory but it's like cutting through spider webs. I can see what's on the other side, but I'm reluctant to go there. Then it all comes in a rush. "No. I'm the SVP of Software Development for AppleCore."

"What about your husband? That was your first thought." Dr. Woodall sounds curious and Windy is even more curious than before.

I have to concentrate, it's still hard to find the answers in my head. "I don't have one."

"So why do you think that was your first thought?" Dr. Woodall seems to be trying to understand something, but he won't tell me what. Did I have a head injury? Is that why I'm here? Something that's making it hard for me to remember?

"No idea. But I have to get back to work. I can't stay here until tomorrow. I have deadlines." I'm seeing my office and the people I work with appear as if walking towards me. They're counting on me.

"Give it a rest, Sage." Windy chimes in. "You've been through a lot."

"You're fine." Dr. Woodall adds. "They aren't expecting you back until next week."

"Why is that?" I ask, not remembering making arrangements to be out.

"You're officially on vacation until then. Everyone thinks you're in a remote place without communications."

"Am I? In some remote place?" Why isn't my mind working right?

"You were in a place where you couldn't be reached." He

confirms.

"But I'm back now. I should call in." I'm antsy to get back to work.

"Until we know you're ready, I won't release you to return to work." Playing the authoritarian. Hmmm.

I'm not sure what he's saying, "When do you expect that to be?"

"We're kind of in uncharted territory here. Until we see how you adjust I just can't say for sure." Evasive. Something going on here and he doesn't want to tell me what. "So what else do you remember?"

"I'm feeling turmoil about my job. Something's wrong there. Did I have a breakdown? Is that what this is all about? Why I can't remember?"

"No, you didn't have a breakdown. Tell me about your family."

Why'd he change the subject of my job? It takes me a moment to change gears to answer his question. "Rocky, my father is an engineer. Named after some movie character. Something about being able to overcome impossible odds. Anyway he's hardware. Worked at AppleCore forever. He got me my job there. Not happy with me."

"Why isn't he happy with you?" Dr. Woodall seems surprised.

"He never forgave me for going over to the dark side – software. Thought engineers had to build something, not just tell it how to work." I grimace remembering he didn't talk to me for months.

"Your mother?"

"Anna Louise. I'm more like her." I see her face in my memory. "She talks with her eyes. You can see how she feels about you. Even though she seldom ever tells you, other than when you're bad."

"Siblings?"

"Younger sister Tabitha." As her image comes to me, the feeling rushes over me. "Oh god. She was in the car." I see the accident scene as my father and I came across it before they removed the bodies and hauled the wreckage away.

Windy steps between me and the doctor, holds my hand. "That was a long time ago. Don't get worked up about it."

"She died?" Dr. Woodall asks carefully.

I nod, and then add, "Anna Laura too." I'm overcome with the memories of loss. Memories of my mother and sister pass by my mind's eye. I can't respond to anything more until those memories release me. I don't tear up. That's strange. I normally tear up when I'm upset, don't I? Dr. Woodall must understand. He watches me for a few moments and then steps away leaving Windy still holding my hand.

"We've done enough for now. I'll be back soon. You need some time to process all this."

Chapter Two

Windy stays with me. Her answers to my questions are very careful. I don't remember her being this way. "What's going on?"

"You really don't remember?" she responds as if trying to be sure what she should or should not say.

"No. Do I have Alzheimers or something?"

"Not that I know of," she responds, trying to be reassuring, but doesn't succeed.

"So why am I here?" I want to know the answers and they aren't forthcoming.

"You were dying." Windy finally tells me the reason.

"Were?" I pick up on the verb tense.

"Dr. Woodall is really quite brilliant. He has just an amazing team here."

I glance out the window, don't recognize anything. "Where's here?"

"You're close to where I grew up. Dallas. We're at the University of Texas Southwestern Medical Center, better known as UT Southwestern."

"I don't live here. So why am I here?" The pieces I'm getting don't fit together.

"This is where they perfected the procedure you had."

THE GHOST IN THE MACHINE

"Procedure? What kind of procedure?"

"Dr. Woodall addressed your health issues." Still evasive, why?

"You seem to think I know what they are. I don't remember."

"Why don't you remember?" She's really making this hard.

"I don't know. You said I was dying."

"You know those super drugs everyone is taking?"

"What about them." This is just maddening.

"Well they caused super bugs to develop that were resistant to them. You just happened to be in the path of one of those trucks."

"Windy. Just tell me." I finally plead.

She doesn't want to but she does. "You had both early onset dementia and a rare and inoperable form of cancer. Bad news is: best guess, you had five years at the most. The good news: you wouldn't remember most of those years."

This is all a bit much to take in all at once. But I evidently knew this. Maybe I just didn't want to remember. Is that what's going on. I don't think so. There's something more here. I follow my intuition. "You've said 'had' a couple of times now. Does that mean I'm cured or just in remission?"

Windy looks about apparently trying to decide how to answer my question. "You definitely don't have to worry about dementia and cancer anymore."

What? How can that be? "I don't know anything that cures either one, except death."

"You're not dying anymore. In fact, you have a very long life ahead of you."

That's a relief. But I've never been one to just accept an explanation like that. At least I don't think I have. "This doesn't make any sense."

Windy smiles that radiant smile she uses to melt men and get her way. "I'll let the doctor explain all that to you."

I process her evasion, wonder what miracle the doctor performed on me, but I should be glad. It's good news. I don't have to worry about my health, do I? "So how are the others?" Since she's not going to give me any more information I ask about my posse, as I call them. Four of us went to Stanford together and have kept in touch since.

Reese was the prom queen and head cheerleader in undergraduate school. When she was going through Stanford with the rest of us all those years ago, that meant she was a math major who wrote algorithms to help retail stores understand their customers as a freshman. She had a successful consulting gig going in her junior and senior years. She married the captain of the football team, who is a people person. That means he manages a billion dollar a year sales team for a money manager.

Windy's parents are rich. They own land in Texas with mineral rights. They build wind generators in the panhandle. Her real name is Wendy, but everyone including her parents call her Windy because she's like a storm coming through the flat Texas plains. She comes upon you unsuspecting. When she leaves, everything is transformed. And it's also a nod to how her parents make so much money – with their wind generators. Windy is her own person. She owns a production house that does computer graphics for movies and commercials. Some of her work is iconic in the business. The everyday person would recognize it instantly. But Windy isn't about bragging. She thinks it would be pretentious to brag. She lets her work speak for itself. It speaks very well for her as she has more work than she can manage.

Delilah is the politically correct one of our group. Her father is a California state senator. Her mother manages his campaigns and

Delilah works on the campaigns and her family's business. Her family owns a beer and wine distributor that feeds a necessary habit for millions of Californians, particularly on football days. And those are nearly every day of the week now that the game has expanded internationally. You can find a professional, high school or college game any time you need to address your addiction.

Mary Colleen or MC, as we have shorthanded her name, is the psychologist amongst us. MC was one scholarship baby of our group. I was the other. MC worked harder to get through Stanford than any of the rest of us, even though she took the least rigorous curriculum. But she was Dean's list every semester and the class Salutatorian. So she had the second highest grade point. She was a drag to be with as undergrads as she had no time to do anything except study. And still we took her in and supported her all the way through. She shares few of our best memories as she was seldom with us then. But she has stepped up since we graduated. She organizes our get-togethers and occasional long weekend trips together. We're also the only two members of the group who never married. She offered to give me a cut rate to help me figure out my issues with men. I told her I'd sign up after she works out her own.

"Well Reese got a new customer who has been just drivin' that poor girl crazy. I mean she's burnin' the midnight oil and still she can't seem to satisfy that woman. You know what I'm talkin' about? She's at her wits end most days I talk with her. And Delilah. You know in a political year she's just up to it. Runnin' every minute. Between polling every single new issue and tryin' to strategize how to be in the media in a positive vein and avoid the big no no's. Well, I don't hear much from her, but she said she was beyond ready to get together somewhere they don't have any media outlets."

"What about MC?" I ask.

"I wasn't going to tell you until I know you're up to it."

"Windy. You know me."

"All right. MC was beaten nearly to death by one of her patients. We're hoping she gets out of the hospital soon. Not sure what she's gonna do. I mean this is a life changer for most folks."

"What happened?" I pursue since she's not giving me much.

"Don't really know. She won't talk about it. Probably needs time, you know. I think she's feeling she brought it on by how she was pushing this guy to own up his role in his abusive relationship. She ended up seeing and experiencing it first-hand."

I feel bad for MC. She doesn't deserve what ever happened to her. She's such a good person. Only wants to help people achieve a stable balance in their lives. At least that's what she always told us.

THE GHOST IN THE MACHINE

Chapter Three

I hear someone at the door and Windy lets him in.

Dr. Woodall. A ready smile, "How's my favorite patient?" Odd, this is a hospital, but no one has come by to check on me other than the doctor. Why is that?

"I'm remembering more. Funny the things I remember,"

"What do you mean?" Dr. Woodall seems unsure if he wants to hear the answer.

"It's like I remember web searches I've done. You know, like webpages suddenly appear to answer questions I'm thinking about. What's really freaky is I can read the pages in my memory. I don't ever remember doing that before."

Dr. Woodall doesn't respond.

"You don't seem surprised." I observe.

He shakes his head. I note he has already moved on to the next question he wants to ask. "Have you remembered any more about coming here?"

Windy's been helping me, but not really.

"I can't explain why it's taking you a while to remember. If you relax and just let your mind wander, I'm sure it will come." Dr. Woodall smiles at me. The smile seems genuine. But why am I even questioning whether it is or not?

"That's a relief." And I am relieved. "I don't feel tense either. I don't really know what I'm feeling other than confused. But what I want to know is how did you 'fix' my health issues?"

Dr. Woodall glances at Windy, understanding why I've asked this question.

"We removed that which succumbed to the disease and replaced it with something that isn't subject to those illnesses."

This makes no sense to me. "I need a little more explanation."

"I have to be sure you're ready. This is not an inconsequential change for you."

Not inconsequential. That doesn't sound good. "So I'm different somehow?"

"Yes. But in a good way."

"Damn it Dr. Woodall, I'm ready. Just tell me."

Windy comes closer in case I need her when he tells me what he's going to say.

Dr. Woodall hesitates, apparently trying to decide what the downside could be by acceding to my wish. Apparently he's still not sure. At least he's thinking I'm not ready. Probably because I'm blocking whatever happened to me. "All right. We transitioned you into a new body."

A new body. Really? "Like someone else's?" comes to mind first.

"No one else has ever had your new body."

I have to think this through. I have a new body, but not someone else's. "How is that possible?"

"You can think of it like a prosthetic arm or leg. We've been giving them to people for decades."

"Yes, but that's different than a whole new body. What are you saying? I have a mechanical body now?" That's just not possible. Artificial legs, arms, hearts even, but not the whole works. "I've never heard of that being done."

"You're the first. That's part of the reason we're being very careful with you."

"What? I'm the first what? First woman? Somebody's got to have done this before you'd put someone like me in a whole new body."

"You volunteered." What?

Windy answers now. "Remember I was telling you about your condition? This was the only option to keep you out of a nursing home probably within a year or two at most."

"So I was losing my mind." I was afraid of this. Maybe the new body didn't fix it.

"You were having increasing difficulty in remembering things, yes." Dr. Woodall.

"So how much did you have to replace?" They had to leave some part of me intact, otherwise I wouldn't be me.

"Everything except your consciousness." What?

"My consciousness?" I still can't grasp what he's telling me.

"Maybe some other time we can talk about how it was done, if you're really interested. But for now the important thing to understand is you have a new body that won't wear down. You won't be sick another day in your life. Over time your body can actually be upgraded. You'll become more capable as technology advances rather than getting old."

"More capable. What does that mean?" I'll need some time to think about what he's telling me. Do I believe it? No, not yet. This is too fantastic. A whole new body? Really?

"We don't entirely know yet. We're working to give you additional capabilities. You'll get them as quickly as they're ready and you're ready."

"So you gave me a robot body and I kept some very little piece of what I was." The reality is starting to sink in.

"That would be one way of looking at it."

"And how long will this robot body last? Have I traded five years in a nursing home for a year?"

"Theoretically it, you, will never die. We will be able to replace any parts that wears out and keep you going."

"Keep me going. Like in a nursing home? Doesn't sound so good. Can I go back to my old body if I don't like this one?"

"Yes. But you have only 30 days to decide. After that, no."

"Thirty days. Why only thirty days?" Seems like an arbitrary amount of time.

Dr. Woodall leans closer and touches my arm. "Your body is being kept alive. It's no longer conscious because your consciousness was transferred. After thirty days on life support we believe your body will have degenerated to the point that reintegration will no longer be possible."

"So I only have thirty days to decide if I want to live possibly forever or die soon." I conclude.

Windy holds my hand, smiles at me and nods with a tear in her eye.

Chapter Four

Dr. Woodall doesn't say much as I work through my situation. He stays with me for a while and then excuses himself. I still don't know what to make of his revelation. Do I believe him? I don't know. Moving my consciousness to a new body just seems so … well, impossible.

Even though I don't feel the need to go to the bathroom, it occurs to me there will be a mirror in there. But if my body is different, do I really want to see what I look like? I study the closed bathroom door for what seems a long time before I decide. From what I've seen of my body, it doesn't look any different. I'm generally the same size, shape and probably height. At least I think I am.

I ask Windy. "Do I look any different?"

"You look fantastic. I'm jealous."

As I open the door the mirror comes into view. I stop dead in my tracks. I'm at least twenty years younger. Firm and tight. And my hair has the same sheen it used to have, long and lustrous. I loved my hair before I started dying it and it became all brittle and lifeless. But that's the easy part. I have lighter skin color, almost Mediterranean. Like a dark tan from a life on fishing boats. And then I see them. My eyes. They're not my eyes. They're not round like they used to be. More elongated. Asian, almost, but not Asian. A penetrating bright blue, but not my eyes and not Anna Laura's eyes.

"What happened to my eyes?" I cry out.

"They're different, I'll have to admit. But it's still you in there." Windy offers.

THE GHOST IN THE MACHINE

I glance at her, "They say your eyes are the windows into your soul. If that's the case, what's become of my soul?"

Windy doesn't answer me, just gives me a hug.

I look at my image further, pull up my sweat shirt and look at my waist. Its firm the way it used to be when I was in my late teens and twenties. Before all the fast food meals and lack of exercise working all day and night to get my degrees and to demonstrate my worth at AppleCore.

Windy glances in at me. "You got a do over. I mean you got a killer bod, girl."

My breasts will tell me a lot. Are they firm? I don't have a bra on and yes they are most definitely my old breasts. They easily pass the pencil test. One more thing to check out. Do I have cellulite? I turn around, drop my pants and look at my buttocks and legs. Twenty years I've lost. How did Dr. Woodall do that? If this isn't a new body, he certainly fixed the obvious bad parts of my old one.

I run my hands over my body. Over my knees and elbows, over my face and through my hair. This body doesn't feel any different, but something's missing in my touch. What's missing? I don't know. "Feeling's different." I remark to Windy.

"What do you mean?"

"Things don't feel the same. Like I'm not getting it all." I rub my fingers together.

"Tell the doctor. He said he can fix things if you tell him what's not right." She's trying to make me feel good about my new self. Is she not sure either?

I think about my body again. It's hard. The skin feels normal and rides over a layer of muscle. At least that's what it feels like. "If it weren't for my eyes, I'd think Dr. Woodall had some kind of time machine. Did he send me back into my old body?"

"Says it's even better than your old body because it won't wear out."

The eyes tell me it's not. I had Anna Laura's eyes then. I'm not me, but I am. Different, but still me. Has to be.

I lean on the sink to get close to the mirror. I look at the eyes. Why are they different? What's that all about? I'll have to ask Dr. Woodall. There's something behind changing the eyes, but I can't imagine what or why he'd change that one thing. Doesn't make sense. I look deeper. I used to look into my mother's eyes because they always told me what she was thinking and feeling. In my case I can't see anything. Just bright eyes looking back at me, curious maybe, but nothing else is coming over. No emotion even though I've got to be a wreck. But I'm not. I don't feel anything in my stomach. And that's the first place I feel things when I'm under pressure. There and my neck. I turn my head like I always do when I'm trying to loosen up my neck. No tightness. I'm able to turn it in every direction. No bones settling into place with a snap. Just a full range of motion. Can't remember how long it's been since I had that. Probably my freshman year in college. That's when the pressure seemed to first take a toll on me. Long nights studying while it seemed everyone else was out partying. Just because I needed to get the top grade in every class so no one would think less of me. Particularly all the male professors who didn't think a woman could make it in their classes.

I look at Windy. "Did I have any idea what I was getting myself into?"

"I was with you for some of the meetings early on. He was pretty clear about what you should expect. He told you he wasn't 100% ready. Never would be. Told you there was a substantial chance something could go wrong and the transfer wouldn't take. Then you'd die because he wouldn't be able to host you in the new body and might not be able to get you back."

"Obviously that didn't deter me."

"Not in the least. Look Sage. We all know why you did this. And we respect your decision. I can't imagine what I'd have done if I found myself in your situation. But here you are and now you've got to figure it out just like you figure out everything else in your life."

"You're all going to help me." I confirm.

"Of course. We're not going to abandon a sister. Just because you're now this superhuman being that will probably run circles around us." Windy is more serious than she wants me to believe.

"I'm still at baby steps. How am I gonna run circles around anything?" I respond.

"Just like any surgery. As you let time heal things you'll be amazed at what you can and can't do."

I nod and turn back to look at my new self in the mirror. It occurs to me there should be a scar or something where my consciousness was brought into this body. But I don't see anything. So how did Dr. Woodall get me into this body? Am I in my head or am I someplace else? If the body really is a machine, the part that is me could be anywhere. I take off the loosely fitting clothes and examine my body from the top of my head to the bottoms of my feet. But there is no scar. No trap door. Nothing that would tell me I'm anything other than a twenty-year old woman. I have to hand it to Dr. Woodall. He did incredible work. But I'm even more curious than before. How did he transfer me into this body? I'll have to ask him.

I stare at myself in the mirror. Damn I look good.

Windy shakes her head. "Where do I sign up for one of them?"

I pull my pants back on and walk back into the hospital room, pulling the sweatshirt over my head. I decide to turn on the monitor wall and see what's going on in the world. I don't even know how long

I've been here. Not supposed to be back at work until next week. But have I been gone for a day or a year? Dr. Woodall hasn't filled in many of the blanks. But then he's hoping I'll remember on my own. Maybe if I know what day this is, something will trigger a remembrance.

The image comes up and the calendar appears in the upper right corner where it always is. September 6, 2045. "My birthday. I'm forty-two today." I remark wistfully.

"Happy birthday. We're all gonna celebrate when you get back." Windy wants me to know she hasn't forgotten.

I'm instantly curious as the image of the Dallas skyline fills the wall and it's not San Francisco. Dallas. Why am I in Dallas? I live in California. Near San Francisco. About a mile from the AppleCore campus where I work. I walk to the office every day. One of the few fitness things I made sure I continue. "So Dallas. Why am I in Dallas?"

"You're here for the medical facility." Windy responds. "Dr. Woodall said this is where they perfected the technique. And of course Dr. Woodall would have to perform the operation where they had all the equipment and trained staff. What did he say? Something about feeling their way? That means they have lots of theories about how you should be reacting. Apparently you're not fitting the predominant theory. That's why they're going slow."

If I had instantly remembered I'd probably already be on my way home.

So why can't I remember coming to Dallas? It's not a place I come to very often. But if Windy hadn't said something and I'd not seen it on the monitor I'd have never guessed this is where I am. Do I know anyone in Dallas? Yes. I know several people in Dallas. Jaime Franklin, Kristin Carpenter, Kat Patel, Charlie Austin and Jamaal Rivers. Oriana's sister lives here. Wait. How do I instantly know who lives here when I can't remember how I got here? Am I accessing the internet? I must have just performed a look up, scanned the directory and noted the names that were in my long term memory. Holy shit. If that's what's happening, that's pretty spooky. "Let me check this out. How many people live in Dallas?" The answer appears in my mind before Windy can answer. "Seven million, three hundred and seventy thousand, seven hundred and twelve as of midnight yesterday. I wouldn't know that. So I'm now a thing on the internet of things." Windy gives me a blank stare.

How do I feel about being grid connected? I'm not sure I like it. I'm sure I'll be happy to be able to fact check everyone in the room faster than they can fact check me. But everyone will also get tired real quick when I always have the answer that is given on the most popular sites. I'll get old at parties real quick. Only I don't think I went to many parties, now that I'm thinking about it. I've not been out raising hell. I've been home trying to keep ahead of my team. Except when Raoul used to come take me out on the town. Raoul. Why do I have mixed memories of him? Oh, that's right. He moved away.

Suddenly my head is filled with the current tasks my team is working. They pass before my eyes one-by-one. The status, who is responsible, the issues they're trying to solve and the next review date all parade before me, giving me an instant overview of the team status. "Holy shit. The team is weeks behind and not even close to delivering."

"Calm down. Don't worry about your team. They'll still be there when you get back. You'll get them back on schedule quick enough if I know you." Windy is reassuring, but she has no idea what she's talking about.

"I've got to get back. They need me. Got to talk with Dr. Woodall about going home today."

Windy settles me down. "Hold on there, Cowgirl. Nothing you do today is going to change a thing. You got to get yourself ready before you just wade back into that grind."

"I can help them get..." I protest, but Windy cuts me off.

"You can get yourself right and then help them. Until you're ready, you'll only be a liability to your team and everyone else you know. That includes me. I'm happy to be here and all. But I got a life of my own I got to get back to. So let's get you out of here as quickly as possible."

THE GHOST IN THE MACHINE

Chapter Five: Twenty-nine Days

Dr. Woodall opens the door to my room. Windy and I are laughing about one of Reese's blonde moments when he enters.

"Good to see you laughing. Good memories I hope."

"It still seems strange I know why I volunteered, but can't remember coming to the hospital or anything specific that led up to the transformation. Twenty-nine days. I have to make a decision in twenty-nine days about going back to the old me." This realization has been eating away at me. It's probably the one thing I'm struggling with the most. Although the instant insights are becoming annoying and probably a close second. Not having time to wonder about things before the answers appear in my mind takes some getting used to.

Dr. Woodall hesitates before responding. "Do you think you might want to?"

"I don't know. I don't know what to do with some of the changes." I answer truthfully.

"No one does." He begins. "No one has had to deal with more than one of the many things you're dealing with all at once. That's why I want you to go slow. Take your time. Adjust."

"But everything is coming at me so fast. Instant answers to my questions. Insights that just pop into my head. And what's with my eyes? They're not my eyes. Why?"

Dr. Woodall smiles. I see he's trying to slow me down. "Which question would you like me to answer first?"

"The speed of everything." I decide to go in order.

Dr. Woodall takes a deep breath. "The speed is a reflection of your processor."

"Excuse me? Processor?" What's he talking about?

Windy moves closer to make sure she's getting the full story so we can discuss it later if necessary. It will be necessary.

"Until now you had a brain that processed information at a certain clock speed. In your new body, the speed at which your 'brain' processes information is about twice the speed you're used to. It's actually capable of higher speeds, but we were afraid you'd struggle at anything faster."

"I'm struggling all right. I don't know how to deal with everything that's coming at me. Why did you think I needed to process information faster?"

"You agreed to it when we discussed what your new body could do for you. As I remember you said being the quickest person in the room would be a decided advantage for what you do."

I can hear myself saying that. "But couldn't you have prepared me for it?"

"We expected you would be able to access all of your memories, so it wouldn't be necessary for us to prepare you. This is a lesson learned." Why is he just so even keel? It almost seems like nothing catches him off guard or gets him upset. I wonder what he's not telling me.

"So I can expect all this info will start coming at me faster once I've gotten used to it?"

"Not immediately, and not until you think you're ready." Damn, that's the answer I would have given. Is he reading my mind? No, if he was, he'd know what I'm not remembering and probably why.

"So how am I getting these instant answers to my questions?" As I remember, that was my second question.

"You're accessing the internet with your thoughts." Dr. Woodall begins. "You pose a question and search engines go to work looking for the answers immediately."

"But how do I see the answers? They're not floating in front of me. It seems more like the answer appears in my mind's eye, or I just know the answer. But how is that possible? I don't have a mind's eye, do I?" I see general information on 'mind's eye' appearing, which I glance through while waiting for his response.

"You don't have a mind's eye. We haven't figured out how to create that, yet."

My mind has gone off gathering dozens of facts for me to consider about direct machine interface research. I've already scanned through it all so I now know more than I ever wanted to know. "Okay. Tell me about my eyes." This is the third point I made.

"You have beautiful eyes. Always have." Is his response.

"Why didn't you give me my eyes? These aren't mine." I stare him down. He finally looks away before answering.

"They're better than 20 20 vision. Much better." He begins, but I interrupt.

"Got that, but you know that's not my question." I let him swing for a moment.

"You're concerned about the shape." He begins hesitantly and softly.

"I can't see emotion in them the way I used to be able to. The way Anna Laura used to.""

Dr. Woodall walks over by the window and looks out before

answering. "Let me answer the second part first. I realize you're used to looking at someone's eyes to read what they're thinking. You're right. You can't see things there anymore. I've been talking with my colleagues trying to understand if there is something we can do about that. Unfortunately, for the moment we don't have a good approach."

"So people won't be able to read me. I've lost that means of communicating my feelings." I'm saddened. There have been many occasions when I counted on someone, usually Rocky, to pick up on how I felt. Now no one will be able to do that. At least not through my eyes.

"I've suggested we intend to enhance things about you as time goes on."

"I don't know what I want at the moment other than to remember what I've not been able to yet. But answer my other question. What's with the shape of my eyes?" I want answers not hedges.

"You have two features that are different from your old self. Your skin color and the shape of your eyes. There's an international medical standards committee. We're pledged to adhere to the standards they set on surgical and medical practices. One of the standards and protocols is for what the committee has labeled 'Immortals'. You are the first Immortal."

"Whoa. Hold on there. You're saying I'm immortal?" This can't be true. He said earlier no one knew how long this new body would last. "Where did this come from?"

"You weren't listening. The committee has labeled you an 'immortal' because you no longer are captive in a human body that has a finite lifespan based on biological limits."

"So no one knows if I'm really immortal." I'm not sure I want to be immortal. At least not yet.

"And no one will until something happens to you."

Windy appears to be totally lost in this discussion, as if none of this had been discussed before the change. I note her reaction and store that to bring it back up at the right time. "So what does all this have to do with the shape of my eyes?" I don't want to get sidetracked.

"The Standards committee has determined that all 'immortals' should have two specific common features, the shape of their eyes and the color of their skin."

"I don't like the implications of what I'm hearing." I begin as I'm thinking this through. "What you're saying is this group of docs somewhere has decided to create a new common racial identity for all immortals."

Dr. Woodall is careful in his response. "Not a new identity, so much as a blending of racial types so that all immortals will share a common racial appearance."

"And in time there will be no further racial separations because when we are all immortal there will only be a single race." I can't believe a group of doctors could make such an important decision for mankind. But then I realize it may take a century or more for non-immortals to die out. But if we really are immortal, that's a very short time.

Dr. Woodall nods reluctantly. "I probably know what you're thinking."

"That a group of docs doesn't have the right to choose what that racial identity should be."

"Is that because they didn't select a specific black identifier?" Dr. Woodall seems to have anticipated my response.

"Even you're sensitive to that fact." Hoping not to come across as a crusading black woman.

"I wasn't part of the committee that made the recommendation, although I support it."

"Because you want to make the world a more harmonious place when there are just immortals left?" I guess as his reasoning.

"Yes. No matter how much we played with the core identity, someone was never going to be happy. I didn't want it to turn into a long drawn out affair, having to consult with every racial identity and finally end up with a horse that looks like a camel so we can please everyone."

"You wanted as few common traits as possible." I guess again.

Dr. Woodall nods, and then looks back out the window.

"So you're engineering a common solution rather than a unique being that reflects the uniqueness each of us represents today." Windy summarizes.

I don't wait for Dr. Woodall to respond. "How long has this standard or protocol been out there?" I ask knowing nothing about it.

Dr. Woodall doesn't look back as he answers, "About five years. You're the first we've applied it to. You'll find people with the eye shape and others with the skin color, but no one has both except you, at the moment. We didn't want people to be able to pose as immortals because they surgically make themselves look like the new immortals."

"You're making me a target, and I don't even know a target for what. I don't know what to expect. Will people be afraid of me? Will they see me as a savior because I can reason faster than they can?" Then I realize. "But you don't know, do you? Your group of docs made a decision. But I'm the first who will actually have to live with the consequences of their decision."

Dr. Woodall still doesn't look at me. "There are a few other things we need to discuss."

"Like?" So much to sort out and still there's more?

"Whether you will want to go back. The window is short. Only four weeks." He turns to me now.

I can't answer his question. "I've been in this body all of a day."

He nods understanding. "Fair enough. Just needed to check out how you're feeling about things."

My response comes almost automatically. "That's the problem. I'm not feeling anything, about the decision or anything else. Will that change?"

Dr. Woodall nods, but doesn't answer with any specifics.

THE GHOST IN THE MACHINE

Chapter Six

Dr. Woodall comes back from the window. Sits down directly in front of me. "You've been focusing on what you perceive to be drawbacks of your new state. But there are a lot of advantages. We discussed many of them before the transformation. Since you haven't remembered those conversations yet, I'm going to go over some of them for you."

I lean back, not sure I'm going to like where this conversation is going. There have been too many surprises so far today. "Like what?" I know I'm coming across harshly, but I want him to know I'm skeptical of anything he says to me right now.

"Let's talk about basics. First of all, you don't need to eat or drink. In fact you don't have any of the equipment that would be necessary to receive or process either food or water."

"How am I supposed to keep…" but the answer is obvious.

"You run on electrical batteries, not food energy."

"Oh great. Does that mean I have a plug someplace?" I'm not liking this one bit. I like food.

"No. Your batteries are very efficient. At normal levels of activity you will recharge once every three days for about fifteen minutes. If you engage in heavy physical activity you may need to charge once a day for the same length of time."

"If I don't have a wall plug, how do I charge my battery?" I know I don't want to hear this answer, but I have to know before I can go home.

"All you have to do is lie down in a special bed. There's an inductive charging coil in the bed. It transfers the power to your battery through what's known as a near field transfer of electricity."

"Inductive charging. Oh great. Now I'm a giant electric toothbrush. What other good news do you have for me?" I'm still not happy about what I'm hearing and making sure he knows.

"You also don't need to sleep."

"But you just said I have to charge up. Isn't that like sleep?" I'm not sure I'm following this one.

"You can maintain full mental engagement while in the charger. You just can't clean the house or throw in the laundry. For anyone who's doing mental tasks, you'll just work right through."

What more can he tell me? No food or drinking, no sleep, what else would a robot not do that I used to? My mind starts presenting answers, so I push him to see who can give me the answers more quickly. "So what else? My mind is already listing things."

"Like?" Dr. Woodall responds.

"No showers, I don't sweat. No pharmaceuticals, prescriptions, doctor visits or hospital stays. I don't get sick. Only minimal heating and cooling of where I am since I don't get hot or cold, except in the extreme. I don't need to go to school, college or university. I have access to the global store of knowledge. I have processors to transform it into action. "I rattle off, even though this is not the full extent of the list presented to me.

"I think you can see when the world is populated primarily by immortals, the foundations of our society will fundamentally change. What underpins our economy will also change since so much we have come to depend on to survive is no longer needed."

"What about the things humans do for pleasure?" I ask. This had come up on my list, but Dr. Woodall didn't mention it.

"Like going to movies?" Dr. Woodall is playing with me now.

"Like going out to dinner or a club for a few drinks. Things we do to socialize will no longer exist. When you think about holidays you think of everyone being home. Having a big meal of all your favorite foods. When you go out, you generally get something to eat either before or after. My god, no more pizza delivery."

"We don't know how people will adapt to the fact that so much we take for granted will no longer be necessary or even possible."

"We won't need to exercise, since we won't be building or maintaining muscle or strength. That means no more clubs, or trainers or sports for that matter."

Dr. Woodall shakes his head. "I think people will continue to play sports. It's a social event more than exercise to maintain fitness. Sports rely upon skills and quickly reading and reacting to situations. If anything, I expect we'll see games speed up as more and more immortals get involved. They will see and anticipate the ball better than we do today."

"Since I have better strength, and I would assume coordination, does that mean I could go out and play a world class game of tennis right now?" I'm curious.

Dr. Woodall again shakes his head, "We don't know. You'll have to show us."

I think through the list of things we've discussed that will be different. "This will all be a major change for me, but not really any change for those around me. Other than they will have to adjust to the fact I won't have to do all the things they do. But will that creep people out such that they won't want to work with me?" I'll need to think this through before I go back to work.

"You won't creep me out any more than you used to." Windy smiles.

THE GHOST IN THE MACHINE

Chapter Seven

"I want to go for a walk." I tell Dr. Woodall.

He looks at me, studies me for a long moment, then rises and motions toward the door. I'm up and through the door in only an instant. But then I have to make a decision. Which way do I go? Dr. Woodall watches me silently. I hesitate for only a moment and turn left. We pass the nurse's station. So they are here, even though none has come in to check on me. That never would have happened if I were a normal patient. I wonder if they're monitoring my core vital signs. But what would they be? Battery state of charge? Processor speed? Memory capacity? But how much capacity do I carry versus what's stored for me in the cloud? Do I have any internal memory other than short term? I need to shut this exploration down or I'll miss what there is to see.

"Where am I going?" I ask Dr. Woodall.

"Does it matter?" he responds, and since I just said a walk, he's probably right. But it would be nice to see a bit of Dallas, even though I don't know anything about the city itself. But then again, am I in the city or a suburb? This is getting nuts! Why am I worrying? I never would have thought about any of these questions before. I've got to figure out how to filter this down to the things I really want to know. Can I do that? Filter my own thoughts? If I'm an internet machine I should be able to do that. Think of the filters I want and turn them on by just thinking about them? I'll have to try that, but not right now.

"What is there to see in Dallas? We are in Dallas aren't we?"

It seems like a long silence before he answers. Probably isn't all that long. Just seems like it because my mind is working so much faster. "Yes, we are. There are lots of things to see. A park, Dealey Plaza where

THE GHOST IN THE MACHINE

President Kennedy was shot, the Stockyards in Ft. Worth, museums..."

"A museum. You pick one."

"Art, natural or social history?"

"Art." I respond. He removes his phone and calls for a self-drive car to pick us up. Then he leads us to the doors at the entrance to the hospital. I feel the sun on my face and see the bright blue sky above. It feels so good to be outside.

The car arrives. Once inside it instantly heads into traffic. I'm used to California traffic, but Dallas is different. Short feeder street and straight up to the highway. Since all the cars are autonomous by law there is no speed limit, only the speed the traffic can safely maintain without an accident. And in Texas that's a lot faster than I'm used to seeing in California. We are in the downtown area, dropping off the highway almost in front of the museum.

I look around at the many tall buildings. The museum is located in the downtown area. A park bridges the expressway linking the city with walking areas. Nice. I'd not seen anything like this before.

As we enter the museum I look for my pay pad to cover the admission. I don't have it with me. But then I realize there is no admission. The museum is free. Another difference from California where everything costs you something. There's even a clean air surcharge on the taxes we pay on our property. Does that mean I own a house? No, a condo close by the office. It's a large condo by California standards. One of the few luxuries I afford myself. Having grown up poor and having lived in a very small house Rocky rented from the Goldschmidts, I always wanted something better. So when the condo came on the market, Jaime told me about it. I didn't really care what it cost. Now Jaime lives here in Dallas and I'm in her old condo.

Dr. Woodall is waiting for me to go on in. I walk down the corridor with grey cement walls. The main galleries are at the other end of the hallway. There are small exhibits along the right side, but they are not of interest. I want to see the featured artist. At the entrance to the gallery is a sign. Vincent Van Gogh and the Dutch Innovators. I've seen many of these pieces in publications and text books when I was in college. Never in person. "Can we go in?" I ask.

I lead the way to find 'Haystacks'. I recognize the brushwork and the vivid colors that were Van Gogh's trademarks. I stare at the picture, taking it all in, drinking it in, and committing it to memory in only a second. It seems like I have been considering it for a long time, when I realize I haven't stopped walking. I'm actually studying the next picture, now. The time is all out of whack. When I've gone to museums in the past I've always stopped in front of each picture. I read the museum painting summaries. Tells me the artist, the time the painting was done and a little about the subject or something particular about the painting. In this case I don't have to stop because my senses are taking it all in so fast. And the internet presents anything I've missed.

Dr. Woodall and Windy stop at Haystacks. They realize I've kept moving. Finds they have to walk quickly to catch up to me. I laugh at them. I'm back absorbing the next painting, the museum summary and glancing ahead. I'm getting more used to the speed of data and information I'm able to absorb, process and determine what I want to do with it. I make split second decisions about whether to simply remember it, formulate a question, or ignore.

I walk through the exhibit even faster. I push myself. I want to see how fast I can devour the entire exhibit. It seems like only a few minutes and I'm in front of 'Starry Night'. It has always been my favorite of Van Gogh's work. There is a clock on the wall outside the exhibit area and I realize we have only been in here for about six minutes. And yet I remember every detail of the paintings. The nature of the brush strokes. The variation of colors. How Van Gogh abstracted elements of the images. Different than the way Picasso deconstructed them. He exaggerated shapes and sizes in such a way that they made the images suggestive of the real thing. He wasn't interested in reproducing what he saw. He was creating a new reality that embodied the nature of the human experience of the time. Where the hell am I getting all this? Oh, yeah. From the internet. Wikipedia? Probably.

I turn to Dr. Woodall. "Did you enjoy it?"

"I'm coming back without you, girl. I need more time than this." Windy remarks as she catches up to us.

"I barely saw it." He sounds curious. "What about you?"

"Every brush stroke and a running commentary of the implications of his work. Let's take a look at what's over here in the side galleries."

They follow me across the hallway but stop as I go in. I turn to look at them.

"I'll wait for you here. I'm sure this will be only a minute." Dr. Woodall shakes his head.

He is right. I walk around the room, take it all in and am back at the entrance in about sixty seconds.

"Did you enjoy it?" He asks as I come out to join them.

"Interesting. Saw some techniques I don't remember having seen before. Not sure I'm a big fan of his subject matter. How he chose to represent it was different."

"Who's the artist?"

"Miro." I respond and start walking towards the entrance. I think I've seen enough of the museum for today.

"Joan?" Dr. Woodall asks.

"Albert, born 2009. Lived in Coppell, Texas, which I think... no I know, is one of the suburbs of Dallas. He died young in a motorcycle accident. Before the laws changed about autonomous cars on the highway and the banning of motorcycles. Tragic death really. He was only twenty-four. According to the historian here, he showed a lot of promise. Actually had a commission he was working for the Tate Museum in London when he died."

Dr. Woodall tries to suppress a smile, but I see he's pleased with all the information I'm bringing to the conversation without having to go to a device to look it up. I must be vindicating all his judgments about consciousness transition.

Windy is just trying to keep up.

As we walk to the exit Dr. Woodall asks, "So what would you like to do next?"

THE GHOST IN THE MACHINE

Chapter Eight

I remember seeing the green of the park over the freeway as we drove in. That makes me wonder. "My visual senses are amazingly acute, but what about my other senses?"

"I assume the way you went through the exhibit you were magnifying the images."

Thinking about it my vision magnifies the image I'm looking at across the street. I'm able to read a very small sign on the side of the building next to the door. Belo Mansion. Don't know what that is, but, oh here it comes. Belo family started and owned the newspaper in Dallas, starting in 1885. The mansion was built in 1890. It served as a funeral home for a short time. Clyde Barrow's body, from Bonnie and Clyde fame, was displayed there for public viewing after his death. It's currently the home of the Dallas Bar Association. Guess I need to simply wait when I don't recognize something as my connections will tell me more than I ever want to know. Got to get back to that idea about filters.

"It works." I summarize for Dr. Woodall. "But what about the other senses?"

"Your hearing acuity also far exceeds that of a person. You should be able to direct your attention to a sound and amplify it."

"How much?"

"You want the specifications of the system? I could just tell you the name of the device manufacturer and model number. Then you could access the information yourself. But I don't think that would be all that meaningful to you. I'd suggest you just try it out and see what you can do with it. Why don't you listen for the sound of a particular bird? In Dallas that would most likely be a robin, cardinal or blue jay."

And even before he finishes his statement I have looked up the sounds of each and been able to hear the sound in my head. I let my attention wander. I'm able to locate each sound somewhere in the area. Seem to be coming from the area of the park we drove by coming in I'd thought of visiting.

I start walking around the museum towards the park, directly behind it. Pine trees line the way. Tall buildings on three sides and the small park on the fourth. I deliberately simply recognize the general nature of the surroundings without wondering anything specific about them as I don't want the flood of information.

Instead I try another sense, that of smell, but nothing. "Why can't I smell anything? I thought with what you've done for sight and hearing I'd be able to smell and recognize each type of flower in the park." I tell Dr. Woodall.

"There are two senses we're still working on. Smell is one and taste is the other. Since you no longer eat, taste isn't as important as it used to be. Smell on the other hand, is a major factor in establishing taste. Maybe that's why we're having so much difficulty perfecting those abilities."

I'm disappointed. "So I'll never…" but Dr. Woodall cuts me off.

"You don't want to think in terms of never. As an immortal you have much longer than a human lifetime to incorporate changes into your new body. You were deliberately built in a modular fashion. We can upgrade you as we perfect enhancements and new abilities. Many of those new abilities will simply be a software upgrade. Others will be hardware change-outs. A thousand years from now you may have an entirely different type of body depending on what we come up with."

I listen to his description of how he or someone designed my new body. It sounds like I'm just a walking computer. I don't like that notion. But I am curious. I seem to react emotionally much slower than I react to facts and data or even decision making. I wonder about that. I'm surprised that nothing presents itself for my consideration. "Something for you to note. When I have emotional responses they occur much more slowly than acquisition of facts and data, which are almost instantaneous."

Dr. Woodall looks at me curiously. "Can you give me an example?"

"I just reacted negatively to how you described my new body. The reaction developed over a few moments and lasted while I tried to understand it. When I wondered about it nothing presented itself to me. Different, that's all."

"So why did you react negatively?" Dr. Woodall is trying to understand my observation. Apparently another of the things he'd not predicted.

"I'm disappointed that I don't have the senses of smell and taste. I'm still trying to cope with the fact I won't eat or drink or sleep for that matter."

Dr. Woodall reacts before I complete my thought. "Understandable. I believe you will quickly adjust. One of the things I don't think I've mentioned is that when you recharge you will remember tastes and smells from your past. So you will experience them even though you aren't experiencing the real time smells and tastes where you are."

I shake my head. "Real time tastes and smells? You've got to come up with a better way of describing all this before you transition someone who isn't a geek like me."

Dr. Woodall seems surprised at my reaction.

I'm off in my head trying to remember the smell of a rose. I remember the smell. That instantly brings back a memory of the last time someone gave me roses. That was Rocky on my sixteenth birthday.

Sixteen red roses. Rocky said that had been a tradition when he was growing up. None of my friends got roses on their sixteenth birthday. So I never knew if it was something Rocky just made up or if it was a tradition. And now here it all comes. A sweet sixteen is a coming of age party celebrating a female's sixteenth birthday in North America, primarily in the United States and Canada.

So, Rocky wasn't bullshitting me. But still strange I was the only person I knew who got roses for my sixteenth birthday. Then I realize Rocky is a sentimental guy. Maybe he was more sensitive to the needs of an awkward teenage girl than I realized. He apparently understood my need to feel worthy of a beautiful present. He must have also understood that I hoped to feel beautiful, even though at that time I felt anything but beautiful. Maybe Rocky was just more tuned into my needs than I realized then. It seemed to me he was at work all the time. The family came second in his priorities. But Anna Laura had once said he felt responsible to ensure we had whatever it was we needed. I guess Rocky took that to mean the money to have what we needed. We lived frugally. And what I needed then was more affection from him. But he wasn't there to give it to me when I wanted and needed it most.

I start walking towards the park again. My head is still spinning with all the conversations we've just had. "What about touch? That's the one sense you've not mentioned."

"You feel things just as you did with…" He stops and changes his mind. "Just as you did before."

"I feel things, but it's not like before. Patchy almost."

He nods as if he expected my response.

Then another thought occurs about touch. "But what about a kiss? Is that the same? Does it feel the same both physically and emotionally?"

Dr. Woodall looks up the street so we can cross into the park as he responds. I can't see his face or his eyes. "You'll have to tell me."

As he turns back to me, right there in the middle of the street, I kiss him on the lips. He seems surprised. It feels soft, but not wet. Need to work on that. But what about emotionally? Nothing. Not what I was hoping for.

People in the park stop and applaud us as a driver honks her horn for us to get out of the way as Windy pushes us across the street.

THE GHOST IN THE MACHINE

Chapter Nine

We pass into the park. A line of food trucks are parked at the curb. People mill around them. I try to remember food truck smells, it's hard to recall smells that you didn't experience often or pay particular notice to. And remembering is so much harder than walking into a room or place and finding yourself surrounded and engulfed in wonderful smells.

"Are you hungry?" I ask Dr. Woodall. "I don't mind at all if you want to get something. I'd just like to sit here for a bit. Feel the sun on my face and let the breeze flow through my hair." I'm already feeling the warmth of the sun and breeze so I know I've not lost the sense of feel completely. But I wonder if my perception of touch can be magnified or controlled in some way. Can I resist pain or even not feel it if I choose to? And at the other extreme can I feel the slightest touch of mist upon my face? Since I'd suggested to Dr. Woodall that he not tell me, I decide I'll just have to experiment to find the answers.

"Are you sure? I feel funny eating in front of you."

"I can't expect people to not eat. You both should get something."

I watch Dr. Woodall order Chinese noodles. Windy is getting a burger. Not what I would have expected from either of them. Windy is California healthy when she's with us as a group. I glance around the park. Many women have their young children scampering amongst the water sprays and climbing on the fixtures in the kid's area. "Grab a table, I'll be right back." I say to Dr. Woodall who still waits for his food.

I walk over to the children's play area and approach the water sprays. It appears that the average age running with abandon through the sprays is about two. Both boys and girls in various states of undress. No bathing suits, just street clothes. I get close hoping to feel the water spray mist. I get too close and the spray hits me square in the face. Yes, I can feel wet. That's definitely good to know. The children have stopped running to see what I'm about to do as a result of getting wet. I smile at them and begin to laugh. The children embrace my laughter and continue their play.

A woman, probably one of the mothers, comes up to me. "Guess you weren't expecting that."

"No," I confirm. "You come here often?"

She nods, "Petal enjoys it. She's gotten to know some of the other kids. So I enjoy the fact it wears her out and she takes a long nap. You have kids?"

"Afraid not." I confirm. I'm not really sure why I put it that way. I've never really had much interest in a family. Always seemed like an impediment to my job and the next promotion. My software products are my children. I launch them into the world and watch them grow. I also watch them be replaced by the new software I develop right behind them. That means I often watch my children die when no one wants to buy last year's model.

"You have time. There's nothing like motherhood to be fulfilled. And to be tired all the time. But it's worth it."

"I'm Sage, by the way, Sage Washington." I hold out my hand to shake hers.

"MeriBeth Lee." She introduces herself. "Don't think I've seen you here before."

"I live in the San Francisco bay area. Just visiting for a few days." I respond.

"Too bad. I'd enjoy another adult out here. So many of the moms are only into their kids. Talk is all about preparing for school and making sure they have all the right educational experiences. Gets old after a while. You know?"

"No, but I can imagine."

A spray goes up. I instantly step closer to it. I feel the mist blow into my face. I grin broadly. MeriBeth shows a puzzled expression.

"Is that what you were trying to do? Have the mist cool you off?"

I nod still smiling. I notice Dr. Woodall sitting and talking with Windy, trying, not overly successfully, to eat his noodles with chop sticks. "Its nice meeting you MeriBeth, but I need to talk with that gentleman over there."

"Hope to see you again before you return home," MeriBeth is not smiling. She turns to figure out what her daughter, Petal, is doing. She's already dismissed me as a passing thought.

As I approach Dr. Woodall he looks up. "Making new friends?"

"Always." I begin. "Never know when I'll need one."

"What am I?" Windy has a big bite in her mouth and tries to make sure it doesn't come out as she talks.

"Present company excluded I'm sure." He responds and takes another bite of his noodles, even though most fall from his chop sticks before he gets them in his mouth.

"I don't think you're supposed to pick them up with the chop sticks. You're supposed to put the bowl up to your mouth and use the chop sticks to push the noodles in." I offer.

"That from Wikipedia?" he asks.

"No. I'm trying hard not to access the official conventional wisdom. That's from memories of Friday nights at my house. My father didn't like Chinese. He always worked late on Fridays because no one else wanted to. So my mother usually had Chinese on Fridays because she liked it."

"Didn't make any difference whether you did or not?"

"Not really." I grimace at the memory.

I watch as Dr. Woodall follows my suggestion. He discovers he's much more successful in transferring the noodles from the dish into his mouth. The consequence, however, is that he finds he has many more noodles to chew than he was expecting. So I smile as he has to chew repeatedly to swallow more and more of the remains still in his mouth. "That wasn't very …"

"No, but we'll both survive it." I don't have time for his apology.

Dr. Woodall decides he has embarrassed himself enough. He takes Windy's papers and napkins and walks over to a trash barrel where he disposes of the rest of his noodles. "Guess I'm not as hungry as I thought."

"Tell me what you smell." I ask him.

I watch as he takes a deep breath and looks about. "Honestly, the first thing I smell is auto exhaust. But we're surrounded by cars and even cars passing below us on the freeway."

I wait.

He continues. "There's a row of pine trees over here. They have a strong scent as you may remember." He looks around. "There aren't that many flowers. Guess I'd not noticed that before when I've been here. Must have something to do with the heat and bright sun. Low lying green bushes. But they really don't have flowers that smell nice, as you're thinking. Some of them have real tiny flowers. Mostly red or white. But I don't pick up a distinct smell."

"What you're trying to tell me is I'm not missing much by not being able to smell the flowers."

Dr. Woodall shakes his head. "How do most people use their sense of smell? Perfume or cologne reminds you of someone you know wears that scent. The rest is mostly food, I think. They smell something like a cinnamon bun and it instantly makes them hungry. Or bacon. Who can resist the smell of bacon cooking? Most smells are triggers to make you hungry. You don't need those triggers anymore. Others are of bad smells, things you don't want to eat mostly."

"I think you're missing the point." I look back to the kid's area and find MeriBeth looking at me. I'm surprised. I would have thought she would be all wrapped up with her daughter, Petal. MeriBeth must be lonely. It's the only conclusion I can draw from her behavior. Someone who longs for connections to others beyond the role based mom's club. I turn back to Dr. Woodall. "I may not need food or water to live, but as a person, smells and food and water are all part of the human experience. You're taking that part of the experience away. Okay, I understand you think it's removing a limitation that people have, but it's also a part of being a person. Removing it as even an option makes me less human in some sense. I don't want to be less human. If anything, I want the same limitations enhanced so I can enjoy them more. Do you understand my point?"

Dr. Woodall doesn't hesitate in his response. "I do. And we've discussed just that for endless hours. We've tried to understand what makes us human and how can we enhance that experience. But at the same time we have an opportunity to redefine what makes us human. We've removed all the physical limitations that the human body puts on us. Some members of the team argued that we should make immortals live only in their minds. Take away all of the burden of interacting and transacting in the physical world. Others went to the other extreme, which was to reproduce the immortal with all of the physical limitations of the human body. Some even suggested you should not be immortal, that we put a clock in you that expires at a hundred years. The problem with that approach is if all men and women chose to become like you, after a hundred years the species would disappear."

"I can tell you I wouldn't want to live apart from the physical world. Being more biology than technology is where I'd want to be. The immortal bit? That isn't all that important to me. In fact, it's actually intimidating. So I'll vote for a slow transition away from the limitations. In fact, if I'm exactly as I was at twenty, I would be very happy."

Chapter Ten: Twenty-eight days

Dr. Woodall takes us out into a hospital courtyard. It's very warm. I see perspiration forming on his collar. Windy fans herself with her clutch purse. "So I should be able to be outside in Dallas during the heat of the day and not wear down because of the heat."

"Theoretically."

"We'll have to do this more often." I observe wishing I was back in San Francisco.

"You planning on staying in Dallas?" He sounds surprised.

"No, I mean in San Francisco." I can see how he would make that assumption from what I'd said, but find it surprising I would make a comment so imprecise that it could be misconstrued. I'm usually very clear about what I mean. Aren't I? I mean I think I am. I have this flashback of someone yelling. They're yelling at me. Why? I said something. Not what I meant, but it just came out. And someone, a man is yelling at me, making me feel foolish. I never feel foolish. How did I ever get into this position? And then the feeling and the image are gone. Nothing more to inform me of what I'd just experienced.

Windy sees my reaction and comes over to stand next to me, ready to help if I need her. "Are you remembering something?"

"Yes. I don't know. Something. A feeling. An image. Just a snippet really."

"Could you describe it?" Dr. Woodall asks.

"Yelling," is all I give him.

"You yelling or someone yelling at you?" Dr. Woodall isn't going to let me get away with hand waving. He wants to know what I experienced.

"Yelling at me, I think. At least that's what I'm feeling."

"Who? Who's yelling at you?" Windy asks.

I shake my head.

Dr. Woodall leans closer. "This might be important for you. Could be part of what you're blocking. You made comments during your intake, it could be related."

He gets my attention. "What comments?"

"You made it clear your career is the most important thing to you. You define yourself by what you do."

"Rocky's the only family I have left." I try to put the puzzle together.

"You rarely discussed things you do outside of work."

"What's wrong with that?" I protest. "I'm the best, the absolute best, at what I do."

"From what you said, I agree. But your degenerative condition started to affect your performance at work. That's all you talked about."

I hear what he's saying, but something is blocking the next reel on that home movie of the yelling. I try to search for it, but it seems someone or something is standing in front of the door to that part of my memory. I want so badly to know. But something in my mind is trying to protect me from something, only it won't tell me or let me see what it is.

Dr. Woodall sees I've not cleared the blockage and seems disappointed. He apparently wants me to get past this memory loss as soon as possible. Is that why he's humoring me by taking me to a museum, park and now sitting outdoors in a courtyard? Is he hoping these stimuli will help me remember and then he can discharge me?

"It's gone, isn't it?" Windy asks.

I nod. I'm let down. The thought of knowing what's paralyzing my mind is scary but I know it's essential. I have to get past this block. I have to move on. I have to re-engage the life I've taken a momentary vacation from. Will I have fixed whatever it was I needed to fix? I still don't know.

"We have all evening." Dr. Woodall offers to help me remember.

"You have all evening. I have all night too." I inform him. "So no discharge today?" I ask and see Dr. Woodall shake his head.

THE GHOST IN THE MACHINE

Chapter Eleven

After the doctor leaves Windy wants to talk. "What do you think?"

"Scary. If I could remember things I'd feel a whole lot better. It's strange I can do all these new things but I can't even remember the discussions that led me to make this decision."

"I was there when you met with Dr. Woodall."

I try to remember her being there, but it won't come. "What did I say?"

"It was pretty much as he described it. You kept sayin' you have to work. You refused to just give up and let your conditions defeat you."

"Is that how I am? Stubborn?"

"You're more stubborn than anyone I know 'cept of course me." Windy smiles.

I reflect on my stubbornness. That was how I was with Rocky. He was always wrong and I knew better on everything. Now I realize that wasn't always the case. "Why did they choose me?"

"You wouldn't take no for an answer. Whatever conditions they put on, you signed up sayin' you'd find a way. I think you just wore them down."

"Should I be afraid?" I ask, not sure.

"Of what? Everything seems to be workin' out as they said it would. I don't see anything says your new body is rejecting you or anythin' like that."

"But what about other people? Will I be a freak? Will people not want to deal with me because I'm always right, at least according to Wikipedia?"

"You were never right. So this might be a good thing for you." Windy pushes me.

"I don't know. Maybe I should have just let fate take me. Maybe I'm trying to fly too close to the sun here."

"You're no Icaris. And he was only a Greek legend anyway. Don't go getting' a big head here girl. You may be a big deal at work, but I know you. You're just that same old scaredy cat who never wanted to do the bar scene with the rest of us. I've heard of guys havin' wing men, but we had to practically surround you to get you out with us."

"Did I do the right thing?" I'm really beginning to wonder.

"Of course you did. You had no choice. We weren't going to just sit around and let you slip away like you did at that one fraternity party where Reese almost got us all thrown into jail."

At first I don't know what she's referring to, but then it comes back and I break into a grin. "At least if you had gone to jail I would have been able to bail you out."

"Well, we're here to bail you out if this just gets to be too much."

"But only for thirty days. After that I can't go back." I reflect.

"You'll know long before thirty days. You get through this week and you'll know."

"Why do you think that?" I hope she's right.

"You'll get comfortable with what you can do. People will accept the new you and you'll get back to it. Won't be surprised the doc will call you up at thirty days and you'll have forgotten all about goin' back." Windy gives me a hug. "Now I'm havin' trouble keepin' awake here. I know you're not tired but I gotta have some sleep. You gonna be okay for a while?"

I hug her now and release her to an uncomfortable chair. I watch her and she is asleep in only a matter of minutes. I could never fall asleep that fast.

I have the night to demonstrate to Dr. Woodall I'm ready to go back to 'it', whatever 'it' is. Software development. Advanced projects to enable new devices to do more, faster and cheaper than ever before in human history. That's what I do.

I wonder about immortal. What does that mean? I'm curious it seems to have two different meanings. One is to have a life that does not end; whereas the second is to produce a work that lives on after me. I'm immortal in that men and women will remember me for something I did or contributed to mankind during my lifetime. So the conventional wisdom doesn't contemplate that immortals will exist in reality. They are focused only on the idea that men and women will reproduce or produce something of substance that will live on long after they have reached their demise. An example comes to mind in William Shakespeare who is still quoted to this day, centuries after his passing.

Now that I have crossed over, how long will it be before there will be hundreds and then thousands and eventually millions or billions of immortals? Not long I fear. And why do I fear it? Because we have no idea where this will lead. I certainly have many reservations and qualms about being immortal. Particularly when aspects of being human seem to be missing from my new existence.

Dr. Woodall said there are those who would prefer to see us as physically housed in a computer server farm and not have a physical form at all. That I can't imagine. I certainly wouldn't want to be rendered as bits and bytes in a server farm. That makes me think of 'The Raiders of the Lost Ark' and the immense government warehouse where the Ark of the Covenant is stored for the rest of mankind's existence, forgotten and inaccessible.

To me, the bigger question is how do I help Dr. Woodall create the feelings, emotions, and sensations that make me human? I don't have the hormonal systems that govern emotions in people. So how do we replicate that? Those on Dr. Woodall's team seem to think emotions aren't important. Can I live without emotions? I've been reacting as if I had them. But my reactions are triggered from memories. I don't really feel them. What do I feel? I don't know.

I know I love Rocky, even though I rarely see him. He's my father. Despite all the negatives about his workaholism, he did what he thought was right for us. He made it possible for me to become what I am, even though he had no idea what that would be. I wonder how he will react when he finds out what I've become. He'll probably freak. I'm his daughter. But the geek part of him will be proud I've been the one to lead the change. To dare what others have not. To lead a revolution.

Rocky wanted to be a revolutionary. What he did made him part of the revolutionary forces. But he was never the one person who stood up to lead something important. Am I that one person? I don't think so. That would probably be Dr. Woodall. He made all this possible. He did the hard work. Lived through the failures and eventual successes that enabled me to become a transformed being.

So I feel love. That's a good start. Do I feel pain? Physical pain? In the old me, the physical pain was a message to stop doing whatever it was I was doing. It was an indicator I probably needed to see a doctor to diagnose what I was doing or what I'd contracted that needed attention. Now I don't know if I feel pain. Why would I? There's no longer a need for a doctor to prescribe medicine for me.

I have conflicted feelings. I have feelings about something or someone. I don't know if the feelings are good or bad. I consider the feelings. But I often don't have enough information to know if the feelings are accurate or just reactions to a limited set of data I have to consider. What do I feel about Dr. Woodall? I kissed him. His lips were soft. He kissed me back so he must have at least a receptive feeling about me. But what did I feel about that kiss? Was there any chemistry? What does chemistry mean when you don't have the hormones that drive feelings? He's a good looking man.

I still don't have any better idea of what I feel for Dr. Woodall. Yes I like him. He seems kind and concerned about me. He's looking out for my best interests, even though he's still trying to figure out what they might be. I'm not sure what they are. So he must really be lost at sea on that front, so to speak. Do I look forward to being with him? Yes. And then there's the whole thing if I'm an immortal. I have to assume he will become one as well. Since he's led the charge on this whole medical procedure I would assume that's a pretty safe bet.

Before the transition, I had signs that let me know what my feelings were. When someone I liked came into a room my heart would skip a beat. I'd feel excited or flush. I could feel something change in me, physically. Maybe that's what I'm struggling with. I'm not feeling those emotionally driven physical reactions.

So if that's the case how do I know what I'm feeling? And the more I think about it, the problem is that I'm not 'feeling' the reaction. I may be having it, but it's all in my mind and not hormonal. Do I need to talk to Dr. Woodall about giving me the equivalent of a hormonal system so I can feel what now I simply remember?

Is the memory of emotions enough? Over time will I be able to live with just memories? Will I care about people? Will I care about myself since I'm practically indestructible? I don't know. This has come upon me so quickly I just don't know what to think.

At the moment I have remembrances of emotions. But I don't know if I can create new emotions without a hormonal system. And if I can't experience new emotions, how will I be able to deal with others? So while Dr. Woodall thinks he's given me all these new advantages and abilities, at the moment I only see that he's rendered me a shell of what I'd been able to feel.

Chapter Twelve

Windy said people will just accept me and I shouldn't worry about being a freak. I decide to test that out. I call a Googlecar to come pick me up from the Medical Center. Our friend Adrienne lives in Dallas now and I gave her a call. She's home and would love to see us. Adrienne will be honest with me. Has the new me fixed the problems I was having?

The car arrives and takes us out into a suburb to a nice house on a tree-lined street. It could be any street in any sub-development anywhere. Her house is small, reddish brick and solar panel roof. Just like nearly every other house on the street. She has interesting flowering plants that line her walkway to the front door. Something like the yellow brick road I would imagine. All one's cares and wants will be resolved here by the Wizard behind the curtain? I hope she will be able to award me the courage I'll need to go back into the castle of AppleCore.

I ring the bell. In only a moment Adrienne is smiling at us in the now open door. "Adrienne! You look great. Is it your hair or did you lose weight?"

"Both." The short pert blonde before us responds almost coyly. She's looking at me, checking me out too. But she says nothing initially. She smiles at Windy. "You look exactly the same as the last time I saw you."

We hug in the doorway. She gestures for us to come in, which we do.

As we enter her cozy living room she gestures toward a couch that faces a window wall revealing a garden paradise in her back yard. The colors seem to represent the rainbow. They're tiered in height so those further away from the window are taller. The illusion is almost a carpet of color, intermingled with green leaves, that ends at a back fence probably thirty feet or so from the house. "You must really enjoy the view from here." I remark.

"Can I get you something to drink? Water, wine, beer?"

"I'm good." I respond as I sit down.

"You have a white wine?" Windy asks. "It's not too early is it?"

"I'm desperate for a glass of wine." Adrienne responds conspiratorially. "So how have you been? What brings you to Dallas?"

Still not asking what she really wants to know. "Good, good. Working hard. Long hours. You know the drill. I'm just here until tomorrow. Came into town for a medical procedure. Tightening some things up. Just trying to stop the clock as much as I can."

She nods as she pours the wine into two large glasses. Apparently she really is desperate for some wine. I wonder why. "You look fabulous. I mean really, you do."

As she comes back into the living room she sips her wine, hands the other to Windy and then asks, "So you have to tell me all about it. Where did you go and who's the doc? I mean I've got to know. I may want to see your doc. I can't get over how great you look."

She sits in a chair next to the couch, balancing her wine, all ears.

"Doc is Bart Woodall. He's from San Francisco, but has a relationship with the UT Southwestern Medical Center here."

"UT Southwestern? Must be cutting edge stuff. They're known more as a research hospital than a clinical one." She seems to be mulling what I'm telling her. She clearly didn't expect this response.

"I'd have to say its cutting edge. Do you agree, Windy?" I'm not sure how to describe the transition so she won't get spooked by it.

"Well you got spectacular results. How long have you been here? Must have been at least overnight."

I'm embarrassed that I can't answer her question as I don't remember when I arrived. Some things are still hazy to me. "A few days." I decide is an accurate response.

"So what all did he do for you? Looks like he removed every ounce of fat, and tightened up your face, but what's the deal with your eyes? They look different."

That tells me all I need to know about my eyes. "That pretty much sums it up." I don't respond to her question about my eyes, because I don't really know how to explain it to her. At least I don't think she'd accept the truth about them. "I feel great and eager to get back to work. But the doctor wants me to go slow at least for a little while. But you know how A'zam is. He's not going to let that happen."

She nods. Adrienne worked with me. She was in Supply Chain. She got married. Her husband was transferred to Texas. We kept in touch but this is the first time we've gotten together since she left over five years ago.

"So what about you? You still loving Texas?" I decide to change the topic and see where she goes.

"Absolutely. It's not California, but no place is. Hotter and no beach. But people are friendly and it's actually pretty easy living here. I have everything I need close by. Schools are good for Alex, who's in first grade."

"Really? First grade already? I can't believe how fast he's grown." I respond.

"I was able to get a job pretty easily. One that lets me work a flexible schedule. So I'm here when Alex gets home. Matt's doing great in his job. Already been promoted, so he's happy."

I decide to test the Happyville description. "So would you come back to California if something opened up for Matt?"

She takes a longer sip of wine this time. "We had the chance. About six months ago. I was ready, but Matt sat down and did the math. What they were offering him just didn't make up for the housing difference, cost of living and taxes. We would have had to change our lifestyle dramatically to make it work. So in the end we decided to stay."

"Sounds like you regret the decision." Windy reacts the same way I do, but voices it.

"Family's still all out there. We see them at Christmas. Either we go there or they come here. We do a week in the summer. But you like to have your family close by. I miss them. Matt does too. But he doesn't say as much about it as I do. He doesn't like me to complain, so I don't anymore."

"You used to?"

"That first year was hard. I'm home with a toddler. Matt's off at work. I'm trying to get some work in while Alex's napping or playing quietly. But it's real hard. Just finding a baby sitter's a big deal. You don't mind leaving him with family. But when it's a neighbor's kid, you know. It's just not the same."

"What do you think the future holds for you? Will Matt's company eventually offer him something that will make it more feasible for you to come home?" I'm trying to understand the big glass of wine.

She shakes her head. "He'll have to change companies to go home. They pretty much have a policy that if you turn down a move that's the last time they'll offer you. Matt said his boss was angry he stayed here. They had a whole plan to bring in someone else to back fill his job. Said he screwed up their whole development program. Matt says things have settled back down, but I just know it's not good for him there anymore. He's no longer a rising star. I suspect, even though he's not said anything, that if the company has a down year he might lose his job."

"Wow. That's tough. So is he actively looking?" Windy asks trying to put pieces together as I am.

"He works in a small industry. Everyone knows everyone and everyone talks. If he put out feelers it would get back and he'd be gone. They expect the good soldier, you know?"

Her comments go straight to the heart of my problem. AppleCore has no loyalty to me, but expects me to be a superwoman. Well, I am now. But that raises an interesting question. Am I doing what I'm doing for the company or for me? Will AppleCore even survive as long as I will? How long would I work for A'zam? Unless he becomes an immortal not very long in relation to my lifetime. And, if he were to transition, does that mean he will be my boss forever? This just doesn't get any easier.

Adrienne notes my withdrawal into thought, gives me a moment, and then asks. "Are you sure I can't get you something? You look like you need it."

I rise, "I really need to get back." I summons the Googlecar, enter the address I'm going to as we walk towards the door. "This has been really great to see you. It's just what I needed." We each give her a hug. She reciprocates, balancing her glass of wine all the while.

We stand for a moment in awkward silence, then I conclude the visit by saying, "The next time you're out, let us know and we'll do lunch. You need to keep your contacts up. You just never know when things will change unexpectedly. That's when you find out who your real friends are."

THE GHOST IN THE MACHINE

Chapter Thirteen: Twenty-seven days

Dr. Woodall arrives shortly after our return to the hospital. He looks at me carefully, apparently trying to decide the state of my mental condition. He comes to a rapid conclusion. "Don't appear to be any the worse for wear."

"Do I get to go home, or are you going to take me out on the town so I can figure out what else is missing?"

Dr. Woodall processes the tone and sharpness of my response. I notice that he twitches at the left corner of his mouth. Don't think I've ever noticed that twitch before. Is that a good sign or one of dread? "Not this morning. So tell me about your night."

"I passed it in anticipation of an early release today." I respond to see what he does with my challenge to his conclusion.

"You seem anxious. Why?" A deflection. Not going to respond directly.

"I just don't see any medical reason why I need to stay in a hospital. I'm not sick, I'm not recovering. I may be discovering and adjusting to the changes, but I don't see why that requires hospitalization. And my work situation demands I get back."

"Just a precaution," He responds. Can't challenge the doctor.

"So tell me what you think is going to happen over time. To me that is." I decide to explore a topic he'd raised the day before.

"Over time? You'll grow both more knowledgeable but also more capable, not like the rest of us who as we grow more knowledgeable, grow less able to do the physical things we used to do. Our physical peak is reached when we transition from teenage years to our twenties."

"The capacity level you've chosen for me." I clarify.

"Yes." He hesitates before continuing. "But in your case, that's just the starting point. As we perfect new technologies, we'll be able to retrofit you to increase both your mental and physical capabilities."

"Could you give me an example?"

"Sure. As we improve the design and performance of controllers, we should be able to increase the speed at which you're capable of walking or running. We should be able to double or triple the weight you're capable of lifting. We should be able to improve your fine motor skills to be able to do even more delicate work in arts and crafts. Fine brush stokes would be one example."

"So I should be able to produce works of art that are more realistic and lifelike than anything we see today." I conclude.

"Exactly." He nods, pleased I'm following his logic.

"And do you see any upper limit to what I will eventually become capable of doing on the physical side of the ledger?"

"Only what the laws of physics would bound. And who knows what we will be able to do to alter those in the future. I wish I could see to infinity, because conceivably that's how long you have. Look at how much we've pushed the limits on both human and machine capabilities in the last fifty years. When you're suddenly talking about fifty thousand or five hundred thousand years, I can't even begin to tell you what the limits could be. No one can."

"What about the mental side?"

"Same argument. You're now a modular being. There's only one part of you that cannot be changed out over time. I think we will be continually pushing frontiers. As we do, you will continually find new and faster capabilities. You'll be like the smart phone that became capable of doing what a super computer did only thirty years before. And you begin to measure that against five hundred millennia. I can't conceive of what you'll be doing in what will seem the blink of an eye to you but many lifetimes to the rest of us."

I pause at the comment about the rest of us, for I have been assuming the rest of mankind will eventually become just like the new me, whether sooner or later. "Do you expect everyone will eventually become immortal?"

"I truly don't know. I'm continually surprised by what men and mankind elect to do with their lives."

"Are you planning to join me at some point?" I'm questioning my earlier assumption.

"I've been more focused on perfecting the technology and procedures than I have in evaluating a personal decision around it. I have lots of time to contemplate what I do over the course of my life to come." Again a non-answer. Why is he not enthusiastically yes?

"Why would you not want to transition?"

"At the moment there's no reason. But there are still many unknowns. I just want to evaluate what we learn together. And what I learn with the others that will be following you soon."

I suddenly have a blinding flashback. I drop my face into my hands. A tall man. I know him. A'zam. The CEO of AppleCore. I report to him. He's yelling. Why is he yelling? He's yelling at me! Why? What did I do?

"A month delay? This is unacceptable, Sage. You're letting things get away from you. Why? What's going on that you're suddenly fucking up everything you touch? That's not like you. So tell me what's going on?"

I can't respond. My mind is working furiously but the words aren't coming. I finally stammer, "Upper limit... to approach... we didn't see. Had to backtrack. Find one that's not... subject to the limits we've encountered." Finally I'm able to get it out and start talking normally. Why am I so afraid? Why can't I even answer a question directly?

"Why didn't you catch this? You've never been behind before, Sage. You're making the whole company look bad. We don't miss release dates. Wall Street is going to hammer us. Do you realize your fuck up is going to cost us tens or hundreds of billions of dollars in valuation? Billions, Sage. This is a big deal. And if you can't fix it you're gone."

I know he's right and has reason to be angry with me. I'm angry with me. But not for the same reason. He sees me as screwing up. I see me as losing control of my mind and body. Suddenly I can't do things I used to do. I find I can't follow a thought all the way to the conclusion. What's going on? Why now? What can I do to stop it? I have to stop it or he will fire me.

"Understood." I respond. I look into his eyes. He's already made his decision. This meeting is just the human resources required documentation of my failure to perform according to expectations. That's why Desirae is here. To witness his notice of my inadequate performance. I have no recourse against the company. I'm a dead woman walking.

The memory fades. The turmoil plays out in the now remembered meeting with Dr. Woodall. I'm back in the hospital room. The memories fresh. The memory of the feelings raw. I look at Dr. Woodall. "I remember."

Windy looks relieved.

"The meeting was with A'zam, my boss. I remember the meetings with you. Now I know why I'm here. The question is do I still have a chance to resurrect my career. Or is it already too late?"

"What happens if you can't?" he asks.

"Then the last thing I'd want is to live forever as a failure." I don't even have to think about this response, it just comes pouring out.

Windy grimaces at my comment. I know she disagrees and will talk to me about my poor self-image all the way home.

"You said you'd hit a rough patch." Dr. Woodall notes for me.

"I need to go home today. Return to work tomorrow. I have to find out if I can salvage things."

"You may not be ready. If you're not, it could all backfire."

THE GHOST IN THE MACHINE

Chapter Fourteen: Twenty-six Days

I'm wearing a killer suit I bought at Neiman Marcus in Dallas before returning to San Francisco. High heels and the whole deal. I want A'zam to know I'm different without telling him how. I've got to make sure that Desirae doesn't deliver the termination letter on my first day back. I'm playing for today. Get through today. Then I'll have a chance to come back tomorrow. One day at a time until I've erased any doubts about my ability to perform.

I walk down the hallway at AppleCore headquarters, a hallway I've walked down thousands of times. I know who sits in which offices. I know what most of them do. I also know who the performers are, and who pretenders. I know who I'd go to in a pinch. Who I'd never go to. I think about the fact that Rocky worked here too until just recently. He's an engineering fellow now. He doesn't have to come in unless he wants to. There's a whole wing of Fellow offices that any can use when in for meetings. When he comes in, sometimes I'll go over and sit and chat with him. He's not in today, I checked.

I go directly to my office where Mindi, my young Indian assistant, is sitting at her desk rearranging my calendar. "Morning." I breeze past her and into my more spacious office. Don't want to act any differently than I would any other morning. She looks up and calls after me. "New suit?"

"Yes. Got it while I was on vacation." I call back to her as I slide into the chair at my desk.

Mindi magically appears before me. "Wow, some vacation. Where did you go? I need a vacation like that." She obviously noticed something's different. Good. That's exactly what I want to accomplish.

"It was fun." I don't answer her question. "When is the team assembling?"

Mindi looks over her shoulder towards my conference room. "Looks like about half are here already. Everyone should be in shortly."

"Thanks for rearranging everything. I need the daily dozen download. And then I'll figure out how we get back on track. Need to get ready for A'zam's staff meeting tomorrow. Is he going to be here?"

The daily dozen are the priority problems or issues the team is working. There are twelve members of my leadership team. One issue each. The requirement is they have to talk about their hardest problem. I need to know how they are going to resolve it today.

"As a matter of fact he will be here for a change." Mindi responds sort of distracted as she studies me. "You have something done to your face? You look great, by the way."

I nod, "Thanks. Can you round up the rest of the team? I think I'm probably going to need more than the usual time this morning." I don't want to continue this conversation as I don't want any specifics out there other than I look great and seem re-energized.

"Sure." Mindi tilts her head to give me another glance and then returns to her office.

I enter the conference room. "Morning." I greet the early arrivers. Generally those who get in first are the ones who are on track. Those who aren't are the last to arrive. I've never been able to figure out if it's to make me think they're doing everything they can to fix things before coming to my meeting or if they think the less time with me, the better when they aren't getting things done.

Oriana is there. She's the one member of my team I know I don't have to worry about. Oriana is the hardest working member and also the most brilliant. A combination I've rarely seen. "How was the wedding?" I ask her. Oriana's sister got married last weekend.

"Great. She had an incredible gown, and it was just a lot of fun. People came in for it I haven't seen in forever."

"Did Scott dance with you?" This is a sore point for her. She's been with this guy for a year and he doesn't want to go out with her. Just wants to screw her at either his place or hers.

"Just one. But it's a start. Maybe the next wedding I'll get another." Oriana is always philosophical about her personal relationships. Seems she's always a mile ahead of the guy. That makes it tough.

The rest of the team comes in almost at the same time. They take their seats around the table.

"Good morning, everyone. Today is the first day. I know it's Friday, but it's the first day of a new approach to what we do. In a few minutes we'll do the daily dozen as usual. But what's going to change, as of today, is we are now an interdependent team. That means anyone behind gets a buddy. Those of you on track will be helping someone who isn't, until they get caught up." I let that announcement sink in for a moment. I already know who I intend to pair, but will wait until we go through the issues to make the assignments.

Robert starts off. "I don't want a buddy." Robert is my problem child. Smart, but just not a good manager. I nod.

"I know Robert." I begin in an even tone. "But this is not an option. We're not performing to expectations. Clearly what we're doing today isn't working."

Robert seems to shrink into his chair. Guess he never thought I'd have the guts to replace him. But I think I've erased any doubt he might have about what I will or won't do.

Oriana is next to ask a question. "Can I volunteer to fix…"

I cut her off. "No. This isn't a democracy. I'll make the decisions about who works with who. I'll be blunt since I'm sure all of you have heard the rumors. My neck is on the line. Pure and simple. I've been willing to give you time to work things out. So now that we're behind, management has the impression I'm complacent. If you haven't noticed, that changes today."

I already know who is most likely to fail and be gone. It's always hard to make choices. You're playing with the careers of people who have families and a life outside what we do at AppleCore. Up until recently I didn't have to worry. The team always performed way above expectations. But maybe I've become a victim of my own success. Always delivering more than I've told management we would. Now I have a hiccup and A'zam wants to show me the door. Does he really think someone else can do more than I have? Obviously that's the case or I wouldn't have gone to the extent I have to ensure I survive.

Oriana is hurt that I won't let her fix things for me. But she can't alone. I know that, but evidently she doesn't share my opinion. I've never thought she wanted my job. But now, for some reason, that thought enters my mind.

The day flies by with the usual crises, resolutions and mini-dramas. As the usual work day draws to a close I'm looking forward to seeing some of the friends I haven't seen since the transformation. We all went to Stanford together, met in freshman English, but chose totally different majors. We ended up in different industries. But we all made it one way or another in the professions we chose. Some of us have titles and thousands of employees doing our work. Some of us run non-profits, have maybe a hundred volunteers who sometimes help and others not. But we're all professional women who came up together. We keep in touch to support each other as we crawl our way to our individual dreams.

Reese, the former prom is sipping her white California wine and telling everyone about someone none of us liked in undergraduate school. "And did you know Beth's no good live-in got her pregnant? She felt so bad about the relationship she had an abortion?" She's also very plain spoken.

Windy absolutely couldn't stand Beth and they were roommates for one semester. "Really? I hadn't heard that. What I heard was it isn't her live-in's, and she got the abortion because she didn't want him to see the child and realize it wasn't his."

"That sounds more like Beth." Delilah, the politically correct one responds. "She just never seemed to be able to talk with a guy directly and tell him what she thinks."

"Let's be fair." MC, the psychologist amongst us wants to moderate the conversation. "Beth has a dependency issue. She has to work it. She can if she chooses. But my superficial observation is she's intimidated by her live-in. Thinks if he leaves her she'll just die. It's a common enough syndrome. He comes to her rescue, ingratiates himself so she feels obligated to serve his desires. The next thing she knows he makes the decisions. Now she suddenly feels totally disempowered."

"Who gives a shit about Beth, anyway?" I fire off to get a reaction. They all know how I am about dropping grenades in the middle of a juicy conversation that none of us really care about. Beth always thought she was better than us. She made a point of letting us know her family could be traced back to the first Stanford graduating class. Her Stanford grad father was a serial entrepreneur. He started and built businesses to a point where he thought they weren't fun anymore.

Beth joined her father's firm when she graduated. Daddy put her on the board of several of his start-ups. And even though her only frame of reference is her Stanford classes, she advises business owners how to quickly grow their companies. Obviously the road has been bumpy for Beth. The group likes to gossip about her. We love to talk about how life hasn't turned out the way she portrayed it when we were all in school together.

"We all do." Windy isn't about to let me derail their fun. "But what's the story with Raoul? You see him recently?"

"He called the other day. But I couldn't make it happen. Work." I answer knowing they're hoping for something juicy from me.

"That's always your excuse. No wonder you're not married." Reese is ready to call bullshit on me. "You want him to spend more than one night you've got to be there for him."

"He's not the one." I respond.

"Then who is?" Windy's right there with Reese. "You're always making excuses. No one's good enough for you. And you're not getting any younger. At some point you're going to wake up and realize you have to decide whether you're ready for a life beyond your little box at work."

"I'm not right now." I respond. "Things have been a bit tense since I missed a deadline."

"You missed a deadline?" MC can't seem to believe I'd failed to do something. "Is something wrong? You have a breakdown? Tell us?"

"Nothing like that." I respond. Windy is the only one who knows all about the transformation. That will be a longer conversation than I'm planning to have with them tonight. I need an emotional recharge, but not a complete therapy session, which is what I'll get if I open Pandora's Box.

"Then what's going on?" Delilah, this time. "Tell us. Who cares more about you than us?"

She's right about who cares for me. I have friends, but only this group goes back as far as college. And my other friends are superficial. We say hello, and ask about kids, work, politics, and the weather. But we avoid anything really personal. Only in this group have I ever gotten into feelings. Only in this group have I let anyone see behind the curtain. And they've all accepted me as I am.

I give a weak smile to Delilah. "You're right. You're the only ones.

It's been a rough time. For a while I was concerned I might lose my job, but hopefully that's working itself out." I shake my head. "I've had to go to extreme measures to stay."

Windy catches my eye as she almost chokes on her sip of wine.

"So next time it might not work so well?" Reese is listening to what she's not hearing.

"You need to tell us about it." MC is playing shrink. She's using the group as a means of getting me to talk, since she knows I'll never come to see her for professional advice. "We want to help, but can't if you're not willing to discuss what you're feeling." Driving right to the feeling level. That's MC.

"What do you mean by extreme measures?" Reese picks up on my last comment. Oops. Didn't want to go there, but now I need to say something.

"I had a procedure." I admit, trying to figure out how I'm going to explain this without revealing too much.

"What procedure?" Reese asks looking at me closer. "Looks like you had your eyes done, but that doesn't explain your work situation."

"I wasn't going to say anything about your eyes, but you need to tell us what else you had done. After all, we may need to do the same." MC offers.

"It was an experimental procedure." I finally decide on. "Can't really tell you much until they go through all the analysis as to whether it's having the desired effects. We're finding limitations and trying to deal with them."

"How is it helping with your work situation?" Reese isn't letting me skate on my explanation. I knew she wouldn't, but need more time to figure out what to say.

"I'm able to focus on work better. Not so distracted. Not dealing with personal limitations I was experiencing."

"Limitations? You?" Delilah is surprised to hear me talk about this since I'd not shared it before.

I nod and grimace with the memory of what I'd been reduced to. But I'd never let them see any of the problems I was experiencing. The degenerative condition was still in the early phases. It became evident when I was under stress. I'm never under stress with this group because, for the most part, they're always very accepting of me. We make each other laugh. "It was all stress related." I try to summarize at the highest level I can.

"I understand. You've got to be in just an absolute pressure cooker with your job." MC tries to read through my comments. But she's also looking me over more carefully than before. I'd deliberately worn loose fitting clothes so they wouldn't see the physical differences other than in my face. But MC is trying to decide what she isn't seeing.

"I'm used to it. Been in the job for a long time. Sure it ratchets up each year, but I've been in the middle of it for so long that shouldn't be the reason. But according to the doctor, it's the culprit behind most physical ailments we experience as we get older."

"Not older, just wiser." Windy remarks as she takes another sip of her wine.

"No, we're not getting older." MC agrees. "But we are coping differently than we used to. When did we start drinking wine? Does anyone remember? Used to be weed. Then vodka and gin. And now it's wine. Same thing, only we're evolving with what our friends are using to cope. Does anyone here really like wine better than weed?"

"I do." Windy joins in. I think she's trying to deflect the conversation to give me more time since she sees I'm not wanting to get deep into it tonight.

"You always liked wine, as I remember." Reese notes. "Your parents went to wineries all over the world. I remember you talking about it, wondering why anyone would want to waste a vacation that way. But don't they own a winery now? Some place near here as I remember."

"They bought a small place." Windy confirms. "Mostly buy the grapes from other growers. But they're learning the business and enjoying it. Unlike us, they have lots of time. And it gives them an excuse to be out here and see their grandkids."

Reese nods, "Yeah. My parents are insisting on having the kids two weekends a month. They say they want the opportunity to properly spoil them. I want my kids to know them and all, but it's a conundrum. The more they spoil the kiddos, the more I've got to do to unspoil them when they come home."

"And as I remember your parents are real stoners." Delilah remarks looking at the rest of us for support. "Is that what you're afraid of? That your parents will rub off on your kids?"

"My parents are free spirits. I'll admit that." Reese begins. "How they raised me was in a different time. The world's just become so much more competitive than it was when we were young. If my kids are stoned all the time their grades will suffer. They'll never get into the good schools. That would limit what they can become so early. We don't want to do that to them."

"That why you shifted to wine from weed? You didn't want them to follow your example?" MC is calling her bluff.

"The people we socialize with are into wine. We still do weed once in a while, but only at home when the kiddos are away and there's no one else around."

"Do as I say and not as I do." Windy points out the hypocrisy.

"It's not like that." Reese responds. "We're liberal with the kids.

We take them everywhere with us. We deliberately look for things they can do to experience all life has to offer. We want them to understand the world isn't one big party. They have to work hard to get the things important to them." Reese sounds defensive, which is unusual in this group.

Delilah nods, "I got your back on that one, sister. We're trying to create a more just future for our kids than our parents experienced. They had to fight for everything. We never had to fight the way they did. But we are working our asses off in a much more competitive environment. I can't imagine how hard Stanford is going to be by the time our kids get there."

"You expect your kids to go to Stanford?" MC asks.

"Of course." Reese responds. "You would too if you had any kids. I wouldn't want them to go anywhere else."

"But what if they decide they want to go to Harvard because they want to be a Boston lawyer?" I ask to keep the pot stirred.

"We don't know anyone in Boston." Reese responds, apparently not really thinking about what I'm asking. "Besides, the valley is where everything's happening. Boston's boring in comparison. At least to me."

"But you just said you're working hard to enable your kids to have a good future. And if the future they choose isn't the one you would hope for, what are you going to do? Would you really say, no you can't go to Harvard because Boston's boring? That seems to fly in the face of what you've said you want for your kids." I continue the thought I think she missed.

"I can't see any of them becoming lawyers." Reese dismisses the question.

"Could your parents see you becoming an algorithms wizard when you were the age of your kids?" MC jumps in to support me.

"My parents didn't even know what an algorithm was when I was my oldest's age."

"My point exactly." MC follows up. "You have to let them discover what makes them happy. What makes them want to get up in the morning and go to work? What's their quest? What do they hope to become? What do they want out of life? It's different for everyone. So we're just saying you need to show them the world and answer their questions. But don't try to convince them your path is the only one. Generally when someone does that, the child rebels. They could end up doing something destructive to the family, themselves or society."

Since MC is the one making this observation, apparently it's carrying more weight. Reese is quiet as she sips her glass of wine. "What else we got to talk about tonight?" Reese finally asks.

"I want to know more about Sage's situation." MC comes back to me.

"Can I take a pass tonight? A lot of moving parts at the moment." I respond, having not touched the glass of wine before me.

"Are you pregnant?" Delilah asks. "That's one of the reasons a woman doesn't drink. And we all know you like your wine."

I laugh. "No chance of that." I reflect aloud. "Doc wants me to stay away from everything I like until we know everything's good."

"Sounds a lot more serious than just an eye job and body sculpture." Delilah notes as she looks even more closely at me.

I shrug to let them know I'm not going to answer tonight.

"Then we're meeting here next week and every week until you give us the whole scoop, Sage. "We're not letting you deal with whatever you got going on alone." Delilah concludes.

THE GHOST IN THE MACHINE

Chapter Fifteen

Today is A'zam's staff meeting. Now I have to take the second step on my road to survival. Even though I have no clear idea what that second step has to be. But it will be taken in the staff meeting. The fact that A'zam will be in the room is a good thing. He has a hard time with difficult decisions when he has to look the individual in the eye. I've noticed that, but never thought I'd be the one he's confronting.

Mindi is back checking me out even more today. She stops by my office, hangs in the doorway giving me a close look-over and absently asks, "You really think A'zam is going to make a change now?"

"We're not performing. What do you think?" I ask her without looking up from my monitor.

"No one else can do what you do. Doesn't make sense." She responds. But is that what she really thinks or is she just being loyal? Never drink your own bathwater is what Rocky always tells me. I may agree with what she just said, but that may be because I'm not seeing me as A'zam and the rest of the leadership team sees me.

"AppleCore has always prospered because it saw opportunities before anyone else has." I begin. "Is A'zam seeing things you and I aren't? I have to guess he is. So that makes it all that much harder to know what to do."

She thinks about my comments only a moment. "A'zam is loyal. He chose you."

I study Mindi's face. I've never done this before. Is it something my heightened perceptions are feeding me that my old mind was just not capable of processing? She seems to be wrestling with something.

"There were lots of rumors during your vacation. But here you are, looking like you're ready to take on the world."

I smile at her, "I am."

"That makes me feel so much better. I wasn't looking forward to having to break in a new boss."

I see that admission was hard for her. But it was also heartfelt. Mindi has always been genuine in expressing what she thinks. "I'm not going to do anything that will cause you to have to break in a new boss, Mindi." I try to reassure her.

Mindi crinkles her face. "You haven't had your caffeine yet this morning. I'm sorry."

Mindi knows I have to have a Starbucks injection to get my heart racing in the morning. She didn't get the double latte. Pumpkin latte this time of year. But now I can't drink it. That realization gives me a moment of panic. How does a leopard change his spots, particularly when I already look so different? Need to be careful and thread this so it doesn't raise further speculation. "No need. Woke up early with the time change and all. So got an early start."

That opened a door I didn't want to enter. "Time change? You never said where you were."

One admission paints me into another corner. How do I get out of this now? "Dallas. I'd never been so it seemed a good place to recharge my batteries." She has no idea how accurate that is.

"Dallas? I've never been there either. Did you like it?" Mindi seems to be trying to put pieces of the puzzle together.

"Different than I thought. Good place to relax." Don't say too much. Better to minimize my responses than to open still another question.

"You go to a spa or something there? You look great like it took off years."

How to answer this without painting myself into another corner. "Maybe we can chat about this another time. I've got to prepare for staff meeting."

"Oh, sorry. Sure. What do you need for me to get you?" Mindi is jarred by my abrupt change of topic.

"Another twenty-four hours?" I suggest. I'm trying to make the point I need to get ready and that my abrupt ending of the discussion had nothing to do with her question.

Mindi nods, seeing that I've already begun to search out information on my display. She heads back to her office.

I look up and close my eyes. I no longer need a display to see what I want to know. It's all presented in my mind. My brain has already begun to organize the facts the way I need them to discuss in the staff meeting. I shut my eyes so everything is easier to comprehend without any outside distractions.

It only takes a couple of minutes. I have all the data in the format I need available for me to recall during the meeting. It used to take me a half day to get ready, pulling the data and organizing it. Now I actually have time to consider what it means before going into the meeting. A new experience. I always tried to grasp what was behind the numbers as I sat in the meeting. But now I have time to thoroughly analyze it before I go in. I can obtain additional data to answer questions without having to say to A'zam that I'll get back to him. This new body may not be so bad.

Normally I would take my notebook with me, where I'd have scribbled notes to myself. But not today. I have it all in my head.

As I walk out of the office Mindi calls after me. "You forgot your notebook." She's almost in a panic, thinking I'd forgotten it.

"Don't need it." I call back without stopping. Mindi must be really wondering what I'm up to. No caffeine and no notebook. I'm clearly living dangerously and out of character. Should I back off and play the part more like I always have? No. I want everyone to know I'm different. Not how I'm different, but that I'm coming at my job with confidence.

As I enter the small conference room, Julia Sommers, the big-boned Chief Operating Officer, has already claimed her seat next to A'zam's right hand. As usual she simply mutters, "Morning." to whomever has entered the room. She knows who it is by the voice that responds.

"Julia." I respond. I never call her that, so I expect she will look up. She does. A quick look catches her by surprise. She decides to study me longer.

"I like your hair. That a new color for you?" I see she's trying to reconcile what she sees with what she knows. Since she doesn't know where I went or why, she's making assumptions.

As I take my seat I respond, "New hairdresser. Last one couldn't quite get it right. You know?"

Julia nods to herself returning to her display to prepare for the meeting. As the rest of the Senior Leadership Team assembles, I get long stares, a few 'mornings' and one pat on my shoulder from Hung Duc, the VP of Engineering, who is sympathetic to the delays in my area. Nothing else.

Chapter Sixteen

A'zam enters the conference room. He seems engaged in something whose presence is not seen. For that reason he enters the room without acknowledging anyone or even seeing who is there and who is not. We have assigned seats. It's obvious instantly who's not present.

As A'zam slides in next to Julia I hear him whisper, "I just met with the last one. I like him best."

Julia, reacts by whispering back, "But that would change the balance. Do you have a plan how we keep the balance?"

A'zam nods as he looks up, then directly at me. He acts surprised to see me sitting there. It takes him a second longer to realize something is different. And about five seconds pass before he responds. "Morning. We have a busy day today. Wall Street is looking for answers to our recent performance downturn. I need those answers from you." He glances around the room to see if anyone is missing. None are. He then looks back at me. "Sage, what advice do you have for us today?"

This had become a joke on the Senior Leadership Team. He always turned to me for 'Sage advice' and I always come prepared with some quip for him. Today I decide to take the offensive and not play the game. "I'm advising you that our newest product will be ready for release on Friday."

A'zam reacts, sitting up straighter with a puzzled look. "What happened? You've been out."

"I've taken the appropriate steps to recapture lost time. My team will deliver as promised."

"But you didn't the last time you promised." A'zam is going straight for the jugular.

"If I don't deliver, then fire me." I'm giving him the rope to hang me in hopes he hasn't already.

The room is silent. Is anyone even breathing? A'zam seems to consider my challenge for a long moment, then looks away before answering, "I may just take you up on that offer." He looks to Julia, who seems as surprised. She doesn't know how to react.

So he plunges on without her. "Friday. Do I gear up manufacturing and our distribution and marketing folks to receive your release? Or do I hedge my bets having been embarrassed last time? What would you have me do?"

"You'll have it if I have to work 24 hours a day to ensure you do." A confident tone I knew he'd not heard from me in a while. But it was the confident tone he'd become used to over the years. I'd given him a month's warning that we might miss the roll-out date the first time around. So he had time to adjust, but chose not to. That was his mistake. But since he doesn't make mistakes, it became mine.

A'zam shakes his head. "Can't do it Sage. I'm not going to be embarrassed again."

"This is your chance to recover with Wall Street." I point out knowing that is all important to him. Only it's clear he intends to tell Wall Street he's making changes to buy more time. I see an opening. "Any other path causes more delays, further eroding investor confidence in your leadership."

The whole team is staring at me now. No one wants to look at A'zam. No one challenges him the way I just have. At least not in front of everyone. And from what I'd heard, anyone who had done so in private was gone the same day. But I have nothing to lose.

A'zam stares at me as he considers my challenge. Seems to be trying to decide how to respond. I don't give him a chance.

"The old Sage is back, A'zam. The one you always counted on when things were sliding away from you. Do you ride the horse that brought you here, or do you change horses not knowing if the new one can go the distance? Particularly on a ground breaking product that person has no experience with?"

A'zam takes a longer look at me. He sees something is different. I know I look a lot more like the Sage he hired. I hope that's enough to convince him. He again looks to Julia who shakes her head ever so slightly. It's funny I've never seen this non-verbal communication between them before. Julia just told him not to change his plan. But I see A'zam consider the points I made about Wall Street and his leadership.

"Suppose I were to agree to the roll-out a week from today." He's considering my offer. "I need to know if everyone can support that. Assuming you were ready the first time around, does anyone have a problem being ready according to Sage's new schedule?"

Julia is handling marketing herself since she has not yet filled the VP vacancy that has been there for several months. The speculation is she's trying to get more hands-on experience since she came up on the financial side of the house. Number crunchers are always invited into the senior discussions, but they seldom have operating experience that allows them put the numbers into context. Everyone I've talked with said Julia is a disaster in marketing.

Julia shakes her head. "I'm not convinced the advertising and marketing campaign has the punch we need, particularly now with the delays. We have to drive a desire for people to want to replace their old units with the new one. It will take several days to get the ads on the air. I'm not sure that's enough time to connect and drive the desire with customers."

I hear the usual buzz words, but they're not in the order I'm used to hearing them. I take a chance, "Are you saying you can't deliver the customers if I deliver the product?"

No one has ever been this blunt in the staff meeting. Julia realizes she's put herself into a bind. She could be the one going on the layoff list if I deliver now and she fails to do so. "That's not what I said."

A'zam enjoys her discomfort. "It is what you said, Julia. Now what's the story? Are you able to deliver the buyers or not?"

She looks around the room like a trapped rat. "We all know there are many factors that determine product acceptance."

A'zam seems annoyed now. "You haven't answered my question and you're giving us what's beginning to sound like excuses. Either you're going to deliver the customers or you aren't. Which is it?"

Julia's response is barely audible. I can easily hear her, but I don't think those around me can. "We will deliver customers. However, I'm not confident it will overcome the concerns about a delayed product potentially having bugs."

A'zam responds as if patiently addressing a child, "If you don't know the answer, go ask your people. What they tell you should enable you to deliver the customers. Listen to them and do what they tell you unless you have better information."

Julia nods almost imperceptibly.

A'zam looks around the room. "I'll pull the trigger before the end of the day, unless something comes up between now and then."

"I'll have the revised schedule, technical issues summary and plan for resolution for you by noon." I respond to put the matter to bed. Now all I have to do is come up with a detailed plan for how I'm going to deliver. Piece of cake. Yeah, right. But at least I got another day.

Chapter Seventeen

The plan went to A'zam at noon as I'd promised. I decided to work with those on the team who were struggling the most, like Robert and Naomi. I was pleased to learn that Naomi was actually back on track. She'd also developed a clear plan to deliver within the new schedule. I asked Naomi if she wanted someone to help her. She said she would gladly take someone if I felt it important, but that frankly if I did, it might actually jeopardize her schedule. She would have to spend time with the helper and not with her module leads who need the most attention. I agreed with her analysis.

I went to find Robert, who was another matter. I called Oriana and asked her to join us.

"Can you show me your recovery plan?" I ask of Robert.

He sends me the document. I quickly scan it. Robert is good at the paperwork, but it's his people skills that limit his success. Something about the plan bothers me so I begin to ask questions.

"You only compile code once a day. Why?"

"So it's compiled when they come in. They don't have to wait. They need all the time I can give them to write their sections. When we're this far behind I can't afford to have them waiting on compilation results." Robert responds matter-of-factly.

"Why do you have them wait?" I'm confused at his logic.

"So they don't have to rework code sections if the compilation fails." Robert is now becoming defensive. I need to keep him from going there as he will just shut down as I've seen him do before.

"That's understandable. But let me ask you a question."

"You already are." He notes to slow me down a bit.

I don't hesitate in my response. "How many times has the compilation failed in the last week?"

"It hasn't." He answers, not connecting what I'm trying to say to him. Have to take him the next step. Damn. Sometimes Robert just makes this whole supervisory stuff harder than it needs to be.

"That's good. It's a sign the code is mature and functioning as expected. That means you're making good progress. But what I'm asking you to consider is: if the code's in good shape, why don't you let the team continue working on coding in a separate instance, but compile every three hours or so? That way you have more completed sections earlier. You'll also discover if you have a problem requiring rework sooner. You may accelerate delivery of the whole product. Even though I asked for product release on Friday, I'm seeing a path to get us there by Thursday. I'd really like us to deliver ahead of the new schedule."

"I don't want to be the one who gets you fired. You know? I mean I'm pushing people pretty hard. We've been at this one much longer than any of us expected. I think there's a bit of development fatigue going on out there, if you know what I mean."

I lean back in my chair. I know the fatigue is hitting him. The question is whether it's just him or his team too? I can't shift the work to others as we don't have time to get new people spun up on what has to be done. It's also always a problem when someone unfamiliar with what someone else has done comes in. No matter how much we ask the developers to document how they build the code, there are always holes or logic differences that don't get recorded. They usually show up later. No, the current teams have to get us over the goal line. But I need someone to give me an independent assessment of where Robert's team really is. That's why I called Oriana, who arrives now.

Robert sees her at his door. His face turns ashen. I know he thinks he's losing his team and have to address that right now. "Hi Oriana. Robert and I've been reviewing his team's progress. I think there's a path to advancing product release to Thursday."

Oriana sits down next to me. "Robert." She nods that she understands.

"What I'd like you to do is an independent assessment of Robert's team. Is getting it done a day early possible?"

Oriana nods again, "Sure. And I'd like Robert to do the same for my team if he has time."

Wow, I hadn't thought of asking Robert to assess Oriana's team.

"I don't know." Robert responds, and then continues, "I think I need to keep close to the team." He shakes his head.

"Isn't Starkes your deputy?" Oriana asks trying to remember.

"Yeah, but I've got him working with Bekka's team. They're my problem children. Individually all good coders, but they just can't seem to get the code they write to compile and integrate. Always the last to get their sections in. They're two releases back of where they should be."

This is worse than I thought. I see his schedule in my mind, see how he intends to have them catch up. I realize what he has proposed is wishful thinking. He doesn't have a credible plan. I look at Oriana. "You know where to start your evaluation." I nod towards the door. Oriana leaves us to begin her assessment. When she's gone I turn back to Robert. "If they're two releases behind, how do you make the schedule?"

"It's all there in the plan." He offers in his defense.

"You haven't given me anything to work with, Robert. I want to give you the benefit of the doubt. That's why I brought Oriana in. She'll be objective. If there's any means of recovery she'll identify it for us. Now I have a choice to make. I can either: take Oriana's assessment and let you implement it, or I can ask her to do so by combining her team with yours. I'll make my decision after I see Oriana's report."

"But she's the one who's assessing my team. She has an incentive to find fault and grow her empire at my expense." Robert protests almost plaintively.

"Oriana doesn't want to add to her responsibilities right now." I inform him. "She has the most difficult deliveries to make. Her team is exhausted. The last thing she wants is to be distracted by solving your problems in addition to hers."

"Then why'd you ask her to do the assessment?" Robert tries to figure out whether he is toast or not. "She should be with her team, helping them."

"She should be. But she's also dedicated to delivering the entire product, not just her portion of it. She knows if she delivers on time but you don't, that maybe her team can get some rest, but we all lose credibility. We've suffered that already."

Robert reflects. What he knows and what I haven't said is the major reason we're this far behind is because his team held up all of the others, time and again. Robert considers what happened and is happening now. "Why are we having so much trouble this time? I don't understand what's changed from all of the earlier releases."

I anticipated this question and have a thought out response. "We've pushed this technology about as far as it goes. There won't be another release for this hardware platform. The next set of code won't have the boundaries we're living within on this set. The alpha team is already experimenting with a new approach."

I think of the irony that I'm having this conversation with Robert about losing his job when I'm in a pitched battle to hold on to mine. I should feel sorry for him, but I don't. I've given him every chance to produce. He's the weak link. He can cause me to fail. I can't afford to let him. Just as A'zam doesn't intend to let me cause him another public whipping by Wall Street analysts.

"I should have Oriana's report by morning, so I'll let you know what I decide then. If you're just exhausted, go home and get some sleep. Have Starkes cover the rest of the day."

Robert nods as I rise to leave the room. I know he won't go home. It would be a sign he's given up. He can't afford to do that now. Just as I can't afford to go home either. Our fates are inextricably linked, only I don't intend to follow him out the door, even though I expect that to be what is in store for him.

THE GHOST IN THE MACHINE

Chapter Eighteen: Twenty-five Days

About midnight I leave and go to my condo. It's a short walk and doesn't take long to get there. I walk into the bedroom. The recharging bed has been installed. Dr. Woodall made the necessary arrangements for me as it had to be shipped from Dallas.

Since I have to charge naked, I remove my clothes to lie down on the bed. Proximity charging is what they call it. The clothes would slow down the time it takes to charge. I feel the charger engage. I close my eyes for the fifteen minutes I have to remain motionless. I'm not resting, but there's nothing to look at so it just makes sense to close them.

I'm instantly flooded by memories. Of the smell of flowers that grew in Rocky's gardens. My mother tended the flowers when I was small. After the accident they grew wild. Within a year they became over run by weeds. I used to love to go walk out there as they always reminded me of my mother. She would spend hours weeding and watering. Sometimes I'd go out and pull the weeds around a rose bush. That particular plant would do much better that year. Bigger flowers, more colorful. The smell I'd inhale would always relax me and give me pleasure. And I'd think of Mother and Tabitha. Mother always wanted me to help her in the garden. I think she would have been disappointed that I didn't tend it the way she did. I was always too busy, studying or reading or going out with friends. It was a big garden. Too much for me when I was younger. I could have kept it up the way she did when I was in high school. But it just never became a priority. I think I also didn't want to spend that much time out there. It reminded me that Mother wasn't coming home ever again. And I missed her then as I do now.

I tried to get Rocky to help me at first, but he would just respond,

THE GHOST IN THE MACHINE

"I don't do weeds."

I would argue with him that he didn't need to do all the weeds, just the ones around the plants. He would disagree that once you get started on something, you need to finish it. Doing things half-way is never acceptable. And if you do something half-way in say a garden, well then what's to stop you from doing something half-way at work? That never works out in the end.

A jolt. I'm sitting at the dinner table with Rocky, Mother and Tabitha. It was the last Thanksgiving we had together. I remember the smells of the turkey, the roles baking in the oven and the pies that Mother made the day before. She always made a pumpkin pie for Rocky and me, and a Raspberry pie for her and Tabitha. The remembrance of those delicious smells overcomes me. I realize I miss those smells. I miss being together with my family. I miss the satisfaction of eating all those wonderful foods, most of which we only got to eat on that one day each year. Mother called it a tradition. It had nothing to do with religion, or national holidays. It was simply the fact that we as a family were celebrating being together and reflecting on the good fortune we had.

I realized I must have been a disappointment to Rocky. After the accident I didn't keep up the traditions. It was just the two of us. I didn't cook much. We tended to pick up fast food separately. Most of the time we were on different schedules. When the holidays came we ordered in and ate together; but we seldom went out. Not even for birthdays. I feel the loss of those traditions. I wonder how Rocky feels about my letting it all go, when Mother had worked so hard to create them for us and make them special.

Another jolt. I'm sitting across from Rocky inhaling Chinese food. I remember the taste of the Kung Pow Chicken. I remember how hard it was for me to use chop sticks to transport the pieces into my mouth. Occasionally Rocky would make a comment. I'd have to put the chop sticks down and calm myself as his comments always put me into orbit then. I'd try again to get just enough nourishment into my body so I wouldn't disappear. I was really thin then because it just seemed there wasn't much need for food. It was more habit to eat than hunger. Maybe I was just too self-conscious that I wasn't overly attractive. None of the boys I was interested in even knew I existed.

I hear the timer. My fifteen minutes of charging are over. It's time to return to work. I have the whole night ahead of me.

THE GHOST IN THE MACHINE

Chapter Nineteen

I'm still trying to figure out why I had memories during the recharge that hadn't come to me in years when I walk into my office. And yet there are echoes of those memories, images that in some cases I don't even remember having seen in the first place. I see an aerial view of the accident site where Anna Laura and Tabitha died. The wet twisted remnants of the dark red Toyota Prius Anna Laura drove every day to work and to pick us up from school activities. It was crushed under a tractor-trailer truck that was forced to stop short, skidding in the rain as it came down a steep hill. The trailer came around into the oncoming lane and flipped on its side landing on the defenseless Prius, Anna Laura and Tabitha. I see the tire marks where Anna Laura apparently tried to avoid the inevitable, braking as hard as she possibly could. I imagine she put her arm out to keep Tabitha in her seat as the car and Anna Laura did all they could to avoid a fate that was not of their own making. As far as I know there were no images of the accident itself, even though most 26 wheelers have had dash cameras for a long time. The dash cam on that particular vehicle had been inoperable for months before the accident. The owner had already been fined once for not repairing it. I know I didn't see that when it happened, and yet I find myself examining the scene of the accident from a viewpoint I never had. What's this all about?

I'm overcome with the same feeling of helplessness I felt that night when Rocky and I came upon the accident on our way home. We were supposed to all meet at the house. Only Rocky was late getting out of work. I had to wait for him at school to pick me up. If Rocky had been on time we would have already been home when the accident occurred. Instead we were less than five minutes behind them on the highway. What I remember most was that when we came upon the accident I saw the license plate number first. The car was crushed, but the license plate was still clearly visible. I pointed it out to Rocky as we slowly passed the accident scene on the shoulder of the highway, in the single lane of traffic moving past the scene.

Rocky pulled over once we were past the tractor trailer so the line of traffic could work its way by. Rocky took my hand and held up his other hand to stop a car so we could cross the lane. A policewoman approached us.

"You can't be here." The stern looking woman, dressed all in blue and wearing a raincoat of the same color, said to Rocky as we came up to the trailer van.

"That's my wife!" Rocky simply replied to her.

"The accident just happened, how do you know it's her?"

"We both saw it. The license plate. CNZ2897. Red Prius. My wife and daughter."

The policewoman looked at me grim-faced, and returned her gaze to Rocky. "Wait here." She took out a walkie-talkie and spoke quietly to someone. We were both in shock. This couldn't be happening.

I'd had an argument that morning with Anna Laura about the clothes I intended to wear to school. Anna Laura told me she wouldn't let me go out in public, let alone to school, in what I wanted to wear. I informed her all the kids were wearing exactly what I had on. I'd argued that she wouldn't want me to be the most unpopular girl in school because I wore clothes from the last century. Anna Laura responded she would rather have me be the last virgin than the first one pregnant in my class.

I'd dismissed her argument and took the clothes I wanted to wear in my gym bag. I changed once I got to school. I was called to the office with a dozen other girls who were dressed the same. I was given detention, but they hadn't called home. I told the Principal I had other clothes in my locker. So Anna Laura and Rocky never knew of my disobedience. But I always felt especially guilty she died on the day I'd disobeyed her. And Tabitha. I'd thought that day I was blazing a path that would make it easier for Tabitha to be her own person and not under Anna Laura's fashion rules. She never knew the sacrifice I thought I was making for her.

I need to see Rocky, but I've been avoiding doing so. I haven't seen him in a month or more. I never know when he's going to come into the office at AppleCore. He comes in when he has a meeting he wants to be involved in personally. Otherwise he stays connected by videoconferencing. As an Engineering Fellow he isn't required to work specific projects. He mentors engineers who are building new products. He helps them solve problems or researches new approaches to solve complex engineering issues. He mostly writes papers that go into the corporate knowledge base. They can be accessed by any engineer seeking creative or different ways to enhance product performance.

I bring up Rocky's calendar on my display. He's not scheduled to come in this month. I wonder what he's working on. I go into his work file. Says he's working on designing Angstrom unit length circuitry for robotic memory chipsets. I wonder how many things Rocky worked on are in my new body. And before I can even complete the thought, the list of components with design features he worked on appears before me. Most relate to my memory storage and retrieval. In fact, I see he was involved in the very features that are enabling me to see what he did in the early design of what I have become. So in that sense he is my biological father and has some paternity, along with a whole host of others in my new self. But then I realize I have as many mothers in my new self as fathers. I really am the result of a whole village that was necessary to create the child that would become the future of the tribe. Or in this case the whole human race if everyone eventually becomes immortal.

I look at the clock, it's not yet one am. Rocky is most likely awake as he has trouble sleeping when he's working on something. I decide to give him a call. He answers on only the third ring.

THE GHOST IN THE MACHINE

"Yeah."

I smile at the recognition of his voice. "You never sleep." I respond, thinking I've now one upped him in that department.

"Sage?" he wants to verify. "What the hell are you doing up in the middle of the night?"

"I could be asking the same of you. What are you working on?" I know what's in the file, but wonder what he thinks he's working on.

"Warp speed." He responds curtly, basically telling me he's not about to discuss it on an unencrypted communication.

"I think someone already solved that one." I kid him. "You need to get out more and find out what the rest of the world is up to." Now I'm serious.

"No need, the world comes to me." I see him gesturing in my mind's eye. "It's all here in this room. Whatever I want to see, know or explore. I don't have to go nowhere. And I owe a lot of that to you, from what they tell me. Keep pushing the frontier on software capabilities. Next thing I know you'll change the world forever and not even bother to tell me."

Does he know? Did someone tell him? Who? I don't want him to worry about me. Don't want him to think he needs to come stay with me. That didn't work so well last time we shared the same house. Even though I feed off his insights when I get frustrated I can't solve one problem or another on my own. He always just says two brains are better than one. Rocky always has a simple approach to solving any issue. I'm off re-inventing physics and he asks me why couldn't I just do such and such? Always practical. Always sees the shortest path between two points. I wish I'd inherited his insights. And now I'm finding myself having to sort out the insights that are an even shorter route to the solution than his generally are. I have to keep slowing myself down because the solutions keep appearing before I know the logic is sound.

"You eating?" Rocky goes days without eating when into a problem.

"When I get hungry."

"Which isn't often." I respond knowing what his answer means. "What did you eat today?"

"Since it's a little after one in the morning, nothing yet." A precise answer. Stop pushing.

"Do I have to come over and make you breakfast?" I know what I have to do.

"About two in the afternoon would be right. Should be just getting up about then." He's trying to get rid of me. What's going on?

"I take it you're in the middle of something."

"You could say that." Evasive. What's he up to?

"Anyone I know?" I ask not expecting to get an answer.

"Dr. Sanderson." I hear the break as he listens for my response. Elizabeth Sanderson is a brilliant physicist at the company and twenty years younger than Rocky. She also has a reputation as an unabashed sensualist. That's a polite way of saying she's slept with nearly everyone at one time or another. "We're working through the theoretical limits of heat transfer in sub Angstrom circuits."

That tracks with what the log says he's working. But at this time of night I'd assume Elizabeth would be thinking of friction causing heat in areas other than sub Angstrom circuits. I guess I shouldn't be surprised Elizabeth would eventually get around to Rocky. He's probably the last one left in the company who's not bed her. "I'll try to have breakfast waiting for you when you wake up. Should it be for one or two?"

THE GHOST IN THE MACHINE

.

Chapter Twenty

By five-thirty I've reviewed all of the files on the various projects in my area. Twelve teams. This review would have taken me days before. Now I'm able to retrieve, parse and zero in on issues much quicker than I could have imagined before. I guess there are some advantages to having access to all company data, and all internet databases to compare, contrast, and determine what I need to do in each area. I've never felt this empowered before. I have the lists and solutions I need to have the teams work all organized in my head. The stand-up meeting this morning is not going to be pleasant for the team until they realize I've taken months out of their schedules by determining their priorities.

I have a car pick me up and deliver me to Rocky's house. It's about seven miles away. Not far, but would take me too long to walk, make his breakfast, and be back in time for a seven-thirty meeting. Since I'm fully recharged and don't get tired, it's no longer out of the question to walk a long distance like to Rocky's place. In fact, I'll plan to do that when I have things under control. Would give me some uninterrupted think time.

I encounter an unexpected problem when I arrive. The home security system always recognized me, but I've changed enough that I don't pass the biometric profile anymore. Since I no longer have an iris in my eyes, I have to go to secondary recognition which is fingerprint. Dr. Woodall had mentioned that they kept my fingerprints for this very reason. Too many security systems were dependent upon them, but that was the only reason. The system wasn't happy it couldn't compare iris and fingerprint, but finally let me in. The monitor has a note for Rocky that I've been allowed to enter with one biometric failure. I wonder how many other security systems are dependent upon my iris recognition. A list instantly appears before me. I file the list and make a note that I'll have to go address each one of them individually, but not today.

I walk quietly through the house to Rocky's bedroom. As I expect, Elizabeth and Rocky are tucked closely together. I wonder how often Rocky has gotten lucky. Not often I expect as I've never found any evidence of a woman in Rocky's tiny house. When I graduated, he moved here since he only needed a two bedroom, one of which is his office. Rocky didn't expect I'd ever want to come back to live with him. He was right. I never did. It wasn't that I was angry with him, I just wanted to get on with my own life. We may be related, but we were and remain very different in how we approach things and what is important to each of us.

I close the door down and go to the kitchen. Guess I really didn't need to come make him breakfast. Elizabeth will most likely make sure he eats something. But I load and set the coffee maker for a full pot of the cappuccino Rocky likes. It will come on at two in the afternoon, just as he requested. I know he often sleeps late, but hadn't known it was that late. He apparently keeps moving it later and later. Last I knew he was generally up around nine. Has it really been that long since I was last over to see him? Of course I'm instantly presented with the exact date that was more than a year ago.

Now I'm feeling guilty that I've been ignoring him. I guess that memory of the crash has me a little off kilter this morning. Still wish I could figure out why that image came up when it did. And of course my brain shows me that the recharge bed is set to present me with memories of smells, tastes, textures, sounds and events that will evoke emotional responses in me. Why? And again the answer appears, because my lack of sensory percepters creates a deficiency of emotional inputs, mostly on the list previously presented.

So the designers of my new body determined that the recharge process was a good time to invoke memories of those inputs. Expectation is I'll keep a healthy emotional state. Really? Does this mean I'm not stimulated to feel the way that leads to most emotional responses? I just don't become aware of the things others react to because I don't smell, taste or feel the way others do. But the question is can I figure out a way to notice the reactions of others so that I can impute that someone has tasted, smelled or touched something that triggered a feeling leading to an emotional response? Of course my mind informs me that it's possible to do so if I simply ask my mind to watch for those behaviors in others. Yes, please do.

I scan Rocky's refrigerator's on-hand menu to see what he's recently been eating. Nothing good for him. Lots of empty calories rather than lean proteins and vegetables. What's this? At least he's been eating smoothies – oops, they're the ones made out of fruit with lots of sugars. Sweet. He always was a sweets person, often ignoring a good meal to hurry to dessert. I select a lean steak, medium rare, whole grain salad with nuts and cranberries, and a persimmon, so he'll have something sweet and healthier at the end. I select that to be ready at 2:15 so he has a few minutes to drink his cappuccino and not enough time to start into his daily project before it will be ready.

A quick walk through of his apartment shows he evidently stopped the housekeeper again. Every time he does that the house gets filthy. He doesn't seem to notice the dust, dirt and disorder around him. He'd said to me one time that he didn't like Rosalinda snooping through his stuff. She was the housekeeper then. The next time I came over she hadn't been by in over a month. The house looked it. No question it has been more than a month since the last cleaning. I simply think I need to hire someone for him and am presented with a confirmation that Janelle, from Domestic Assistants will be by to clean the house at 4:00 today. The confirmation also notes she will be debiting my account rather than Rocky's for her weekly cleaning until further notice. Knowing Rocky, any interval less than a week will probably be disastrous. I wonder if Elizabeth changed the sheets on the bed before she would get into it. Doubt Rocky had changed them since the housekeeper left. But then again, maybe he did so in anticipation. Sometimes Rocky surprises me.

The car is outside. I take a last look around. I spot a note on the security monitor Rocky left for me: 'Sage, I know it's futile to ask you not to order breakfast and a new housekeeper, but I really don't need your help just yet. Someday I'm sure I'll have been reduced to such a condition, and then you can exercise your power of attorney to let me die peacefully. But until then I'd just as soon be responsible for my own encounters with the Heath department.'

I'm shaking my head as I pull the door closed behind me. I ensure it locks and the security system engages. I'm not quite to the car when my communicator alerts me to an incoming call. Shit, it's Raoul White. At my approach the vehicle door opens. I climb in as I answer. "Raoul. A bit early for you isn't it?"

"I'm in New York, so it's about nine-thirty here. How are you Sage? I see you're taking this on your mobile so I can't see for myself."

"Just going into work. I have an important meeting coming up at 7:30, so I need to be ready."

"What's it been? A few months?" Boy is he blowing smoke.

"More like a year. I actually thought you must have gotten married or something." Raoul only calls me when he's horny.

"I was in a relationship for a while. What about you?" He's probing. Definitely horny.

"You know me, married to my work. You still doing the same thing?" Maybe I can head this off.

"As a matter of fact I did change employers. Now with Acceleration Labs. Got a new chip line that's going to blow away the competition."

"Really? What does Morningstar say about your new product?" Morningstar is a ratings agency that sends out independent evaluations of new technology products.

"Four stars." Raoul responds proudly. "Highest rating in our class. And we're still early in our lifecycle, so it will be a while before anyone catches up. By then we'll be on our third generation and putting distance between us."

"Shoot the information over to Robert. He'll do the diligence and I'll let you know if we have any interest." I respond hoping this is just a business call.

"Speaking of interest, going to be in your area next week. You up for a visit?" Nope. He's horny.

"Which days?"

"Thursday and Friday, thinking I could stay the weekend. That is if you could put me up."

Then it occurs to me. I couldn't sleep with him if I wanted to. Holy shit! How could I have not even noticed? And without it and hormones am I even a woman? I look like I always did, so I must be a woman. But no vagina? My mind fills with studies of women who lose their reproductive capacity and yet remain a woman. I'm sure the reports are meant to reassure me so I shut down the search and realize I've been leaving Raoul hanging out there with a very long silence.

"I'm not going to be able to get together. My father's health is in decline." A true statement, but not to the point. "And he's scheduled for testing to see if we can figure out how to make him more comfortable."

"Through the weekend?" Raoul doesn't want to buy my excuse.

"Only time they could get him in as he's on a deadline for the company. Couldn't miss a whole week." That is also true as I'd gleaned that fact from his work log. In fact, I was surprised he made time for Elizabeth. Normally Rocky can only do one thing at a time. But then again, maybe she really is helping him with angstrom length circuit heat dissipation.

"Call me if something opens up. I'll come down." Raoul doesn't want to accept my excuse.

"I'll let you know." I leave it and click off.

Chapter Twenty-One

As I expect, the stand-up wasn't pleasant. Everyone except Oriana seems to be in a daze when I hand each their key problem to solve today, and a most probable approach to solving it.

"Where did you come up with this?" Jermaine asks

"Your reports."

Oriana is the next to ask a question, "Why this approach?"

"A correlation of the issues across the products and a review of the approaches each of you have taken. We need to take a leap of faith that what I'm seeing will clear the way to delivery."

"But you've never been this specific before." Jermaine again. He's the one most bothered that I've pointed out he wasn't as close as he thought, or at least wasn't taking the shortest path to delivering a product.

"We will miss delivery if we don't do something different. This isn't a reflection on you. It's a necessary step so we don't blindside the company again."

"We're making progress." Robert this time. I was probably the most proscriptive in what I'm having him do. Oriana had shown that he was totally out of touch with his people. He's managing a schedule that no one bought into.

"Robert, Oriana has a copy of your assignment. She's responsible for your team's delivery today. I can't wait for you to figure things out any longer. I want you to spend the day analyzing why I came up with a very different set of assignments for your team than you did."

THE GHOST IN THE MACHINE

It almost seems like the air has been sucked out of the room. No one expected I would be this hard on Robert. I start noticing several of the team members getting flush in the face and others won't look anyone else in the eye.

Robert hasn't completely understood the implications of what I've just said. He finally asks, "Do you have some time today I can come talk with you about this?" He holds up the assignment I've given him.

"I'll be in my office this morning, but will be making the rounds of each of your teams this afternoon. Not to interrupt what you've got to deliver, but to observe, to see if people are engaged and working the right things. I've sent you each a breakout of who on your teams need to be working which aspects of the problem. Those are only a suggestion, but if any of you fail to deliver today, I'll be asking questions."

"I get that we've screwed up." Oriana begins. "But this almost seems like remedial 101. What gives?" She's never been this outspoken before the whole group. She's probably been hearing the rumors about me. Probably wondering if this is a last gasp attempt to keep my job. Does that mean Oriana thinks she has a chance to replace me? I can't rule that out no matter how close we've been.

"We don't have time for a debate this morning." I look up at the clock on the wall behind them. "We're going to succeed together if you complete your assignments on time." I look straight at Oriana in case my suspicions are correct.

I see Robert has figured out that by moving him out of the way, I may have saved him the embarrassment of a very public firing. Oriana also has figured out that she's on the hot seat, having to fix Robert's issues at the same time delivering her own team's product.

Jermaine breaks the mood, "I don't know about the rest of you, but I got to get to work." The team files out, all except Oriana who approaches me privately.

She glances around to make sure no one else hears. "How did you do this? I've been working day and night to figure this out."

I put my arm around her shoulders, "So have I," literally all day and night.

"But your approach is so simple, why didn't I see it?" Thank you, Rocky.

"In time you'll see what you don't today."

"That sounds like you're talking about wisdom." Oriana seems to be trying to explain something to herself she never thought she'd have to account for.

I nod to the clock, "You have the biggest bite to chew and everyone else now has a head start."

She nods to herself, "I hear you."

I watch Oriana walk away with her head down, trying to figure out how I could have turned the issues around so quickly. I've bought another day.

I return to my office. Mindi pokes her head in. "A whole new you."

"Pardon?" She's out of context and I'm not sure what she's referring to.

"Tough as nails. Haven't seen that in you since your first year." Has it been that long?

"No one's questioned whether I could deliver since then." I point out.

"Welcome back. I actually like this version of you better. Democracy is great if it doesn't make any difference who's leading. But when the chips are down, I'd rather be following someone who has the track record to be successful." Mindi almost seems relieved.

My communicator rings. A'zam. "What the hell is this file you sent me?" He's not angry, he's more curious. I never send him files of technical information.

"Transparency and traceability." I respond.

"My Greek is not current." He's telling me to give him the long hand version.

"You have the complete file on how we will begin loading the software tomorrow."

"Two days ahead of your new schedule?" A'zam sounds like he doesn't trust what I'm saying.

"In twenty-four hours I have put in place a full recovery plan. It's detailed down to individual coders, with full transparency. What you don't see is that you can port this software into the new hardware the beta team is completing."

"What you're telling me is you no longer have the problems you were experiencing?"

"Brand new me, better than ever." I need to reinforce a termination would be premature.

"Friday will tell us a lot," he wants me to know I've not proven myself just yet.

"More than you think." I have to ensure he won't listen to HR and act pre-emptively.

Chapter Twenty-Two: Twenty-four Days

Dr. Woodall should be in his office by now, if he's not on rounds. I place the call.

"Morning Leesa. Is the doctor in?" Leesa is his nurse. She supposedly was in the surgery where my consciousness was transferred.

"How are you feeling, Sage?" She hasn't answered my question. Apparently stalling to see if he comes in.

"I'm good. Learning a lot about what I can and can't do, and that's the reason for my call."

"Oh? Which are you concerned about?" Leesa is wondering if she can help me.

"What I can't do. Seems you didn't give me all the physical attributes I had when I came in."

"Something you no longer need or something you might want anyway?" She knows exactly what I'm talking about but doesn't want to go there unless I make her.

"So is the doctor in?"

"He's normally in about now. Do you want to hold for him or should I ask him to call you back?"

I look at the clock, just after 8:00 am. I need to start breaking down the work on the upgrades I expect A'zam to ask for.

"Why don't you…"

"Here he is, just a minute Sage." And Leesa puts me on hold.

It takes about a full minute, a long time for me, before Dr. Woodall answers. "Sage. I wondered how long it was going to be before you called in. You've actually gone longer than I expected."

"When did you think I'd call?" I'm annoyed. He thinks he's praising me but he's also dissing me that I couldn't make it without calling.

"I gave you twenty-four hours. So what can I help you with today?"

"Got a spare vagina anywhere?" I ask sarcastically.

I hear him exhale into the communicator. "I was hoping you'd give us a little more time on that one." Apparently not.

"So the answer is no." I summarize.

"We have a prototype, but I don't think you'll be satisfied. That's why we didn't include it in the beta release."

"Meaning me." I interpret.

"Yes." He admits. "We knew you'd probably like to have one, but for some people it's not a priority. Given your history, it didn't seem to be."

"Meaning I'm not married and not generally sexually active." I summarize.

"Actually, I think the way you put it was, 'occasionally active.'"

"Well the occasion called me up today and asked when." I'm trying not to be sarcastic, but he keeps setting it up so it just comes out that way.

"How much time can you give us?" He sounds distracted as if

consulting a schedule. "The more the better."

"I know you'll never be done. When is the beta release currently scheduled?" I know way too much about how these things usually go.

"Next year. We're struggling with the software to simulate hormonal triggers. It's tough when you don't have any."

"You want me to develop the software for you? I could go to a few X-rated movies and probably have it ready in a few days." I kid him.

"Somehow…"

"So I'm just supposed to remain celibate for a year or more while your guys in white coats try to figure out what turns a woman on?"

"That's an eons old problem." Dr. Woodall admits.

"Then I suggest you work on a variable control system." The problem is all too obvious to me, but apparently not to the good doctor.

"I don't understand your comment. How do you mean that?" He really doesn't have a clue.

"Every woman is aroused by different things and to different degrees. You don't want a singular solution where every woman responds exactly the same to every stimulus."

"Is that important?" This is worse than I thought.

"How many different women have you slept with?" I think I'm just solving a typical software problem, little did I know.

"Is that relevant?" he doesn't want to answer. Why?

"You're a virgin?" I'm amazed.

"No, but I'd probably describe myself as having limited experience." He's trying to rationalize.

"It clearly makes it hard for me to talk about what arouses a woman if you have limited experience." And I'm wondering what else he doesn't know about what it means to be a woman.

"That's why we have a team working the software." He's struggling and I don't realize to what extent.

"How can I help you?" I ask, legitimately wanting to. He chose me out of the thousands willing to cross over into a world no one understands even now.

Dr. Woodall hesitates. "I'm not sure. I assume an orgasm for you is a lot like an orgasm for a man. But I'm getting a lot of feedback that's a poor assumption. What insight can you give me?"

"Not remotely in the same ballpark." I should know as the queen of long foreplay. "A woman has to be romanced and slowly aroused. A slow hand is much more likely to get me there than someone with the pedal to the metal. Do you know what I mean?"

"I understand what you're saying." I doubt it.

How do you explain sex to someone? "It's a total sensory experience. It comes down to physical appearance, and smells, and touch, especially touch. If you touch my inner thighs and not my clitoris that's an arousal accelerator, at least for me. And it's a touch all over my body. Kisses, hugs, massage of my neck and legs. Running your fingers through my hair. Massaging my feet, that's a major relaxer. Being relaxed is essential. I can't do it if I'm tense. All of that's foreplay before we even get down to the 'bring me to an orgasm' part."

"Okay. So how do we do this?"

"If you're going to be the one who determines how orgasms are delivered for the rest of eternity you better understand the range of experiences. Otherwise you'll sentence the rest of us to some mechanical process no one cares about." I regret my comment as soon as it comes out of my mouth. But he needs to get some folks involved who've been there if there's any hope for the rest of us.

I listen to the silence and his breathing. "You're right. I'm probably the worst person to be leading this project. I'll turn it over to Aggarwal."

"He a Chippendale? You know one of those dancers who turn on women?"

"I don't think…"

"How about a woman?" I suggest. "She might actually be able to talk from experience."

Dr. Woodall sounds curious. "Would you help the team?"

I've got more at stake than any of them. "Of course I would." What have I just signed up for? Orgasms aren't exactly my forte. I'm not sure I'm going to like having very frank conversations with a bunch of folks I don't even know.

THE GHOST IN THE MACHINE

Chapter Twenty-Three: Twenty-three Days

I work through the day and night. Havens, our test director, sees me prowling the floor about four am. Everything has been integrated and running through the test protocols for hours now. Everything is working, with minor bugs his team has been able to quickly troubleshoot. So everything is on track and a delivery should be no problem.

"Why you still here?" Havens asks me. "Don't you trust I got your back?"

I look up to him as he is at least six inches taller. I note his eyes are tired, while mine are not. I hope not to explain to him why I'm not more tired than he is. He had a chance to go home and get some sleep before coming in. "Not worried at all. I'm trying to understand the few bugs you've come across in real time. Want to correlate things. Understand where our vulnerabilities might be before A'zam asks ."

"I'll give you a complete summary in the morning." He offers, hoping that will be enough.

"That's about two hours from now. I might as well stay through." I observe.

"You need sleep. We all do." He genuinely sounds like he's got my best interests at heart.

"I appreciate your concern. But they pay me the big bucks to make sure it's right the first time, you know?"

"Gotcha, boss lady. You can watch to your heart's content."

I return to my office as the server sends reports. I'm able to identify each and every potential issue. I send a note to Havens on what to look for. He clears each one and sends me a note. By 8:00am the team is in the conference room for the stand-up. I call Havens to join us.

"Good morning." People are looking at me. What's the problem?

Mindi leans in. "Did you go home last night? You're wearing the same outfit as yesterday."

At least I know what the issue is. "No, I didn't." I look up at the team. "Havens is with us to give you a status."

Havens moves into the room. "Nothing major. Like most of the other releases. A nit here and another there. Nothing we haven't seen before. I want to compliment you. This is actually the cleanest I've seen in a while. Did you have someone scrub it for you? First time I can remember a compile going through completely without several restarts."

Members of the team glance around, surprised they are getting such a positive report.

"This mean we don't have rework today?" Jermaine asks.

"This means we're ready to deliver and you've got today off." I respond. "And your whole teams. We nailed it the first time. Doesn't get any better than that."

As the team files out of the conference room with the first day off in months, Oriana approaches me again. "Did anyone not follow your suggestions?"

I shake my head.

"Guess you proved your point."

I shrug. Then, "Robert's people are now your people."

"He resign?" I'm actually surprised no one else asked about

Robert in the meeting. Probably too afraid of the answer.

"He now has a team of buyers in supply chain." I respond.

"Quite a change." She notes.

"Better than the unemployment line." I respond. "Robert's been a valuable member of the team. I apparently didn't mentor him well enough."

"Robert never understood how to manage a development team."

I'm surprised at her cold response to Robert's situation. Apparently she doesn't think she will ever end up in the same place. If she becomes an immortal she probably won't.

"You and I both owe Robert a lot." I try to soften the change.

Oriana glances around. "He's been steadily falling behind. Why did you stick with him?"

"Everything's more complex. Some of us have been able to surf the technology wave. But suddenly the next wave became much higher than Robert had ever seen. He couldn't stay up on the crest. So in the end he still would have had to swim to shore."

Oriana nods. "And at some point all of us are going to find ourselves in the same place. Is that what you're telling me? That I should be sympathetic to those who succumb first because someday that's going to be me?"

I think about her question for a moment before responding. "I don't know. We have to be a lot smarter to solve the next group of technical issues. If any of them were easy they'd already be solved."

"You solved this one pretty easily."

"Fast, not easily." I reflect on all it took to pull the plan together. No one else could have done it as fast as I did. At least not until another immortal is christened.

"How did you do that? Two weeks ago you couldn't have if your life depended on it."

She's asking the twenty-four thousand dollar question. "Necessity is the mother of invention." She's not satisfied, but I'm also not going to tell her what happened on my summer vacation. "You need to get some sleep. I've been running you pretty hard for a long time."

Oriana nods, not happy I'm not willing to give her the secret of my success. Not yet. Not when I still think she's trying to figure out how she can replace me.

Chapter Twenty-Four

I monitor the burn in testing throughout the day. Havens has it well under control. No major issues. It will be ready to release at the end of the day. Well ahead of schedule. I send a note up to A'zam informing him we will release at 6pm. I transmit a note to Havens to let half the team go home now, and the rest then. They can have the next day off having worked 24 hours straight. This wasn't the first time they'd done so. I'm sure it won't be the last.

What I don't know is how A'zam will respond to my keeping my pledge. He said Friday. Customer acceptance will tell the tale. That would mean I have a job through the week. Probably into next week, too. At least as long as it will take for the company to assess customer acceptance of the new product.

I keep myself busy on the software for the next generation hardware systems. This is what I'd promised A'zam I could deliver ahead of schedule. In my mind there's no way A'zam is not going to take me up on my suggestion. No one else can deliver gen three at the same time everyone else in the market is releasing gen one.

I'm sitting at my desk about one am, when I finish the plan. I read through to see if it closes. Does everything tie together? I've written an algorithm that checks all that for me. I wait to see what adjustments I need to make. After a few minutes the message comes back up on my screen. The plan closes. So now I have six and a half hours before the morning stand-up meeting.

I can ask myself questions. See what my mind delivers to me as answers. Or I can listen to music, scan the catalog of several major museums, or... But then I remember Mindi reminded me I'm still wearing the same outfit from yesterday. If I don't go home and change, it will be even more noticeable. Don't want to call attention to how little sleep I'm really getting. Don't want to open that can of worms.

If I go home, change clothes and come right back I'll still be in by two am. I can start research on cutting edge circuitry to see what Rocky is really up to. Give me some insights into how software can take advantage of those hardware breakthroughs

Since I'm just running home for a few minutes I decide I don't need to take anything other than my communicator. I drop it into my pocket. I let my mind start the search as I walk out the front door and into the street.

Did Rocky eat the breakfast I ordered for him? I don't know. In only an instant I get a confirmation from his food service that he did indeed consume the steak. He didn't eat much of the grain salad. And the persimmon? Didn't touch it. Although it appears Elizabeth took it home with her as it left the premises intact. I'm surprised Rocky didn't want the sweet finish to his breakfast. But then again, maybe Rocky didn't recognize it was sweet. Probably just thought it was some fruit I'd ordered for him. I'll have to ask the next time we talk.

What was Rocky's last paper about? "Maximizing Current Flow in Angstrom Unit Length Circuitry." As I walk back to my condo I quickly glance through the paper where he basically identifies heat dissipation as the biggest limitation to current flow and capacity. Maybe Elizabeth really was helping him with his next paper. I'll have to make sure I read it. See how Elizabeth may have contributed to his understanding of heat dissipation.

And that reminds me I still need to engage with Dr. Woodall's team on the control systems for the emotional responses necessary for a vagina to deliver an orgasmic experience. I start thinking through that problem. Do I really have enough experience to give a full and complete answer to the question? Would it be better to do focus group research with women across a broad spectrum of orgasmic responses? But how would you find the right people? Take out an ad in a local or national newspaper?

You'd have to profile them to get the range of diversity. Even that might not be enough. After all, there are differences between societal, ethnic and religious groups. At least I think I remember something to that effect. But who is doing that kind of research? Mostly sociologists and psychologists. Probably working under grants. Maybe I'd steered Dr. Woodall in the wrong direction. Maybe I'm totally inadequate to answer the question of how do you create a set of universal turn-ons that lead to orgasms.

Of course the list of institutions doing research on human sexual response presents itself to me as I turn down the street where I live. I start reading through the list to see if I recognize any. I actually don't recognize any of the institutes that have been established at several major universities. Some are looking only at domestic sexual practices. Some are dedicated only to primitive societies. And then there are those who are interested in comparative sexual practices around the world. Those are the ones Dr. Woodall should probably consult. I make a note to myself to send him the list. My mind has already taken care of that. I read the note and realize I would have put the subject a little more delicately. Not "Comparative Human Sexual Response Stimuli Across a Multi-factorate and Trans Societal Framework."

Well, I've totally embarrassed myself with Dr. Woodall.

I'm close to my condo. A man steps out of the bushes in front of a neighbor's place, startling me. Should I be afraid? I glance back to see who it might be. I notice a knife in his hand. Yes, I should be. I keep walking. A little faster. It's about one-fifteen in the morning. No one else is out on the street. Not even the police. The man comes up behind me, carrying the knife. What do I do? Something. It appears he's about to put his arm around my throat. If I'd had a heart it would have been racing. I remember the heart racing feelings from movies. But nothing obscures my thinking.

My left arm comes up to block his arm coming around my neck. I spin and punch him in the head with my right hand closed in a fist. Did I really do that? Is he surprised or have I actually hurt him? He drops the knife. Do I punch him again? He steps back and falls to the ground. No, I don't. I kick the knife away. He doesn't move, so I step on his groin with my high heel, and watch the man convulse to protect himself. The knife lies close enough he could retrieve it. So I scoop it up, and walk away quickly, looking over my shoulder in case he recovers. I don't want him to follow so I take off my heels and make a run for it.

Once inside my condo, I drop the knife on a desk. What do I do? Call the police? What are they going to do? I should, but I really don't want to get involved. Hopefully the man won't come looking for me, and even if he does I can probably outrun him. This is a very different conversation I'm having with myself than I would have had if it was the old me. I'd have been petrified. Now I'm more annoyed I've got to be more alert coming home. Why?

Chapter Twenty-Five: Twenty-two Days

I work through the night from the house. Occasionally I stop and think through the attack. But I come to no conclusions. I'm reviewing the latest technical research from a wide range of universities and various professional symposiums. I need to get a sense of the direction of research in addition to specific technical papers that tell me how to achieve much higher levels of performance. The research universities give hints, but seldom do more than build crude prototypes. I don't have time to let them scale up their experiments. I have to correlate findings and see what is common. How do I get results from mere indications? I take chances, that's how. But I have to have a pretty strong indication I'm right before I go spend a ton of money on having people code solutions that are only speculative. I'm totally immersed in this research and my analysis of it when something draws my attention to the sun coming up. I check the clock. Six am. I need to get back to the office before the seven-thirty stand-up.

The bathroom catches my attention as I stand up. I used to shower every day. I haven't showered once since the transformation. I don't sweat so my clothes don't get dirty the way they did. But I couldn't smell it even if my clothes were rank. What do I do? Mindi already noticed I didn't change them, so I need to do that. But what about a shower? What would a shower do for me? I'd get the dust off if nothing else. Dust? Really? I probably ought to shower just to see if it improves my appearance.

I shed my clothes and get into my shower. I notice the temperature of the water doesn't register as much as it used to. I'd wait for the water to get warm before getting in previously. But now it just doesn't seem to matter. Cold or hot, no difference. I'll have to ask Dr. Woodall about my ability to perceive the differences in water temperature. That's something I would have thought they would have addressed, but guess not. I feel the water running over my body. Somehow it's not how I remember a shower. It always seemed a shower had a relaxing aspect. The heat would relax my muscles. I would look forward to that release. I also enjoyed shampooing my hair. Rubbing and rinsing out the shampoo and conditioner. Maybe because it was one of the few times I really rubbed my head. I loved to comb my hair, dry it and then brush it as it dried. It always seemed to gain a luster when it was clean and brushed out. Would it look the same way now? I don't know. In fact I have to think for a minute before I even remember what it looks like now.

The water running over me seems to have no effect. I feel it, rub soap on my skin and rinse off. But the feeling I used to enjoy just isn't there. Another thing to talk with Dr. Woodall about. And of course my mind has already sent off a note to him. 'What about sensory perceptions? Whole body perception is not what it used to be. Example: a shower.' If only my mind would phrase these a little more delicately. But then again, maybe Dr. Woodall is just glad to be getting the information about opportunities to improve the immortal experience.

I shut off the water and grab the towel. Need to dry my hair first. No sense drying my skin if water is dripping down from my wet hair. I feel the towel drying my skin. Again, the feeling is not what I remember. But is my memory accurate? I don't know. It just seems to be different. I have to assume I don't have anywhere near as many nerve points in my new skin as I had in the old skin. If that's true, it would explain why the feeling isn't as pleasurable or as intense. Another compromise from what I was to what I've become. Not a big deal, just something else that's likely to fade in time as I get further and further removed from the experiences I had before. What I now experience will be the new norm.

Selecting clean clothes from my closet, I quickly dress and return to the bathroom to further dry and brush out my hair. This seems closer to what I remember. I feel the tug at my scalp and the pull on the brush as I run it through my hair. I look in the mirror and yes, the luster is there that I remember. And the hair doesn't seem to have the brittleness my actual hair had from dying it to hide the gray hairs that kept trying to find their way to the surface. It looks more like the hair I had when I was twenty. And I thought my hair was my best feature then. Although it always seemed the guys were more interested in my boobs. Never understood that fascination. Maybe it was because my boobs were larger than most of the girls. Not a whole lot, but they were prominent and stood up then. No sag like what happened the last few years. They're standing up again now. Same size, same firmness. Only the nipple is always prominent now. No control over that. But I guess it's better to be prominent than to sag.

As I finish looking at myself in the mirror I realize I'm seeing the twenty-year old version of myself in all respects except my mind. I'm way ahead of where I was then. Where I was even a week ago. I should be glad of that fact. It's giving me an advantage without which A'zam probably would have terminated me. But I'm still adjusting to the difference. I'm learning how to control what is presented to me and in what form. Still too much information. Too much for me to really get a clear understanding of what I need to know to make decisions. Got to find a way to streamline the data coming in response to my thoughts. At least it's better than the first few days. Still a long way to go.

After finishing brushing out my hair, I take another look at myself. There are definite advantages to the transition. I've not looked in the mirror much other than to put on facial crème or eyeliner in a long time. I need to pay attention to how I look. Hadn't thought about doing so in a very long time. No need, but now I have the goods to strut. That is if I had a place to strut my assets. AppleCore really isn't the place. AppleCore is all about the mind. It's about what I can contribute to products and customer excitement. I've done that really well for a long time. Now I have the ability to push the envelope even further. Maybe my appearance isn't such a big deal. Maybe I should continue to hide my new assets. But why? Maybe I can do both. Might be interesting to see what effect a whole woman would have in the SLT meetings.

I reach for the cabinet where I keep my deodorant. But I don't
need it anymore. A deodorant is to hide body odors. But do I even have
a body odor? I don't know. I can't smell anything. I remember what I
used to smell like, but that's another thing to send to Dr. Woodall. And
yes the note appears in my mind as it goes out into the ether. 'Body
odor?? Should I have a distinct human odor? Maybe this is something
we could work on??' I guess my mind is getting less formal with the
doctor. At least the communications are becoming less formal and more
cryptic. Why is that? Does it mean I like him? Yes, I do, but what does
that mean? Does it mean anything? Probably not. Whatever I'm feeling
is based on memories of what I should think and feel, not current
feelings. On the other hand, I'm looking a whole lot better. Maybe I can
get his attention once I get a vagina. In the meantime, even if I do look
great, not having a vagina is a substantial limitation. Maybe I can
engage the team to speed up the development. I'm the technical expert
anyway. But then again, maybe I shouldn't be in a big hurry. I've got
time. More time than anyone else, in fact.

Then the accident reminds me that time is not given to anyone.
Anna Laura and Tabitha weren't as lucky as I've been. They were just
coming home from another day. Suddenly they were no more. I now
have infinity to look forward to. Why was I chosen to be the first person
to live forever, when Tabitha had only nine years? She was so much
smarter than I was then. Why Tabitha? Why didn't Anna Laura decide
to pick me up rather than her? Then we would all be alive. It would
have taken her longer to get to me than it did Tabitha. But then again,
she might have come earlier. If she had would we have died? Tabitha
would have been the one Rocky got a job at AppleCore. Would Tabitha
be the one to make the leap into the unknown? Would I have been the
older sister who unfortunately died at a young age? I don't know how
that would have happened. Tabitha wasn't interested in technology. At
least she wasn't then. But at nine years old, who could tell what she
would have become? Particularly if it were just Tabitha and Rocky. But
knowing Rocky, he would have instilled the scientific method in
Tabitha even if she wanted to be a ballet dancer. Rocky can be
persuasive, even if he doesn't think he is.

And Anna Laura? If she was still alive, what would have happened to all of us? Would I have still had the drive to do all I've done? Would I be where I am now? Would I have used her to shield me from Rocky's view of the world and life? Would I have gone off and been an archeologist in Peru? Or maybe open a cupcake shop on Main Street? What would have been different? Everything would have been different. I'd not be as emotionally hollow. I'd have had her continuous and unconditional love all those years when instead it was just Rocky and me.

I used to see Anna Laura's eyes when I looked in the mirror. That was her best feature. And she gave it to me. But now they're gone. I have these other eyes that don't tell you anything other than I'm awake. Tabitha got her intelligence. I got her eyes. Why didn't I get her intelligence? There have been so many times I made the wrong choice. If I'd been a little smarter. Not a lot smarter. Just a little smarter, I could have avoided so many situations with Rocky that drove us apart. I needed him in ways he couldn't understand. And even now I need him. But I can't tell him. He wouldn't understand, even if I tried to explain why. Rocky lives in his head. All the social stuff always seems to elude him. I'm still amazed he figured out a way to get Elizabeth Sanderson to stay the night. But then I only have to think for a moment to realize it wasn't Rocky. It was Elizabeth who figure that out. I wonder how Rocky felt the next morning waking up to find Elizabeth in the place Anna Laura had been for a short time in his life. Strange I'm sure. Just like the first time I woke up to find Raoul next to me. That was the time I was disoriented thinking it was Tabitha in bed with me. We'd shared a bed in San Francisco because it was only a two bedroom house. Tiny even by today's standards. But Anna Laura made so little as an elementary school teacher that with Rocky's AppleCore salary it was all we could afford.

A spritz of hairspray and I'm out the door, on my way back to work.

THE GHOST IN THE MACHINE

Chapter Twenty-Six

Record time for a stand-up meeting. Five minutes. Everyone simply told me to let them get back to work. We're now delivering a product upgrade every day to one or another product. We were only delivering one a week when I left for my transformation. The team has responded well to the challenges I've given them. I don't need to give each of my team leads a detailed work assignment for each of their team members anymore. Each team lead is doing it. Once they knew what was needed, they picked up the approach and have been running with it.

Julia comes by my office. I'm talking with Mindi about what I need her to prepare for me for the Senior Leadership Team meeting. "Excuse me? You have a minute?" Mindi looks up and nods that she can come back later.

Julia comes into the doorway, but doesn't sit down. The power position. If she sits down in my office then I have the power. I'm at the desk. If she stands, she keeps the power because she's standing over me looking down. Body language. Always an important part of any communication. We too seldom see it anymore, because so much of communication is over a device. I'm sure Julia is feeling insecure. I delivered ahead of schedule. She wasn't ready with the marketing blitz. Not my problem. But it is my problem. Julia thinks I made her look bad to A'zam. At the same time she did so much to make me look bad before the transformation.

"Do you need something before the SLT meeting?" I ask to try to frame the discussion. I want to let her know we both have to get ready.

"Actually I want to talk with you about the product release schedule."

Exactly where I thought she'd go, "We will be on or ahead of schedule from here on."

"But that causes marketing to always have to be ahead of schedule, in case you exceed plan."

"Marketing should have a schedule that starts ahead of the release schedule. When it starts can be arbitrary. You know. Such and such new feature coming soon. And when we firm up the release date then your campaign includes the roll-out date."

"Yes, yes. We do that. But with new releases every day, it gets confusing to the public. They don't know if they should wait for the next release we're saying is coming, or buy now based on the new release we dropped today. We need to find a way to create more separation. We're seeing sales drop off some because of feature fatigue."

I nod, understanding of the issue. "We discussed the possibility of staging releases in different markets to rotate from one to another. Create separation by not making all new features available globally on the same day."

Julia rolls her eyes. I can almost hear her thinking, been there, done that. "A'zam doesn't like that idea. Says if we have a good marketing department we shouldn't need to stage the roll-out by market. He thinks we only maximize revenue if all customers have equal access to all feature sets."

I hear her dilemma. "Have you considered doing a simulation? Provide the results to A'zam? Show him what the effects will be before you make the change. I do that with our software."

Julia nods to herself. I know she's seen the simulation data. I make it available to the whole senior leadership team. "Hadn't considered that. Do you have someone who could run a simulation for me?"

"Robert just moved over to supply chain. He could. I'll send him a note to contact you."

"I appreciate your help. But it still won't solve my basic problem. You've introduced uncertainty in your delivery dates." Her voice hardens as if she's trying to find a way to make sure she doesn't back down from me. For some reason she has to make me change what I'm doing. Why?

"Delivery dates have never been cast in stone. The development process doesn't lend itself to certainty. Sometimes we're early. Sometimes we need more time. That's never been truer than now. We're pushing the limits on some of the technology. I'm having to build roadmaps to transition to entirely new approaches to some of the feature sets we want. We can't get there from where we are." I respond deliberately ignoring the warning signs.

"I understand. But you're not a team of one. The rest of the organization has its own rhythms. When you accelerate the rest of the organization has to scramble to try to keep up. Doesn't matter whether it's marketing or supply chain or our channel partners. We simply have to find a way to get back into rhythm."

She has a good point. However, I always thought it was the job of the rest of the organization to keep up with the fastest schedule we can achieve. It drives higher revenues. But as she points out, I'm just one part of the larger organization. I might as well let her tell me what she wants me to do. I need to get this discussion over with. I'm not ready for the SLT meeting. Time is quickly running.

"What do you suggest?"

"I want you to hold your releases until the scheduled dates."

"Do I get to request adjustments to the release dates? Example: if I know now that I'll beat a release date for something a month from now by a week. Can I ask to move it up now? That gives the rest of the organization three weeks to adjust their work."

"No. We set the schedule quarterly and we stick to it." She has to win this one. Why?

"Even if one of our competitors comes to market before we do?" I have to clarify. We've always accelerated when we find someone gets out ahead of us. We don't want to give up too much initial market share to a competitor. Takes too long to recover.

"We will look at exceptions on a case-by-case basis." Not giving even an inch when she knows we will make those exceptions. A'zam must have come down hard on her over her slow response to my early release.

"Fair enough. You have anything else? I need a few minutes to gather data for SLT." I'm trying to retain some semblance of autonomy here. She reminds me she out ranks me. I better fall in line.

"There is one more thing." Oh, oh. What now? "Who's doing your hair?" She steps further into the room to get a better look.

"Glenn over at Hair Raising Adventures. I thought that was who you were using."

"Really? Glenn? I changed to Roberto. Glenn just couldn't seem to keep the color consistent. But he's done a really good job with you. I'll have to consider changing back."

"I'm happy with him." I think I'm done. Bad assumption.

"Jacqui's happy with him too. But that's because she's sleeping with him. Guess he pays more attention when he's getting more than just a tip."

"Jacqui's sleeping with Glenn? Didn't know that. Anything else I need to know about who's getting a better deal?"

"You know there's a rumor about you." Oh shit. Where is this coming from?

"There's always rumors about me. Which one is it this time?" I'm already pulling data in my mind for SLT. Is she trying to make sure I'm not prepared for the meeting?

"That you were sleeping with A'zam, but he got tired of you. Rumor was that's why you got behind on the schedule. But everyone's wondering who you're sleeping with now?"

I give Julia the sweetest smile I know how. "Julia. Thanks for bringing this to my attention." I cut it there even though I have more thoughts I know I shouldn't express.

"Rumors, Sage. You need to control them. Information is the only way."

"Oh, I agree..." Don't say anything more.

"Don't get angry with the messenger." Julia got what she was after, which was to put me in my place. She wanted to make me angry. But that didn't work. Now that she has her little victory for the day maybe she'll leave me alone in the SLT. I can hope, anyway.

I smile as best I can.

THE GHOST IN THE MACHINE

Chapter Twenty-Seven

For some reason my mind dumps an unrelated story into my awareness as I'm walking back to my office with Wallace. "Glad we actually got something done today, for a change." He concludes.

I nod absently. The story gathering my attention is about a man who turned up at the hospital a few blocks away with a head injury. He died shortly after being admitted. There was no indication of what caused the injury or why he suffered it. The story is a warning to people to be cautious at night in our area, even though it has traditionally been thought to be very safe. Apparently the man ended up at the hospital about 2:00 am. The article also has a picture of the man. I instantly recognize him as my attacker. Did I kill him? Oh god. My heart should be racing now, but of course it isn't. What do I do? But then my logic kicks in. Did something happen to him after our encounter? Had to be. I didn't kill him. Whatever happened must not have been too long afterwards. He entered the hospital less than an hour after he attacked me. I didn't hit him that hard. Did I? No. I couldn't have. I couldn't kill someone.

I wonder what I should do if anything. I don't want to draw attention to myself. What should I do if someone saw what happened? What if the man knew who I am? What if he said something to the hospital doctors about me before he died? I don't know quite how to handle this. I don't have enough information. Ironic that I have a direct feed into the internet. I'm swimming in data. And yet I don't have enough information to know what I should do.

Nothing. If there's an issue, let it come to me. No sense going and looking for trouble.

"What are you going to do about the marketing mess Julia left you?" Wallace is drawing me back into the present.

"Oh. I haven't given it any thought yet. I'll have to assess the situation first." I respond, still only half back into the conversation.

"Don't sit on it. You've got a time bomb there waiting to go off." Wallace looks around to see if anyone is listening in, like Julia, I presume. "She's been trying to make all the decisions. Overruling her staff. The good people all have their paper out to go someplace else. If you don't get in and convince them you're not Julia, you'll be doing it all yourself in probably only a matter of days."

"Didn't know it's that bad." I respond, but already my mind is displaying reports and data on the marketing department performance. I'm scanning them as we continue to walk. Then I see report after report from one... "Landon Banerjee. What do you know about him?" I ask Wallace, who muses for a moment before responding.

"Landon is probably the brightest guy in the department. Not only bright, but incredibly creative. You lose him and you have major problems. Particularly if he shows up at a competitor."

No need to say more. This is an emergency. "I'll catch up with you later."

As I come into the marketing department area I scan for names on offices. Landon's is all the way to the end of the row. Low man on the management totem pole. Several people I don't recognize turn to watch me. I walk through their area heading for his office. I'm sure one of his colleagues is texting him that someone is on the way to see him.

I poke my head into the office of Landon Banerjee. Picture on the wall of a guy holding a cricket flat paddle with a helmet and face cage on the wall. "Landon?"

He peers over the computer screen, which is deliberately set so people walking by or coming into his office can't see what's up on his screen. "Who wants to know?"

I walk in and extend my hand to shake his, "Sage." Something pops up on his screen. I can tell he's looking at my picture and the announcement I've been given responsibility for marketing. His eyes are wide as he looks back to me. Then embarrassed, he rises to his feet.

"Sorry. I didn't recognize you. What can I do to serve you today?"

"You can start by sitting back down. I wanted to stop by and chat to let you know I'm intending to promote you to VP of Marketing for AppleCore."

Landon Banerjee continues to stand. He looks at me without answering. I'm not sure if he believes what I just told him. I am sure he knows I have the authority to do exactly what I suggested. So the instant thought I have is I may be too late to save him. So I plunge ahead, "Is that something you would be interested in?"

"Miss…"

"Sage. We're on the same team." I respond letting him know I'm a different kind of sheriff.

"I cannot answer your question as I don't know what you are proposing, exactly." He finally responds after another long silence.

"I am proposing you move down this row of offices to the empty one on the end. Then you call a staff meeting. You announce to everyone you have an impossible job. That is to devise a whole new approach to build market share and product loyalty. That you will be getting a new product or upgrade every day. That you will be responsible for coordinating everything we do to let customers and potential customers know what our products are and what's coming out next and when. So you convince people to buy what we make over all the other products in the marketplace."

Again Landon Banerjee looks at me blankly as he thinks about what I've suggested. "Why me?"

I decide to go no bullshit. "Because I need someone who doesn't care about tradition, or image, or who is who. I need someone who will use creativity and imagination to catch the attention of the public. And with all the information floating in the ether, that's become an incredibly difficult proposition. I've reviewed what you've done for us. I've seen what you've proposed. I've also seen what you've been given authority to deliver. There's a vast gulf between the quality of what you've proposed and what we've let you do. From what I see, you're the only one capable of giving me what I want. Does that answer your question?"

"How have you reviewed all of my work when it hasn't been released to the market?"

"Not your concern. Everything I've reviewed is what you've delivered for us. I intend to flood you with products you're going to have to deal with."

Landon Banerjee looks me in the eye. "I have heard of you. But you present risks. I am not prepared to take risks with you."

"Why?" I ask.

"I intend to ask someone to marry me."

"You'll report directly to me." Landon Banerjee is listening, but I can't see a reaction. Nothing. Not like, yes I can do this, or it's too late for me to go back now. "I do understand about wanting to get married and wanting to have a family. That's very important. It will ground you. I need someone responsible for all that we do in marketing grounded above all else."

Still nothing from Landon Banerjee. I'm probably too late. At least I tried, but then I've got a bigger problem. I'll have to rebuild the department from the ground up. I don't know all that much about marketing, but will quickly have to learn.

"Could you assist me with one minor problem?" Landon asks

almost embarrassed. I nod. "Would you put in a good word for me with Miss Mindi? I love her but I am not sure she loves me."

"Like my assistant?" I ask and Landon nods.

THE GHOST IN THE MACHINE

Chapter Twenty-Eight

Back in my office, Mindi comes in, "The report satisfactory for the SLT?" she asks.

I'm looking at her thinking about Landon Banerjee. For whatever reason they don't seem to go together. Mindi is forthright and outgoing. Landon strikes me as an introvert who has trouble talking with people. And yet he communicates ideas powerfully using media. A contradiction. But I've seen it over and over again. People used to talk with people. It was the total experience that built relationships and made it easier to do business. People knew each other. They understood who they were dealing with because they socialized. They would talk about kids, and parents and friends and neighbors. Some people talked politics and religion, but didn't have as many friends as they did converts. But it was a personal relationship that made the world work. And I am the biggest offender of changing all that. I develop the software that runs the devices that intermediates communication. It's all text and video now. Heaven forbid someone would be in the same room with the person they are communicating with. That went out decades ago. And Landon is the wizard of media. He knows how to package a message, with graphics, sound and soundbites that sell. And he does that better than anyone I've seen. He just hasn't been given an opportunity to show what he can really do.

Mindi, on the other hand is a throw-back. If Landon is all electronic, she's all high touch. She needs to be in your face, looking you in the eye, and reading your reactions. She studies your posture, your state of nervousness, whether you'll hold someone's gaze or look away. She is all about the subtle cues that Landon works without. She needs to make contact, to reassure, to let the other person know she understands how they feel. Mindi sympathizes with their plight, whatever that might be. Mindi is a rock of stability and caring. In my brief moments with Landon, there is no reading him. He lives in his head. He doesn't display his emotions, reactions or thoughts. And maybe that's why he needs Mindi. Maybe Landon needs someone who can bridge the divide, reach across and reassure the electronic wizard that he is all right when maybe even he isn't sure.

"You're reflective today. Something come up at the SLT?" Mindi wants to know what's going on.

"No. Just thinking about you." I set the trap.

"Me?" Mindi genuinely seems surprised I would dwell on something related to her. She's indispensable, but also invisible. That's the role she staked out for herself. We've never really discussed it. I've simply become the beneficiary of her attention and care.

"Do you know Landon Banerjee?" Mindi blushes.

"Landon is it?" She's trying to set a tone in our discussion that tells me not to take him too seriously. But is that because she really doesn't care for him, or because she doesn't want others in the middle of her personal life?

"You know him?" I repeat my question since she implied an answer without giving one.

"Yes." She drops her voice an octave as if she's being punished for knowing the man.

"Tell me about him. I've been given marketing. From what I see he's brilliant. At least when it comes to marketing." Got to sound neutral while putting in the plug for him.

She looks at me curiously, "Landon?" she seems to think more about him. "He's creative. Yes, I would agree with that. But no one has ever said he was more than an ideas person. He's not taken seriously. He's never managed a whole campaign. They simply wouldn't let …"

She catches herself realizing she's not talking with one of her Hindu friends.

"We're not talking about 'them' anymore. I'm responsible for marketing. I have to select a Vice President to run the area. From what I've seen, I think Landon has the ideas and ability to transform what we do. But I would agree. He needs a strong staff behind him. I'm not sure we have that anymore."

Mindi shakes her head, probably without realizing it. She's indicating to me she knows a whole lot more about the marketing department than she would from working with me. I have to assume she has gotten that read on things from Landon. But what really is the nature of their relationship? Will she tell me or keep it protected?

"Thoughts?" I ask since she doesn't respond.

"What do I know? I'm just an administrator in software. Marketing? That's not what I do."

She doesn't want me to think she knows as much as she does. Or maybe when it comes out that she and Landon are romantically inclined towards each other, she doesn't want me to think she tried to influence his promotion.

"But you know Landon. Am I misreading him? Is he someone who can do what I need him to do? Just as there are many things I've come to rely on you for?" Not personal, but giving her the opportunity to say what she thinks. Character reference more than skills reference.

"Landon. How do I tell you about Landon? He is unique. Quite brilliant and quite helpless." She realizes what she said. Quickly backtracks. "I don't mean that in a negative sense. He is quite capable of doing what you want. But he needs someone to keep him organized and focused on what must be done… every day."

"So he needs someone like you, just as I do. To keep things straight."

Mindi laughs. "No. You are easy in comparison to Landon. He would come to work naked if someone did not lay out his clothes for him."

"Who does that?" I try to see how she responds.

"His mother lives with him. She is the one who organizes him in the morning." Mindi smiles thinking about Landon's mother and what she must go through to get Landon out of the house and on the way to work.

"So you make it sound like he's a real challenge. Too much for me to give him the opportunity?"

Mindi looks me straight in the eye. "He will make you proud."

"Does he make you proud he is your friend?" A push again, not hard.

Mindi blushes, which tells me what I need to know. "Not proud. I'm honored to be his friend. I know someday, if not now, Landon will do something quite remarkable. And then everyone will see what I see and know him to be a good man. A brilliant man, who can transform society through the images and words he chooses."

"Would you marry him if he asks you?" catches Mindi off guard. She looks down, believing she has gone too far. That she needs to retreat.

"Marry him? He has not asked nor have I sought more than a friendship." She tries to soften the position she finds herself in.

"He will ask you. He asked me to put in a good word with you for him so you will say yes."

Mindi blushes again. She looks away, embarrassed I have caused her to reveal her feelings for this man. Embarrassed that I now know more about her than she would have me know. But that is only because she is part of my team and not an equal in her eyes. She thinks I would not care about her happiness on a personal level, only her happiness on the job. That's a pretty poor statement. She thinks I segment my friendships by work and outside work. What she doesn't know is I have very few friendships outside work. My day time family is much more important to me. I spend many more hours with them. But she doesn't see that. She can't understand she is a part of my family. More so than anyone except Rocky.

"So does my word for him carry any weight?" I ask smiling at her. I reach out and touch her hand. "I want very much for you to be happy. If Landon lights a smile in your heart, then it is good. If not, then maybe someone else will do that for you."

I see a tear in the corner of Mindi's eye. She wipes it away hoping I've not seen it. She smiles at me although she is choked up. "But who lights a smile in your heart?"

She has me. No one. "We're talking about your happiness."

Mindi nods faintly. It becomes more pronounced the longer she nods. "I see so much potential in him. Like a rough diamond. You look at it when you first dig it from the ground. It is nothing. A piece of glass, or so it seems. But you polish it. Soon the brilliance comes through. And suddenly you know you have a thing of beauty in your hands."

"Then follow your heart. If he is the one, when he asks you know what to say."

"But what of your heart? Are you following it? I see no one who excites you. No one you absolutely must see to make your day complete. No one who makes you more than you are alone. Why is that Sage? Why are you alone when you have so much to offer?"

How do I tell her about the years with Rocky? The years after Anna Laura, when affection had died? I am self-made. To depend on someone else would be an admission of weakness. How do I tell her

THE GHOST IN THE MACHINE

without reducing my value in her eyes?

Chapter Twenty-Nine: Twenty-one Days

The posse meets at the usual watering hole. Delilah starts things off with her glass of white wine in hand. "I think we should dedicate this whole evening to Sage, who hung us all out last time by saying she had a procedure but never asked us to go with her, or even tell us about it in advance. That wasn't in the spirit of this group. We take care of each other."

"I really don't think I deserve your undivided attention. There has to be something else we can talk about."

"Nope. I said last week that we were going to meet every week until we got the whole story. So spill the beans girl. We're waiting on you."

"She had more than just a minor procedure." Windy has decided to force my hand. I don't know how much she intends to share, but she's not going to let me just skate like I did last week.

"How do you know?" MC is all over her.

"I was with her." Windy confirms.

"I'm hurt." Delilah pouts. I didn't mean to make her feel bad about it.

"I had to travel so it would have been a real imposition."

"Travel? I'm all about travel. Where did you go?" MC this time.

"Dallas." I confirm.

"Dallas? What's in Dallas?" Reese asks now.

"A Medical Center that specializes in what I had done. In fact, I think it's the only place that does that kind of procedure." I'm trying to make them understand I'm not mad at them.

"Come on now. What kind of procedure do they do in Dallas they can't do here? I mean we got big hospitals. Huge ones and gigantic ones. They do all kinds of procedures here. What did they do there they can't do for you here?" Delilah is unhappy with my explanation.

"It's a little hard to explain. But it appears to be working. I'm feeling better, getting refocused at work, and even Raoul called."

"Oooh, Raoul called. Sounds like it's gonna be boogy time at Sage's house. Reese, you still got that video camera so we can tape these sex Olympics?" Delilah is getting into my situation, painting it in the most absurd colors.

"Ladies, I think we need to give this young lady a little space. She's been through a lot and we're just making it all that much harder for her to explain things to us." Windy cuts in, unhappy with the direction of the conversation.

"You were there." Reese points out. "So why don't you tell us what she had done?"

Windy looks at me and I don't give her any indication what I'm thinking. I know if I shake my head she'll tell them everything. But if I just play it like I'm not happy she'll be more likely to not give them everything. I still think this has to be a gradual introduction of the idea. "It was pretty major, but the good news is her recovery was very quick."

"I don't know how." Reese shakes her head. "I mean just your eyes. That had to be a lot of cutting and healing. They got something that speeds up the healing?"

"They don't look puffy at all." MC looks closer. "And you've got to be what? Fifteen pounds lighter? That's a major drop so I got to believe they did lipo or something to get that off you."

"And you're still not drinking." Reese notes for everyone. "You sure you're not pregnant?"

"Medicine I'm on." Is my full and complete response.

"Well, you better get off that medicine quickly." Delilah chimes in. "I'm not comfortable you're just sitting here watching us get sociable and you're not. I mean we have much better conversations with you when you've had as much as we have. And not only that, it helps us all forget what the others said. You'll probably even remember some of this in the morning, only we won't."

"As soon as I possibly can, I promise to have a drink with you." I watch Windy who knows what I'm really saying. She won't look at me.

"You did it again, Sage." MC notes. "Got us off talking about your procedure. Since you don't seem to want to discuss it, why don't you just give us the name of your doctor and we'll look him up and see what his specialty is?"

Since consciousness transfer is not on his website, I looked, I think this might actually be a compromise solution. They'll see he specializes in a wide range of terminal illnesses. That was me, but not anymore, unless I go back to my old body. I'll have to come back to that question again soon, but right now I'm not seeing a major reason why I'd want to. But I also don't think I'll be unemployed soon. That could change everything I'm thinking. "Dr. Bart Woodall." I give them.

"He's in Dallas?" MC asks.

"San Francisco." I respond.

"So you went to a local doc who did your procedure in Dallas." MC tries to think my procedure through. "Doesn't make sense, but I'll look into it."

THE GHOST IN THE MACHINE

"And just why is it you don't want to tell us what this is all about?" Windy prompts me.

"I was dying."

Chapter Thirty

A'zam stops Mindi in the hallway the next day. "I've been meaning to stop by. Do you have a minute?"

"Of course." The last thing Mindi wants to do is talk with A'zam of whom she is afraid. "With what can I help you?"

"Nothing. I just want to talk with you for a minute. I'm trying to understand what's going on with Sage. She seems different since she came back from her time off."

Mindi immediately knows what he wants. "Different? I think she's the same. She needed the time off, to recharge her batteries as she put it. But she's back fully engaged."

"Really? You think she fell behind on the flagship delivery because she was just worn down?"

Mindi hears the implied question. "When was the last time Sage took a week off, before now?"

A'zam has to think, which is what Mindi intends. "I don't remember."

"I've been her assistant for almost ten years. This was the first time in all the years we've worked together. The increasing pace of new products has to take a toll. The fact she could recover so quickly is amazing to me. Especially since she's increased the pace tremendously since her return."

A'zam thinks he hears an opening, "But if she got wore down before, how long at this pace before she wears down again?"

"She needed to delegate more. She needed to save more time for herself. I see she's doing that. More planning and talking with her team to pick up things she used to do. I think she learned the lesson."

"You're not just bullshitting me, are you Mindi?"

Mindi smiles, "Have I ever... 'bullshitted' you?" She almost has trouble getting it out as she never uses crude language.

A'zam straightens up. "No. I rarely ask you for anything, but you always get it right."

"Thank you." Mindi responds. "Have I given you the reassurance you seek?"

A'zam decides to change tactics, "That's what bothers me. You're reassuring when we both know Sage was on her way out. And now she's suddenly indispensable. Why?"

"Judgment, A'zam. You made a judgment without facts. Because she struggled, you assumed she was done. She wasn't. She just needed time to reorient."

"What do you mean 'reorient'?" A'zam thinks he hears what he's looking for.

"Sage is amazing. She's delivered exactly what's needed for a decade. That's a very long time by any standard. She's a great leader. She compliment's her team. Whatever they need to succeed she provides."

A'zam cuts her off, "Except on the flagship product this last time around." He knows I had a problem and isn't convinced it was an anomaly.

"Once in ten years? Give her credit. She took a few days off and had it fixed in two days after her return. What more can you want?"

"Perfection. That's our standard. No mistakes. Particularly not ones as big and noticeable as this disaster has been. I don't know what to do. She seems even more capable than usual. But she screwed up. What am I to think? Is it going to happen again next week, next month or next year? I have to assume it's going to happen again. It's only a matter of when. I've got to make sure it doesn't. And there's only one way to do that."

Mindi is surprised A'zam is this frank with her. What is he trying to accomplish? Is he looking for Mindi to confirm something? Or is he hoping she will reveal something inadvertently? Mindi isn't about to do either. But she knows A'zam is cagy and difficult to predict. "You don't need to worry about Sage. She's back at one-hundred and ten percent. Maybe more."

"That's not my problem, Mindi. For how long? That's the question I have to answer."

Mindi thinks as quickly as she can, but this is a hard question to answer. "Sage is at the top of her game. If you make a pre-emptive move she will go elsewhere and eat your lunch."

A'zam swallows hard. "Has she said anything?" He looks about since they're standing out in the middle of a hallway and others are about.

"About?"

"Leaving."

"She wouldn't say anything to me. If she were going to go, you'd never see it coming."

A'zam is still dealing with Mindi's insight. "But she's different. What happened when she was on leave? Where'd she go? What did she do? You talk. She must have said something to you."

"That's where we disagree. Sage is the same. As to where she went? The only thing she said to me is she visited friends in Dallas.

What happened? She was able to rest up as far as I can tell. What did she do? I don't know. She usually tells me about the long weekends she takes with her friends. But this trip was different. She went alone and really didn't have much to say about it."

"Why do you think that is?" A'zam isn't going to let Mindi not answer.

Mindi gathers herself since A'zam is holding on like a bulldog. "She had a promise to you she had to keep. She doesn't take those things lightly. I'm not surprised she hasn't said anything. In time she may, if the right situation presents itself. But she's never been one to talk much about herself. You know that as well as I do."

A'zam seems to consider her response. "Tell Sage she needs to give you a raise. She clearly under-appreciates your loyalty."

A'zam returns to the executive suite, turns to the right rather than going to his office straight in the back. Desirae Abdullah, his Human Resources VP is in her office. A French woman married to a French Algerian, she is adept at straddling cultures and conflict.

"Desirae. What have you been able to find out about Sage?"

"You may have had cause before her time away. But based on her performance since she returned, wrongful termination would probably be the finding in a court case."

"Let's see what she does with Marketing. She might struggle again since this is her first time through. And Julia left it a total mess."

"I thought that was what you were thinking." Desirae confirms.

"How do you explain the turnaround?" A'zam shakes his head. "I've never seen anything like it. Almost like she was completely rejuvenated. Is there any medical treatment that would explain it?"

"I'll have to research it. Nothing comes to mind."

"Do that. And if you find a satisfactory explanation I have a few other members of the SLT that could benefit from whatever she did."

Desirae makes a note to herself. "I wonder."

"What?" A'zam isn't going to let that open ended statement go.

"Probably nothing. Just something I remember reading about a long time ago. Worth asking a few questions, but probably not something that would be ready for prime time."

"Is it something we could turn into a new product? It's getting real hard to keep coming up with new devices and features. There's got to be a limit to what we're doing. So we need new things to feed this beast."

"I don't have any idea. I've got to get out and ask some questions. See if anything came of research that was going on. Last time I looked at it they weren't making much progress. So probably nothing."

"I'm counting on you to figure this out." A'zam sounds more worried than usual. "If she flames out I've got to see it coming."

"At the moment I'm more worried about Wallace than Sage. He's making noises like he's underappreciated. He's keeping up with Sage, but gets none of the credit."

THE GHOST IN THE MACHINE

Chapter Thirty-One: Twenty Days

I'm lying on the recharger. I imagine that for someone with normal senses this probably isn't very comfortable. A metal frame with a thin, but strong plastic covering. The coils are exposed on top. There can't be too much material between the recharger coils and the coils in me that pick up the electric charge. It's strange to think about what's inside me. When a biological person I would think about my heart and stomach. Those are the acceptable organs. It's good to have a kind heart and strong stomach. We think about how the things inside us make us the person we are. But the organs we think about are ones that simply sustain us in the lives we chose to lead.

If we are concerned about others, the kind heart enables us to help. If we are doing unpleasant things, the strong stomach helps us get through them without having to back away. And at the same time, if we are only concerned about ourselves, we have a hard or cold heart. We don't care about others and chose not to help. Those conceptions are all metaphorical. Our heart only pumps blood and is neither cold nor kind. The same with our stomach, although a sensitive stomach may betray us when we are doing something distasteful. It is the emotional response to what we are doing that causes the reaction. Not the thing we are doing itself.

I have neither a heart nor a stomach, not needing either to function. What does that say about me as a person? Am I less likely to be concerned for others? No, I'm the same in that regard as before the transformation. Does that mean I am, as a person, driven more by my consciousness than my physical being? Does my consciousness define me as a person, and not my body? What about what I know? Almost everything I now know is stored in a memory. It's processed by a computer chip which may not even be in my head.

In fact, I wonder. Where is my new brain? Is it where my heart used to be? Embedded in my chest? That would seem logical as it is the most protected part of my body. But maybe out of tradition it's still in my head where my brain used to be. Maybe the designers of the new me, kept with the notion of humans having a brain in their head. Maybe.

But sometime I'll have to ask…. No I didn't want to send that note to Dr. Woodall, but it's already gone. And here's his answer. 'The computer processor is in your head where your brain used to be. Need to be able to get to it easily for upgrades of chips, memory and processing components.' Didn't know he would be up working this late. And another message from him, 'I'm often up this late. I take it you're recharging. That's why you're finally getting around to wondering these things?'

I'm having an email exchange based just on my thoughts. I really have to be careful what I think. It goes out before I realize what's happening. And then the next jolt of smell remembrances overcome me. That cologne Raoul wears? What is it? Elon Musk. I'd forgotten he wore that. Said it makes him feel electric. A really poor pun, but sometimes you just have to go along with a guy's sense of humor. And Raoul does have a strange sense of humor. He can still make me laugh. At least I think he can. He did the last time I saw him. He has all these really weird insights into people. Attributes crazy thoughts to someone. Socially unacceptable thoughts. You know they aren't really what that person thinks. At least you assume they don't think what Raoul suggests.

When he gets on a roll it gets to be really funny. But the first insight or two cause you to scratch your head. What's he talking about? But as he gets into it, he finds a way to push the exaggeration further and further. You can't help but laugh. And his routine is always person specific. If you didn't know the person, you wouldn't get what he's saying about them. He must be able to notice little things that the rest of us take for granted. He's able to pick up on those things and take them to their illogical limits. But what he's picking up on, everyone else must see, but not think about. Otherwise it wouldn't be believable and therefore funny.

Another jolt. The remembrance is the taste of Tagliatelle with a lamb ragout. Like Rocky and I had at the Zeppelin Cooking School in Orvieto, Italy. Just incredible layers of taste. That meal is still with me all these years later. I was a senior in high school. Rocky had to deliver a paper at a conference in Rome. He brought me along so we could share some quality time since we'd been sharing none. Rocky was at the top of his game in circuitry design. He was in demand to share what he was doing with the industry. The Rome conference was the only one the company agreed to let him address. Over four thousand people showed up to listen to what Rocky had to say. It transformed the industry. All of a sudden it was clear Rocky had advanced the state of the art pretty much all by himself.

But that was the boring part. We got into Italy on Thursday. His address was on Monday. So we had a couple days in Rome. With the weekend available to travel. Someone at work had told him about this little mountaintop community. They said it was typical of the small cities of Italy. It was supposed to be a great place to see what the tourists seldom see. So Rocky packed up and got us on a train to Orvieto. When we checked into the hotel, he asked at the desk what there was to do. We were told they had a great cooking school right next door. The hotel proprietor was friends with Chef Lorenzo. He could get us in. We could help make our dinner and learn about how Italian food is prepared at the same time.

Chef Lorenzo was welcoming and an interesting guy. He was married to an American and spent time in the US. His English was excellent and his cooking knowledge incredible. Said he taught Etruscan cooking. The Etruscans lived in Orvieto before the Romans came out and conquered the area before the time of Christ.

We met the apprentice chefs who were working with Lorenzo before going into commercial kitchens around the world. Each shared a technique they used to prepare parts of the meal. When everything was done, we were invited to eat what we had all prepared from scratch. Just incredible food. It opened my eyes to what was possible. The experience gave me a much better appreciation for the meals I am served in restaurants. It also gave me insights into Italy and the people there.

Another jolt. I remember the feel of a soft blanket against my face as I'm trying to sleep in after a long night of sleeplessness. I always have the problem of an overactive mind. I find it hard to shut down when working a problem. I want to solve the problem and move on. And when I finally resign myself that I'm not going to fix it then and there, I collapse into bed exhausted. But I'm never able to fall asleep. My mind isn't going to stop in the middle of solving the problem. It's going to find an answer even if it means I'm not going to get any sleep. I can't tell you how many times that happens to me. And in every case, by morning I'm pulling the covers up over my head, trying to block out the morning sun that streams into my room. That is when I feel the softness of the blankets against my face. It's a feeling I enjoy. Usually by the time I pull the blanket up, I have an approach worked out that might solve the problem. At that point my mind is willing to rest for a bit. Let me go to sleep. I enjoy that feeling of finally being able to relax and go to sleep. I'm totally spent, over tired and unable to keep going. And I know my mind would keep going if the rest of me is willing; which it never is.

The soft blanket. How many times have I woken up to find myself drenched in sweat? And I lay there. Still exhausted after several hours of sleep. It isn't physical exhaustion so much as it is mental. I push my mind as far as it will go on its own. I've reviewed every option my mind could entertain to find an answer. My body reacts to the ordeal my mind is going through. And the result is the sweaty condition I find myself in the next morning. And then I have to go wash the blanket and all my sheets. There is always a price to pay for the overnight struggles. It's never been easy. Would I do it all again? Yes. Can't kid myself on that one.

AppleCore has been my dream job ever since Rocky said the company was hiring new grads and I should take a look. I don't think he thought I'd follow through since we never talked about where I would go to work. He just assumed I'd go find a job at Wal-Mart or Costco and that would be all I'd ever do. He never took me seriously until the day I was made a VP. Suddenly I was higher in the organization than he was as an Engineering Fellow. He came by my office just to check it out. "So this is where all the big shots hang out." He said that first time. He could have been a big shot if he had wanted to go into the product side rather than just engineering. But engineering was where he was comfortable. That was where he stayed.

Another jolt. This time it's the smells of Raoul as we made love. That same cologne in my nose. It had an arousing effect on me. Phenomes, I think, is the correct term for those smell triggers that arouse a woman. Raoul didn't arouse me as much as some others had. It took a while for me to respond fully to his touch and kisses. But when the release finally came, he was surprisingly gentle. He would help me prolong the contractions. Kissing my body in sensitive places I didn't know existed. Touching me gently. Caressing the contours of my now relaxing body. All those sensations. I miss them. And I wonder if I'll ever be able to experience anything like them now. Particularly when Dr. Woodall installs my new vagina with hopefully appropriate software to simulate the human sexual response. I'm supposed to help in developing that software. But I'm really out of my depth. What do I know about recreating something as personal and intense as an orgasm? And yet all of the immortals to come after me will either thank me or damn me for what I help deliver.

I wonder how Dr. Woodall smells, and even before I finish the thought, I'm making sure I don't send an email to him asking that question. But I remember he said he was working on smell capability. A retrofit sometime in the future. But is it like next month or next century before I'll be able to perceive smells like everyone around me? I never thought about what I miss not being able to smell things. And now all I have to go by is memories of smells. It's hard. It's almost like I'm in a bubble. All of the things I used to react to, are indirect. Seen on a television screen so I know they're there. But I'm not reacting to them. I'm reacting to seeing others reacting to them. I'm not sensing or feeling what they're feeling. I'm only reliving a memory. But Dr. Woodall says to be patient. My experience will only get better. I hope it gets better soon.

Chapter Thirty-Two: Nineteen Days

I'm sitting in my office deep in thought. The pages of reports, journal articles, email, and code architectures pass before me. I retain all of it. I'm on the trail of something important. I'm tracing through the choices we've made. I'm getting a bad feeling we've gone down a rabbit hole. I'm retrieving more and more articles and artifacts from other development projects, trying to see what isn't evident yet. Is there something that limits us on our functionality in a way we aren't anticipating? The code structures have become more and more complex. And I'm the one who has driven us in that direction. That's why I have to understand where I'm taking this product family. Am I creating a limitation that will haunt me if I don't fix it now?

I accelerate the speed at which I'm working my way through the materials, circling back and comparing code modules with those we have abandoned on other products because of discovered limitations. Mindi comes into the office. I can't stop now to find out what she wants.

A journal article catches my attention. The author contemplated a different architecture, a more open architecture. Is that the answer? I don't have enough information yet, but it looks promising. What about the other product?

I continue to follow the threads. I have no idea how long I work through all the information, but I'm seeing a feasible way to avoid the perceived trap. Oriana comes in, says something, but I'm still working through the solution. Suddenly I'm there. I know what we have to do!

"Been like that all day. Doesn't respond to anything." Mindi is explaining to Oriana.

"Oriana." I turn to look at her. "I'm sending you an email with instructions. We have to re-architect the section your team is coding. The specifics are in the email."

Oriana says to Mindi, "She comes up with some wild stuff now."

Chapter Thirty-Three: Eighteen Days

After spending the day re-architecting code sections with Oriana's team, I decide to give the team time to work through the changes. I need to get out of the office as I'm spending way too much time here. People are making comments, wondering when I was last home. Can't have anyone suspecting I'm not my normal self. Would open up too many questions I'm not ready to address.

As usual I walk to my house, keeping an eye open for anyone who might want to rob me after the earlier incident. There haven't been any further reports about the man dying, so hopefully the case has been closed. But somehow I doubt it. The police rarely give up trying to solve what they think might be a crime. After all, if someone killed the guy on purpose, then they need to find the person before someone else is killed. I put the incident out of my mind as not worth worrying about. I have other things to consider. Time is running down before I have to make an irrevocable decision. If I go back to my biological body I'll not be given a chance at a later time to make the change again. That will be it. As I walk past the spot where the man emerged from the bushes, I see the events once more in my mind. Almost like a videotape. It all happened so fast, but the interesting aspect of having photographic memory is I can play it all back slower. See what I didn't the first time. For instance the knife. He walked up to me carrying it pointing down and away. He apparently was trying to decide how to use it to commit the robbery. Was this the first time for him? I don't know. I react when he gets close, spinning and building the momentum of my right fist that hits the man on the left temple, above his eye. Both eyes roll back as his head whips back from the impact. He lets the knife fall from his hand, stumbles backward before collapsing to the ground. I step forward, kick the knife away from him, and step on his crotch with my high heels. He practically sits up as I do so, but drops back to the ground. I stoop to pick up the knife and get away from the man as quickly as I can.

By the time I've reached my condo I've examined the incident a dozen different ways and still come to no conclusions. I need to set it aside, keep vigilant in a way I've never had to before, but circumstances have changed. My neighborhood is no longer the safe haven I've thought it to be. I have to act accordingly. And then I think about my reaction. Before, I would have been a nervous wreck, probably needing a glass of wine or something to relax when I got home. But now I don't feel tension, I don't feel stress in the same way I did before, where it would manifest itself in tight muscles, headaches and feeling 'uptight'. Now it's all an intellectual thing for me. I think about it. I remember things, but I don't feel the reactions to what happened. Am I really even physically reacting at all?

Candles always helped me relax, smelling the odors, feeling the warmth, looking at the bright light. So I decide to light a candle and see how I react. I do so and sit down to experience it. I see the light flickering and see the wisp of smoke and heat rising. I even hear the crackling of the flame as it bursts wax before it melts and turns into a shimmering molten covering over the candle wax itself. I remember the smells, but they aren't there. I can't perceive the smell now. And the remembrance and the absence are a stark reminder that I'm not what I was. I'm different now, better in some ways and deficient in others. And who knows how my abilities will change over time? Will I eventually regain the abilities l lost? Or will I simply adjust to the new reality? Only able to experience my memories. No longer experiencing the real thing when it comes to smells, and taste, sex, child birth and other things I'm still discovering.

Funny, it's been a long time since I thought about child birth being an experience I could have. Since I've never met someone with whom I'd want a family, it hadn't come up in a long time. But now that it's one of the things I'll never be able to experience, I've come to wonder about it. Wonder whether I'll regret that loss in the centuries ahead when I have no family. Rocky will pass on at some point and then I'll be alone.

For centuries.

But just like smells and tastes, I'll have the memories, but not be able to create new ones. I'll not experience smells or tastes that I'd not experienced before the transformation.

I extinguish the candle. No sense wasting it. The effect I was looking for isn't there, even with the memories of the smell. Maybe it's something to do with how the smells interact with the human nervous system, which I also no longer possess. I'm missing so many things. Things I just took for granted. But they were the things that informed my understanding of the world around me and my experience with this life.

Dr. Woodall. I need to call him. I glance at the clock. I've talked to him this late before. I make the call. "It's Sage, Dr. Woodall. Do you have a minute to talk?"

"Sage. Yes. Always for you. What can I help you with?"

"Remember our walk in the park? You said you were working on smell?"

"I remember. We're making progress, but these things take time."

"I understand, but do you have any idea when I might…" How do I explain this without it sounding like upgrading a computer?

"Part of the issue we're dealing with is there's only one of you out there. There will be more soon. But it will be years before anyone who invests in creating this capability will be able to recover that investment through sales of systems."

"Believe me, I understand that. But there must be some way of accelerating this work so I'm not blind to smells for decades. And it's not just smells. I need help with taste and touch. I know I'll never need to eat food, but there must be some way I can experience how things taste. And touch, textures elude me right now. I can't tell if something is soft or hard except at a very general level. None of these are impairing my ability to work or live my life; but they enrich the experience. And for now I'm limited to remembrances. I lit a candle tonight. I could remember how a candle smells, but at the same time I'm feeling the absence of smells. Do you understand what I'm saying?"

A short silence before Dr. Woodall answers. "It was a compromise. We could have held up allowing anyone to transition until we had everything perfect, or we could offer an 80% solution. We chose the latter, knowing you and those who come after you will experience life without some abilities you're used to as the technology is perfected. That's the important thing to focus on. You have time. More time than anyone else alive, at least at the moment." Dr. Woodall waits to see if I have a response. I don't so he continues. "I know your history is to be impatient. That's part of what defines your success. But now I'm going to ask you to be patient with us. We want it to be right when we … give you this capability."

"You were going to say something else." I challenge him hearing what he was about to say.

"Yes, I was going to say retrofit you, but that's not what we're doing. We're giving you the ability to smell. That's what a doctor does." An odd way of putting it. I wonder why he chose it.

"So when should I look forward to this capability?" I ask.

"I'm not promising, but we hope it will be ready for a trial run soon. Originally I wasn't going to ask you to perform that trial run, we were going to do it in the lab. But I've changed my mind because of this call. You're right, I have a responsibility to you to try to make your experience better. So, soon."

Chapter Thirty-Four: Seventeen Days

Professor Reinhardt Schroeder, PhD. is lecturing. Discussing robotics and the human condition. I'm in a relatively large lecture hall at the University of California at Berkeley. I became aware of this lecture and decided I need to better understand what Dr. Woodall is telling me about my future. Universities are supposed to be doing the pure science research, not the applied type. They normally look at the distant future, the leading edge. They test theories and eliminate unpromising areas for research. And I'm all about theories and research. I'm all about finding new capabilities for software and systems that aid and augment human existence at AppleCore. So now I need to spend a little time trying to understand more about the voyage I'm on personally.

"What does it mean to be human? Are we the sum of the sensory inputs we experience each and every day? Are we more in that we balance spiritual and cognitive conceptions? We're feeling beings. We are said to be ruled by emotions. But robots don't experience emotions. They can't love or be sad or experience joy. They process data and make decisions based on rule sets. Rule sets we create for them. So if you ask me, can a robot ever be human? I would have to say not in my lifetime and probably not for a very long time thereafter."

"Professor." I call out from my seat a few rows up and to his right. He nods to me. "This is the Kurzweil year." Professor Schroeder nods and smiles. "The year of the Singularity. What do you think is the likelihood of a man-machine future for mankind?"

"An interesting question." The professor begins. "Dr. Kurzweil wrote that book a long time ago. Much has happened since then to re-shape the future he foresaw. But also certain things he assumed have not occurred. A singularity where man replaces the human body with either a robotic one or goes even further to become a presence on a computer node is a fanciful notion. It would be a remarkable transition for mankind to shed the limits of the human body. It would create a race of immortals. But what kind of existence would they have if there were no humans with whom to interact?"

I continue the line of questioning, "What do you see as the major limitations to replicating the human body with a robotic one?"

"How would you transition the consciousness to the new host?" He replies flatly.

"But what if that were solved? What is the major limitation of the robotic body that we can produce today?"

The professor nods to accept the assumption. "Okay if we were able to transition your consciousness, the new host has solved balance, locomotion, coordination, sight, hearing, voice and the ability to interact with the internet for information and communication."

"What's missing?" I push. Others in the audience turn to look at me, curious why I'm following this line of questions.

"A series of physical sensors and systems, but those are less interesting questions than how the new being would deal with moral and ethical questions. You would have spiritual issues to deal with. What is this being's relationship with God? If you have a being that lives forever with periodic upgrades, what role does it play in relation to the non-immortals and the other immortals, at least until such time as everyone has become an immortal?"

"Have you created a master race?" I deliberately use words I know will evoke a reaction in the audience. I hear the stir of people in their seats.

"There are many ways you could describe the new bifurcation of society that would occur. Yes, you would have a probably increasing number of people who have superior intelligence. They can instantly access and process any information. As new processors are released, faster processing speeds. That means they will be able to out-think and make decisions from more perfect knowledge. Yes, the non-immortals would have a difficult time keeping up with those who have transitioned. But that is at the pure cognitive level. The other things that make us moral and ethical beings is the more interesting question. Where do ethics and morality reside? Is it part of the consciousness or part of the memories stored in the computer? Are moral and ethical decisions programmed into the immortal or do they reside in that part that would transition from the biologic being? Something that has yet to be defined?"

I could answer his question but choose not to as I don't want to draw attention to the fact that this leading edge academic is actually trailing where medical science and robotics have already arrived. "I know this is probably not your area of expertise, Professor. But for a moment let's suppose the moral and ethical aspects of human behavior reside with the consciousness that transfers. In that instance we become superhuman in some respects and less than human in others. How do you see that sorting out?"

The professor wrinkles his brow, trying to follow my question. "Could you be more specific?"

"If human consciousness transfers to a robotic body, certain perceptions are lost. Certain feelings can only be replicated through memory because not all the same sensors will be available to the new immortal. Without a nervous system or hormonal or adrenal glands, the new immortal lacks many of the stimuli that the biologic human experiences. Reactions are different, delayed or based on memories of having those biologic systems that create feelings, stress reactions and emotions. The new immortal may live forever, but unless software and robotic sensors can replicate the experiences in a similar fashion, your new being cannot experience life as we know it."

"That's a very insightful analysis. How did you arrive at those conclusions?" The professor queries.

THE GHOST IN THE MACHINE

"It goes back to the less interesting part of your discussion. Morals and ethics may be in the headlines of robotics, because they are more nebulous than smell, taste and touch, but they are less informative of the non-biologic human experience than those mundane sensory perceptions which are currently missing from your robotic host."

"But why would an immortal care about smell, taste and touch if they have no need to eat?" The professor wonders aloud, apparently hoping someone else would answer.

"Because it's part of the human experience. If you're transferring consciousness from a biologic being who has had those experiences, that being will miss what informed her or him. Memories will haunt of a Thanksgiving or family dinner. Smell is one of the most powerful inducers of memory. We've seen a smell invoke emotional reactions to detailed and complete images particularly for individuals under stress. Combat situations are typical. And they invoke Post Traumatic Stress responses. So if your new immortal doesn't come with the whole package of sensory perception capabilities, that entity will be haunted by the memories and the lack of congruence to their current reality."

The professor wants to change the subject and get back to his lecture. He clearly knows he's out of his depth. Somehow he has encountered someone who has given the subject a great deal of thought. "What you say, in a given scenario, may be the case. But the fact of the matter is, at the moment, we are speculating. There are no robotic humans to test out your theories. I'm pleased you would join us this evening and pose questions that will give us all reason to ponder on the range of possible non-biological human possibilities. There are more unanswered questions than answered. And while your vision of the future seems reasonable, I can assure you it is not one of the more probable futures we need to contemplate."

"And why would you say that professor?" I fire back.

"We really must move on, Miss. So back to my lecture."

I'm no longer listening, realizing Professor Schroeder is not a leader in his field, but just another professor repeating what every other professor who has not done leading edge research is reciting for the edification of the uninformed students interested in the topic.

"Moral dilemmas will be handled differently by…" has the professor returning to his lecture. I gather my things. As I walk down the stairs to leave the building a young man comes up behind me.

"Do you work for one of the robotics companies?" he asks. He's dark haired, dark eyes and dressed like a student. He holds out his hand to shake. "Moshe."

"One that dabbles, but that's not what we primarily do." I admit.

"You sure have more insight than the professor. You have any jobs open there? I'd like to get in on the ground floor. Particularly where it comes to the Singularity, if that's what you're after. I read that book like five years ago. It was like wow, this is what the future could be. And I've wanted to find a way to get involved in the merger of consciousness and robotics ever since. That's why I'm here. But as you can see, not many folks here are really leading the charge."

"What are you studying?" I respond, curious.

"Neurocognitive sciences, mechanical and electrical engineering and robotics. That's not how I started out until I decided the faculty wasn't strong in robotics. So I decomposed the skill sets I thought I'd need. I've been devouring the components so I can create the whole myself."

"Are you entrepreneurial?"

"Yeah. That's me. Entrepreneurial. Whatever that is. So you got a job for me?"

THE GHOST IN THE MACHINE

Chapter Thirty-Five: Sixteen Days

A'zam wanders into Julia's office. Julia, of course, is surprised by his appearance. She waves for the glass monitor screen to blank itself. Images of New Mexico Badlands appear instead of the data sets she was examining. A'zam glances at the screen from the back and asks, "You take those pictures on a trip?"

Julia isn't following his question, glances around the office trying to figure out what pictures he's referring to but doesn't notice the screen. She looks back at him blankly.

"The badlands on your monitor. You take those?"

Julia finally connects. She looks to see what picture he's referring to. "No. Just something I found on a website. Thought it an interesting place to contemplate."

A'zam is unusually casual today, "And what have you contemplated about it?"

"Peacefulness. Quiet. Nature."

A'zam nods to himself as he makes an odd face completely unnerving Julia. "Do you ever go to lectures?" He asks and engages her eyes with his.

"Lecture? Like a graduate course?" She's trying to put together where he's going.

"I'm curious what our academic friends are working on. So I try to make it a point to attend a lecture once a week on something related, but not directly in our wheelhouse." A'zam reveals.

"Didn't know you were doing that." Julia responds honestly.

"Not something I advertise. You know if I can slip in and out unobserved I don't have to get into endless conversations with people looking for a job or take a pitch on a new product someone has cooked up and thinks we should build here."

"Makes sense. To answer your question, no. I don't go to lectures. I spend time reading journals to get the same insights."

A'zam shakes his head. "You don't. That's why I go. In an article you only learn what the author wants you to know. You don't get an opportunity to question their assumptions and conclusions. You don't get the texture of their research, whether it's really leading edge. Doesn't give you insights as to whether they are taking you into opportunities or simply sidetracking your thoughts and investments."

"You make a good point. I'll try to get out more."

A'zam flares for a moment. "Don't _try_, Julia."

She leans back in her chair, "I'll start next week." And she has another thought. "Anything you'd recommend I sit in on so we're not duplicating effort?"

A'zam shakes his head disgusted. Moves on to the point he came to make. "I attended a lecture at Berkeley last night. On robotics."

"Who lectured?"

"Reinhardt Schroeder. An interesting guy. A top mechanical engineer who's gotten all caught up in ethics and morality."

"Sounds like you didn't think much of the lecture." Julia notes wondering why A'zam would remark on someone clearly not that interesting to him.

"On the contrary. There was a very interesting discussion." A'zam hesitates searching for the right words to describe what he heard and saw. "Unexpected, really."

Julia listens to his carefully selected description, wonders why. "In what way?"

"Someone in the audience noted this is the year Ray Kurzweil predicted the Singularity between organic and robotic man. And that spun the discussion off in a… very unexpected direction."

Julia wonders why this would catch A'zam's attention. "Tell me more."

"Schroeder tried to dismiss the whole Kurzweil prediction. But one person in the audience kept stripping away his dismissal. Penetrated to the very heart of what it would be like to have achieved the Singularity. It was clear Schroeder really hadn't given it much thought."

"Do you think there's something there for AppleCore?" Julia thinks she finally understands why this lecture was so intriguing to him.

"I do. It seems we're marching towards the Singularity an inch at a time. But what if…"

"What if we could make the leap and capture an emerging market?" Julia completes the thought tentatively, afraid she might be wrong.

"Exactly." A'zam is pleased she has understood what he saw. But at the same time, that's not enough. "But how do we exploit this opportunity? We create tools that extend the senses and understandings of biologic man. But how do we incorporate all those tools into the actual robotic man? There's a whole range of fascinating opportunities alluded to last night."

"From a competitor?" Julia jumps to the assumption that would unsettle A'zam in this way.

"Think about it." He ignores her question. "If you have a robotic body, your senses no longer need to warn you of danger. They're used for awareness, but of very different pieces of information. You no longer need to worry about eating something that would kill you. You don't have to worry about walking on a broken bone, so a sense of pain is no longer important. Your internal organs won't kill you if they're damaged in some way. So your perceptions are very different."

Julia nods reflectively.

"But at the same time, if you've transferred consciousness to this robotic body, if it's still you in there and your memories have come with you." He stops to modify his thought. "You experience things that form the basis for your decision-making. And if you are no longer subject to the same limitations, you don't need to worry about all those things your body used to worry about for you."

"So where are you going with this?" Julia is lost.

"If the Singularity involves moving a person's consciousness that has evolved over a lifetime, that consciousness approaches the world based on experiences. If the senses are no longer feeding those same experiences, the new bio-robotic being encounters dissonance. That being remembers cues and feelings that are no longer there in exactly the same situation. So the new bio-robotic person reacts to memories of feelings and pain and taste and smell, but doesn't perceive them in the same situation."

"So you're saying these new bio-robotic people need a shrink. That's not exactly what we do."

A'zam shakes his head. "Unhelpful."

Julia regrets her flippant comment.

"We can provide the sensors that replace the senses the robotic body doesn't have, but the person inside expects to frame their experiences. This could be a whole new product area. Particularly as more and more people cross over, or transition or whatever they're going to call it."

Julia needs to recover. She goes on the offensive. "You didn't answer my earlier question. Who was talking about this at the lecture?" Julia wants to know who the competition is for this new opportunity.

"Sage." A'zam responds almost in a whisper.

Julia reacts as if slapped. "Sage?" Why in the world would Sage be into robotics? "Why isn't she bringing this to the leadership team?"

"Wrong question. Why has she become more of an expert than the professor who's making robotics his life's work?"

Julia shakes her head. "I can't imagine."

"Why are you so obtuse, Julia? Think about it."

Julia acts as if slapped once more. "I'm…"

"A month ago we were about to terminate Sage because she couldn't keep up. Now she's running circles around everyone. And suddenly we find out she's an expert in something that doesn't track with what she does."

Julia is still reacting to being called obtuse. "I don't think…"

"That's the problem. You don't think. I need you to get with Desirae. Find out what Sage has done, probably in Dallas, and how we profit from it. And this better be your highest priority."

THE GHOST IN THE MACHINE

Chapter Thirty-Six: Fifteen Days

Dr. Woodall let me know the day before the virtual meeting on robotic sexuality was to take place. I was busy all day and didn't make time to prepare. But of course my brain scanned the literature and websites for relevant information, so when the time finally arrived I did have something to pull on. However, I didn't feel good about what I had. Too esoteric. Too theoretical. Not enough personal analysis of the situation to really make a case for how this aspect of my robotic being is going to function. And then I find out there is only one other woman on the call. Really? A dozen men and one woman to figure out how sexuality should work?

"Dr. Aggarwal, I wouldn't suggest that an orgasm should result in the same sensations for a male and female." Lidia Belmare protests. An Italian psychotherapist, she's an expert in the psychological neuroses that result from sexual dysfunction. And that makes her an expert in what the experience should be for both male and female sexual systems, as they are labeled in the materials sent out in advance of the virtual meeting.

Dr. Aggarwal seems taken aback that someone would disagree with him. He's now the lead research engineer on this project. A biological engineer who crossed over to robotics late in life, he was thrust into this leadership role because Dr. Woodall asked him. "Nonsense. There needs to be symmetry. We have an opportunity to make the sexes equal. Why would we want to perpetuate a difference that is related to the physical needs of reproduction? That's no longer a factor. So we have a blank slate to create anything we wish." Should have kept Dr. Woodall.

I can't hold my tongue, which probably isn't a good idea.

Normally I want to get a better lay of the land. Who has influence? Who has good ideas? But Dr. Aggarwal is just so removed from his subject I can't stand by. "Dr. Aggarwal. I don't have your resume, but I do have insights you don't since I'm the only one here who currently is waiting for the fruits of your labors."

"I concede your point." Dr. Aggarwal clearly would prefer not to.

"I understand your perspective of the biologic ties that no longer pertain. But we do not intend, at least in the near term, to transition consciousness of a person without a reasonable history of existence."

"And your point is?" Aggarwal is aggravating.

"My point is you intend to make the experience the same as the male experience currently. You're proposing to force all women to experience the sexual world as you do. If there is to be a migration I propose it should be the other way. Force all men to experience the sexual world as women do. A slow arousal from multiple sensory and hormonal inputs, which builds over time to a crescendo."

Aggarwal shakes his head, "Not possible. It would neuter the aggressive nature of man that forces him to seek success and drive for it."

"And are you prepared for a world where women are as aggressive and ruthless as their male counterparts? Where there is no balance between drive and relationships? Where feelings give way to complete and utter drive to succeed?"

Aggarwal shakes his head. "Why do you see this as an either or situation?"

"Because it is. At the moment, without your wonderful device I don't experience feelings of love or hate, pain or joy. I remember those feelings from when I was a biologic entity. I apply my memories to the situation. But I can't feel any emotion that's not a memory. That's no way to live. And feelings are what drive us to success. If we feel good about how we look, or how successful we've been because we mastered something, we push onward into the unknown, expecting to repeat the success we've had."

"But you no longer have the need for feelings." Aggarwal protests. "Why can't you function on data and information? What's the purpose of feelings in a being that isn't subject to the dangers feelings help us manage?"

"Have you ever had intercourse with a sheep?" I ask because he has no idea what he's talking about and I have to get his attention.

"Of course not." Aggarwal dismisses my question.

"Then you don't know what it's like to have a sexual relationship with something or someone who doesn't react to feelings." And still I don't think he understands my point. "Are you married?"

"What does that have to do with our task?" Aggarwal responds, now feeling under pressure.

"Because you are the beneficiary of your spouse's reactions to you. She or he responds to cues you provide. Cues about your sexual interest. Cues about how you perceive them. You demonstrate your interest, which flatters that person and causes a reaction on their part. The sexual encounter is just that. It's the result of differing perceptions, reactions, and biologic processes. They are complimentary, in that they are different, but reinforce the outcomes for both partners. It's not the same. If they were the same, neither would experience what they do."

"I understand the point you are making. But that is the way it is now. We have the opportunity to change that for the better."

"Better according to whose definition? Yours? Who else believes that removing the complimentary nature of sexuality would make it a better experience for either?" I challenge.

"She has a point you must consider." Lidia Belmare chimes in. At last.

"I am giving it consideration." Aggarwal responds, but then continues. "It's an important point we must recognize, but it's not a limitation. We have already changed the immortal prototype to harmonize racial identity. We have eliminated physical ailment and limitations. We have created a high functioning being capable of sustained high performance. Performance at levels we could have never contemplated before. And here we are. An achievement that is unparalleled in history. And we have the opportunity to make it better. To make the immortal the crowning achievement of mankind. And we have the opportunity to eliminate sexual bias and sexual limitations in the functioning of immortals."

"But the difference in men and women is what has enabled our race to grow and prosper." I respond. "Those differences have enabled us to continue to raise our standards of living, to raise whole populations from poverty, sickness and short lives. If men alone inhabited this planet, wars would have killed off everyone centuries ago. Women are the moderating influences in life. We focus on relationships, and feelings and emotions. Men seldom build the foundation of a society on those elements."

"I might agree with much of what you have said." Aggarwal hesitates, probably wondering what my next attack is going to be on his premise. "But I still don't see how all you have suggested pertains to the sexual experience we are seeking to define and create for immortals."

"A woman looks for a man who is strong, smart, and cunning to be successful. But she also looks for the man to be caring, not only of his wife, but of his children. If the man is self-centered, then she will be left to feed the children and herself. Not an attractive proposition." I offer knowing Aggarwal has already dismissed Dr. Belmare, but hoping two of us together will be harder to blow off.

"This whole discussion is unhelpful." Aggarwal responds, looking for the men to bail him out.

"I recommend you let me build the software prototype." I counter.

"Why would I do that?" Aggarwal seems affronted by my suggestion.

"Because if you don't, AppleCore will make a more appealing version. You can either work with me or you'll find yourself unremembered and a non-contributor to the final immortals project."

THE GHOST IN THE MACHINE

Chapter Thirty-Seven: Fourteen Days

Oriana pokes her head into my office. "Got a minute?"

I look up, even though reading documents in my head. I figured out that it freaks everyone out when I come up with answers to questions they are all furiously trying to find on their mobile devices without consulting one. So by looking down, everyone thinks I'm reading from a device just like they are. "Hi. What's up?"

Oriana stays in the doorway. Normally when she wants to talk she comes in and closes the door. But not today. "Got time to get a coffee or something alcoholic?"

"Whichever you prefer." I answer knowing I'm not going to be drinking either one.

Oriana brightens, "Let's go out. This may be a more than a coffee conversation."

That doesn't sound good. I'm instantly scanning Oriana's delivery statistics in my head, but everything seems to be on track. "Sure. Got a place in mind?"

Oriana nods and I follow her out to a Googlecar. "You look stressed." I observe hoping it will give her an opening to give me a clue about what's on her mind.

"I'm probably more tired than stressed. You know you get to a point where it all kind of blends together? I thought there's no way someone fifteen years older than me can keep up this pace. I'm feeling the effects of it and you don't seem to."

Right to the point. "I may just be better at hiding it."

THE GHOST IN THE MACHINE

As we get into the Googlecar Oriana continues her thought. "Am I crazy or has the pace of deliveries been accelerated to ludicrous speed?" Oriana asks.

I wonder what the actual increase in pace has been. My mind instantly presents me with: "We've doubled the rate of delivery, well, actually it's up 97.3% over a month ago." That's effectively doubling the deliveries.

"Why?" Oriana can't fathom why we needed to.

"Because we intend to appreciably move the needle."

"More hand-waving from the Senior Leadership. Do you have any idea what the toll has been on the team?"

I can see it's been having a toll on Oriana. She is my absolute best 'go to' person. She's always been able to find a way when no one else on the team could. "Tell me."

"Sure you're showing us shortcuts we didn't know existed. Those short cuts have been the only reason the whole team hasn't quit on me. But you're pushing us beyond our comfort levels. I mean, quite frankly, half of us are amazed at what you come up with. The other half is so lost they have no clue what they're doing. They just code it and go home."

I hear what she's saying. The team had always had an integral role in defining our solutions and the approaches we take to solve some of the hardest problems. But now, in the interest of faster deliverables, I've taken away their role and left everyone as just a coder.

"What do you suggest?" I ask.

Oriana glances at me. "Do you really care what I suggest?"

"Absolutely. I've always valued your thoughts and ideas." I'm surprised at her response.

"Until you came back from your holiday I'd have agreed. But now? I don't know if you care about anything other than yourself. At least that's kind of what the team is telling me. I have to agree with them."

Holy shit. This is much worse than I thought. How have I been missing the clues? It's almost déjà vu to that lecture. And then the call on the sexual software. I've become more insensitive than I thought. Am I missing the cues or just not looking for them anymore? Have I lost the perceptions of feelings that others have? I noticed Oriana was stressed. But only when she reached out to me to bring it to my attention. "I hear you."

We pull into Jack's loading zone. We depart the Googlecar and walk into the bar in silence. She spots a table. We migrate towards it before a couple can get there. They show their unhappiness about being slow. That's not my problem. I guess Oriana feels the same. We sit down. Oriana orders two beers.

"I'm still not drinking. Taking medicine that doesn't go well with it."

She waives off the second beer. "So what's going on with you? I've never seen you this way." Oriana begins. I know I have to give her something, but as I start to respond I'm not sure what I'm going to say.

"Good or bad?" I begin to buy time.

"I don't know yet. You amaze me every day. You did before your vacation." Oriana situates herself differently on her chair, uncomfortable about the conversation. Probably afraid I won't take it well. "It's almost like somehow someone gave you a steroid shot to the brain. Now you're a mile ahead of the rest of us. You're wearing us out trying to keep up."

"And you're not, from what you said."

Oriana has this pained look. She grimaces and responds. "I sort of am, but I'm having to put in mega hours to figure out where you're taking us. After a longer day than usual at work, keeping everyone else focused, those evening hours of added research. Well, it's just killing me."

"I'm sorry." I admit. And I am. I have no idea what the effect of my transformation has been on the team. And now that I know, I have to do something I really don't want to. Damn logic is making me act differently than I would have if I still had hormones ruling my psyche. Taking that into consideration I finally continue the public thought. "What do you think I need to do to get everyone back on the same page?"

"You obviously are seeing things the rest of us aren't. Personally I think you need to give the whole team another day off. Go home. Sleep. Play with your kids or sleep with your spouse. Whatever it takes to get back to an even keel."

"And then?"

"You need to explain to us what you've done. Why is the architecture morphing in front of our eyes? The tried and true approach has been abandoned in favor of something many of us don't understand. And you know the team. They'll go through hell and walk out the other side if they think it will result in a better product. But frankly, we're already in hell. Worse, we suddenly realize we have no idea how to get out."

I look at Oriana skeptically. "You really think if I do a presentation on the new architecture it will get everyone back on the same page?" I don't think so.

Oriana gladly accepts the glass of beer and instantly takes a sip. Guess she thinks she needs reinforcement to continue the discussion. "Well, that and you've got to slack off the pace. You're jamming changes on us we're not comfortable with. What's made this team so special is we understood what we were doing. We understood how what we were doing made the product better. But now…" Oriana shakes her head. "Now… most of us are left wondering what the hell we're doing."

"But it all comes together." I conclude to clarify what she's saying.

"Yes. But we have no idea how or why. We're not robots."

Does she know what I've done? No, but her comment hits too close to home.

"We need to understand what we're doing." She continues. "And how it makes the product better. You're not giving that to us."

"What I hear you saying, and correct me if I'm wrong, is I need to explain how the code works. I need to show everyone why it's a better approach than what we've done in the past. And then I need to slow things down. Give the teams more time to absorb the changes. Put out the product based on greater understanding of what they're doing."

Oriana shakes her head. "I can see how you'd draw that conclusion. But truth be told, we need to be part of the team again. When you define the coding each person is going to do, you take away the creative inputs we, as team leaders, used to have. Now we're just delivering what you tell us to. We're managers. We're not part of the team. You've assumed what all of us used to do. We're left without the creative part we all came here for."

I have to think this through. "Go back to letting the team leads define what each person codes."

"Let us create the product within your guidelines. Yes." Oriana concludes.

THE GHOST IN THE MACHINE

Chapter Thirty-Eight: Thirteen Days

Mindi didn't say why Julia was calling the Senior Leadership Team together, but I go anyway since I expected to find out how we were doing with our deliveries. Julia is sitting where A'zam usually sits. What's this all about?

The usual small talk while we wait for the rest of the SLT to arrive. But then I look around and realize everyone is here except A'zam. Julia begins.

"A'zam will be away for a while. Since he doesn't know when he will return, the Board asked me to assume the role of acting CEO." Julia announces. "You have your targets. I simply expect you will execute to deliver against those targets. Are there any questions?"

Hung Duc, the SVP of Hardware Engineering looks at Julia quizzically. "What you mean do not know when return? He sick?"

"No, Hung. He's not sick." Julia responds as if she had expected this question. "He had a last minute opportunity to go do something he's always wanted to do. So he took it. Not one of those things you can plan for. Serendipitous. That's about all I can say about it."

"Why all say?" Hung is not satisfied.

"A'zam asked me not to discuss it."

"Why now? Always know everything before." Hung is unhappy. I would have pursued the same questions, but Julia would never have accepted them from me.

"Maybe we need to start doing things differently, then." Julia responds.

"Wait A'zam?" Hung pursues her.

"No. I don't think that will be necessary. I have full authority to do what I think prudent. So I intend to interpret that authority liberally." Julia sets out so we all know we can't hide behind what would A'zam do? Julia looks across the team as A'zam would have done, to see if anyone has a dissenting opinion. Only she's done her best to squash any independent thoughts.

"So no adjustments to the schedule." I venture with thoughts of Oriana's fatigue still ringing in my ears.

Julia shakes her head, not intending to deign the need to answer the question.

"But if I need to make an adjustment, what's the protocol?"

"Up or back?" Julia responds. Since I've advanced the schedule there's no longer a simple expectation that everything always slips.

"I've pushed my teams pretty hard. I need to back off for a bit to give them a chance to catch up." I respond.

"So a slip." Julia drills.

"Depends on how you look at it. We still haven't advised the market or stores of our advanced schedule. We only pulled it forward last week. And we will still beat the original schedule the market is expecting. So not a slip, merely an internal adjustment while I get my team comfortable doubling the delivery schedule." I respond, knowing I need the support of the rest of the team since Julia isn't exactly a fan.

"Give me a break, Sage." Julia shakes her head. "You're lapsing back into the same old failure syndrome. You promise a delivery date and then the next thing we know you can't make it. What's different than last time? Nothing. You're failing in your job. You're failing to live up to your promises. We can't count on you. So I'm removing you from your role effective immediately. Oriana will assume your duties."

Alix shakes her head. "I wouldn't advise that."

"What? Who are you to tell me what to do?" Julia is indignant.

Alix stares Julia down. "If A'zam had used that criteria to judge you when you still had marketing, you wouldn't be sitting in that chair now."

Julia blushes, shakes her head, "Different circumstances."

"Maybe." Alix responds. "But if Oriana can't deliver to the new schedule, which is not likely if Sage is backing off, then you haven't gained anything."

I have to hand it to Alix. She laid it all out there for me. The only question is why. What's going to happen now that she has? Will Julia replace her too? Julia looks to Desirae, as head of HR. Desirae gives her an almost unnoticeable head shake. Basically advising Julia not to go there. Petra, the CFO won't return her look, basically saying 'you're on your own here'. Alix has backed Julia into a corner. Julia doesn't know what to do since she's been in this role for all of a few hours. This is the first decision she's had to make. I'm glad I'm not sitting where she is. But then again, I'm totally amazed at the whole discussion.

Julia decides to test the whole group. "What about the rest of you? Am I the only one who's uncomfortable with Sage?"

Hung Duc seems ready to put Julia in her place. "Sage pushing us. Go beyond we do before."

"I agree." Wallace, the head of manufacturing weighs in. "I know Oriana. She's good. One of our best. But she's not ready to step into Sage's role. You pull the trigger on this and you'll put us right back where we two weeks ago. Wall Street questioning everything we do. Personally I can live without that."

Petra has heard enough, "Give it a rest, Julia. We don't need Wall Street questioning our forecasts. I spent way too much time on that last time around. Just got my life back. If Sage's delay isn't visible to customers or Wall Street I say we give her a pass. We only act if she can't keep the 'adjustment' invisible."

Not the outcome Julia was hoping for. She looks at me. "You must have more lives that a cat." She grimaces. "I'll need updates from you at Noon and Six every day. Any indication of an impact to product release you'll be history. Am I clear?"

I nod without voicing what I'm actually thinking. I must have really pissed Julia off when A'zam gave me marketing and took it from her.

"Am I clear?" Julia almost shouts at me.

"You have erased any doubt as to your intentions." I respond.

Julia doesn't know what to do with my response. So she does what she usually does with information she doesn't want. She ignores it.

"All right then." Julia looks at each of us individually. "We stick to the plan, stay coordinated and deliver according to the forecast. No more adjustments. Got it?"

Wallace seems in a rare mood, feistier than usual. "Are you planning to do the quarterly update to Wall Street and the Analysts in A'zam's absence?" This is a trap question as to how long A'zam is likely to be gone.

"I'm preparing for it, yes." Julia responds dismissively.

"Not what I asked. Are you planning to deliver it?" Wallace looks at me, then back at Julia. "As I see it, A'zam wouldn't let you present it given he expects to announce an acceleration on new product releases. He will want to deliver that news personally. And if that's the case he'll be back within two weeks. And if that's true then I don't think any of us have to do anything differently. He'll be back before we could implement any changes anyway."

"He be pissed we change anything." Hung Duc adds.

"Do I have to remind you I'm in charge?" Julia sees the revolution and doesn't like the implications.

"Most of us are pretty well aligned, but you always seem to be the outlier. Why is that, Julia?" Wallace asks.

Julia tries to gauge the level of support Wallace has.

THE GHOST IN THE MACHINE

Chapter Thirty-Nine: Twelve Days

The art exhibit features contemporary and experimental artists. I'm trying to get out of the office. Focus on something other than work for a while. Not that I think I need to, but Oriana's warning that I'm driving the team too hard is a wake-up call. I need to respond appropriately. Mindi had mentioned she was coming by here with Landon Banerjee. So that relationship seems to be progressing. Mindi even said she was surprised how much she likes Landon. Seems once someone recognized his talents he became much more confident. Also less reticent to express his thoughts and feelings. He'd never approached her because he didn't think he was worthy of her. But once he was chosen to take over marketing, suddenly he was.

I wander into the gallery, even though it's in a sketchy part of town. I'd have thought Mindi would go to the main galleries downtown. But then again on what AppleCore pays her, she probably couldn't afford to buy anything in downtown galleries. Here the artists aren't as well known. That translates into greater affordability. And interesting enough, I'm seeing some pieces that intrigue me. Don't know as I'd want them in my condo, since I really have very little art on the walls or anywhere for that matter. Rocky again. Telling me art is for those who have more money than they know what to do with. Money is spent on education, clothes and food. And in that order. Probably why Rocky and I rarely shared anything other than cheap fast food. It took me a long time to recover from that poor diet. I had to work harder than anyone I knew to get into shape when I finally got into college.

I thought studying should be the first priority. But there was a physical education requirement to graduate. I had to get into shape to get through it. I had to work harder than I ever imagined to do just that. The last thing I wanted to do was run. My Phys. Ed. Instructor confided it was the quickest way to achieve the levels of fitness required. By the end of my sophomore year I was running five miles a day. I could get into a zone running. It freed up my mind to think about my studies. Who would have thought I'd actually like it? And the weight loss was flattering in a way I'd never imagined.

I stop before a painting I can't figure out. What's it trying to say? Landon Banerjee and Mindi come up beside me. "Oh, hi." I smile at them.

"You look puzzled." Landon remarks.

"Well, yes. Look at it. How would you describe it?" I respond totally at a loss.

Landon looks at the description tag next to the painting. "Double Helix at Sunset. Seems to be a geometric shape imposed on a landscape. Pretty elementary if you ask me. Maybe that's what puzzles you. You're looking for meaning where there is none, at least none beyond the physical representation presented."

"You like art, Landon?" I respond intrigued by his description of the piece.

"Very much. I aspire to be an artist, not just a marketing hack. No disrespect meant."

"None taken." I reassure him. "So is that why you always have a different approach to the visuals you use in the marketing campaigns? Visuals that arrest you even if they actually have nothing at all to do with the product you're selling?"

"Art can inform you in conscious and unconscious ways. The trick is to find ways to cross between them and inform on multiple levels."

"Is that why so many artists use mind altering drugs to distort their perceptions? To see if they can inform themselves on multiple levels?" I ask.

Landon considers my question. "Distorting your perceptions is one way of doing that. But for many artists, the use of drugs is an attempt to loosen the ties that bind us to the familiar. The drugs distort perception. They cause us to look at the familiar in unfamiliar or non-traditional ways. We are attempting to see the world differently.

It's like the old discussions of centeredness. If you are a male you look at the world through male eyes. If you're old you look at the world through old eyes. But if you're young or a child, you look at the world full of wonder, not understanding everything you see, and trying to make sense of it all. But as a child until you see something more than once you have no idea of the context it exists in. So artists try to replicate that unexplained perception. Being open to what is, and not necessarily having to explain it or see it in context."

"Sounds like you've given this quite a bit of thought." I respond.

"I am an artist. What I do for AppleCore is to try to apply that artistic eye to what we do. I seek to find the childlike quality in our expressions that engage people of all ages."

I think about my own situation. "But what if you couldn't distort perceptions though use of drugs? How would you free yourself to see the world as a child? How would you gain an artistic appreciation for an image?"

Landon considers my question, but Mindi is the one who finally responds. "Through faith. If you believe the gods will guide you on your earthly journey, they will also reveal the inner truth of every image you see. The gods will provide you the insights, understandings and inspiration to represent concepts, ideas and human desires through the images you create. You just need to have faith."

"Mindi is correct." Landon notes. "That is what we are taught. And that is what we must believe. However, we also understand that not only must we believe, but we will be shown what we are destined to see. It is our responsibility to put ourselves in a position to see it. That is not something we can expect the gods to do for us. We must be engaged in the process. We must seek out the truth. We must explore, examine, reject and accept what we are led to see. And not everything we are led to see is what we are destined to see. Life is not linear. We must follow the path to the many dead ends along with the many rewarding experiences before we will have the opportunity to achieve what we are meant to achieve."

"Fate." I respond.

"We believe in predestination. But we also believe that each of us have the freedom to take different paths to find that predestined place in the world. Predestination does not guarantee when we will arrive there. In fact, many arrive at their destination so late in life they are not able to fully take advantage of what they are predestined to achieve. It may be only a fleeting moment of joy. If, on the other hand, we make the prudent choices earlier in life, then we have a much longer time to experience the joy of our predestined end."

"I didn't know you were such a philosopher, Landon." I say as a compliment, but he darkens.

"I am an artist, not a philosopher. Philosophers try to explain the world. That is not a worthy cause as the gods will never permit us to understand why. Since it is a shared experience that we live, no one is fully in control of the outcomes. And that is why it is futile to try to explain life, existence or what becomes of us during our journey through this life and beyond."

"Let me ask you a hypothetical question. If you, as an artist were able to live forever, how would that change your art?"

"Live forever? I don't understand your question."

"Art has a shelf life. It's an expression of a certain point in time. It expresses what men and women feel and experience in a given transient situation. The situation they are in, changes about them as they record their impressions of it. So if you were going to live forever, how would you change the expression? How would you record something that is only a single moment in time when you have all eternity before you?"

"You mean, like you never die?" Mindi asks.

"Exactly." I respond. "This is hypothetical, but I've often wondered how a different time horizon for the artist changes the expression itself."

Landon Banerjee nods to me as he gets a far-away look. "Timeless expression." He looks to Mindi and smiles. "You are always in the middle. So you would not show beginnings or ends. No babies or grandparents. Animals I suppose because they are always there for you. Jewelry because it lasts many lifetimes. The sun in the sky, but not a sunrise or sunset. The expression becomes compressed. It would need to go to the inner structure of things. Molecular. And galactic at the same time. Infinite space that we travel forever. Abstraction. Over time weather erodes that which is familiar so the art would come to show the morphing of familiar objects into the future which is different in many respects."

"And what of filters?" I press the discussion. "Without altering our perceptions would we create a 'Starry Night'?"

"I don't know. The world would become very crowded if people lived forever. Worse yet if we still procreate at the same rates we do today. My country is a good example of what that would be like."

"What do you think, Mindi?" I want to bring her into the conversation.

"I can't contemplate a world where we don't die. It would change a fundamental assumption as we go through life. It's our duty to become responsible adults, to raise the next generation as we contribute to society, and then to make way for the next generation to lead us as we decline in our old age."

"But what if… what if we could change that expectation? What if

THE GHOST IN THE MACHINE

we could have forever to refine our art and contribution to society?"

Chapter Forty: Eleven Days

Julia has been expecting me, or at least it seems that way when I arrive at her office, which is right next door to the vacant one A'zam usually inhabits. I remember the first time I visited A'zam there. The size is meant to be imposing. It calls attention to the importance of the resident. And while there were stories of how A'zam's predecessors had decorated that space with rare and exotic remembrances from around the world, A'zam did not. A large office with white walls, white rug and large teakwood desk. The desk is what draws your eye. It looks plain from a distance. But as you approach it, you see the very shallow carvings of the designs found in the Blue Mosque in Istanbul. The floor to ceiling windows overlook a Japanese tranquility garden with coy pond and low growing sculptured and bonsai plants.

Julia's office is the opposite. Smaller and crowded with a conference table and chairs. Her walls are covered with photos of powerful people she has met upon one occasion or another. All intended to impress the visitor that Julia is someone who is connected. But Wallace and I'd come to the conclusion that Julia couldn't call on any of them if she needed to. Most would have no idea who she is. Photo ops are a dime a dozen. Connected people don't need photos to commemorate their relationships.

"Morning." I offer.

Julia looks up and regards me as if an alien from planet Zorp. Not quite believing I'm actually here, although she knew I'd have to make the obligatory stop. Given that the leadership team hadn't backed her on sacking me, it was going to be an awkward meeting whenever it occurred. "So are you on schedule?"

"Yes." Is all I'll give her. I don't want to tell her all I've had to do to thread the needle of unhappy and exhausted teams and the promised delivery schedules.

"How is that possible? Just yesterday you were telling the SLT you couldn't." Her tone is accusatory and not at all friendly.

"I always try to exceed expectations, so sometimes it's necessary to lower them." I try to put what happened into a context she could accept, or at least I hoped she could accept.

"Even though you didn't need to. And in the process you made me look a fool. And not just a fool, but a weak fool." Nope. She won't accept it.

"Julia. No one thinks of you that way. My guess is everyone thought you were trying to show decisive leadership. Take action rather than die from a thousand cuts. No one thinks the lesser of you for that reason."

"But they do think the lesser of me for other reasons?" She pounces on anything that can reflect badly on her. Got to be more careful what I say.

"You've established your value over the course of your career. One decision is not going to make or break you." I try to deflect.

Julia apparently decides this conversation isn't doing either of us any good. "So why are you here?"

"If you remember, I set up a team of new hires and gave them a senior design engineer as a resource."

Julia searches her memory and finally nods. "I remember Hung Duc saying he wanted to try that but we didn't give him the resources. Why was that?"

"Hardware is different than software. A new grad or even a team of new grads won't be able to design something totally new right off the bat. Software is different. Code is often modular. A new grad can string together code elements. In the process she can create a new functionality without years of training and experience."

"I remember something about that. So what did you want to talk about?" Not really curious.

"My new grad team delivered a prototype code that does some interesting things. I think it's worthy of consideration for our next update."

"Has it gone through the usual testing and validation?" Julia's resisting the idea. Why?

"More extensive than usual, as a matter of fact. I challenged them to break it. Said I wouldn't take it to market until they did and fixed what they broke. It took a while, but they finally found a way to shut it down and made the necessary fix. Been running in the lab successfully since."

"Why should we give this priority over what we have scheduled?" Still looking for a reason not to put it out there. I don't understand. A'zam wouldn't have put me through the twenty questions test.

"Not saying we should. I'm recommending we release it as a surprise in addition to what the market is expecting to see this next update. As you know marketing has been advising of the next feature set with each release. Since the scheduled release features are already known, don't want to disrupt that. Just give them more than they're expecting."

"How much would you increase the price to reflect the additional value?"

"I wouldn't. The market is expecting certain features at a certain price. If we change what people are expecting it could work against maximizing the value of the release."

"So you'd just give it to them for free. Why would we ever consider that?"

"To reward people for being loyal customers. They've been buying our feature sets for a long time. We make a lot of money from them because they do. So give them more than they're expecting."

Julia shakes her head. "See, that's where you don't understand customer psychology. Once you give them something for free, they'll come to expect it every time. When you don't, they'll be disappointed. Then they'll not buy the next feature set, waiting to see when we give away something for free again. It would undermine the whole feature set upgrades business model."

"I understand your thoughts. How about we let this team continue to work new feature sets and when they come up with something interesting, like they did this time, we give it away too. That way we can do a special advertising campaign about this new grad team. How we're adding their features for free. Then the customer will come to expect that only when this team comes up with something will they get it for free."

Julia shakes her head. "We need the customer to pay for everything. Any deviation undermines our business model. We've spent decades building a brand that evokes quality in the minds of the consumer. You may pay more for an AppleCore product, but you won't get anything better. We start giving things away, people will start to wonder how good can this be? Can't have all that much value. Maybe I should go look at the competition."

Obviously I disagree, but I can't really argue with her any more. "All right. How would you like to proceed with our new grad product suite?"

"A separate advertising campaign around them. Might feature profiles of the team as individuals. Where they went to school, hobbies, things like that. And even talk about their contributions to the team and the products they're delivering. Make them rock stars. You know? Maybe we even name an app after one of them. Julia's app. See? Catchy name. People identify with it. That drives demand. We make it a separate roll-out between scheduled feature sets. Maybe we even consider it a premium product we charge more for to pay for the advertising campaign."

Julia's trying to convince me she understands marketing. I'm waiting for her to take it back. If she does that will tell me A'zam is going to be away longer than just a few weeks or a month. "I'll have Landon's team work it up and send you the concept sheets."

Wrong thing to say, "Why did you promote him? He's not qualified to run the team."

I could say the same about you, but I won't. "Landon is an ideas guy. I want him to feed creativity into the group. See if they can amp up our advertising to make it stand out more in the crowded ad spaces. If the first campaign doesn't work, I'll take another look at that decision. Don't worry. I'm monitoring results closely."

"I want him gone. I don't like anything he's done. He's not AppleCore. He doesn't have the right sensibilities. Not for our customers. He'll destroy everything I've done." I didn't realize how much she's internalized A'zam's vote of no confidence on her running marketing. But he still left her in charge of the whole company. I don't get it. Need to step carefully.

"Are you going to the Silicon Valley Masquerade Ball on Saturday?" I change the subject. "You were there last year. Seems I remember you went as a Bell."

"Yes. I was the Belle of the Ball. I was going to go as Mother Teresa, or Saint Teresa, but my husband said he didn't want anyone to think he was living with a Saint. So I'm still thinking."

"I won't this year. Too much to do here." I rise and leave her office.

THE GHOST IN THE MACHINE

Chapter Forty-One

I've known Beth since we were in high school. We were physics lab partners. That was when I discovered she was brilliant. Not in a conventional way, mind you. She's brilliant because she sees everything in context. She sees how everything relates faster than anyone I've ever met. Everything she learns she contextualizes. She's able to quickly decide what to do next to build upon it. I wanted to hire Beth at AppleCore. She chose Symbol Ventures. Since we're now competitors we don't see each other much. High School reunions and things like that. Sometimes we run into each other at conferences. We always chat, but we never talk. Can't. We're competitors working some of the same areas for our respective companies.

But when I called Beth and asked if we could talk about something non-product related she agreed. So here we are, having a drink at Shorty's Sushi and More. Not a place anyone in the industry would hang out. Don't want to start rumors. And of course Beth is having her usual glass of Chilean red wine. I'm having one too, only I'm not drinking it because I can't. Is that one of the things I need to talk to Dr. Woodall about? Some means of drinking alcohol for occasions like this where it eases the conversation. Could empty the tank when I recharge if we can't figure out a means of recycling it for some other use. Of course I see the confirmation of the email to him.

"I could really use some advice." I begin after the obligatory exchange of whatever happened to… from our class and people we both know in the industry.

"You?" Beth seems surprised. "I always thought you were the one who had it all together. And why me? What could I possibly help you with?"

"You've seen what we're doing." I begin, not wanting to be too specific.

"Rolling out advanced feature sets at a pace that must be killing your teams."

"And that's what I need some advice on. I am. Killing my teams. I'll start experiencing turnover if I can't figure out some way for them to become more comfortable and more confident with the pace." I admit, even though I probably shouldn't be saying this to a competitor. But I trust Beth. She wouldn't take advantage of my situation when she learns the specifics in confidence.

"You think I have a better handle on how to fire up teams than you do? We're no-where near you at the moment. We're all jealous. You leap frogged over several things we had in development."

I grimace, embarrassed I've made her job harder. I wanted her to join me in the first place, and she chose the different path. "What do you do when someone gets to the burn-out phase?"

Beth sips her wine, thinking how to answer my question without giving away anything that would be proprietary to her company. "You got your MBA. The profs told us you need to get to know your team as people. What drives them? What do they want, for themselves, for the families and from the company? And respond accordingly."

I nod. Re-read that just this morning amongst all the other sources I was consulting from the searches my mind was doing for me. "I've gone over all the textbook stuff. What I'm really looking for is the human side of all this. Personal experience. The nuance you don't get from all the classroom discussions of people who are trying to learn, but don't really know. You and I've both been in the trenches for a long time. We've been making mistakes and learning from them. And you always learned better than I did. You always saw things I didn't. And that's what I'm hoping you can help me with." I plead my case.

Beth nods again, takes another sip of her wine. She looks at me over the rim of her glass as if trying to size me up. She wants to understand what I'm really asking. She's trying to decide what she can share and what she can't.

"I've actually followed that textbook approach most of my career." She muses. "I try to get to know my team members as friends. And you have all kinds of friends. Some are close and some are those you just say 'hi' to, and ask about their family. I try to keep it personal. I'm a friend, I care about them, but I'm also the boss. We have things we all have to deliver for the company. That's why they pay us to be here. It's not a pension. We're here to deliver product the company can sell to pay our wages. If the products don't sell, the company doesn't need and can't afford quite so many of us."

Beth sips her wine before continuing. "So we're all in the same boat together. We all need to help each other to put the best product we can out the door. We know that paydays only come when we're all successful together. I try to build an interdependent relationship. But I always keep it such that if someone leaves or takes another job in the company that we survive as a team."

She takes another sip and considers a bit longer. "I'm just rambling here. If this isn't helpful tell me. I think I understand your problem and sympathize. It's just you must be so much further out there than I am. I should be asking you these questions. You're living it today."

"No, no. You're being helpful." I reassure her. "But think of a situation where someone was just at the end of their rope, so to speak. You've taken him or her about as far as that person can go on their own. Smart. Good degrees and have delivered great product for you in the past. But you've taken that person past their comfort zone. You're asking him or her to do something beyond what they know how to do on their own."

Beth sips again. Suddenly I understand why she sips. She wants a mechanism to buy some time to think the question through. At the same time she wants something to stimulate her thoughts in a creative way. The wine is that outside stimulant. It helps her think in different terms as her mind reacts to the layers of taste in the wine, the bouquet of different scents, the colors and legs on the glass as the wine settles back after the sip. I'm seeing all this because my mind is working so fast I have to keep it occupied as I wait for Beth's answers.

"I probably shouldn't mention names here, but in this case you know the person I'm going to discuss with you."

Instantly I know, "Robert."

Beth nods. "Robert was a star for us for a long time. He understood our architecture and how to deliver functionality. He was good with his team, although I came to discover that most were a lot smarter than he is. Everyone was happy as long as the team stayed ahead of schedule. Probably why Robert was a stickler for schedules. He gave us daily earned value estimates that always seemed to be accurate."

I nod in agreement, having seen exactly the same behavior in him.

"Because of his great team performance I gave him a particularly difficult assignment. He seemed to welcome it at the time. But half way in, he ran into problems. He couldn't figure out how to code a crucial element of the solution. He came to see me. I gave him some advice as to how I would approach the problem, but I didn't want to solve it for him. It's the feed a man a fish he eats for a day, teach him how to fish and he feeds himself for a lifetime. That's what I've always tried to do with my teams. Robert was no different."

"But he failed and quit." I comment, knowing what happened.

Beth nodded with a grimace. "He's the only member of my team I couldn't turn around when they got into trouble. Everyone wants to solve the problem themselves. Robert couldn't face up to the fact that he couldn't. For whatever reason. He just didn't understand what he needed to do."

"Robert's now in Supply Chain for us. Same scenario. Unfortunately. But if you still had Robert on your team, what would you do differently to bring him along into uncharted territory?"

Beth furrows her brow at my description, "You're pushing your team beyond current technology, aren't you?"

I have to be careful now. "Let's just say I've had some insights."

Beth seems to consider the question in a whole new light. "Hmm. You're making them fly blind. And you're being real proscriptive on the coding aren't you?"

"Had to. My team leaders couldn't see how to get there. But they have to get the work done. I can't slow down to show them what I've seen because it keeps changing."

Beth shakes her head, "How are you able to do that?"

"Trade secret. Sorry." About the only thing I can go back to she will respect.

"So let me get this straight. You're giving your team leads coder assignments to deliver modules they don't understand. You're pushing them to double their delivery rate and you wonder how to keep the team together. Am I right?" Beth is having an 'oh shit' moment.

I nod, pick up my glass of wine to humor her, but don't drink as she thinks this through.

"You have to take the time to talk with each member of your team individually. Every coder. You need to reassure them they won't lose their job. But everyone has to let go of what they know. They have to embrace a time of change. It's like the Indiana Jones movie. They have to step off the cliff and have faith you're leading them into the Promised Land and not to their early death. Only then can you succeed."

Every coder. Hmm. I've got a lot of work to do. And I'm the one stepping off the cliff first.

Chapter Forty-Two

Recharge night. I walk up to the door on my condo. I find a note from the city police. They are investigating a death in the neighborhood. Interesting way of putting it. Not a homicide. That would mean either they haven't figured out what happened to the man, or they're trying not to alarm folks in the neighborhood. To be conservative I need to assume the latter. They would like to schedule a call to learn more about anything I might have seen or heard that night. Otherwise they'll send someone over to try to catch me at home to discuss what I might know. They're making it abundantly clear they will not let me not discuss the situation with them.

I set the note aside and drop my clothes to the floor before climbing into the recharger bed. I feel the tingling of the recharge across my back. That makes me think my batteries must be in my chest cavity. I would have thought they were in my buttocks to situate the weight of the batteries close to my center of gravity. Then I realize they probably are, but the magnetic coils that pick up the current are probably in my back to give them more surface area. It's strange to think of how my robotic body works when I've spent next to no time thinking about how my biologic body worked. At least until it didn't work as it always had. Suddenly I was spending way too much time trying to understand the prognosis. I didn't want to be just another person parked in a nursing home waiting for the end to occur.

The first wave of sensory remembrances hit me. This time it's the smells of sweaty bodies, analgesic balm on sore muscles and the wind in my face. I'm running track in college after I began to pay attention to my body. Because I wasn't much of an athlete in high school, trying to make the jump into intercollegiate athletics at a ranked university was impossible. But somehow, in my junior year I made the team as a middle distance runner. That meant I might run anything between a half mile and two miles. I hated the thought of it, but discovered I actually did like the peacefulness and solitude that came with the practices and even the meets. Sure I had to be competitive to be on the team. I found I actually ran faster when I was alone with my thoughts. So I'd not focus on the meet itself. I was able to relax and let my body do what it could do. I thought about everything except what my body was doing at that particular point in time. Sure I had to focus in on the last hundred yards of any race to figure out where I was. Could I pass anyone who was ahead of me before the finish line? Usually I could. It seemed I never tapped into the real well of physical strength and speed that my body had hidden from me all those years before I tried to get into shape in college.

And I won more than one race, particularly in my senior year. By then I'd discovered that my best event was the mile. If I hung with the leaders through three and a half laps, then took off, I'd usually end up first or second at worst. Two miles just took too long. Since I wasn't paying attention, by the last lap I could be anywhere in the field. The half mile was all about positioning. I had to be no worse than second at the end of the first lap or I had no chance. Everyone was saving for the last 220 yards.

But the competitive side apart, what I really loved about running was the time alone. I loved the wind in my face. Fresh air. Deep inhales. The wind blew my hair. It would trail behind me like the Mercury seen on old fashioned dimes that Rocky had shown me. They were supposed to represent the god Mercury, which meant swift because the planet Mercury orbited the sun every eighty-eight days. So Mercury orbited the sun four times for every year on Earth. That was an amazing fact to me. A year for every season on Earth. So Mercury was fast. And I was fast. Or at least as fast as most of the other women who were running for their university track teams. I was right there in the thick of things with them. But it was the time alone. Thinking about what I was learning. How to create new applications of tools that men and women needed to be more productive in their lives. And I almost sit up.

What tools do I need to create to make my AppleCore teams be more productive?

The first thing I decide to do is adopt that old Mercury dime symbol for my team. We are going to be the ones who deliver new products four times faster than everyone else on Earth. Perfect. And I'm going to sit with each member of my teams to get to know them as people. Who are they? Do they have a spouse and kids? Dogs and cats? Where did they go on their last vacation? What do they like to do as a family? Do they get enough time off? Do I need to do something about that? How do they feel about the technology we're putting out there? Are they comfortable they know enough to do their work? Or do I need to set up courses on campus they can attend to help them stay current with where we're going? I'll probably have to teach those courses myself. I've done that before. No problem.

I feel the jolt of a new stimulus. Suddenly I'm remembering the scents of a steak dinner with Rocky at one or another steak house. Rocky never spent much money on food. It had to be a chain steak house where the main course was a semi-grizzly steak with mashed potatoes and gravy, mushrooms and some kind of corn, usually creamed or on the cob. That was always followed by some kind of fruit pie. Often it was peach or cherry. Although Rocky wasn't a big fan of cherry pie. Never understood why. But he would always select whatever else was on the menu.

Why would Rocky take me out to a steak house? It was always because I'd done something good. Finished first in my sixth grade class in overall grades? Steak dinner. Finished first in my overall grades in high school? Steak dinner. Graduated with honors from Stanford? Steak dinner. I even got one when I finished my dissertation towards my doctorate. He didn't take me out when I graduated, probably because he was working a proposal. He was putting in seven day weeks at the time. But that was alright. That's how it went then. I had to respect that Rocky needed to make a living to pay our bills. And it seemed that the discussion at those dinners was always the same.

"I'm proud of you. Your mother would have been if she were here today."

Rocky: how do you have any idea what Anna Laura would have thought if she were here today? She probably would have wanted me to do something entirely different than I'm doing. She would have been more concerned about the kind of person I was becoming rather than whether I was number one in the class. I'm not dumb. I'll do fine even if I'm number ten and not number one.

But for Rocky I always had to be number one. No other choice. As if I could make a choice. Mine was not to decide if I wanted to do something different. I had to achieve what Tabitha never would. I had to achieve for both of us. And I had to please a ghost. One whose approval I'd never have again. But Rocky knew what she would approve of. Rocky was now both mother and father, even though I was sure he had absolutely no idea what Anna Laura would have wanted for us.

And that steak. The smell comes back. The taste comes back. The texture of the meat on my tongue as I chew it. How long has it been since I've had a steak? Years. I never wanted a steak after I finished my dissertation. It brought back too many memories. I always went for the fish or the pasta. Sometimes lamb because I could convince myself it wasn't like a steak. It was a chop or a leg, but not a steak.

Why do I avoid steaks? I should have wanted them as a testimony that I was achieving something. Doing something that was seen favorably. Doing something that would please my remaining parent. But I knew. Nothing I would do would please Rocky. He expected me to follow him into research. He expected I would be a mini Rocky. An engineering fellow who enabled some, but not all, of the AppleCore successes. Pure research is his thing. But it isn't mine. And the day that I told him I was going into software I'm sure was the single worst day of his life. Other than the day he lost Anna Laura and my sister in that crash. He just looked at me and asked a single question: Why?

I answered that everything I saw said software was where the differentiators were going to be. The hardware was just the vessel that carries the software and does what it says. Just like our lives were the vessel that carried our family and Anna Laura was the software that told us what to do. Rocky didn't like that analogy. Said he never wanted me to use it, ever again. I promised. He finally relaxed, but I'd never seen him that angry before. And not since.

It's hard when you disappoint a parent. At the time I thought he might excommunicate me from his life. But he didn't. He accepted the fact I was going to waste my genius on software where no one would be able to appreciate what I brought. But I think I've proven that assumption wrong. I think he even enjoys coming by my office to see where I sit in the hierarchy of the company. I think he enjoys the notoriety he has since his daughter is a Senior Vice President. Meanwhile he continues to work as an engineering fellow on hardware solutions my team empowers with our software and operating systems.

Another jolt. I'm flooded with the scents of candles burning. They're in my living room. I'm smoking weed with Raheem. He brought the weed. Said Middle-Eastern weed was much better than the shit we were getting out of Mexico. We were all there. The whole group. Reese, Delilah, MC and Windy. I think Raheem slept with all five of us that night. Not sure about that, but it seems to me that was what happened. But we were all just beyond any high we'd gotten from our usual dealers. Raheem was right. The Middle-Eastern shit was potent. I still have no idea how he was able to keep going when the rest of us were like in La La land.

Do I even remember him coming inside me? He was big, that I remember. I was sore the next day. So not sure I was all that wet or turned on. If I were, it probably wouldn't have hurt quite so much. But I do remember the orgasm. Seemed to go on forever. But maybe it was a quick one and the weed distorted my understanding of what was really going on.

The alarm goes off. My fifteen minutes are up. Why did it go off when I'm in a memory I'd like to remember more?

Chapter Forty-Three: Ten Days

Jermaine comes by to see me. "Hey. How's it going?" I ask.

"You want to hear what you want to hear or you interested in the truth?" Jermaine is not happy.

"You should know by now I always want the truth." I respond to make it clear whatever is circulating with the team isn't accurate.

"Then I'm surprised you don't know the truth." Jermaine is unhappy with me, but not necessarily for the right reasons.

"How do you know I don't know the truth?" I push back.

"'Cause if you did, you'd be doing something about it. At least that's the way you used to be. But now? Man, I don't know."

"Why do you think you're here?"

"To get you to do something about it." Jermaine is hopeful.

"Let's see if I am. You're lost. You're frustrated because we're doing shit you don't understand. We've gone way beyond the stuff you've been working. All of a sudden you're just a go between me and your team. Your team mates ask you a question. You have no idea how to answer. That's making you feel like you're not a member of the team anymore. You're just someone relaying shit to your team. You're expected to deliver the code elements not knowing if what you're getting is the real deal or some drivel that won't do shit. Am I right?"

"You know all this, why you asking me? Why ain't you fixin' it?"

"I'm hoping you're here is the first step towards fixin' it." I respond.

"Okay. Lay it on me. What's gonna change?" Jermaine wants to get right to the heart of things.

"I'm hearing you want to be part of the solution and not part of the problem."

"Absolutely." Jermaine responds enthusiastically.

"You want me to lay out the architecture, lay out the solution we're working towards, break up the module elements by team, and let you figure out the rest." I respond

"That's what you used to do. But now you're driving us to solution sets none of us understand. How can we deliver what you want if we have no idea how to get there?" Jermaine is still frustrated.

"That's why I broke down your work assignments by coder. So you could see what was required." I respond. "I was hoping you could examine and follow the new logic. Evidently that was a poor assumption."

"We're not stupid." Jermaine responds. "But I've never seen anything like what you're asking us to do. How did you come up with this shit? I mean, I can't follow where you're going. Neither can anyone else on the team. You've got to back off, let us catch up. Then maybe we can work together to get where you're taking us. But this working in the dark? Shit. I'd rather be selling dope to kids. At least I'd understand what I was doing."

"Thanks for breaking that down for me." I respond before I realize he may take it differently than I intend. "I'm not being facetious. I understand what you're saying. We're going to do things differently. Every morning, instead of getting your assignments for the day, we're going to discuss the architecture and the deliverables needed. We're going to discuss shortcuts and differing paths to achieve the functionality. We're going to work this as a team. I'm not going to do your work for you, anymore. We're back to being the team we were before. Think you can handle that? You're going to have to work harder. You're going to be learning in real time."

"No. I welcome the change. I know what you were trying to do. You pushed us out of our comfort zones. We needed to step up without slipping schedule. You de-risked the whole thing by giving us the break downs so we could learn from you. This next week, you'll find out which of us are successful in learning from you. I can probably tell you right now who was and who wasn't. So I hope you continue to doing the breakdowns, because some folks are going to need them in the short term. At least until we all catch up."

"You're telling me you won't need them?" I ask, not quite sure what I'm hearing.

Jermaine sort of nods sort of shakes his head. "I hope I don't, but for a while I'll check what I think against what you think until I can defend going a different way."

"That's fair." I respond. "How do you think the others will take it?"

"We all want to be part of the solution." Jermaine responds. "At the moment we're feeling like the step kids. Nobody wants us, but everyone's expecting us to do what needs to be done. I can't explain it better than that. You know?"

"Got it. So what else do you need from me to make your job easier?"

"Easier?" Jermaine seems mystified by my choice of words.

"Yeah. I've made the job a lot less rewarding to you and the team. I'm trying to fix that. But we still have twice as many deliverables as before. So how do I make it easier for you to do what we're asking?"

"No one's ever asked me that question in all the time I've been here. You sure you want to?"

"Absolutely. You need more time with your family, we'll see what we can do. You need to take some courses on current architecture? Done deal. You need more bodies on your team, you need different expertise, and you need anything? Tell me what it is and I'll see what I can do."

"I need my old lady to be nicer to me when I'm home. How you gonna fix that?" Jermaine thinks he's got me.

"What's the source of the tension? Not home enough? Not willing to look after the kids and give her a break when you are home? She want you to fix dinner one night a week? She want you to go to church with her? I need to know why she's not being nice to you."

Jermaine smiles. "Truth? Probably all of them. But I don't expect you can fix everything."

"Which one would you want me to fix?" I ask.

"Being home more would probably fix most of the rest of them." He admits.

"You have a big team. Why don't you promote Samantha to be your deputy? She's got the teams doing the hardest tasks. She's also right on schedule. I think you under-appreciate her."

"Samantha?" Jermaine seems surprised I'd pick her off his teams. "I always thought of Antoine as my second. He's been with me forever."

"Antoine's good. No question. But think about it. Samantha seems to have a better touch with the team. Antoine seems to be more focused on the schedule. You need someone who gets down in the trenches with folks, talks about what they're having trouble with, and giving them real solutions."

Jermaine looks at me quizzically. "How can you tell all that when you're never out with my teams? I mean, you seem to have a better handle on them than I do. And I'm with them all the time."

I smile at Jermaine. "I've been talking with everyone. They haven't told you?"

Jermaine gets nervous, "I've been hearing about your conversations. Just didn't think you'd get that level of feedback."

"Think about Samantha and Antoine. I'll support you either way you decide to go. But before you decide, you should ask your team who they think would do a better job. In the end it's your decision. But you'll have to deal with the consequences of a wrong decision. Particularly if the objective is to make your life easier."

Jermaine is not happy with how this conversation has gone. "Why now? Why didn't you authorize hiring a deputy a month ago when I asked for it?"

"We've doubled our production rate in the last month. When you asked, we couldn't justify it based on sales and deliveries. With what we've done in the last few weeks we can now."

"All comes down to dollars, don't it?" Jermaine nods to himself.

"The more we deliver, the more we can ask for. We need new people, we can ask. Might not get exactly what we want, but there will be a response. Let me know what you decide on the deputy role and I'll start the paperwork."

"How'd I ever get so far behind?" Jermaine asks himself as much as me.

"You didn't. But the world accelerated and now we all have to keep up."

THE GHOST IN THE MACHINE

Chapter Forty-Four

I place a call to the police department.

"Yes, this is Sage Washington. You left a message for me to call you. Something about a man dying from my neighborhood."

"Just a minute Ms. Washington. I'll connect you with Detective Thomas." I'm on hold for a long moment. I'm in my office at work reviewing the progress of the teams across the board. They're holding their own even with me taking, on average, a half hour of productivity out of each coder as I've done my rounds. What I'm noticing is the productivity after my visits has actually gone up. Guess this strategy is working. At least for the moment.

"Ms. Washington. This is Detective Stuckey. Do you have a few minutes?"

"What happened to the other guy? The one the receptionist was putting me through to?"

"Oh. She's on another call. Rather than have you wait they asked me to pick up."

"Fine. What can I help you with?"

"A man checked into the emergency room not far from where you live a few nights ago. He suffered a severe head trauma and died shortly thereafter."

"Your note mentioned something to that effect." Minimize. Don't give them too much and don't volunteer anything.

"What we're trying to understand is if you saw or heard anything that night that might help us understand why this gentleman died."

"What time are you talking about?"

"It was about 2:00 am when he arrived at the emergency room."
Facts and data.

"I was confronted by a man that evening who wanted to rob me."
I offer. Don't know how much they know at this point and need to build
plausible deniability.

"Could you describe him?"

"It was dark and it happened quickly. So I'm afraid I can only say
he was taller than me, which is 5'6". He was a white male, not skinny,
but not heavy-set. That's about all I can remember."

"You didn't report this incident to the police." Detective Stuckey is
unhappy.

"No. He didn't get anything of value and I was unhurt, so I didn't
report it." Is that sufficient reason not to report an attempted mugging?

"Most people would want to make sure your assailant wouldn't be
able to strike again."

"As I said, he didn't harm me and he didn't get anything of
value."

"I see. How did he confront you?"

"Came up behind me as I walked home from work."

"What time was that?"

"Some time after midnight." Don't be too precise.

"You were working that late? What do you do?"

"I'm an executive at AppleCore. And yes, I frequently work that late."

"Have you ever asked for police protection?"

"No need. I live in a safe neighborhood." I respond trying to make it sound convincing.

"Until a few nights ago." Detective Stuckey reminds me.

"As I said. Wasn't a big deal. I grew up in a rougher neighborhood. Guys like him were never something you couldn't handle."

"So he came up behind you. What did he say?"

"I don't remember him saying anything." I'm trying to play this straight.

"Then how do you know he was going to rob you?"

"He had a knife." I respond.

"You saw it?"

"I have it. Has his finger prints on it if you'd like to compare them to your guy."

"You have it?"

"Yes."

"How did you come by it?"

"I disarmed him and picked it up when I left."

"Are you a martial arts expert?" Detective Stuckey is fishing now.

"No, but I grew up in a rough neighborhood. I learned how to take care of myself early in life. This guy wasn't much of a bad guy. You know what I mean? Probably strung out on dope or something. Didn't take much to take away his weapon and send him on his way."

"So tell me how you disarmed him." Details, details.

"I kicked him in the groin and watched him go down. I picked up the knife and went home."

"Could you give me a little more detail?"

"He was holding a knife. I kicked him in the groin and he went down. What else is there to say?"

"You talk about this so matter-of-factly. Like it was no big deal."

"In my old neighborhood it was no big deal. Now in my new neighborhood it might be for some folks, but hey. I'm just someone who grew up in the 'hood and it was an everyday occurrence. So it didn't rattle me. And in my old neighborhood, calling the cops didn't make no difference anyway. So we good?"

"I understand your perspective. Now you said you still have the knife. Why'd you keep it?"

"What was I supposed to do with it? I mean if I'd left it there he might have picked it up and come after me. I figured without a weapon he wasn't a threat to anyone except his dealer for non-payment."

"Could I have someone come by and pick it up?"

"I'm at work now. Probably best if I drop it off to you. I'm not home much when I'm not sleeping and with my work schedule I need all the sleep I can get."

"What do you do for AppleCore if you don't mind telling me?" Detective Stuckey is still trying to decide if there's anything here or not.

"I'm the senior vice president of software development."

"For a product line?"

"No, for the whole company. I only live a few blocks from the offices. I bought my condo for exactly that reason. So I could walk back and forth." Stop talking. Too much information.

"I understand. I'm sorry to be bothering you. I know you have an important job. If you could drop off the knife that would be great. Just mark the package to my attention and I'll take it from there."

"And your name is?"

"Stuckey. S-t-u-c-k-e-y."

"Anything else you'd like to know?"

"Did you see anyone else out when this occurred? Anyone in the window of a house, lights on or anything that would give us a direction for someone who could corroborate your story?"

"At that time of night I never see anyone. For this guy to show up had to be a fluke. I've been walking that way for years and never seen anyone. That's why I assume he was on something. Probably got disoriented and lost. As for people in their houses? Can't tell you. I don't remember seeing any lights on. But there have been so many nights – I just don't remember any."

"We'll continue checking with your neighbors. Maybe someone saw or heard something. That's usually how we solve these kinds of cases. Someone comes forward and fills in the missing pieces."

I decide to turn the tables to see what they're willing to share. "The guy who died. Who was he? Anything about the guy who attack me line up?"

"We really don't know. No identification. He didn't say anything when he came in. Just got in the front door and collapsed before he even got to the desk. They rushed him into the emergency ward, but he was dead before they could do anything."

THE GHOST IN THE MACHINE

"So could have been anybody." I note.

Never should have volunteered the knife. Now this will go on and on and I could have stopped it here. Won't do that again.

Chapter Forty-Five

When I got the call from Dr. Woodall to come in I was curious. He wouldn't give me much information over the phone. Just said he had some updates I needed. So I made my excuses at work and headed off to his clinic.

When I arrive Leesa shows me where I'm to meet the doctor. It's an examining room. Only this room is larger than most. It has instruments built in along one wall. Some of them I recognize, others are completely foreign to me. But the examining table is the same kind I remember from when I was young. The doctor would always tell me to climb up on the table as it was too high for me to just step up and sit down. So the first thing I think of when I see that table is, 'climb up.'

I sit down and wait only a few minutes before Dr. Woodall joins me with a resident by the name of Grayson. I know his name only because he's wearing a name badge on his white jacket. Dr. Woodall, on the other hand, isn't wearing a white jacket. In fact, he's dressed more casually than usual. A golf shirt and slacks. If he'd been wearing golf shoes I would have thought he was squeezing me in between the front and the back nine.

"How are you adjusting?" is his first request.

"I'm feeling fine." I respond just to see how he reacts. He takes a long look at me and raises an eyebrow.

"Are you? Feeling anything?"

"I remember feelings, mostly. Feelings of not liking to visit the doctor. And having to crawl up on the examining table. I never liked to take off my clothes for the doctor. And I never liked to come in when I was sick, because I was sick and that's what I associated with a doctor's office."

Dr. Woodall smiles at me. "Fair enough. Memories. I take it you've been having lots of memories because you're experiencing sensory deficits."

"I'm having lots of memories because that's the only way my mind can complete the situations I find myself in. I look for smells because my mind tells me I should smell something here, either good or bad. My mind tells me to expect a loud noise after a flash of lightning. My mind tells me I should be attracted to a good looking guy, but nothing triggers the feelings I'm expecting."

"Tell me about the lightning. Why'd you bring that up? You shouldn't be having a problem hearing." My turn to smile.

"I was just checking to see if you're listening to me. But it does illustrate the point that my mind tells me things I should expect. I look for them with the appropriate sensor. But some of them aren't there or aren't working to the same level as I'm used to. So I'm constantly feeling out of synch with my surroundings. Like there should be more."

Dr. Woodall turns to Dr. Grayson. "You'll remember this day for the rest of your life. You're talking with the first immortal."

Dr. Grayson nods as he looks up from the chart he's been reading. "Nice to meet you. Sounds like you're having some issues with the adjustment. Nothing serious?"

"Depends on what you think of as serious." I shoot back. "Missing senses and the things that generate feelings is really quite disorienting. I'm getting better at filling in blanks from memory." I respond.

Dr. Woodall rises and walks over to the machines against the wall. "I'm going to ask you to lay down now. Since taking your clothes off embarrasses you, leave them on. We're going to do an update, but that will require me to take you offline for a short while. I'll explain what we've done when you come back up."

"Why afterwards?" I ask concerned that there might be negative consequences of what he's going to do to me.

"It will be easier to explain when you can experience them. They'll make more sense to you when you see, hear and feel the differences."

"But this is my body. You wouldn't just perform surgery on a patient and explain what you did until afterwards."

"Except in an emergency, you're right. But in this instance, what we're going to do in the updates are things you've either asked for or we discussed before the transition. The main thing is how everything works together. Individually I don't have any concerns. But when all of the updates go live and begin to interact, that's where I get concerned. There may be something, a side effect, a software conflict where one update cancels out another. We just don't know. We don't have a live test bed to try all these things out on simultaneously before we upload them to you."

"So there may be side effects." I note. Still don't like the way he wants to do this, but he's the doctor. "All right. Just want you to know I'm not in favor of doing it this way. So in the future it would help if you give me a little more notice. I'd also like a full explanation of what you're going to do and a chance to say, no, I don't want to do that."

Dr. Woodall seems to consider my complaint and then nods. "Fair enough. Next time we'll do it your way. So would you please lie down so I can get started?"

I comply with his request, but also ask, "You in a hurry to make a tee time?"

Dr. Woodall shakes his head. "Why would you ask that?"

"You're just dressed like you just came back from or are on your way to play golf is all."

THE GHOST IN THE MACHINE

He glances at what he's wearing, raises an eyebrow and puts his hand over my eyes to shut them. "Just relax. Read the Encyclopedia Britannica while you're waiting."

"I already have. What else do you suggest?" I tease him.

I feel the loss of all sensory inputs. I'm not thinking, I'm not feeling, I just am. Floating as if suspended in a dark room. Nothing permits me to gauge time or what is occurring in my surroundings. In fact, I have no idea where I am. But I am. I just am.

Then a jolt. I encounter the rush of information to my brain. My sensors come back on line, one at a time. First is vision. I see Dr. Woodall and Dr. Grayson looking at me curiously. Then sound comes back. I hear the high pitched wine of the machines in the room. I hear the doctors both breathing. I hear voices down the hall. "Are you going out with Ali tonight?" a man's voice I don't recognize.

"Don't know for sure. She may have to work late." Another voice.

And then a new sense. A pungent smell. I pull back away from it, whatever it is. Then I see an open container with a candle burning in it. I'm smelling something in the room. An actual smell. Not just a memory. I can smell the different colognes on the two doctors. I smell the shampoo each used. In fact, they apparently used the same kind of shampoo as the smell is identical. I can smell the perspiration on each of them. They're anxious, apparently wondering what I'm experiencing. Whether whatever they did is going to work harmoniously. And then I smell my own dress. It smells musty. Not from sweat, since I don't, but because I've worn it several times in the last two weeks. I smell the sheet on the table I'm sitting on. It smells of chlorine, apparently bleach to kill bacteria. And I could just go on picking out the new smells. There are so many. My mind wants to catalog each one. Make sure I remember it. But I need to see what else Dr. Woodall did for me.

"Can you read the Encyclopedia Britannica for me?" Dr. Woodall asks.

"I've just loaded the whole thing into memory, so I can answer any question you might have."

"The Capital of New Zealand." Dr. Grayson asks

"Auckland."

"You have a new memory and processor. Double the speed and four times the memory."

"Impressive. So I can work twice as fast and solve much harder problems. I should really be hell on wheels at work now." I say more to myself than to the doctors.

"I also installed a prototype device for you to check out for me."

"Prototype." I don't like the sound of this. Something half-baked is not what I want to have to deal with when I've got to find a way to get my team to up their game.

"Dr. Aggarwal delivered the first immortals vagina. It's not hardened and the software isn't quite where I think you want it. I would like you to try it out and give us feedback." I'm angry. Why did he go ahead and install something I was going to build myself?

"Is this why you wouldn't tell me before you installed it? Afraid I'd veto it? Well, I would have."

"Hold on. You agreed to be the beta site for anything we develop that enhances your experience. So you really have no choice, contractually. But I want you to look at this the way a scientist or an engineer would. What's good about it? What needs to be improved? How can we make the experience better? We think the hardware is in relatively good shape. It's the software we really need your feedback on. You're the best person to do that for us."

"Despite the fact I'm making a competing product at AppleCore?"

"Yes. We welcome your investment in helping us get a

particularly important feature correct. All we want you to do is to confirm for us where we are in the development cycle. Are we near a release product or do we go back and completely re-engineer the software?"

"Or wait for my release. You know Dr. Aggarwal and I aren't exactly the best of friends."

Dr. Woodall nods. "But you're also a particularly ideal candidate to give us the right kind of feedback."

"So we going to do it here? On the table?" I challenge him.

"That would be a breach of ethics. Sorry. You need to resume the sexual life you had before. Tell us if this enhances that experience or limits it and how."

I have to laugh.

"What's so funny?" Dr. Woodall is confused by my behavior.

"I never thought I'd be having such a dispassionate discussion about sex." I think back to the first time I did it. Feeling guilty I was doing it behind Rocky's back. But the attraction for Graig was so strong I couldn't say no. I was a jumble of hormones and feelings and when he touched me I just tingled everywhere. And when he touched my vagina I discovered new aspects of my body. "Will this be like the first time? Or will this be like the first time Dr. Aggarwal did it?" I have to ask.

"To be honest, probably neither. The device should handle the mechanical part of it. You'll experience an orgasm and hopefully so will your partner. But what we can't say is whether the feelings you'll experience will be what you want. And that's what you'll have to tell us."

"So does the software pick up the other sensory inputs? Particularly the smells? The touch part of it? Is there any emotional impact I can expect?"

Dr. Woodall shakes his head. "I think the best thing is for you to try it out and tell us what you think. I can run down how it works. Even have the software team tell you what their design criteria were. But in the end this isn't about engineering elegance. It's about how you feel."

"Okay. I'll try it out. But don't expect me to call you up in the throes of ecstasy to give you a full description of its fidelity with the real thing. And also don't expect a report soon. I don't exactly have a harem of guys waiting to come satisfy me."

"We also upgraded your vision with Infrared, thermal and hyperspectral so you can see in the dark and you can see temperature sensitive places. The hyperspectral should give you clues to how people you're with are reacting to situations by changes in body temperature."

I'm surprised at these upgrades. I don't remember asking for them. "Do I really need them?"

"Actually we discussed them before your transition. I told you they were close. You asked for them as soon as they were ready."

"And how am I supposed to use them?" I don't remember the conversation at all. I'm not happy with Dr. Woodall. I think he's trying to use me as a test bed. That's not something I remember signing up for either.

"I'm sure you'll figure that out. You seem to leverage every other capability we've given you so far. You've been much more resilient than we thought. Most of us expected you'd be in every few days looking for one adjustment or another. And you've just adjusted to the new body."

"Sure you won't reconsider trying out my vagina with me. For medical research?" I'm trying to push him to reconsider. With my extra senses I'm finding him more attractive than before. Maybe the software for the vagina is tieing everything together. What happens if I actually get horny? Maybe I ought to try masturbation before I invite someone in.

THE GHOST IN THE MACHINE

Chapter Forty-Six

I have the Googlecar drop me at my condo. Since I can smell the mustiness of my clothes I decide I need to shower and change. Don't know how much of what I'm smelling is from dirty hair and dusty skin. As I enter the bathroom, I let the clothes drop and turn on the shower to warm up. I take a look at myself in the full length mirror. Damn, I wish I'd looked this good when I was trying to get dates. But that was before I'd scared most men away. At least that's what I think happened. Most men didn't want to try to compete with me. Don't need more androgen. If anything more estrogen might be a good thing, even if it is only software and not the real thing. But somewhere in the back of my mind I've also harbored the thought maybe I pushed the guys away. Maybe I didn't think I needed anyone. I'd basically been on my own since Anna Laura died. Rocky was there. But I always thought he was more of a handicap than someone who promoted a balanced psyche. Maybe that was because his own psyche was shredded when Anna Laura died. She completed him. She enabled his ability to live in his head. Enabled him to imagine great things and go find a way to make them real. And when she wasn't there, he couldn't do it anymore. Maybe I don't want to find myself a shell of what I could be because I lost the one person who completes me.

And now that I'm going to live forever, unless I decide to go back and take my place with the people waiting to die, I need to start thinking about relationships. Are they important? Do I need one, or many? And is that one person who completes me a guy or a girl? As an immortal changing out the equipment must be the easy part. I've got to open myself up and explore the full range of relationships. But in the end, I'll bet I go back to being alone. Anna Laura's and Tabitha's deaths at such an early age scarred me in a way I've never really spent any time thinking about. And maybe that's why I keep Rocky at an arm's length. And Raoul. Can't become dependent on either for anything. Most importantly not for emotional support.

I walk into the wall of rain coming from the shower head. I smell the mist in my nose, feel the wetness. Hurray! I feel wetness. I didn't last time I showered. Another improvement. I'm liking the new me better and better. This is much closer to the experiences I lost when I transitioned. Well, at least it's much closer so far. And my hearing and sight are much better than when I was biologic. I think my smell is too, but I've still got to test that out. I was almost overwhelmed with smells in the hospital, but that may have just been as a result of the sensor turning on and my brain synching and picking them up. Does it have a filter that makes it less sensitive so I can go about my daily work without constantly being overwhelmed with smells? Or maybe my brain makes that adjustment. Maybe it will still pick them all up. But I'll pick and choose which ones I want to consciously think about.

The water feels good as it runs over my body. I run the bar of soap over me, lathering up, washing away all the dust and activating all the touch sensors. The firm wet pressure on my body feels good. I definitely need to take more showers. Time to shampoo my hair. I rub it into the hair and feel the texture of the hair in my hands and fingers. I feel the gentle pressure on my scalp and head. This too feels good. Showers are supposed to make you feel clean and smell good. But I'd forgotten how they open up your body to feel the touch. To feel hands on you. And that makes me think of my new vagina.

Do I want to see how it works when it's just me? Not now. I'll save that for a future shower as a reward or punishment if it doesn't work as advertised. I think I'm actually afraid it might work well. Then there's no need for me to design a better software experience. But I also need the time to be able to evaluate it properly. So whatever I do is based on objective facts and not subjective thoughts. I've already been out of the office longer today than planned. Dr. Woodall said the update wouldn't take long. I believed him. Now I don't know if I can trust him in the future not to do something I wouldn't approve of. But what's he really done? He's made me feel better about myself already. And I haven't completely explored the updates.

Time to use the conditioner. Rub it into my hair, over my scalp. Rub my head. Oh, that feels good. And now rinse it out, rinse out all the negative thoughts. Make today a great day. Fix things at work, begin to define the next feature sets I need the teams working. Lay out the high level work partitions to get the teams going. Got to be a good day. Did Dr. Woodall also upload 'The Power of Positive Thinking?' I don't know why all of a sudden I'm having all these positive thoughts.

I turn off the shower and dry myself. Again I feel the sensations of the towel as it dries my skin. He must have activated more sensors, probably software that fills in the holes between sensors with calculated values to make the sensation continuous. It wasn't last time. Everything was a point. I feel pressure here, but not any around it. Then I feel pressure here, but not around it. Yes, this is much better. But why didn't they think about this approach initially? Why did they put me through an initial experience that had so many discontinuities with what I'd experienced as a biologic being? Dr. Woodall told me why. They really weren't ready to do a transition. If I'd not shown up with the need to do something immediately they wouldn't have done it yet. He said they were close on a lot of things, but would have been much happier if I'd waited a year. But I couldn't. If I'd waited, A'zam would have released me. I'd probably be sitting in my house waiting for the phone to ring as my body progressively disintegrates around me.

I have to make a decision about going back to my biologic body. There's not a lot of time left for me to decide. It's kind of like Rocky. It's reassuring to know he's out there, even though I really don't see him that often. But I'd feel the loss if he weren't. Knowing I can still go back is reassuring. When it comes right down to it, I don't know yet what I'm going to decide. It will be hard. Particularly if Dr. Woodall does another upgrade before it's time.

Who knows how much better this will get? And maybe that was his strategy all along. Maybe he wanted me to experience the raw transition into an imperfect immortal, so that I get a taste for how much better it can be. Maybe that was how he intended to convince me to remain. Interesting strategy. It's clear he doesn't want me to transition back. It would be a failure for him if I do. Would discourage others who are waiting for the next unit to be ready.

I smell the clothes hanging in my closet. None smell all that great. I pick out a sunny dress, shoes to match and a leather belt. I look at myself in the mirror again. Certainly is an improvement over what I'd become before the transition. Just not wearing those heavy glasses changes the whole look of my face. I'll never have to wear glasses again. I gather up the rest of the clothes in my closet and hang them on the back porch. I send a note to the drycleaner to come pick them up, and head out the door.

But then I stop. Another thought comes to me. If my touch is so much better, can I taste anything? I go to the refrigerator. There's an open bottle of wine still in there from the night before I flew to Dallas. Haven't opened the refrigerator since I came back. I find a glass, put a little wine in it and put my nose into the glass. Smells like a Petite Syrah. Was that what I was drinking that night? Think I opened the bottle just to celebrate my last night as a biologic being. That certainly sounds odd. I sip the wine into my mouth. Yes! I taste it. A Petite Syrah. Definitely a Petite Syrah. I spit the wine out into the sink. I can't swallow it because there's no place for it to go in my body. Or can I? I don't think so. Dr. Woodall didn't say anything about giving me the ability to eat, but he also didn't say anything about my upgraded touch. Oh, I'm so happy to feel things again, to be able to taste, smell and have it all come together into feelings. Yes, I'm having feelings. Being happy and feeling positive. Those are feelings. But then my logical-self kicks in. How did they do it? What else is different than before? I don't know, but I'm certainly looking forward to finding out.

Now I go out again, closing and locking the door behind me. The fresh air, the sun warming my face. Yes. I can feel the warmth of the sun better than before. Another improvement. And then the rush of flowers and pine trees fill my nose. I distinguish many different types of flowers, different pine trees and my mind is racing to tell me what it is I'm smelling. Geraniums, Chrysanthemums, roses, how many different roses? The list of the different roses I smell and see around me grows by the moment. I look up at the trees. Again my mind begins to identify each and every one as I glance around me. It's amazing there is so much to see, smell and experience in just this short walk I've made so many times over the years. Usually in the dark. I'll never walk this way again ignoring all there is about me. And I know I'll be trying to identify flowers and trees and bushes I've not identified on previous walks. Looking for the differences, looking for what's new, what's beautiful, what smells just amazing?

Now I push all that into the background. I need to think for a moment about work. It's late in the afternoon. The teams will be leaving soon if they haven't already. So I'll have time to think through the next set of designs. Then I realize my mind has let me run thoughts in the background while I have forethoughts on something. That means I can pick and choose what I want to think about without stopping what my mind is doing in the background. That's new. I was only able to focus on one thing at a time before. I smile. Dr. Woodall apparently decided I need to be able to multi-task.

I now understand. Apparently my body was going to a male, or should I say the first transition was going to be a man. I got that body and all the male limitations. Is that why there was no vagina? They were planning for a penis and I showed up. Since they didn't have a vagina ready they didn't give me either. Better to be neuter than have male equipment when the transitioning consciousness is female. But how much of an issue is that? Can I really choose to be a male? To have a penis? To have all the feelings and experience the world the way a man does? I don't know. How much of my female consciousness is a result of the memories that were brought over? How much was the consciousness itself? Is there a difference between a male and female consciousness apart from memories? Are the role differences a matter of what you learn, rather than what you are? Again, I don't know.

THE GHOST IN THE MACHINE

Email to Dr. Woodall. Another question from Immortal number one. But I doubt he knows. It's a matter of experimentation to determine. But who would want to transition without bringing memories over into the new you? Why would anyone want to transition into a new being, without a memory when so much of what defines you comes from the experiences you have growing up, interacting with your family, friends and strangers? I don't think I would have wanted to transition without my memories. Without them, I wouldn't have been able to fill in the blanks between remembered experience and what I'm experiencing now. But then again, there wouldn't be a comparison. I'd only be experiencing the world as my new body permits me to experience it.

I close my eyes and let the sounds, smells and warmth of the afternoon sun fill me with a world I'd not experienced before. I'm hearing conversations across the street. I'm hearing people in their houses talking to pets. I'm hearing the buzz of bees as they search for pollen, and snakes in the grass that are moving to new places where the sun can warm them. I open my eyes again. I think about infrared. And suddenly the colors of the scene around me change, towards the blue end of the scale. And I'm seeing auras around trees. I zoom in on a flower and can see the pollen drop off the legs of a honeybee as it launches itself skyward. My vision picks up the heat of the honeybee. This is amazing.

I walk into a man, who has tried his best to avoid the collision. My vision comes back to normal scale. I smile an embarrassed smile. "Sorry. Not looking where I'm going."

The man glances over to see what I was looking at, "Not a problem, but do you mind me asking: what were you looking at so intently?"

I nod to the rose with the honeybee. "The Alissar Princess of Phoenicia Rose."

The man looks across the street, "Which one is that?"

"Come with me." I lead him across the street to the rose and stoop down to show him. "Its registered name is Harsidon. It's a garden shrub. I know, most people don't think of roses as shrubs, but that's actually what they are. They grow into a bush. That's your first indication. It has a star rating of three and a scent rating of two, which is unfortunate that it doesn't smell as good as it looks, but you can't have everything. The pedal size averages eight centimeters with three to seven flowers per cluster. The plant averages 110 centimeters in height by 90 centimeters wide. The color is always pink with a red center. It's a semi-double flower at first cream with ruby centers, transforming to pink with burnished centers. Its blooms bring to mind the fluttering of butterflies. And it's usually used for borders and cutting."

The man studies the flower as I describe it, then looks back at me with a new appreciation. "You certainly know your flowers. What do you do for a living? You don't look like someone who works in gardens."

"Why? Because I'm not wearing blue jeans and hiking boots?"

"No. In reality, you look delicate. A lot like your Alissar rose." We rise together. I see an appreciation in his eyes I haven't seen in a very long time. I instantly realize I've been dressing down, not feminine. I've not wanted to call attention to my attributes. But now I'm all for it. It's nice to see someone react to my conscious choices.

"You live near here?" I ask, wondering why I've never seen him before.

"Not far." He's not that interested. Time to move on.

"Hopefully I can give you another rose lesson sometime we bump into each other." I give him the smile I use when I want someone to think good things about me.

He laughs. "Hopefully we won't just bump into each other. It's been a real education. I'll be looking for your Alissar rose every time I walk this way. Thank you for going out of your way today."

No exchange of names or promise of anything. But he has that look of interest. Either in a relationship or married and just doesn't wear a ring. Oh well. There are billions of fish in the sea. I nod to him and begin the rest of my journey to work.

There certainly are advantages to instant information about anything I want to know about. I decide I need to watch where I'm going. Not get so distracted. So I decide to focus on my new and improved hearing. I select the sound of car tires on the street as the electric Googlecars ferry their passengers to their destinations. I try to separate out the individual tires. Can I count the different sounds, divide by four and estimate the number of cars that are within my hearing range? I can as I instantly know there are four hundred and twelve cars within my hearing range. I wonder how far that is? It's quite a bit larger area than what I could hear before. But other than being a fountain of useless information, what good is it that I can hear so much and so far? Will the next version increase the frequency separation and increase the range? I don't know. But I can expect Dr. Woodall will continue to improve and expand the capabilities I will have.

I wonder when Dr. Woodall will transition himself. Who would he ask to transition him? Someone who has assisted him I would expect. But how long will he wait? The fact that he would be able to do so much more, to accelerate the development of capabilities has to be something he would consider. I have to think he will do it relatively soon. I'll have to ask him about that the next time I see him. And then I think about being attracted to him at the hospital. Was that real or was it the fact he'd enabled my ability to feel again? Was I just adjusting, or is he really as attractive as it felt at that moment? I'll have to check him out again and see.

The AppleCore offices loom up ahead. I feel disappointed I have to go back to work. I'm enjoying just being outside, learning so much about what I've taken for granted for so long. I'm feeling happy to be alive. That makes me think I should be grateful as well. If I'd not met Dr. Woodall I wouldn't be feeling happy. I wouldn't be learning and growing and wondering about so many things. I'd be waiting to be fired. I'd be wondering how long it would be before I'd be going into a nursing home. I'd be dreading the sunrise because I'd have to face another day of decline, of lessening powers of observation, or reasoning and contributing to society.

Yes. I have a lot to be grateful for. Smile girl. It's a great day.

THE GHOST IN THE MACHINE

Chapter Forty-Seven

I'd agreed to meet the posse after their work hours as I no longer really have work hours, since I work through the night. I'd not given them much detail on why I was dying. I know I need to fill in those blanks. Especially since my time before a decision about transitioning back or not is getting closer, and without a job, eternity seems like a long time. I know I'll need their support on that decision.

"So you're in remission on your cancer." MC is quizzing me.

"And the dementia is no longer an issue." I clarify.

"I don't know how you get there from where you were. I'm not a doc, but I know enough about different diseases that there really isn't a cure for either of what you have." MC informs everyone.

"You're right, there isn't. I have to make a decision. Whether to stop what's making me seemingly healthy again or go back to a disease and pending death.

"Is there some problem with what you've done?" Reese wants to get back into this conversation.

"I don't know. I'm the first who's had the procedure. The doctors don't know what the long term effects are going to be."

"As long as you don't die from it, aren't you better off?" Delilah wants to simplify what she intuits is really complex.

"And you're still not drinking." Reese points out. "Sure you're not pregnant?"

"No fear of that." I respond.

"So no Raoul?" Delilah asks, curious. "I imagine he'll be wondering why he ever left you once he sees how great you look."

"That would be nice, but I don't expect to be seeing him anytime soon."

"I think you need to tell everyone more about your decision so we can help you." Windy chimes in. She's been sitting on what she knows each time we get together and it must be just killing her.

"So you think I need to tell everyone about my old body." I confirm.

Windy nods and takes a sip of her white wine.

"Old body?" MC jumps at the description.

"My old body is basically in a cooler somewhere in case I decide I want it back."

"A cooler. So this isn't you we're looking at?" Delilah doesn't believe what I'm telling them.

"This is a totally new body. Only thing that's original is my consciousness."

That description is greeted by a long silence as each considers my situation.

"So this a clone or something?" Reese is trying to follow my description.

I shake my head. "It's robotic."

"All of it?" MC asks, disbelieving.

"It is." Windy confirms for me. "I was there. Her body is robotic and that was the only way she could recover from her illnesses."

The entire group sits contemplating the news. Each takes a sip of their wine and work this information through in their mind.

Delilah is the first to ask a question. "So that's why you got a decision to make. Live as a robot or die as a person."

"Sort of." I confirm. "I'm still a person. The same one you know. I just have a different body."

"How long have they been giving people robot bodies?" MC is thinking beyond just my situation. "Are there a whole bunch of people like you around and we don't even know it?"

"I am the first. Although they're getting ready to transition others." I confirm what little I know.

"So what do you think? You going to keep it?" Reese asks.

"I don't know. Lots of advantages, but I've been struggling with the limitations. And I still don't really know all of them." I answer as fully as I can.

"What do you think, Windy? You were there for the whole thing." MC asks.

"I don't know. She's not been talking to me any more than she's been talking with you since we came back from Dallas. On the surface, if I can live a relatively normal life in a different body that sounds appealing. At least in comparison with the thought of dying pretty soon. But I don't know how she's been adjusting to it all."

"It's been hard. But it's also getting better. This is the first time I've worn a dress in forever. I'm beginning to feel more like a person and not a ghost inhabiting a machine, if I can use that analogy."

"I can't imagine what you've been going through." Reese declares. "And you haven't been sharing this experience with us. Maybe one of us will need to do the same thing. You were fine six months ago, and now everything is different. Even if you go back to your old body, you'll never be the same as you were."

"I didn't think about that. I was scared. My whole life was falling apart. Everything I'd worked so long for was slipping away."

"We hear you Sage. But you didn't let us hear you when we could have helped." MC is angry with me. Angry I didn't go to her when she could have helped.

"I've got to get back."

"You're going into work now?" Windy looks at the clock.

"I was out for most of the morning and don't sleep anymore, so this is productive time for me." I stand up and gather my things. "Think of the questions you have about my dilemma. Next week? Same time same station?"

Chapter Forty-Eight: Nine Days

I'm out in the lab. Something has me confused. I'm looking through lines of code thinking there's something I've missed, or something I took the wrong approach on. But what is it? Why am I coming to this conclusion now?

Jermaine sees me in the lab and pokes his head in. "Heading home. Everything looks good."

"Hey, Jermaine. You're the Wiz when it comes to geo-locational apps. Come here and walk this through with me."

Jermaine looks up at the clock. He turns around and motions to somebody behind him. In a moment I have him on one side and Oriana on the other. "What are you looking at?" Jermaine asks.

"This is the code Moshe and his team developed for the new grad project. Its bullet proof and works like a champ. But something about it bothers me."

"That's never a good thing." Oriana rolls her eyes.

"What's bothering you? Is it the functionality, or the response time or search approach they took?" Jermaine asks looking over my shoulder at the code, but not at anything specific.

"This reminds me of the global dictionary. You know. The one that could translate any language into any other."

"Yeah. I remember that one. We started over. That was back in the day when we had slack in the schedule. We could afford to do that. Don't you know I'd love to have that luxury now?"

"Stop complaining." Oriana responds. "Those days aren't coming back."

"Not as long as we're using current tools and following coding conventions that limit reuse." I observe.

"What are you talking about?" Oriana responds. "We're using the latest tools and reusing code elements and modules as much as possible."

I shake my head. "We're going to push the envelope again on this next feature set." I glance up to see Jermaine's reaction. I have a pretty good idea how Oriana is taking this news.

"Hold on. You can't do this to us again." Jermaine steps back away from me. Holds up his hands. "You pushed us up a level and things are just beginning to settle out. I mean folks are still trying to really understand what the hell we're doing, how we make our devices dance and sing the way we are. You change the rules on us again, you're going to have a mass exodus."

I hear what I expected when I started seeing what my slower and less-capable-self had missed. "If you were in my chair, what would you do if you saw a different way to ratchet up our capabilities? We have an opportunity to really put distance between us and the competition, but only if all of us step up. So what would you do?"

"You're asking me to crawl inside your head and figure out what you haven't?" Jermaine pushes back. "Wait a minute. That's what they pay you the big bucks to figure out. I just push code out the back door as fast as you all define for me what I got to do."

"But you were both critical of me for pushing too hard. For not consulting you on what and how your teams were going to approach the code and solutions. So I'm asking."

"But you need all the team leads here, not just the two of us." Oriana points out.

"I'll do that in the morning. But for now I'm putting the problem in front of you. Giving you a head start in helping me find a solution. What do you see I don't?"

"Let's dissect the problem." Jermaine begins, buying time to think what to say.

"This high school biology?" Oriana asks.

"No, smart ass. I mean we got to go back to the basics. You said something about tools. Oriana thinks we got the latest and greatest. Is she right or is there something out there that can automate parts of what we do so we can work faster?"

"Assume I'll have some new tools for you in the morning." I respond.

"Who's gonna teach our teams how to use them?" Jermaine responds.

"I will. No problem. Keep going."

Oriana looks at me like I'm crazy, but reserves judgment. "Well, if the teams can automate some of what we do, then we can focus on the really hard stuff."

"Who defines the hard stuff?" I ask anticipating an answer.

"We will. That's what we do." Oriana steps up. "And if you automate some of the routine work, help us define reusable modules that leverage performance and reuse, we can clearly deliver a whole lot faster than we do."

"So if we were going to start this new approach tomorrow, what would you need on your desk when you come in?"

"Automation tools and training materials." Jermaine begins.

"Partitioned work assignments with notated architecture

documents so we can see exactly how we need to proceed to create these reusable modules." Oriana concludes.

"That all?" I ask.

"Would certainly make it easier for us to do our jobs." Jermaine notes."

I only need a moment to absorb their recommendations. My mind is already racing on the new tools. I push that to background. "Okay." I get up and give each a hug.

"What?" Jermaine isn't sure he believes what I just said, even less the hug as it's been a while since he got one of them from me. Even Oriana has a quizzical expression.

"I'll do my part. Tomorrow when you come in, you just need to be ready to do yours."

Chapter Forty-Nine: Eight Days

The SLT meeting is subdued. Apparently Julia has been making life hell for those who didn't back her in the question of whether to sack me or not. Wallace's report was simply a head nod when Julia asked him if he was on schedule for deliveries. Alix won't look at me. She has been looking down at her hands throughout the meeting. Petra studies her spreadsheets and has not been engaged in any of the discussion. Usually she has a comment or two on everything.

I decide it's time to spice up the meeting. "Julia. I have an update I'd like to give."

"I already have your report. Don't think it's important to waste everyone's time on it."

"You see. Now that's where we differ. I think it's important for everyone to know when I'm changing the functionality set we're going to deliver next."

"Hold on now. That wasn't in your written report." Julia protests.

"That's true. However, we live in a rapidly changing world and market. Just before coming into this meeting I was given some market intelligence from Landon Banerjee. Symbol Ventures is going to release a new functionality set next week that contains some things our current release doesn't. That could result in customer defection, something we've all been working hard to avoid."

"We don't react to the competition. We lead the market." Julia recites an old company mantra that was set out a long time ago.

"Are you ready to explain to Wall Street why we didn't release a product set that could have prevented customer defections? Every defection carries over on our top line sales for months, if not years." I respond. Petra suddenly becomes very interested in this discussion.

"We can't knowingly watch the competition get a leg up on us." Petra remarks.

Again, Julia's lack of experience in this role gets the better of her. "What research have we done that would indicate a single feature set would result in a loss of core customers?"

Unfortunately only she and I've managed the marketing department recently so it's her word against mine. And Banerjee hasn't done a specific study for me on that topic yet. So I'm scanning the literature as I stall my response. "As you know, AppleCore hasn't engaged such a study. But the broader academic studies show on average, across multiple industries, feature set leadership ensures a ninety percent customer retention. That's been the justification for us investing as heavily as we do. But that same literature and set of academic studies show that when a long term market leader falters and an upstart gets to market first with a new product, the incumbent loses, on average, 25% of the new product sales to the first mover. They also lose ten percent of the upgrades and first time adopters."

"Damn it Sage, where do you get all these statistics you're always using? And how do we know they're accurate?" Julia is getting upset I always have a response to her questions. She doesn't have the data in front of her. That's because she doesn't know what questions to ask.

"Happy to give you the citations and you can validate any as you wish." Is my not too subtle response to her exasperation.

"Okay. Let's accept them as correct for the sake of argument. Then you're saying we have to scrap our feature set. Roll out something our customers aren't expecting? You argued against just that at the last SLT meeting."

"What do you think, Petra?" I ask. Not a wise thing to do if I'm trying to diffuse Julia, but at this point it wouldn't make any difference anyway. She's never going to be my best friend, or even friend for that matter.

"The company has always taken the conservative approach. Ever since we introduced our communications devices that changed the whole marketplace."

Julia's smug expression shows she thinks she's won the debate, but then Petra continues. "But we all know business models have a lifecycle. We've been studying our customers and the market to determine: when do we have to eat our young? And by that I mean, when do we cannibalize our existing sales to move the business model to a new model?"

Julia's expression hardens. "What are you going on about Petra?"

"I'm saying you're both right, depending on what you think the future will bring. And in that case the future will prove one of you to be prescient and the other out of touch with our markets."

"Who do you think is right?" Alix asks.

"I can't tell you. I clearly don't want to forsake revenue if there is no threat. But on the other hand, I don't want to hold on to every dime, only to see the dollars evaporate. We have to react if the customer is embracing a different business model."

"If you were Queen for a Day, what would you recommend?" Alix is impatient.

"I would either take one feature out of the current feature set to include it this time around, or I'd include it in the next feature set and advertise the hell out of the fact our superior solution is only a month away."

"Dividing the baby." Alix notes and withdraws from the conversation.

Wallace joins the discussion for the first time, although it's been clear he has been listening intently. "I'd recommend getting it out there. Take Marketing's recommendation on what to delay."

We all nod agreement.

Chapter Fifty

I've rearranged my office so my desk faces the wall. This is so I can think through things without having to always have my head down like I'm looking at a monitor. If I turn my head to the right I can see out the window to the same Japanese courtyard that forms the back of A'zam's office. Only my office faces it from a different corridor. If I go up to the window I can see into his office. I never do that anymore. I'm just not that interested in who's in talking with him. And since he's been gone, no one has been using his office anyway.

I'm reviewing the market research study Landon Banerjee just finished for me on new product opportunities. I hear someone at my door. I turn around to find Raoul smiling at me. "You been someplace?"

I shake my head not following his question. "Not recently, no."

"I mean since the last time I saw you." He's trying to find something to get the conversation started. In the past he's never had to search very hard. He's a salesman at heart. Spends most of his time talking to strangers and people he only sees once in a while.

"Not really. What brings you to California? Thought you'd been moved to international sales with most of your trips to Europe." I'm remembering the conversation after the last time he was by loving and leaving me, quite literally. And then he disappeared for a year.

"Global sales conference in San Francisco. First time here in five years. You said you were going to be dealing with your father. Guess your plans changed?"

"A lot has changed in the last year." I'm wondering how he talked his way in here.

THE GHOST IN THE MACHINE

Mindi comes to the door, the look on her face tells me she got the call from the lobby.

"Thanks, Mindi." I let her know it's all right. Raoul comes in and sits down in the chair I usually occupy at the end of my conference table. He swivels around so he's facing me. Same suits as always. He looks like a salesman with the bright smile, deep tan and longish dyed blonde hair. He has a moustache now. That's new since I last saw him. Pencil thin. Usually don't like moustaches shaved that way. If he wants facial hair it should be trimmed and neat. Not reduced to something artificial like his.

"Can you sneak out for a late lunch?" he asks. But he's thinking a different kind of lunch. Raoul's always in a hurry. Not much for foreplay. He wants to skip to dessert. "I need to get back up to the city. The meetings start this evening." He informs me.

"Can't you skip the introductory meetings?" In the past he would have.

"No can do. I'm the chairman of the event. I have to be there to kick everything off. Have to stay because I moderate the sessions. So I'm pretty much tied up for the whole thing." He's explaining why this is the only opening on his dance card. If I want to dance I need to take advantage now. I had the rest of the afternoon set aside for wandering around. By that I planned to go out on the floor and talk with coders. I planned to reassure them. Get their feedback on how the new tools and approach are working out. Are they taking pressure off? Are people more comfortable with the pace we've set? Can they keep it up? And what more do I need to do to help them get ready for another ratchet up I'm planning.

Raoul stares at me. I've gone back to work in my mind. Guess he's not the attraction, distraction he used to be. Either that or the new feelings I experience still haven't figured out attraction to men. That moustache is putting me off. Need to get beyond it. "I need to chat with Mindi for a moment." I rise and go out to the outer office.

Mindi begins, apologetically, "He said he wanted to surprise you."

"It's fine. But give me a heads up next time." Mindi either knows or suspects why Raoul comes around to see me. We don't do much work with his company. "We're going out for a quick bite. I should be back before the second shift comes in. I'll do my walk arounds then."

Mindi gives me a disapproving look. "Another late evening for you."

I shrug. "How's Landon?"

Mindi smiles, but looks away. Not a good sign. He must have done something she's unhappy about. "Landon is Landon. He's decided you're his role model. You promoted him. You believe in him. So he works all the time, just like you. I seldom get a whole evening with him. Would you talk to him? Let him know it's all right to spend time with me?"

"Sorry I'm such a bad role model." I touch her on the shoulder to let her know it will be okay. "I'll stop by to see him when I get back."

"Thank you. I don't want to distract him from his work. But I'm getting lonely waiting for him."

I nod as I turn back to the office and Raoul.

We walk to my condo. Even though Raoul is chattering away about the antiquities of Rome and the decadence of Paris. I've assigned listening to him to a background processor. I only do that in case he asks a question. I'm looking for my rose. I know where it is. I've been scanning the flower beds to determine whether there is another. Usually they plant more than one of the same kind fairly close together. But I've not been able to find another like it.

"Have you been exercising? You look great by the way. Even better than the last time we got together."

Background processor kicks in, "Not as much as I'd like. How about you?"

"Are you upset with me for wanting to see you and taking a chance you'd be here?"

Change the subject. "Do you know anything about Roses?"

Raoul glances around. Apparently notices the rose bushes along our path. "Probably not as much as I should. I know they're beautiful, just like you. Don't smell all that much. But you smell good, so I guess you're more attractive than a rose."

Keep it coming. Need to find out if you get me horny. "You like my cologne?"

"Love it. Isn't that the one I gave you?" It isn't but I knew he wouldn't remember.

"Of course. Do you think I'd forget you?" Of course I forgot you when you dropped me for some Parisian or Roman goddess you sweet talked. But I've got to stop having these thoughts. He'll never get me turned on.

Raoul smiles, proud of his power to keep a girl wanting more of him, at least in his mind. I spot the Alissar rose. I smile thinking about it. But I want him to think I'm smiling about him. Raoul puts his arm around me. I wait for a reaction. Nothing. "You've lost weight. I wondered when I saw you. I like the new you, by the way. You were gorgeous before, but now…" he doesn't complete the thought. He can't. Anything he says will be a negative about how I used to be.

"When does your meeting start tonight?" I'm wondering how much time we really have. It will take him at least two hours to get to the city this time of day.

"Seven. We have plenty of time. I want to relax and enjoy you as much as we have in the past." He wants to enjoy me. I guess that was a slip of the tongue, and I know the tongue is coming because Raoul likes to French kiss.

I notice Raoul has picked up the pace. Not a lot, but noticeably. He's in a hurry. I'll bet I hardly get in the door before he'll be ripping my clothes off. If this lasts ten minutes I'll be amazed. So how do I get him to slow down?

"Did you bring some weed?" I ask. He used to.

"Oh, I can't. I've got to have it together for my meetings." I'm just a bonus for him on this trip. He's not really here to see me, he's just trying to keep his harem current by touching us once in a while so we don't go find someone else.

"You need to relax if you want to enjoy me, otherwise you'll come and go and forget you were even here."

Raoul is feeling trapped by his own bullshit. "All right." He checks his vintage Rolex. One of the things about him is he wants everyone to think he's eminently successful. "One joint."

I hug him, gently, just to let him know he made the right decision.

THE GHOST IN THE MACHINE

Chapter Fifty-One

As I close the door behind us Raoul turns into me for an embrace, looking for a kiss. I smell his cologne. It used to turn me on. Will it now? He presses his lips against mine. He unbuttons my blouse. I let him fumble for a moment before gently pushing him back. I disengage from his kiss.

"First thing is shave that moustache." I point to the bathroom. A razor awaits.

In a minute he is back with a clean upper lip. "Joint?" I remind him.

"I know. The back porch because you don't want the smell in the house. But I want to see you, so let's sit out there in the nude."

"Funny. The neighbors will love that." Not going to happen, Raoul. I take his hand and lead him out to the back deck. It's screened in so we sit out here without anyone seeing us. But I'm not letting him get hard too soon because in the past he hasn't been able to keep it up all that long.

Raoul lights the joint and inhales. Not as deeply as in the past when he wasn't in as much of a hurry. He holds it out to pass over. I shake my head. "What? I've got to mellow out but not you?"

"You don't want me mellow. It will just take longer." I offer as my defense. Since I don't breathe I don't know how I'd be able to smoke.

Raoul nods. Apparently remembering the last time we made love. It seemed to take me a long time to have my orgasm. I've wondered more than once if that was the reason it took him so long to come back.

THE GHOST IN THE MACHINE

Probably the other women he's sleeping with don't make him work that hard. Raoul takes multiple short puffs on the joint. He's not talking between. That means he's feeling pressured. Wants to get on with it. I try to slow him just a bit.

"So how are Parisian girls compared to those you've had in Rome?"

Raoul holds this one for a moment longer as he thinks how to answer my question. "Amazing. Each in their own ways. There's just a different attitude about sex over there. It's almost like making love is an art form. They can't get enough of me. We go on and on and on. Amazing. Just amazing."

Raoul has had enough. He stubs out. Reaches across for me. Takes my hand. Leads me back into the house. As soon as he has closed the porch door he is on me again. Kissing me as he unbuttons my blouse. I slip his jacket over his shoulders. Let it drop to the floor. He has my blouse undone. Goes to work on the cuff buttons as I undo his shirt. I rub my hand over his hairy chest. He shows a taught smile. The buttons are undone. He slips my blouse off my shoulders. Raoul holds it up, twirls my blouse like a matador. Maybe he had a Spanish girl or two in there somewhere.

I get his shirt up. Out of his pants, off his shoulders, as he goes to work on my bra. A single snap and it goes limp on my shoulders. As he pulls it away he looks at my breasts. He clearly doesn't remember them looking taught and firm like they do now. He seems to be trying to understand why I'm so much firmer and younger looking. But it's been a year. I'm sure there have been a lot of women.

Raoul kneels down. He kisses my nipples as he pulls my skirt and panties down at the same time. He looks directly at my vagina. Leaning forward he kisses the inside of my thighs. Then higher and higher until he finds my spot. He runs his tongue over it.

I pull on his arms. He rises. I kneel. Undo his belt. Open his pants.

Slowly bring the zipper down. I'm greeted by his hardening self, trying to get out of his pants. I let the pants drop. Then bring the underpants down to his ankles. He comes fully erect as he steps out of his underpants.

He gently pulls on my arms to rise again. He stands there, erect, looking at me in the strangest way. Almost admiring, as if he can't believe he's going to make love to me. We come together. His tongue is in my mouth, searching for my tongue. He's slowly pushing his tongue in and out. Not too subtle. My mouth is moist, so the software does respond to sexual cues. I just hope they've given me enough moisture to last until we're done.

Raoul steps back. Picks me up in his arms to carry me into the bedroom. It occurs to me that I haven't changed the sheets since I went to Dallas for the transition. I wonder if they're clean. As he carries me to the bed he sees the recharging bed. He doesn't say anything. Not worrying about sheets, he sets me down on top of the blankets. In a moment he crawls over top of me, leaning down to kiss me again. Full tongue. In and out. I know the only way I'm really going to get a good understanding of how the vagina works is to bring him to a quick external ejaculation. That way he will have to work back up to the second one. My dilemma is if I use my mouth to bring him, which is what he prefers, what do I do with the semen? I can't swallow it. I can't get out of bed, spit it out and wash my mouth out, can I?

I take his erect member in my hand, start rubbing the head. It's already hard. I feel it begin to throb as more blood pumps in anticipation. I push him over onto his back, grasp the throbbing rod and squeeze, but gently. I still don't have a good gauge of my strength. He stiffens, what seems to be every muscle in his body, before the contractions begin. He holds the tension for only a second before he begins to relax. Problem solved, he couldn't wait for me. As he relaxes more, murmuring, I get up, wash my hands. Bring back a towel to clean him up. A little housekeeping on his stomach and legs. I toss the towel aside.

THE GHOST IN THE MACHINE

Raoul crawls up on me again, kisses me on the mouth. Then proceeds to kiss my cheeks, my neck and then breasts. He kisses the nipples. He used to have to kiss them several times to get them to stand up. Now they're in that position permanently, although I expect he thinks they're just reacting to him. He doesn't linger on them the way he used to. He works his way down my body, kissing as he goes until he's face-to-face with my vagina. His tongue explores me. He continues until he feels a response. He's impatient, but I know he needs time to recover from the first ejaculation. I'm hoping the weed also has slowed him down. But given how fast he came, it didn't seem to have any impact on his arousal. Am I that hot? He certainly was never that aroused before.

I feel a tightening in my abdomen. Apparently they installed something that replicates the stomach muscles when they installed the vagina. A rhythm begins with what seems like a tightening and relaxation. The pattern continues. It gets more intense, although maintains about the same rhythm. Raoul slides up next to me. Slides his finger inside me. In and out. In and out. I feel the finger is wet and slippery. The lubricant is working. I wonder what it is, but set that aside. I need to fully understand the feelings. I'm getting aroused. Is it like before? No. It's different. I don't feel the flush in my face. The increased heart rate. I can't. What else is missing? The stomach muscles seem to be tightening and relaxing on their own. I'm not sure the arousal is a result of the touch or the overall experience, including the emotional aspect. Stop analyzing. Let it go. Just experience it. Figure it out afterwards.

Raoul continues exploring me using his finger. Gentle pressure. Back inside and out, in and out. I feel a rush, or so it seems. My stomach muscles tighten, I feel like I'm riding the crest of a wave. Raoul pushes himself inside to ride along. The contractions come over me, strong, violent and rapid. Raoul tries to keep up. Thrusting deep. In and out, in and out. He's kissing me again. Tongue trying to keep up with the deep thrusting.

The crest of the wave moves on. I'm contracting a little more slowly. The contractions remain strong, pulling him deep inside. He gets harder just before I feel his release. Not quite synchronously. Feeling his contractions within me. He keeps thrusting deep. Deeper. Harder. As if he's trying to push all the way to where my uterus would be. I'm glad I don't have to worry about getting pregnant. I wonder if Raoul's even thought about that possibility. He doesn't seem to care, if he has. Harder. Deeper.

And then my contractions lessen. He notices. Backs off his thrusting to be shallower, gentler. He continues rising as I contract. Coming together as I rise. This after sex, sex is nice. More gentle. Not as frenzied. A nice feeling of senses alive. Satisfying. I continue. So does Raoul.

He rises to get a different angle with his gentle thrusts. He's trying to see if we can have a second orgasm. I acknowledge the possibility as I move to help him achieve contact. Again I feel the stomach muscles begin their gentle tightening and relaxing. Raoul notices. Rises a little higher to try to stimulate me even more. But instead of speeding up his thrusts, he continues the slow and gentle movements. It's more arousing than the first time. It doesn't take long before the contractions begin again. Strong, but not as violent. Slower than the first time. More pleasurable. I feel Raoul harden again. He thrusts deeper. Long slow thrusts. Not hurtful. Almost languorous. Long thrust as we come together. Then we pull away before coming together again.

By the time Raoul has his second orgasm I'm nearly done. I'm slowing, so I consciously speed up to help him. This orgasm is shorter, less intense for him as well. I feel him getting smaller. Then he stops thrusting as he pulls out. He looks down at me with a contented smile. Kisses me on the mouth. No tongue. I'm surprised. He then kisses my nipples. Finally rolls over with a big sigh.

I reach over. Run my hand across his chest. He takes my hand, kisses it, seeming content. We lie next to each other. I used to crawl up on his chest, but I expect he doesn't have time for that today. And I'm right. He leans over, kisses me again, and gets dressed.

I decide to do the same comparing this to last time.

Chapter Fifty-Two

I'm still comparing orgasms when I walk into my office. Mindi looks up from her desk, smiles at me. I look at the clock. It's still early. Raoul just never takes that long.

"Julia wants you to come see her as soon as you get in." Julia? Why would she want to see me now?

"Where did you tell her I was?"

"Late lunch with a vendor. I told her he came in unannounced. You rearranged your calendar to accommodate him." I'm glad she did that. Otherwise Julia would be having a fit that my calendar isn't current.

"She say if I need to bring anything she wants to go over?" Trying to see if I need to prepare.

"Nope. Just come by as soon as you get back."

I nod, not able to figure out what Julia's up to now. A'zam can't get back soon enough. I need him as a buffer. I slowly walk around the corner to her office. As I approach, her admin, Sharon, nods for me to just go on in. I'm surprised when Sharon follows me, closes the door behind me before returning to her desk.

"Sage. Glad you weren't long. Come over and sit down." She motions to the conference table although she doesn't get up to come join me.

"You and Tom going to the Opera this weekend?" I decide I need to do the social chit chat to see if I can take the edge off that I hear in her voice.

"No. We saw Madam Butterfly in New York about a month ago. So not really up to seeing it again so soon. Are you?" At least she's willing to chit chat.

"No. Holding out for La Boehme. I usually only do one a year. I understand they're bringing in the lead for La Boehme from the Paris Opera, which should be a real treat."

"But it's so sad, don't you think? All the young radicals die." Where's she going with this?

"Everyone dies in the opera. Just comes with the territory." I respond not really thinking through her question.

"But that's a theme in society, don't you think? I mean all the young radicals who start up new companies based on great new technology generally get bought out at an early age." This doesn't sound good.

"That where A'zam is? Trying to create the next AppleCore?" I'm trying to steer this conversation if I can.

Julia shakes her head and smiles. "He's not the reason I wanted to chat. You've become an embarrassment to me." Knew this wasn't going to be good.

"Wall Street doesn't think so." Got to find a defense wherever I can. One she can't ignore.

"It's a good thing no one from Wall Street is in our SLT meetings." She lets that sit for a long moment. "But those who are, think it's perfectly all right to disagree with me."

"We all disagree with A'zam. You've disagreed with A'zam. That's why we have the meetings. To discuss. Come to agreement on how we are going to execute this business. If your opinion was the only one that counted there'd be no reason to have a meeting. We'd just send you a status report with the decisions that need to be made. Wait for your response."

"That's not exactly true. As long as I'm the CEO, my opinion is the only one that counts."

"But you can't run the company by yourself. You should welcome disagreement. A'zam does." I respond feeling I'm not going to win this time, no matter what I do. No supporting cast to back me up.

"A'zam isn't here. We don't know for sure when or if he will be coming back."

Whoa. That's the first time anyone has raised any doubt about A'zam returning.

"And I've made a decision. For the good of the organization I need to make a change. You've become a distraction. A lightning rod if you will. I can't get people to focus on what's important. Oriana is taking over Software. You're terminated effective immediately."

So Julia wins. What I've been working so hard to prevent happened anyway. Just not for the reasons I thought it would. Might as well call up Dr. Woodall and tell him I want to go back. I don't want to be unemployed for eternity. And once the word gets out I was let go at AppleCore, I'll not be able to get a job anywhere else.

Maybe I'll spend the rest of eternity as a professional vagina tester.

"What are you thinking?" Julia's probably concerned I might have already come up with a way of saving myself.

"Thinking about time."

"That you're going to have lots of it?" Julia smirks.

"No. Really about how little you have left. You have no cause for your action."

"You failed to carry out a direct order." She comes right back.

What? "What are you talking about?"

"I told you to fire Landon Banerjee. I'm looking at the company roster. He's still the VP of Marketing. You disobeyed a direct order."

"As you disobeyed a direct order from A'zam to fill that role. You want to go down that road, you'll find it's a slippery slope. I began a search for his replacement, but wasn't going to leave the department without leadership until we got the right person. That was A'zam's biggest complaint when you led the area. The lack of leadership. I learned from your experience."

"No matter. You're still out. You've littered the place with causes of action. I'm not at all concerned about justifying the change." She isn't about to let me rattle her. Got to try a little harder.

"You should be. Particularly if A'zam returns." I see her reaction although she tries to hide it.

"Anyone who opposes me, as you have, will suffer the same fate."

"Wall Street will punish you within a month as feature set deliveries slip again, which they will once I'm gone."

"Oriana is brilliant. She's the only reason you have the track record you do." Julia's still trying to understand how her decision can be attacked. That's the only reason she's letting me continue talking.

"Have you asked her if she still believes that?" I wait to see her reaction. A furrowed brow. She's wondering why I'm saying this. "As you said, things changed when I got back. Not in my absence. When I got back. If Oriana was the solution, why didn't they get better while I was out?" I see the seeds of doubt entering her thoughts. "And if she can't keep up with the doubling of production releases we've already advised in the market, who takes the blame for that? Not Oriana. The acting CEO, who's in over her head and doesn't know enough to know it."

"I think this discussion is over. Clean out your office. I want you gone in an hour. Leave your badge with Mindi."

"You reap what you sow." Are my parting words as I leave her office.

THE GHOST IN THE MACHINE

Chapter Fifty-Three: Seven Days

The call from Oriana came earlier than I thought. Not even nine-thirty. I'm searching the media for any current references to A'zam. Any kind of sighting, gossip, anything. The only thing I've found were the releases from AppleCore. A'zam took a leave of absence. Julia is acting CEO until his expected return. The releases were vague.

"Morning Oriana. Enjoying the view?" I'm referring to the Japanese garden from my window.

"I don't have time for that. How long is this going to last? It's crazy." Oriana is clearly stressed. And she's only had the job for a few hours.

"What did Julia tell you?"

"Until further notice. Go figure it out, she said. I figure it out I get to keep the job. I don't, someone else will have it. Big of her. Shows a lot of faith." Oriana sounds like she's not a fan. Until now I thought they were close friends. Julia certainly implies they are.

"She's on a short leash. So I wouldn't get too excited about any of it." I hope that will calm her down, but I also know it could put her into orbit.

"What do you know I don't?" Oriana is beginning to realize there's a whole lot going on she doesn't see.

"I'm doing my homework now."

"Let me know what you find out. Got to figure out how to get a firm footing here, 'cause I certainly don't have it at the moment." Oriana needs to settle down.

"Relax and tell me what's going on. I'll give you any insights I have."

Bingo. My mind dumps an article: A'zam, or someone who looks very much like him, seen in a restaurant in Dallas having lunch with several unidentified men. Dallas? There's nothing going on in Dallas. What's he up to?

"It's like the place just shut down. I can't get anyone to focus. Everyone's running around trying to figure out why you're gone. What does that mean for all the changes you just made? Do they continue trying to learn the tools? Learn the new architecture? Or just wait to see what happens? So nothing's getting done." I hear her anxiety and fear. Fear of failure. Probably the first time Oriana ever thought it possible to fail at something. It's scaring her to death.

"My recommendation is you start with your team. Get them restarted first. Let people see others getting back to work. Be as calm and reassuring as you can be. I know you're not calm at the moment. The panic will pass as things get going again."

"Sounds like you don't think you'll be coming back." Oriana is asking a fair question. I'd want to know that too if I were in her position.

"At the moment I don't know what to think." Don't want to give her too much of the conversation with Julia, because it's important Oriana not trust her.

"All right. Is it okay if I call you as I need advice?" Oriana is covering the bases in case I do come back.

"Absolutely. Just think of it as you've been given the rest of the teams. Do what you'd do in that situation. The rest will come."

Oriana hesitates, "Oh. There's one more thing. Mindi told me Julia fired Landon Banerjee this morning. She said you'd want to know." That was to be expected.

"Thanks. Tell Mindi I'm sorry." And I am.

Oriana is gone. So much for the transition. Time for me to get back on the hunt for A'zam. Dallas. The person who saw him wasn't able to confirm. No other appearances at conferences, or affairs. Without a secondary confirmation it isn't a story, just a possible sighting. But then I come across a reference to Symbol Ventures having a development office in Dallas. They bought a small company there that's doing work on teleportation using particle beam technology. Very theoretical stuff. They've actually built a model of how it could work. Alix said she heard he was doing something with them. Could this be it?

I continue scanning for references to him. Nothing since he took his leave. What was Julia trying to say that he might not be back? That could be more of a hope or a bluff on her part. Who knows? But I guess I shouldn't pin all my hopes on A'zam returning and rescuing me from my current situation.

Doing product development is so much easier than trying to divine what's going on in the Board room and behind closed doors in the C-suite at AppleCore. So this opens a whole new avenue of thought for me. If I don't go back to AppleCore where could I go? My first thought is no one would want me. But is that really true? If it is, then I definitely need to go transition back into my old body. I can't sit home like this as an immortal. I just couldn't do it. So where could I go?

THE GHOST IN THE MACHINE

Chapter Fifty-Four

Once word got out that Apple released me, Reese didn't want to wait a whole week, so the posse heads out to Tyree's Table, a place where good looking guys tend to hang out. The problem is the good looking girls hang out there too. So the competition is usually stiff. But the people watching is always fun for those of us who aren't taking the singles scene seriously. Although with my new job as the official immortals vagina tester maybe I ought to.

"So Raoul just shows up unannounced, big dick in hand saying give me a hand?" Reese is asking.

"Pretty much." I acknowledge.

"Not much ego there." Windy doesn't like Raoul, even though she's never met him. Thinks he's a jerk who's only looking for sex. She's right, but that never stopped me in the past.

"Not much there, there, either from what I remember." Delilah dated Raoul before I did. In fact, she introduced us when she was done with him. "But then I think someone said he was augmented before he started sleeping with you."

"Really?" I didn't know that. "So does that mean we had a mechanical dick screwing a mechanical vagina and neither of us knew it at the time?" Hmm.

"Don't think I want to contemplate that." Delilah shakes her head.

"No. I heard that." MC responds. "From one of his friends."

"I didn't know he had any friends. Particularly any who you'd know." Reese is teasing MC.

"Yeah, well. He was infamous locally before he got too big for us here and went off to screw the world."

"I don't know if I can handle all these allusions." I protest.

"Well, that's what you get for sleeping with the slime ball. You go a whole year, the good celibate sister. Jerko comes to town and you don't even get a free meal off him. I mean you need to have some self-respect."

"It was an experiment. You know? I was trying to figure out if I still know how to do it after all this time." I protest.

"I got lots of guys who'd be happy to share your bed. But you never seem to have any interest." Delilah has been more than willing to share her good fortune.

"If I don't go back to work soon, I may need someone to pay my bills for me." I note.

"You mean like a sugar daddy? Wow. Never thought Miss Brainiac would stoop so low as to come down to earth here with the rest of us." Delilah acts surprised.

"Not that I have a problem now." I note. "But you know a girl's got to look to the future. Yesterday shows things can go from the best of times to the worst of times overnight."

"I wouldn't think Jerko represents the best of times. You can do so much better than him. Think about it. He lives in Europe most of the time. He sleeps with anyone who doesn't say no before he can get his tongue down their throat. And he doesn't care about you. If he did it wouldn't be a year between saying hello." Reese is always the practical one, we think of her as the mother of our group, if we need a mother.

"All right, all right. Send me pictures and I'll think about it."

"What do you mean think about it?" Delilah's not going to let me sit home. "What else you got to do except check out men? I mean it's not like you got to punch a clock or something. Look Windy will give you the keys to her ranch if you want to go be alone. But you been alone practically your whole life. So when are you going to join the rest of us here. Have a relationship with someone who cares about you?"

"I'm not sure that's possible." I respond honestly.

"Reese found someone. If she can, you can." Windy points out. When Reese was dating she was notorious for having unfailingly bad taste in men. Either they were complete jerks who were only trying to get into her pants and dropped her as soon as they succeeded, or they lacked confidence and had trouble performing in the bedroom. The ones who were smart or professionals always were completely self-centered and expected she would be their slave with privileges. Any thought of having a career of her own was just out of the question. She was almost as hopeless as me when she met her husband, Tariq.

"Hey!" Windy isn't happy I haven't said anything in response to her observation about Reese. "You're not getting away retreating into your head. You're here with us. You owe us your undivided attention."

"Okay. Yes. Reese got lucky. We should all be as lucky as she is." I respond a little annoyed that I don't believe I ever will.

"Bullshit." Reese doesn't like to think it was all luck. "I worked my ass off trying out all kinds of guys until I found Tariq. He didn't fit any of the profiles I had in my head. And it wasn't until I put that all aside that I was open to someone like him. Yeah, I'm lucky now. Lucky I didn't prevent myself from being happy. And that's exactly what I see you doing. You're preventing yourself from finding someone who you can be happy with."

"People used to say someone who can make you happy. But that's not what you said." I note to the group.

"People don't make others happy." Reese continues. "It takes two. If you're not receptive to them, nothing they do will enable your happiness. When you look at someone, your test should be whether you could be happy being with this person, sharing a life, but not being a possession." Reese seems glad she got that off her chest.

"How long did you look before you found Tariq?" I respond, wanting to temper her enthusiasm a bit.

"Too long. It was hard work. But any relationship is hard work. It's never all rainbows and roses." And I instantly think about my rose on the way to AppleCore. "So you have to get started today. You see that guy over at the bar? I want you to go to the ladies room. Say hello to him as you pass by. See if he responds when you come back."

I shake my head. "Not going to do that."

"Why not? You protecting your virginity?" Windy again.

"Look. I appreciate you seeing a window of opportunity for me to change things in my life, but from what's going on at work that's going to happen whether I want it to or not."

"What does that mean? Do you have a job or not?" MC asks me.

"At the moment, I don't." I shrug. "I don't."

"You should talk with Beth. You were always upset she didn't come to work for you. Maybe she was upset that you didn't come to work for her. Maybe now's your chance." MC continues.

"Or at least she can tell you whether the rumors of A'zam going to work for them are true." Reese responds.

"What rumors?" I pounce. "Haven't seen anything to that effect."

"They're all over town." Reese responds. "Nothing confirmed. That's why they've not shown up anywhere. But everyone's talking about it. Some real estate person said he's putting his house up for sale."

Windy's checking the time. She has a client coming in and was only going to stay a short time. "So what do you need from us, regarding your decision?"

I hesitate not sure how to respond. "I guess I know what I don't want more than I know what I do want."

"And what don't you want?" MC dives right in.

"To be unemployed forever."

"Meaning if you can't find another job you'll just go back and die." Windy summarizes. "That's not you. You're not a quitter."

"This is only my first day off and already I'm going crazy without something to focus on." I admit.

"Then focus on something. Anything. What have you always wanted to do if you just had time?" Delilah asks.

"You said you always wanted to travel." Reese tells me from what she remembers. "Maybe you could set up an importing business."

"Yeah. An import business and my family will buy wine from you that you source from different wineries around the world." Delilah suggests.

"Get with the plan girl, you aren't going to just sit around waiting." Reese summarizes.

THE GHOST IN THE MACHINE

Chapter Fifty-Five: Six Days

I'm sitting in my kitchen in a top and shorts, researching wineries and the regulations around importing when the phone rings. Mindi is on the line. "Can you come in now?"

"Right now?" I respond, caught off guard. Not sure I want another confrontation with Julia.

"Yes. A'zam asked me to call you. SLT is in a half hour. He wants you there."

"He's back?" I'm about to burst with hope. But then I temper myself. Just because he's back doesn't mean anything has changed.

"This morning. Haven't seen him, but people say he's different."

"Different? In what way?" I'm wondering about Dallas now.

"Gray hair's gone. People say he looks like he took years off. Must have been some holiday."

Hmm. "Need a shower, but I'll be right along."

I'm tearing my clothes off as I sprint towards the shower, a quick lather, rinse and shampoo. I'm drying my hair while also still getting dressed. I'm done in fifteen minutes. New record for me. And I'm out the door smelling the soap and shampoo on my skin and hair. Why do I notice them now when I never did before? Maybe I just appreciate them more. Or maybe it's my sense of smell is so much more acute that I can't avoid it as much as before. I spot my rose on the way, zoom in on it and look at the center, which is where the honeybee pollinates the flower. I think of Raoul pollinating me. But push that thought out of my mind as I finish the short walk to AppleCore.

THE GHOST IN THE MACHINE

Mindi is waiting for me with my badge at the door. "They just got started."

"They know I'm here?" Mindi nods. "Good. Is Oriana in the meeting too?"

"No. A'zam asked me to tell her not to come today."

As I enter the Leadership Conference room, I instantly know where A'zam has been. Same almond eyes, same Mediterranean skin. The gray is gone from his now longer and fuller hair. I wonder if Dr. Woodall did the transition. Was A'zam in line ahead of me? Am I in the body he was supposed to get? That explains why I didn't have a vagina to begin with. It actually explains so much I've pretty much assumed it was true.

"Sage." A'zam greets me. His voice is different, deeper. I wonder if that was a custom tweak to the standard model. I thought they were supposed to replicate you exactly except for the racially identifiable differences they've hybridized. Namely our eyes and skin color.

I nod as I take my seat between Wallace and Alix. I glance at Julia who is clearly not happy to see me. I smile and nod to her. She looks at A'zam as if he were a space alien, which he almost is. I wonder if Julia knows where he was. What happening to him. I wonder if she has any idea how fast he will be able to run circles around her? Or is she the next person in line to cross over? Was that the deal? He goes first. If it's successful then she gets to go? Hard to tell what's going on.

"I'm hearing software is in turmoil. Fix it Sage. Today."

"Yes, sir." I respond without elaborating.

"I'm also hearing we're all out of synch on product launch. Julia since you screwed up marketing what have you done to fix it?"

"It's not…"

But A'zam won't let her respond. "That's what I thought. Nothing." A'zam turns back to me. "Sage! Fix it."

"Can I rehire…"

"Yes. Tell Banerjee I personally asked we rehire him."

Wow. He got up to speed quickly. But then I shouldn't be surprised. I wonder if he got the upgrade chip to start.

"Now I need to know from each of you what we need to do to get back on track." He skips over Julia and starts with Alix. "Supply Chain?"

"If I can get Wallace and Sage in a conference room for a half hour I'll be good."

"Schedule it. Sage you need to get back with your team so we'll skip over you. Wallace?"

"Half hour with Alix and Sage and I should be good too. It's all about coordination at this point." Wallace isn't hiding his contempt for Julia's decision.

"Petra?"

"I'd like to sit in on the production coordination meeting so I know what to say when the analysts start calling with the news you're back." She responds.

A'zam realizes he's holding the rest of us up. "Okay. Get us back on schedule. I want a report by the end of the day on where we are. Sage, you give that to me. Thanks everyone."

"Can I ask a question?" I ask to get everyone to stay put for another minute.

"Sure. What do you want to know?" A'zam is trying to decide what I'm up to.

"Didn't the production planning meeting take place while I was out?" A simple question.

"Oriana didn't have the details we needed, so we cancelled it." Wallace answers. "Not her fault. Just a poorly planned handover. There was nothing she could do."

"My fault." I answer. "I should have called her in when I knew she was taking over."

Julia stops in the doorway realizing I just took her bullet, but not understanding why. She doesn't look around, but walks out.

"Lesson learned." A'zam notes. "Any of you out, even for a couple days, you make sure your replacement is fully up to speed."

We all nod. "How about 3:30 for the coordination meeting?" I suggest. Everyone notes it in their diary.

As I come into the office, Mindi's waiting. "Oriana went back to her old office. Do you need me to get you anything?"

"Access to all the systems. And then I need you to call Landon."

I see Mindi hold her breath. "Landon?"

"Yes. Tell him he's late for work. Julia may have given him a day of vacation, but I'm not the pushover she is. I expect him in working when he's working." I turn to go into my office and then pause. "Oh, and tell him to come by to see me when he gets in. I need to talk to him about the current campaign. And tell him A'zam personally asked for him to get back to work today."

Mindi is beaming as I duck into my office. Now where to begin? I'd actually had a secondary processor working that problem because I had no idea how long it was going to take to get back to work, if I was going to be coming back to work. Now the plan is before me. I dial Oriana's number.

"Come see me when you get a chance. I'm flexible until 3:30." Probably hiding out since her time in my chair was a disaster. Not her fault. Julia just had no idea the situation she was putting her in.

I write a message to the entire software team, now that I have internal mail privileges again.

"Team. I'm back. We're back. No time to waste. You know what I expect. We're now a full day behind. I'm sorry that happened. But I need you all to step up now."

THE GHOST IN THE MACHINE

Chapter Fifty-Six

A'zam is in the software lab when I get there. It's almost midnight. He doesn't need sleep any more either. "A'zam." I acknowledge him. He nods back to me and continues the discussion with the lab supervisor. "I don't understand why it takes you so long to validate the software. Do you need to automate some of the tests?"

Oriana begins to answer the question for the supervisor, but A'zam cuts her off. Oriana looks at Jermaine standing on the other side of A'zam, but Jermaine just shrugs.

The supervisor, a young woman by the name of Patrice also shrugs, but in response to A'zam's question. "I can't say, Mister A'zam. I'm given the tools and testing protocols. I just run the tests and provide the results to Engineering."

"So no one asks you how you can do your work faster or better?" A'zam responds.

"Oh sure. They come through with their teams. They take some of my testers off line. I've got to figure out how to make up for them not working for a day or two. But it's when they got follow on stuff to go do that it kicks my ass. I can plan for the day or two. But when it turns into a week, I can't recover. So if you'd just stop improving me, I'd get my work done and you all'd be happy again."

I shudder as I listen to the discussion. Oriana is red faced. Jermaine looks around uncomfortably. Patrice and I had a discussion along these lines over a year ago. I challenged her then to find a way of recovering schedule. Apparently she didn't want to find a way.

A'zam looks at me. "You got this?"

I nod. "What have you learned since you returned?" I ask.

"Our efforts to move everyone forward are lagging badly. We have more people who are 'can't get there' than 'sure, that's easy.'"

"Nothing we do is easy." I respond.

"Granted. But that's no excuse. We spend a lot of money getting the best and brightest. So who are all these other people?"

"If I can be blunt, you're only beginning to see what I've been seeing for the last several weeks. I've pushed the envelope beyond the comfort zone of even our best and brightest. That's why we're struggling. But it has nothing to do with the ability of our people. It has everything to do with the fact that you and I are seeing new ways to advance the state of the art. And I've been merciless in pushing that agenda. It's taken me a while to learn how to slow down. Something you'll come to value more than you do now. But I have to get everyone on board, even though that's hard. I can see the end goal. They can't. Does any of this make sense?"

A'zam smiles at me. "What took you so long?"

"Sir?" I'm not quite sure what he's saying.

"To figure out what your real role is."

I don't like the implication that I've not had it right even though I've been in this job for years. "You saying you think I've been screwing up all this time?"

"Not at all. You've delivered some remarkable products. But until now I've never heard a clear statement of what you're trying to accomplish other than turn product. Anyone can do that. I don't need you to create software for us. I need you to lead us into the future. And for the first time it sounds to me like you've turned the corner on knowing what that means."

"If I've been screwing up, where have you been all this time?"

"Waiting for you to figure it out for yourself." I don't like his tone, but I understand.

"That the most efficient way to do it?"

"That's not the question. What would it take for you to learn how to lead? For me to tell you? No. I know what works for me. Becoming a leader is something you have to discover for yourself. And it's unique to everyone. What makes you a good leader is your ability to inspire, to catch the imagination of your teams. To push them beyond what it takes for them to deliver excellent products that no one else can. You're out talking to your teammates. I've not seen you do that since you became the SVP. I'm sorry you had to go through what you did to get to this point. But I'm glad you did."

"Wait, wait, wait. Why didn't you tell me any of this in my reviews? I mean I could probably have saved a whole lot of time if I'd known what you just told me."

"Wouldn't have made any difference. You weren't ready. You thought you were doing a good job. In reality you were doing an adequate job. But just barely. You didn't know what it takes to be a real leader. You did what you thought was important. You mentored people so they could use the tools and organize the work of their teams. But you didn't demonstrate how to inspire the teams to produce more than they think they can. I know people are capable of doing much more. And it's only when they're properly challenged that they finally decide to step up."

"We're doing that now." I note.

"Yes you are. But only because you discovered you're capable of doing much more than you ever expected you could. Doesn't make any difference that you're now an immortal. What matters is that whether biologic or robotic beings, we have to decide to push our capability frontiers. I'll make you a bet. You can do all these things you never could before. You've had several weeks now to figure out how to exploit your new abilities. But have you pushed those capabilities to the limit?"

How is he seeing so much more than I am? But then I realize, he isn't. He doesn't have the technical expertise to make those judgments. So why is he saying this to me? And then it's evident. He's trying to challenge me to be more than I am. That's what a leader does. He's modeling the behavior I should be exhibiting. He's not mad at me. In fact, he's probably amazed, if I can use that term, at what the team has produced. But he's pushing me to do more, just as I'm challenging the team to do more. The difference is he's dealing with another immortal who works at his new speed. I'm still dealing with biologic humans who need time to absorb what we do in a few moments. "Got it." I respond.

Oriana turns to Jermaine, "Do you have any idea what they just said?"

Jermaine shakes his head. "They were jabbering so fast I have no idea what they were talking about."

A'zam and I both turn to them realizing we've been talking at multiples of normal speech speed, but it just seemed like a normal conversation to us.

Chapter Fifty-Seven

I wasn't expecting the call from Beth. I'm sitting in my office reviewing the progress of each team member. It's clear there's an immediate effect on those I talk with individually. Their productivity is way up over those I haven't spoken to. I need to redouble my effort to get out and talk with everyone.

"Hi Beth. How are you?" I respond, seeing her name on the caller ID.

"Good. We're ahead of plan and working some fascinating technologies. Far bleeding edge stuff."

"That's what you're better at than anyone. I confirm." And then I remember our last conversation. "And that discussion we had. It really has helped. Thanks."

"Good to hear. You going to the Masquerade Ball?" I just had this discussion, but that was with Julia. Not an auspicious start.

"No. I rarely go. You need someone to go with who's a good sport and willing to take a lot of abuse." I decide to push it back to her.

"Actually I'm going this year. Like you I usually don't. But the company is looking for a few good people to take us to the next level. So I have a few 'discussions' with folks set up for the ball this year."

"Your husband's not going?" Beth's husband is a patent attorney. Not much imagination. I suspect the same is the case in bed. But Beth more than makes up for it, I'm sure.

"Not this year. He's working that big Korean infringement case. It's just consuming him. Don't think we've gone to a single social engagement since July."

"Too bad. Those cases go on for years sometimes." I note.

She changes direction. "Heard there was a dust up over there. Someone said you were in the eye of the hurricane." Interesting way of putting it.

"We're past that now. A'zam's back." Down play whatever she's heard.

"It's no secret, we're looking for a Chief Operating Officer."

"You'd be perfect." I respond without thinking.

"I'm not a candidate. The Board want's someone to infuse new blood. Since I've been here as long as you've been at AppleCore, I'm pretty much seen as the enemy." Surprising, but I was getting to the same place before…

"It's hard to be a prophet in your own country."

"That's the case here. For sure. But I didn't call to commiserate on my situation. We've had a candidate from AppleCore apply for the job. Someone you work with closely."

"Julia?" I'm not sure why I phrased my response as a question.

"Yes. Although you've never said a word about her. I take that to speak volumes, by the way. I've heard other things on the street that make me cautious. Should I be?"

"Julia is an intelligent and thoughtful finance professional." I stop where I can be positive.

"Except she's your sitting COO." Beth waits for me to respond, but I don't. "Not a ringing endorsement."

"Rocky always told me to convey the meaning in as few words as possible so there will be no misunderstanding."

"Is she the reason you got off track?"

"I can't comment on internal affairs of the company."

Beth seems to be making notes as I hear the click, click, click of her device. "Thanks for that. I have another question for you. What would it take to get you to come over to Symbol Ventures?"

"As COO?" I ask to make sure I understand what she's asking.

"Yes." Yup, she's going where I thought she was.

"I'm not sure you're ready for me." I try to push it away without sounding negative about the idea. I know there aren't all that many who get this chance to change companies at this level.

"But if we were. What would it take?"

Evidently when they heard I was removed. They waited to see if A'zam would reinstate me. Boy. The word sure gets around fast. "I haven't given that question any thought. You'll have to let me think about it."

"And do some research. You'll be impressed by what you'll find out. We lead the industry in every segment AppleCore doesn't. We have an aggressive plan to displace you in several. We should catch you in sales within the next five year plan."

"I think if you ask anyone at AppleCore they would tell you Symbol Ventures is our biggest competitor. You don't have to sell me there. But why go to number two when I've just turned up the heat in the whole industry?"

"That's exactly why to go to number two. A chance to even the playing field. To help number two become number one. To substantially change how mankind uses technology." Good argument.

"…But I can do that where I am." Still not good enough to make a change.

"Think about it. COO. In line to be a CEO wherever you might want to go in five years. And I've been authorized to tell you we will double your salary and give you complete freedom on all product development, hardware, software, firmware and even vaporware if you want it."

"Vaporware?" I've not heard that term before.

"Thought that might get your attention. I can't tell you anything about it over the phone. But if you come in for a chat we can discuss it with a confidentiality agreement in place."

"Beth, I'm really flattered. And you know I waited for you to apply at AppleCore once I got here. I've wanted to work with you in forever. But there's never a good time to make a change. We're both on a treadmill of sorts. When it's a good time to move, no one wants you. When it's not, everyone wants you. My dedication to my teams is why you want me. But if I was the kind of person who would leave them for a job that would only be better for me, then I'm not the person you want. That's why you need to make the Board understand you're the best candidate. You want me to talk to them for you? Send them my way."

Beth assesses the truth to my observation. She knows I'm right. Knows she's the right person for their job. Although it seems her Board doesn't understand the fundamental truth to leadership. "I had to try. Thank you for listening and telling me exactly what I needed to hear. I've been doubting myself ever since I was informed the Board didn't want me in the job. At first I thought it was just an excuse. But I was able to confirm it did come from the Board. I may ask one member to call you. I'll send you details if I decide to go that way. You're a special friend."

"So are you Beth. I wouldn't have listened to anyone else."

Chapter Fifty-Eight

I'm surprised when Rocky wanders into my office. He looks around, as if impressed. But he shouldn't be. He's been here more than once. I haven't done a thing to it other than turn my desk to the wall. "What are you up to, child?"

Rocky always makes me feel like I'm ten years old when he refers to me as 'child.' "Just trying to keep the company alive long enough to pay your pension like always." That's a joke between us. When I first got the top software job, Rocky came to my office and asked me to be sure to keep the company alive long enough to pay his pension. That was ten years ago. He's still collecting a paycheck and not a pension. I look into his eyes. They aren't as bright as the last time I saw him. Cataracts maybe? Or maybe he's just getting tired. More lines in the face too. I think the loss of Anna Laura added twenty years. After the accident he always seemed to be tired. But then again, maybe that was because he was only sleeping about four hours a night. Even his hair seems thinner than before. Why am I noticing all the effects of aging on him? Maybe because I have to make a decision about whether to suffer that fate or not. "How are you feeling?" I ask.

Rocky sits down in a conference table chair. He sits slowly as if trying to avoid aches and pains. Rocky has been working at a stand-up desk for most of his life because he always had a tender back. That's why I'm surprised to see him sitting. "Fine, fine. Can't kill an old bird like me." He sits perfectly still for a long moment, looking at me. "What happened?" Rocky's upset.

"What do you mean?"

"Your eyes. You have your mother's eyes. But you don't. Not anymore. What happened?"

I get up and close the door. I return to sit next to him at the table. "I had surgery. A couple weeks ago."

"I heard. People say you're not the same. They say you're working all night and all day. They say all of a sudden you've been able to solve problems we've been working on for decades. And you're doing it overnight. People are afraid you're going to burn yourself out."

I reach over and put my hand on his. "You don't have to worry about me. I'm not going to burn out. I probably should have told you before the surgery. But I wasn't sure it was going to work. Anyway, I'm fine. Really fine."

"What was this surgery you had? Female problems? Cancer? What was it?"

I think for a long moment, trying figure out how to tell him in a way he'll understand. "Rocky, you know those angstrom unit circuits you've been working on?"

Rocky nods wondering why I'm going there.

"I have a whole bunch of them in me."

Rocky's eyes flutter. He tries to understand why I'd have his circuits in me. "Why?"

"You said I don't have mom's eyes anymore."

Rocky's trying to tie the two statements together. They don't come together in his mind. "I don't understand."

"Do you remember Ray Kurzweil's book on the Singularity?"

Rocky straightens up. "You replaced your eyes?" He's not sure about whether that would be a good thing or not.

"I replaced everything except my consciousness." I let that sit a moment. "This is a completely robotic body. Right down to the angstrom unit circuits in my processors that you designed."

Rocky looks more closely than before. "How would anyone know?"

"That's the idea. They don't want anyone to know the difference. But I am different. And…" I hesitate. "I'll live forever."

"Why isn't this all over the media?" Rocky still isn't sure he believes what I'm saying.

"Because I made them sign a confidentiality statement. They can't put anything out until I make the final decision."

"Final decision? What final decision? You've already become the robot." Rocky shakes his head.

"I'm not a robot, Rocky. I'm still me, only I have a robotic body. They transferred my consciousness and all my memories. So I'm exactly the same person I've always been. Only I have certain limitations and abilities I didn't have before."

"But you'll live forever." He confirms apparently wanting to be sure.

"Yes. Unless I choose to go back. Which I have to decide about soon."

"Why would you go back if you're the first? If you're going to live forever? You have to go on. You have to carry on for your mother and for Tabitha."

"And for you, Rocky?" Is this what he's thinking? I have to carry on for him? This always happens when the two of us get together. Rocky says something obtuse that just completely ticks me off. And he just did it again.

"I never had a son to carry on our family name. You're it. And you don't seem to have any interest in having children."

There is a silence as Rocky considers what to say next. "So this is our chance. Our line can go on. You're already the first. That means you're like Eve in the Garden of Eden. Don't you see it?"

I have to admit his line of thinking had never occurred to me. Eve? Me? Or I can go back and let A'zam have that honor. The first immortal who stayed immortal.

"Rocky. You got me doing it again. I'm focusing on stuff that doesn't matter. Who cares if our line dies out with me? Nobody. If we're gone, we're gone. Your patents and papers will persist. You'll be the member of the family that's remembered. That should be all you care about."

Rocky looks at me sadly. "I've been a disaster as a father. I know that. Every time I see what you've become I marvel at how resilient you are. I thank god you have your mother's genes and spirit. I'm past the point of anyone caring about me or what I've done with my life. And that includes you. Angstrom unit circuits. Big deal. When the next researcher reduces them to sub-angstrom units then I'll be as forgotten as the guy who had the mile record before the current guy. Yesterday's hero is no hero. But you have the chance to always be a hero. Someone's hero. Because you won't die."

I never expected this kind of lecture from Rocky. He's a deep thinker. I've always known that. But this is all coming in a conversation where he hasn't had a chance to research or really think about it. I guess I underestimate him. "I'll think about what you said. But Rocky. It's important you not tell anyone about me."

"Why?" Rocky isn't happy about this condition. I'm not sure why.

"Because I haven't decided. I don't want any publicity. I don't want any pressure from anyone as to how I'm going to make my decision. It's got to be my decision. For the right reasons. It's got to be because it's right for me and me alone."

"That's only because you don't have anyone other than me. I've never counted in your life." He's doing it again. I'm not going to feel sorry for him. "But you need someone in your life. Someone who will make all the sacrifices you make worth it. And right now you don't have that person. That makes your decision selfish. I hope you understand there will be someone in your life at some point who will make you as proud as you make me."

THE GHOST IN THE MACHINE

Chapter Fifty-Nine

Oriana sits with me in my office. The Japanese garden beyond frames her as we discuss the progress the team is making. It's a peaceful backdrop for her. It's also in contradistinction to the tension she exhibits.

"I still don't know why you promoted me when I made such a mess of things while you were out."

"You didn't have a chance to do anything while I was out." I smile at her and nod. "Now can we get past this and deal with what we can affect today?"

"One other thing." I guess the answer is no, we can't get past this, at least not yet.

"What?'

"What happened to A'zam? He apparently went wherever you went. He has the same eyes you do. And that exchange between you in the lab? What was that?"

I guess I need to start telling important people in addition to Rocky. "Have you ever read the Singularity?"

She thinks for only a moment before recalling. "Kurzweil's book."

I nod. "I'm the first."

Oriana looks at me more closely, apparently trying to recall what she can of Kurzweil's book. "That's why your eyes don't blink. It's been driving me crazy watching you." She stops and thinks another moment. "What's it like? It must be different."

"It is. As you point out there are things I don't have to do anymore. But there are also things I miss and things I can't do and things that are just different and probably will never be the same."

"What about processing? Everyone said it wasn't possible. But whatever you have must be much faster than the brain. That's why you and A'zam…"

"Yes. He's the second to transition, at least as far as I know."

"Why you?" Oriana apparently realizes how her question sounds and she backtracks. "I don't mean to be disrespectful, but of all the people in the world, why were you chosen?"

"I wasn't chosen. I volunteered. I was dying. Not quickly, it wouldn't have happened overnight. But I was getting to the point I was going to have to resign."

Oriana nods once. "It was the talk of the whole team. Everyone wanted to know what was wrong with you."

"And when I came back I took the fun out of being here."

"Yeah. Everyone's unhappy about it. We're getting so much done. We're pushing the envelope. Everyone's excited, but exhausted. Now you seem to remember things you'd forgotten. At least that's how we interpreted it. And now we find out you're the first. Holy shit."

"There's just one thing. You can't tell anyone what I just told you."

Oriana wrinkles her nose. She clearly doesn't like that restriction. "Why? You should be proud to be the first. It'll energize the teams if they know what's going on."

"And the whole world. When the word gets out I won't be able to do anything except answer questions about what it's like to be a robot. I'm feeling a lot more like a ghost in the machine. And for the first two weeks I couldn't feel anything. The software wasn't ready when they transitioned me. So please, don't say anything."

"You're waiting for more of you. So you won't be the only one."

"Do you think you can sit on this for me? I would really appreciate it."

Mindi buzzes me. That means I have an important call. Oriana starts to get up. "It's Dr. Woodall." Mindi informs me on the intercom.

I motion to Oriana to stay and push the button. "Good morning doctor. Haven't heard from you in a while."

"I've been in Dallas."

"I know. A'zam looks better than ever." He doesn't respond. "What can I do for you?"

"I need you to come in. Today if possible. I'm afraid I got busy and you're overdue."

"For what?"

"We'll discuss that when you come in."

"And I want to discuss everything before you do anything this time. No more surprises."

THE GHOST IN THE MACHINE

Chapter Sixty

I'm sitting in the same examining room. I've decided it's the only one for immortals. That would make sense if there's only two of us. But I don't know that for sure. Dr. Woodall's resident, Dr. Grayson comes in first. "How are you feeling?"

"You know that's probably not a relevant question to be asking. Have I noticed any malfunctions, might be better." I kid him.

Dr. Grayson puzzles on my response, "You may be right. I'll have to remember that. You know you go through med school and they teach you bedside manners. The first question is always: how are you feeling? But you're right. Doesn't apply in your case." The machines scan my body and interrogate my computers. After only a minute or so, the printer spits out the readings for Dr. Woodall.

"Excuse me. The doctor will be right in." He takes the readings with him so I don't get a chance to see how I'm functioning. Is everything working within normal ranges? Am I using 100% of my processing capacity? How much of my internal memory am I using? Are the controllers working within normal limits? Very different data than what a doctor normally looks at.

Dr. Woodall comes in carrying the papers. Dr. Grayson follows right behind. "Sage. Thanks for coming on such short notice. The good news is your readings indicate everything is fine. Nothing to be worried about. If there were, we'd just swap out the relevant subsystem and send you on your way."

"So you have a spare of every part of me here?" I'm surprised.

"Only those most subject to failure. But we can get any part we need from the manufacturer here in town."

"Good to know. So what do you have in store for me today that was so important?"

"Several things. Mostly software. Can be all software if you prefer. And then we need to talk about next week."

"Next week?" I'm not following his comment.

"Your thirty days are up on Monday. If you're going to transition back to your biologic body it has to happen then. That's your last chance. I've already scheduled the hospital to perform the operation. That ensures you have that option, right up to the last possible moment."

"So. I go back I'm confronted with chronic deterioration of my memory and bodily functions. I can expect to live five years or so."

"No assurances on the five years. That's just a guess as you know."

"What happens to my body if I chose not to go back?" I hadn't asked this before.

"It's a fully functioning unconscious body. It's just like a person in a coma. Under the laws of California it's a living person who can never regain consciousness. So you have the right to have us disconnect the body from life support. It will die in a matter of days. Again, since it's unconscious it won't feel a thing. Once the body has expired, it will be made available for medical research and then cremated according to your wishes."

"So I signed papers to that effect before the transition? I don't remember that."

"It was amongst all the papers you signed that day. I answered your question about cremation, but that was all that came up."

"That was a very stressful day." I note, more to myself than the doctors. "So I only have a few days to decide." I'm confirming what I think he wants me to know.

"Yes. And to take away any pressure, the operating room is scheduled, your body will be available and you can elect to back out right up to the scheduled time for the procedure."

"What are the risks? Since you've never transitioned anyone back before." I suddenly realize I have no idea if I'll be a vegetable immediately or be in the same state I was when I transitioned the first time.

"You're right. We don't really know. What we believe to be the risks are that somehow we're unsuccessful with the transition. Your consciousness could be lost. In that case you would cease to exist, as far as we know. That's the worst scenario. We don't expect it, but it's possible.

"We think most likely you will transition back, wake up in your old body and be able to resume your normal activity within a day. Your body has been on life support all this time. That's why we think it might take you a day to get back to normal. Get weight on the muscles again. Thirty days of inactivity will leave the body weak, so you'll have to take it easy for a while.

"A third possibility is you will have impaired functioning. Parts of your body could shut down as a result of the life support period. This could accelerate the deterioration you experience. You could be emotionally impaired, unable to experience feelings you used to have. It could even hasten your passing. We can't properly assess the probability here, because it will be unique for everyone who transitions and comes back."

"Two out of three don't sound particularly hopeful. The best result is just going back to what drove me here in the first place." I summarize.

"True. But those things you can't do as an immortal, you could do again as a biologic entity."

"Like what?" I'm not sure I'm following his logic since it all sounds gloomy to me.

"Like have a child. Even if you only live five years, you could bear a child that would live on after you. That child might make a substantial impact on the world, just as you have."

"I'm not even in a relationship." I shake my head. "Not likely anyone would want to have a child with me."

"You might be surprised who would step up. When your story gets out, you'll be famous. The first person to transition. The first person to transition back. The world will want to know about you. And if you transition back you'll be amazed at who will want to be a part of your life."

There's that word again. Amazed. Guess I better prepare to be amazed. The doctor thinks I will be either way. A child. That's what Rocky wanted for me. Was he only encouraging me to remain immortal because it's the next best thing to having a child? I'll have to think about this. "You know I never wanted fame. I didn't do this for any reason other than to be able to work."

"You told me that."

"But you've given me some important things to think about. And thank you for setting it up so I have that option right up to the end. I appreciate that. Now what else you planning to do to me today?"

"Your sexual upgrades. We've reviewed the software you submitted. We find it acceptable. So we will upgrade that today and hope you have the opportunity to test it out. We're also adding additional memory, the data shows you're using the maximum capacity at times, so we're expanding that. We're going to add another math co-processor and another main processor. Those will double your speed and processing power. You keep pushing the limits of what we gave you last time, so we're going to challenge you to double again. We also have a retrofit that will allow you to drink a small amount of liquid and hold it until you can discharge it. It's not a lot of liquid. About the equivalent of a glass of wine or glass of beer. If you choose water, that will be diverted to your gland tanks for use in providing moisture to your mouth. Small tweaks but getting you closer to what you remember."

"You said it could be just the software if I choose. What other software do you have to install besides mine?" He hasn't given me everything. I'm still suspicious he sees me as a test bed and not much more.

"Software upgrades include advanced filtering capability. So in essence you think of a question, the advanced filtering will search all relevant sources and present you with the highest probability answer. If the question is somewhat nebulous, it will give you the pros and cons of the top three answers. It also has math accelerators so you'll be able to compute much faster. You'll be able to do higher order math in your head. Beyond that we have software that better simulates the responses to emotions, improves your touch density, I think we're getting closer to the biological density."

"Okay. Let's do it all. I'm curious about how the additional computing power will lead me to insights I'm not having."

Dr. Woodall gently pushes me down on the table. In a moment my sensors go blank. I'm riding that state of consciousness where I'm floating with no inputs. No sight, no sound, no time.

When I come back up vision is the first. I see the doctors looking at me. Curious I think. Wondering if I'll act any differently. Then sound. I hear the hum of the computers in the wall machines, the different frequency hum of the lights and the rushing air of the HVAC system. I also hear the breathing of both doctors. I sit up smiling that I have a new set of abilities to test out.

THE GHOST IN THE MACHINE

Chapter Sixty-One

I leave Dr. Woodall's office to go home. I need to recharge and shower. Even though I don't need to shower because of body odor, I just want to feel clean, to redo my hair and change into something that smells fresher. With my smell capabilities enhanced I've become much more aware of how I smell. I don't have the same smell I used to have. A lot like having a head cold. Maybe I'm overly conscious of that. So I try to keep the soapy and shampoo smells fresh. I use more cologne. I don't know if anyone else has noticed, but I feel better about myself as a result.

I decide to recharge first, dropping my clothes and climbing into the recharge bed. Dr. Woodall told me that the bed had been refurbished to include moisture and lubricant infusion or drainage during the recharge. When I lay down on the bed, tubes connect to the tanks in my lower back and neck to refill. They have automatic sensors that determine the amount of fluids in each and top them off or drain. Both top up to replace what was used in my kissing and sleeping with Raoul.

I feel the coils in my back engage with the charger. It's a pleasant feeling, almost like one of those massage chairs found in certain novelty stores. It doesn't relax me as I still don't feel physical tension not having muscles that get tight with emotions. It doesn't soothe either. It just has a pleasant feeling that I'm coming to enjoy.

And the first sensory memory hits me. Where am I? I'm in a restaurant with Rocky, Anna Laura and Tabitha. What am I? About nine I think. I smell the steaks cooking. Melted butter for the corn on the cob. The plate is placed before me. The smell of the gravy on the mashed potatoes fills me with anticipation. But we have to wait until everyone has their meal. Tabitha's hasn't come yet. She only wants a hamburger. I never understood why she doesn't like steak. A hamburger is the same thing, only in a different form. But she wouldn't eat steak so Rocky gave up ordering one for her. He let her order what she wanted. Rocky was always easier on Tabitha than he was on me. Anything I did he didn't like would have a swift and harsh punishment. Maybe he thought he had to be hard on me since I was his first. As a parent he still had his training wheels on when I was born. But by the time Tabitha came along he had the hang of it. He was more relaxed with her.

The steak was fatty. Rocky could only afford to go to places where they served the inexpensive cuts of meat. That meant they were very fatty. The cooked fat gave the steak more flavor. But I didn't like the taste or thought of eating fat, so I always cut it away. That didn't leave much to eat. I wasn't going to eat that fat. Rocky wasn't going to make me. Anna Laura agreed with me because she did the same thing. Rocky ate some of the fat, but would cut away the rest. I would remind him of that.

I liked to eat the corn on the cob. At least until Anna Laura took me to an allergist who pronounced me allergic to corn. Anna Laura told the doctor that she'd never heard of anyone with a corn allergy. Lots of people are allergic to it and just don't realize it. The sensitivity becomes more apparent if they look for it. So Anna Laura would cook corn for everyone else and give me peas. At first she always cooked them too much. I asked her if I could cook them for less time. Then I got so I really like peas.

The mashed potatoes and gravy I liked before the accident. But afterwards I lost interest in them and weight because I wasn't eating them. We didn't sit around the table and eat like we did when we had a family. Rocky would take his food into his lab in the garage. I'd eat mine as I did my homework. We didn't talk much because Rocky buried himself in his work. I only had my school work. So that's what we did most nights.

Another jolt. I'm riding in the car with Anna Laura on my way to ballet class. I feel the sun on my face through the window. The trees in our old neighborhood pass by. The drought made the trees look brown. I'd see pictures of the same trees in other parts of the country where the drought hadn't had such an impact. It was the same with the lawns. I'd seen pictures of green lawns. People used lawnmowers to cut the grass because it would look shaggy if they didn't. But in our neighborhood we couldn't water the grass because of the drought. We were lucky to have enough water to shower and wash clothes and dishes and cook with. That was about it.

The air was dry. On hot days the air would burn the inside of my nose. And I'd sweat a lot. I used to get embarrassed at how much I sweat. I knew I didn't smell particularly good. There would be big wet spots under my arms. Sometimes on my back and around my neck. Savannah never sweat. She was in my class. A blue-eyed blonde with a rich father and the best clothes ever. Her mother would take her down to LA to buy clothes on Melrose Avenue. We'd seen the clothes on television shows. Everyone was jealous of Savannah. That was exactly the way she wanted it. But the fact that she couldn't sweat was a problem for her. She couldn't stay outside for very long because she couldn't deal with the heat. So she was excused from physical education classes. She never had to go out for recess. A big black air conditioned Tahoe SUV brought her to and picked her up from school. She was like a princess or something. All the boys loved her.

Another jolt. I'm walking home from school with Teddy. I must have been sixteen with hormones screaming in my ears. Teddy was in my class. He'd transferred in from New York at the beginning of that school year. His father came out to work at AppleCore. He was an executive or something. Teddy never said exactly what his father did. The only thing he ever said was his father didn't know or work with Rocky. I was surprised that someone who worked at AppleCore didn't know Rocky. I thought he knew everyone there.

Teddy lived a block over from our house. It was a nicer section than where we lived. His house was newer and bigger. And the rumor was it cost like a million dollars or something. That was a lot more than our house. On his first day at school, I was walking in as usual. He was at the corner where our streets intersected. I introduced myself. He did the same. Probably the only reason we became friends was because I got to meet him before anyone else in our class. We always found a reason to walk home together.

Teddy always looked at me in a special way, like he appreciated me. But he never touched me. Except that one time I nearly fell when I wasn't watching and stepped into a hole. He dropped his books and grabbed me to hold me up. It was as if all my senses opened up to him at once. A flower recognizing the sun for the first time. I have no idea how he felt, other than his face reddened slightly, like he was embarrassed. But he held on to me longer than he needed to. I thought about that touch often afterwards. It was like forbidden candy. I knew it would be a problem if Teddy and I ever did it. He probably would never walk home with me again. And as much as I wanted to do it with him, I was scared of losing the time with him every day. Savannah, who was still in my class liked Teddy. He was the new kid. She wanted him for her own.

Another jolt. I'm sitting in the dark in my house. This was probably only a month ago. Is that all it was? I'm sipping a glass of red wine. Trying to remember how we built a particular module to our geo-locator code. It's like sitting in an aquarium. I can see the fish on the other side of the glass. But I can't touch them. I can't talk with them. They see me and I see them. It's as if we are in separate worlds that we will never traverse.

Why can't I remember something so simple? The worst thing is I know I could a few months ago without a problem. It would have been right there as soon as I thought about it. That's the way my mind has always worked. But now... have I made the right choice? Do I really have a choice? This is only going to get worse. I can't live this way. I can't go on failing myself, and my teams and the company. I can't do that. The transition is the only hope I have of ever getting back to my old self. Dr. Woodall tells me not to have any expectations about what that new self is really going to be like. Nobody's been there. It's got to be better than sitting here in the dark, drinking red wine and trying to remember something so simple.

Then I have a glimmer of what I'm looking for. It's there in my mind. I know it's there, but I can't get to it. What did the doctor say? I have plaque on my brain cells that interfere with the transfer of electrical impulses. Plaque. Why can't I go to the dentist and have it removed? But the doctor says that's not the way it works. I've got to be patient. There's a lot of research going on now. Some of it looks promising. In five or ten years there may be a treatment that can slow or reverse the process. Five or ten years. That's the problem. I probably won't live long enough. Another disease somehow invaded my body. So I have no choice. I have to transition. If I want to keep my job, if I want to solve problems, if I want to deliver solutions and if I want to go on with life.

The buzzer goes off and my time is over in the charging bed. I'm unsettled by the memories, particularly the last one I've put out of my mind.

THE GHOST IN THE MACHINE

Chapter Sixty-Two: Five Days

I feel recharged. I'm refreshed from the shower. A new dress that's been in my closet forever. I would never wear it to work. I thought I needed to be less feminine. In fact, it's been in my closet so long it's probably already out of fashion. But I don't care. I'm trying to make a statement with my appearance. I think I look good so that's all there is to that. Besides, no one at work ever compliments me on my appearance. I'm trying to see if I can get someone to do so.

I walk into work. There's the Alissar rose. Next to it is a Rosa Ingrid Bergman. It has very large, moderately fragrant flowers up to 3.9 inches in diameter. Their color is a warm, velvety, dark red, described as currant to cardinal red. The well-formed flowers have a full, high-centered form and 26 to 40 petals. They appear solitary or in clusters on long stems from June to September. The blooms are long lasting on the plant and as cut flowers.

The shrubs are upright. They reach a height of 24 to 39 inches, and a width of 24 to 26 inches. The medium-sized dark green foliage is semi-glossy and normally healthy. The cultivar is heat and rain tolerant. Winter hardy down to -30°C. Disease resistant. It sounds like a very hardy, very pretty rose. Different in appearance to the Alissar rose next to it.

So now I have two roses that I'll look for when I come home tonight. Maybe I'll start looking for others to think about as I make my daily trek in both directions. Something more to test out my new capabilities. But it's time to start thinking about work. What do I want to get done today? I want to set aside time to review the design approach and architecture in light of my increased computational capability. I should really be a math wizard now. But that's not the focus for today. It's more about architecture, and tools.

I'm at the door and into the building. The guard looks up and smiles at me. He never smiles when I come in. Maybe he notices the dress. Maybe this will be a good day yet. Even if it is the evening and not the start of a new day. I take the stairs, preferring to walk rather than ride, even though I'm no longer concerned about exercise. Even a robotic system needs to be used, often and harshly to ensure it maintains the full range of flexibility and adaptability.

As I come into the office, Mindi has gone home for the day. Not unexpected since she said something about Landon was coming over for dinner. She said he was going to come back into work afterwards. That doesn't sound good for Mindi's love life. But who knows? Maybe he'll stay long enough that they can enjoy each other.

Chapter Sixty-Three

Desirae works late, I wonder if she's still here? My mind tells me she's still on line. I wander down the hall to her office. I see her with her back to the door. I knock.

"Sage. Come on in. I was going to come see you before I go home tonight. So this saves me the long trip down the hall." She smiles at me. I always liked Desirae. She's never phony. She tells you what she can and what she can't. She answers questions immediately without having to screen what she's going to say before she says it. I like that. She's real. Seems interested in what she can do to help whoever she's with.

"Did you see Samantha took a job with Symbol Ventures?" I ask as I sit down across from her.

"It just came through. In our systems I don't see terminations or resignations until the person's last day. Someday I'm going to get that changed, but it's just not high on the IT priority list."

"I think there will be more. Sounds like Symbol Ventures is putting on a full court press."

"So we need flexibility to match offers." Desirae goes immediately to where I want her to go.

"I think so. We also need to step up employee communications. We've got to let people know how important their work is here. Appeal to their sense of loyalty and importance. Anything we can do to make people feel wanted and appreciated. Does that make sense?" I need to make sure Desirae sees the situation as I do.

"Yes. And you're not the only one who's been asking us to look at that."

"Good to know. We're pushing people hard. I don't want to lose the good people in particular. Anyone who goes over will make a dent in the lead we've established. Particularly if they take tools or architecture with them."

"How do we stop that?" Desirae is asking a good question.

"I don't know. If someone really wants to, there are a dozen ways, if not more." I'm recognizing our success has forced the competition to take desperate measures. They need to either slow us down, by hiring our talent, or reduce the gap, by using the same methods and tools. And they can get both by hiring the right people.

"So it all comes back to me. What HR can do to slow or prevent an exodus of good people?" Desirae is right there again. This is why I like her.

"One thing I've been thinking is the need to hire more people. We can afford to with the huge productivity jump we've achieved. But it's always an issue of diluting the efforts of the folks who are cranking away. We bring in more people and our productivity drops until they get up to speed. But I've been mulling that problem. I'd like to propose setting up a pirate organization. One that's completely separate from the main team. They don't affect anything we're doing because no one from the mother ship comes over. The model for it is the new grad team and the work their doing."

"Let's take a look at it and talk more."

"I figure two heads are always better than one. You see things I don't. I'm just a software geek. The people part, well, that's all you."

Desirae shakes her head. "Been hearing about your little visits with your teams. One-on-one, even though you and they don't have the time for it. You're making the investment in relationships. I see it having a high payback. Looking at the productivity reports. I can pick out who you talked to on what day and by the amount of improvement I can even tell if you saw them in the morning or the afternoon."

"Didn't know anyone was paying attention to that." I respond surprised.

"That's my job. I have to know what our team members are thinking, feeling and what they're likely to do every time we change something. What we're talking about is nothing new. We've been dealing with these same issues since the first year. We had a pirate team a long time ago, as I'm sure you know. It worked out then. I expect it will probably work out again. But as you point out, for very different reasons."

"But it's not enough." I know we've got to do more.

"I agree with you. Everyone on your team has been struggling to keep up with the changes and expectations, which you arbitrarily amped up the day you got back. You need to prepare people when you want them to change what they're doing. You didn't do that at all. You seem to have realized what you're doing. But I think your teams need a breather from more change. You think you can do that?"

"No. I can't. In the next week we're going to introduce a whole new set of automation tools. More than three-quarters of what they're doing today will be automated. So they'll be spending that time doing the more creative part of coding. They'll be focused on how to link feature sets in new and exciting ways. We're going to completely change the game and everything they know. And that's just next week."

Desirae's shoulders drop. This is not the news she wants to hear from me. "Do you have any idea how hard you're making my job? You'll have people doing almost completely different jobs, using different tools and following what is it? The third major architecture change? All within a month? Give the people a break. This isn't reasonable."

"It may not be reasonable, but it's necessary." I'm not going to back away from what we have to do. If I decide to go back, this will be my last chance to advance the state of the art.

"You're sounding more like A'zam." She then realizes how that sounds. "Oh, I didn't mean that in a bad way. I mean neither of you are content. Neither of you are willing to play it safe when it comes to our people. You want to challenge every person here every day. If anyone's not stepping up, then move them or let them go. I'm just not used to that approach." Desirae sounds tired.

I hear her. "Let's go back to the idea of a new team. How long until we could get them on board?"

Desirae doesn't miss a beat. "They start a week from tomorrow."

"What? I don't understand."

"A'zam knew you'd eventually get to this decision. He hand-picked the people and sent the team leaders to Dallas this week to go through the same treatment the two of you did. The rest of the team will go through it as soon as the people in Dallas can handle them."

"What do you know of Dallas?"

"Southwestern Medical Center, Dr. Bart Woodall. That's about all. A'zam said he will fill me in when it can be released. Apparently that's Monday. He can't tell me more." Thank you A'zam for respecting my agreement with Dr. Woodall and the medical center.

"This team will am…" I'm about to use the word amaze but I decide not to. "This team will push us well beyond anything we're capable of today." I summarize.

"A'zam said amaze. Looking at the two of you, whatever it is, I hope I get my chance soon. I could certainly use a face lift and tummy tuck."

"There's a little more to it than that." I know she's poking around to see what I'll tell her.

"I've guessed that. And so have most of our employees."

THE GHOST IN THE MACHINE

Chapter Sixty-Four

A'zam is in his office. Of course he would be. Since he no longer sleeps why would he be anywhere else? I smell his mustiness as I come into the office. Apparently he's not been retrofitted for smell yet.

"You can shower, even if you don't think you need to. I shower every day now."

A'zam turns around from looking out at his dark Japanese garden. "Shower?"

I come across the room and stand next to him facing out at the Japanese garden. "Can you smell anything?" I ask. He seems confused.

"No. You can?"

"Comes with the first upgrade."

A'zam motions to my dress. "To what do I owe this transformation from the Sage we knew and loved to one who is a vision of loveliness?"

"That came with the first upgrade. The second helped even more."

"Something to look forward to. Maybe they'll even replace the hair on my chest."

"It's getting better. You just need to push the limits and tell them what works for you and what doesn't. The docs listen."

"So you're two generations ahead of me?" A'zam doesn't seem pleased.

"You'll catch up quickly. Just don't short circuit the adjustment time. It's tougher than it seems."

"The voice of experience. It was damn hard to discover what you'd done. No one would talk about it. But this is the future. AppleCore is going to lead the way."

"Yes. Desirae was just telling me about that."

"I've respected your confidentiality agreements." He sounds defensive.

"Thank you for that. I mean that sincerely." And I do.

"Why thirty days before a release?" I'm sure he's guessed since they must have given him the same option to go back. He's just looking for me to confirm.

"And you chose that as the day our immortal team comes to work for the first time."

"If we're going to create the future we can't wait for it to get here."

"Did you purchase all of the transition slots available? And for how long?" His strategy is becoming clear to me.

"Woodall wouldn't agree to more than a year. Believes that when the news gets out they'll be inundated with requests and appeals from all sorts of people. Wouldn't provide an exclusive until I wrote a check bigger than they ever considered. They're building a whole new hospital in Dallas just to perform transition operations. Fortunately for us, it will take a year before it opens. All the docs who can perform the operations will have learned on our people. And we also have an option to get half of the slots there for five years."

"By then will everyone at AppleCore be an immortal?"

"No, only about 45,000 team members over five years. And that's if we use all of our slots. I think it's still to be determined if everyone needs to be an immortal. Finance, supply chain, legal? Can you imagine having the same general counsel forever?" A'zam laughs. He's on his fifth general counsel in ten years.

"You've been busy. An unbelievable strategy. No one will be able to catch us."

"I'm amazed you volunteered. That was a bold step into the unknown. But AppleCore is already benefitting more than even you realize." A'zam is never this forthright, what's up?

"And the competition is already coming after us. I was talking with Desirae about people leaving. We have to minimize and mitigate it." I have to temper his enthusiasm.

"I knew it would happen. I knew you would talk to Desirae. I also knew you'd come see me about now. I was probably off a few hours. But Mindi said your doctor called and you had to go see him. So your second upgrade was today. Notice much difference?"

"It's getting interesting." I don't like being manipulated, but it seems A'zam has me all figured out. "So what's your plan? That we release a new product a day? And then what? One every hour, every minute? Where does it end?"

"It doesn't end. Nothing ends. We just adopt a different market strategy. After we blitz the market and drive out the competition, we actually release fewer products, further apart but with much greater jumps in technology. We then get back to premium products we can charge a lot for. And as there are more and more immortals, we'll provide software and hardware updates that are built in. No external devices. We'll set up automatic payments. We download over the air and debit the account without the individuals even being aware they've been upgraded. People will no longer have to make a choice. It becomes automatic."

"So you already have an exclusive deal with Dr. Woodall and Southwestern?"

A'zam nods. "You gave me the idea for that when Dr. Woodall mentioned you wrote software he then uploaded for you. Today I think. That got us into a discussion and another check. Dr. Woodall is one of the wealthiest men in the world today."

I wonder if that was why Dr. Woodall installed the vagina prototype without telling me. Had he already made his deal with A'zam? "Is there anything else I need to know about Dr. Woodall and Southwestern and AppleCore?"

A'zam shakes his head, "That's about it. I'm trying to buy the company where they're building the robotic bodies, but we haven't agreed on a price yet. I also have the Merger and Acquisition team looking at companies with promising technologies we might be able to incorporate in the future. You know that recharging bed is a pain? Not literally, but I hate to have to lay there for fifteen minutes. It's a complete waste of time. So we're looking at a recharging chair so you can recharge anytime you sit down."

"But then you'd miss the memories of things you can't experience now. That's a big part of the transition. Coping with what you've lost."

A'zam looks at me critically. "I don't get that. Who cares about Thanksgiving dinners? I get to live forever. Giving up smells and food and showers…"

"You need to take one. And every day because those of us who are around you aren't pleased to smell you when you smell musty."

"Musty?"

"You get dusty. Your hair's a mess, and your clothes need to be cleaned. You want to smell and look like you would normally. You're an executive. You need to look the part. It's important. Believe me, been down that path."

"Yes, mother." He smiles but turns serious almost immediately. "Now there's another discussion we have to have. That's about your role here."

"I'm happy turning out more and more advanced products."

"I'm not happy having you turn out more and more advanced products. You're the one who got us started down the road to what I believe will be the most exciting time in our history. I wouldn't have looked at this for... who knows how long? Now this could easily replace much of what we're doing with an onboard platform. We've been looking at how we get the same functionality in a biologic person for decades. Now it becomes relatively easy. Board level for the most part."

What's he saying? I'm not qualified to do what I do anymore? He going to have me go on tour and tell my story so people will buy our products? I don't think I'm going to like whatever it is he has in mind.

A'zam waits for me to respond, but I don't, afraid I'm going to say the wrong thing. "Do you have any idea what I'm suggesting?" he asks.

"No." As Rocky said, as few words as possible to be perfectly clear.

"I want you to take over all product development and production."

I'm not sure I heard him correctly. "Reporting to Julia?"

A'zam isn't happy I brought her into the discussion. "Reporting directly to me. I intend to focus on how we grow into new markets. The immortal market is the first. We've already made a huge bet based on two of us. And with less than a month of experience. I intend to set up different operating groups to address each one. You'll have the responsibility to follow along with my efforts, to get the infrastructure and people in place quickly so we can get first mover advantage in every case."

"But what of Julia? She's the COO?" I don't want a replay of what

I just went through.

"Julia is no longer a member of the senior executive team. You don't have to worry about her."

"You don't know Julia, then. She'll find a way."

Chapter Sixty-Five: Four Days

I'm sitting in my office later that morning when I get a call. Not one I'm expecting. "Raoul. How did your conference go?" Social talk. What do I want to do with him?

"It was kinda rough to start out, but it got better. Kind of like us. At least that's how I took your reactions to me."

Is he apologizing? No, but that's about as close as he gets. So why the call? "I'm glad your conference got better." I respond. Need to be clear I'm not talking about us at this point. Let him hang wondering.

"Yeah, but what about us? You okay or am I persona non-grata?"

Direct question. Means he's still in town and want's to come by. "I didn't expect to hear from you for another year. That's what happened last time." I remind him without answering, but giving him an indication, just the same.

"Not that I didn't think about calling you, but when you're half way around the world, I mean, what's the sense?"

"You would have found a way If I was important to you." Push him and see what he says.

"You're important. Why would you think you're not important? It's just you're here and I'm not anymore. That makes it hard, you know what I mean?"

I'm waiting for him to make a more direct link to getting hard because that's all he's really interested in. Why did I ever sleep with him in the first place? Oh yeah, there hadn't been anyone in a long time. And he was the only guy who really seemed interested then. But what

I'm realizing is I was the one who really wasn't interested. As Reese said, I wasn't willing to do the hard work of finding the right guy. I settled for the guy who pursued me, even though he wasn't looking for a relationship. And maybe that's what appealed to me about him. I wasn't looking for a relationship either.

"So where are you?" Time to find out if I'm right about his motivation to call.

"That's the good news. I'm still in San Francisco. I need to make a presentation here today 'cause my West Coast guy resigned to take a job with a competitor. The meeting was already scheduled."

"So you have time to fit in me before you leave for more than a year this time."

"Fit you in." He corrects me, only I said what I meant. "That's not the way it is. I want to take you to dinner. Any place you'd like. I've not been as attentive as I should have been. You got that right. I'm not real good at keeping in touch. So I owe you. Let me take you out. We always have a good time."

I have the software I developed now. Do I want to do a direct comparison? Would eliminate the uncontrolled differences between two guys. But I'm just not sure I want to let him screw me. I'm sure that's how he sees it. He's a salesman. He's trying to sell his dick right now. Am I buying? And if I don't go back, is this how it's always going to be? Screwing but no relationship?

"Can't do dinner tonight." I finally respond.

"Then let me stay with you tonight. I don't have a hotel because I wasn't supposed to be here. I'll entertain myself until you get home."

"That doesn't work for me either, Raoul." Do I really want to cut him off? Just the fact that I don't really want to sleep with him should be enough. But is it? "You've never tried to be anything more than a casual friend who wants privileges. Well, your privileges are revoked.

Have a good life with your Parisian and Roman girls. Hopefully you'll never meet Mr. Syphilis." Did I really just say that? This is going to be interesting. What's he going to say? He's a salesman. He's not done yet.

"Sage. How can you say that? You've made it abundantly clear you look forward to our time together. You rearranged your whole day last week just so we could do it. Your behavior doesn't match your words, and I always go with behavior."

He can't believe I wouldn't want to do it with him again. Not surprising from someone who can't empathize. "Then observe this behavior." And I hang up on him. Oh shit. Did I really want to do that? Yes I did. I'm glad I did it.

The phone rings again. Shit. Raoul. Do I answer or ignore it?

"Obviously you don't believe behavior either." I answer.

"Sage. I'm sure it was just a call failure. You'd never just cut me off. We have too much of a good thing going. And besides, it may be a while before I get back. You're not going to want to think about how we could have gotten together and we didn't take advantage of the opportunity when we had it."

"There's one problem." I let that sit there to see how long it will take him to ask. It takes about five seconds.

"There's no problem. I can handle it if it's a long time before we get back together after tonight. But we owe it to each other. We've been doing it for a couple years now. It took a while for us to get it down, but now that we do. I mean, we can't just throw away all that time and emotional energy we've invested in learning how to please each other."

"Good line. I bet you had to think about that one for a long time."

"It's not a line. It's the truth. One thing I've learned about you is you're no bullshit. You say exactly what you think. You act on what you feel. And I know you got feelings for me. You showed me that a couple days ago. That was no casual encounter. That was built up passion."

"Funny, that's not exactly how I'd describe it. More like a dump and run on your part."

"Sage, baby. That wasn't kind. I told you when I got here I was on the stage in a few hours. I couldn't stay the night, even though I would have if I could have. You know you mean a lot to me. I don't know anyone quite like you."

"That's for sure." Although he has absolutely no idea of what I'm referring to. "But that's unfortunate for you. Now you're going to have to go back to those boring Parisian and Roman women. The ones who are just lying in wait for your return, with their legs spread in anticipation of a short and rough visit for a few Euros. We're done, Raoul. I won't answer next time you call. And Mindi won't bring you up. I'm finally getting some self-respect. I no long need or want you in my life. Good-bye." I hang up, leaving the phone behind.

Chapter Sixty-Six

Because I left my phone in my office, not wanting to hear from Raoul again, Mindi comes to find me out on the floor talking with Jermaine.

"Sage." Mindi interrupts when I've finished. "You have a call. From your doctor?"

"Let me know how that works out." I conclude with Jermaine and follow Mindi.

When we're a ways down the hallway I ask Mindi, "Did he say why he was calling?"

"No, but apparently it's important enough he said he'd wait for me to find you." Does that mean my body died and I don't have an option to go back anymore? Why would he hold for what could be a long time?

I arrive at my desk. "Dr. Woodall. Hope I didn't keep you waiting too long."

"I wanted to talk to you about Monday." He begins. Has something come up that we can't do it then? Is he moving it up? This doesn't sound promising. "We're all learning this time. So we want to be thorough. Make sure we don't overlook anything that might affect the outcome."

"So everything's okay?" I ask tentatively, thinking I'd not heard anything that was a problem.

"The preparations are progressing as expected, yes. Nothing on our side should be a problem to transition you back, if that's what you want. So, first of all, have you made your decision? It's not an issue if you haven't, but if you have then that simplifies things for us."

Is he going to ask me every day until I do? I didn't expect this. Hmm. "No. I haven't."

"Not a problem. As I said, you have until the scheduled time on Monday. So let's talk about how you're feeling about being immortal. We've talked about how some things aren't the same. We've made a first attempt to make them better. And they'll all get better still as we learn more about how your system works. Especially where things aren't as you want or expect. You may actually decide you want things to be different than you remember. And that's fine. We don't expect everyone will want to be the same. In fact, your consciousness pretty much guarantees you won't be the same. And that's a good thing. We want immortals to be able to complement each other. To have different perspectives and insights."

"That's good to know." I respond deliberately not answering his question.

"But how do you feel about your new condition?" He waits for me this time. Guess he figured out what he was doing.

"I thought I wouldn't really have a choice because of the diseased condition of my biologic body. I volunteered because I want more than to simply disintegrate in a nursing home somewhere over the next five years. But you've raised an important distinction between being immortal to carry on my family or to have a child to carry on the family. To tell you the truth, I hadn't considered that. A family has just never been a consideration for me. But you've convinced me that it could be. One I need to consider carefully. Not dismiss it because of what my life has been like until now."

"I'm glad you were listening. Once we release your body, we don't want you to regret your decision. But on the other hand, if you decide to cross back, we want you to have a plan for how you're going to address your medical conditions. Ensure you're ready to accept that fate."

"Why did you use the word 'fate'?" I ask, zeroing in because I'd not considered my fate before. I thought my fate was to die once I was diagnosed. I'd changed my fate by transitioning.

"Some people believe in fate. Others don't. In this case your medical diagnosis is pretty clear. What will happen to you if you go back isn't substantially in doubt. You may have five years, a little more, or maybe a whole lot less. No one can predict that accurately. We're only going on what we see in other people with similar conditions that have progressed to the same point as your condition."

"What about medical research? Is there anything on the horizon that might change the prognosis?" I ask. I've been given one answer in the past. I want to see if anything's changed, or if Dr. Woodall is aware of anything. Dr. Zapach, my neurologist wasn't.

"Nothing I'm aware of indicates a possible change in your prognosis."

I consider his response, since it's what I expected and change the subject. "Have you ever heard of an Alissar Princess of Phoenicia Rose?"

Dr. Woodall doesn't respond but I can tell he's listening closely.

"I've walked right past one going to and from work for probably a decade. Never noticed it. Had never heard of it. And now I can identify and tell you all about every plant on that short trip if I just want to take the time to look and think about it. I didn't have to transition to do that. I just had to decide and do it."

"Tell me if I'm wrong, but what I think I hear you saying is: You don't have to be immortal, or have all the super sensors we're giving you to live a full and complete life. You just need to decide to do it?"

I hesitate wondering if that's it. I finally nod. "From the work point of view, this has been a phenomenal journey for me. Immortals will transform our society in only a few short years. You'll be amazed, if

I can use that word, at what's going to change. From that point of view I'm already leading the charge. The only question remaining is do I want to continue leading that charge until the laws of physics stop us?"

"But that's your work. That's never been an area of concern for me." Dr. Woodall responds.

"Then what are you worried about?" I'm not following his concerns.

"The one thing you've never really addressed with me. Your emotional health. How are you feeling? You were real upset with your emotional limitations. Have you even tried to see if that's better? Are you finding it easier to build and maintain relationships? Whether friendships, caring or loving relationships? Are you feeling connections with others? Have the limitations of the software and systems you inhabit so limited them that you just can't connect?"

"At work…" but he cuts me off.

"I'm not worried about you at work. There's lots of positional and power dynamics going on there that make it not a good indicator. Your personal life."

"I don't have one. It's just me and sometimes Rocky. And sometimes my posse, at least that's what I call them."

"What about the guy you slept with?"

"He's gone. I realized I didn't need him anymore. Probably because it wasn't a relationship."

"That's good. It means you're growing in ways you weren't before. I'm glad for you."

Chapter Sixty-Seven: Three Days

The posse was surprised I called them and asked to get together tonight. They didn't hesitate even though I told them I was going to ask a question they had given up ever expecting me to ask. We met for drinks at the Back Porch Saloon, a country western bar that we enjoyed going to because all the guys were outrageous in their behavior.

"What's so important you needed us all here?" Windy is the one to kick things off once the drink order goes in.

"You know the decision I have to make in just a few days. And I need your help in putting it into context."

"What's the question?" Reese is really giving me the hard stare.

"If each of you had to decide whether to have another child so you can raise it, influence it and guide its decisions, or watch your kids have their own kids and know that you can only indirectly influence what kind of people they will become, which would you do?"

Windy jumps in. "I see where you're going and that's an interesting question. Hmm. I'll give you my perspective. I'd have another kid. I just like being a mother. It's an experience that's tryin', it's frustratin' and it's hard. But you never have another opportunity to be able to create something the way you do when you shape, guide and instill values in a kid."

I'm not surprised that's how Windy would come down on the issue. With her family riches and Texas attitudes, she always thinks she can create more, have more, and influence whatever she wants. The one I'm most curious about is MC. She's always been the mystery for me. "So what do you think MC?"

"So if you go back are you thinking of having a kid with that scumbag Raoul?" She instantly accuses me. She's never been one to hide how she feels about him. And she's been outspoken about the fact she thinks he just uses me. She's never offered to help me find someone better. But I always thought she didn't think I'd be a very good wingman for her when she goes out trolling for guys.

"Raoul is gone. History. So no."

"Really? I don't believe you." Delilah is always the suspicious one when it comes to relationships.

"In fact he called. I told him never to call me again."

"You didn't? Really? MC's not sure I could be that strong. "I hope you did because it's long past time for you to get on with your life. It was worth coming tonight just for that news alone."

"So what would you do, MC?" I'm trying to get the conversation back on track.

"I'm getting too old, especially for diapers, and midnight feedings. For having to take this kid with you everywhere. Always being too tired to want to make love. I'd miss the nights out with all of you and dinners and shows. No. I'd be happy to sit and watch the next generation to see if they do a better job of running the world than we have."

"That's because you're a freaking shrink and all you ever do is try to stop people hiding from reality." Reese and MC are the closest of friends amongst us, and that's why she'll let Reese say that. None of the rest of us could get away with it without hurting her feelings.

"Don't complain. Without me keeping you engaged in the world you couldn't buy your cheap wine tonight." MC has always been able to give as good as she gets.

"I think I know how Reese will answer my question, but Delilah. What do you think?" I say to encourage Delilah. She is always looking to please us, so I make sure she knows I won't be unhappy with her answer either way.

"The only thing I want to be doing at midnight is have an orgasm or sleep. I don't think I want to be cleaning up Cheerios from my kitchen floor, or having to go shower three times a day when the kid spits up all over me or craps her pants and they run out when I pick her up. I'm with MC. I'm good the way things are. I don't want to mess with Mother Nature either. It always seems the kids with the most physical and adjustment issues are the ones that come late in life, when your body's not quite ready for the wear and tear they put on you. You know? I mean it's tough. And the other thing is the last one always gets away with murder because it's like I didn't kill the other ones with neglect so I won't kill this one either. That's not good. You need to be involved with them or they feel like you don't love them or something. I couldn't do that to a kid. And I wouldn't want my perfect life disturbed with the earthquake another kid would cause. You know? No. I'm perfectly happy to keep my life the way it is now. I worked long and hard to get to this point. You can have your kid if you want. You've never had that pleasure. But for me. I'm way past that."

Delilah surprises me. She's like Mother Earth or something. She's so caring to everyone's kids. And even though her husband left her a long time ago, she's never been out of a relationship with someone. And she's been real good about picking guys who are good to kids. But I guess I can understand she would get to the point where she wants to move beyond the potential role of arbiter of every argument, the supporter of every school cause and worrying about where they are and what they're doing six nights a week.

Now it's Reese's turn. I look at her and she doesn't wait for me to ask. "I think this is a bogus question. You don't care about kids. So why do you want to know what we think about kids? You already know. You said you knew how I'd respond to your question, but you don't. You're making an assumption about me, just like I'm making an assumption about you now. So I'm not going to answer your question.

I'm going to sit here until you tell us what you're going to do."

I think about their answers and the turn in my life just since we last met. "I don't know yet. I was hoping you'd give me a strong reason to consider going back. But you haven't. Dr. Woodall said it could be up to five years, but it could be a whole lot less. The only reason I can see is to have a kid. As the doctor pointed out, I just never know what that child might become. So am I selfish and just live my life, or do I give someone else a chance?"

"Knowing that someone else is going to grow up without its mother." Windy points out.

"If you had a strong relationship with a great guy, I could see it." MC offers. "One who understood the situation going in and loves you enough to carry some part of you forward. But all you have is Raoul. Not a good idea."

"I'm glad I'm not you." Reese summarizes without giving me her thoughts. She's upset with me that I assumed how she would answer my question.

"I'm going to be totally selfish here." Delilah changes the tone. "I don't want to lose you from our group. We've been through everything together."

I take Delilah's and Windy's hands, they take the others and we just make the circle for a long moment, transferring strength to each other. I smile at each one weakly. "Thank you for being here for me."

Chapter Sixty-Eight: Two Days

Rocky is pouring himself a cup of coffee when I open his kitchen door. He looks up. He holds up the pot to see if I want any and I shake my head. "What brings you by so early in the morning for me? Not so much for you. You've always been an early riser."

"We need to talk." I respond knowing he's not used to talking with me.

"I didn't do it. Whatever it is you think I did. I didn't. And she wouldn't tell you even if we did it."

"She?" I ask.

He frowns, "I thought you knew about me and Elizabeth. You do. You were here when she was. I know you know. It's nothing. I could never replace your mother."

Nice to know I'm not the only one sleeping around without a long term game plan in mind. "I'm not here to talk about you and Elizabeth." He seems relieved. "I'm here to talk about me." I see confusion and an insecurity about how to deal with me. Rocky always wanted to just pass me off. Let me figure it out myself. I'm not going to let him do that now. He brought me into this world. He owes me the benefit of his experience in life. Not sure it's all that relevant, but every so often Rocky comes up with something I need to consider. At the moment, I need to consider every perspective I can gather. I just don't know what I should do. Neither alternative is straight forward. Both have advantages and disadvantages. And I'm running out of time to decide.

Rocky takes a sip of his hot coffee. It burns his tongue as he does every day. I see him licking his tongue on the inside of his mouth as he tries to get it to stop burning. Some things never change.

"So you want to talk about you."

I nod.

"What about you?"

"Do you remember what we talked about when you came by my office?" I ask not sure he really does remember. I've noticed from time-to-time he forgets things. Just like I used to.

"Some movie you'd watched. Something about robots maybe?"

"It wasn't a movie, Rocky. I have a robotic body now. And I need to decide if I want to keep it."

"That's great. You should have a good time." He's not understanding me.

"Rocky. Tell me this: Would you rather die when you get old or live forever?"

"I wouldn't want to live forever as an old person. This is no fun. I can't remember things like I used to. I feel all these aches and pains. I can't do the things that were so easy, like going for a run or playing a game of baseball. Getting old is no fun. So no. I'll be happy when my time is up and I don't feel all these limitations anymore."

"But what if you could go back? What if you were twenty again and you'd just met Anna Laura? You have your whole life ahead of you, but you could never have me or Tabitha. No kids. Just you and Anna Laura?"

"No kids? I don't know about that. Anna Laura and I talked a long time before we had you. Had to figure out how we would raise you. Were we going to be tough on you or let you explore the world for yourself? What activities could we afford to get you involved in? She wanted ballet and I wanted sports where you learn team work. We disagreed more about you kids than anything else. We could always find something we could agree on except when it came to you and your sister."

"I didn't know that." I respond, surprised he would tell me this.

"She wanted to be hard on you. Thought you needed structure. Rules. Moral guidelines. Almost like she thought she could give you a handbook to life. I never thought that was possible. We'd argue about her wanting you and Tabitha to be just like her. Same morals, same beliefs, same approaches to life. And I always said you need to find your own way. Anything we impose on you will just backfire. At some point you'll reject it and go off and do what you're going to do anyway. I was always afraid you'd reject us in the process. Then we'd lose you and your sister."

And after Anna Laura's death, I'd done exactly what he was afraid I'd do, but not for the reasons he thought. I reacted to him giving me freedom to find my own way, mistaking it for him not loving me or caring what I did. All the time he was doing what he thought was best for me, according to what he believed about raising kids. And when Anna Laura wasn't here to balance him out, it got all out of whack. "Are we as close as you'd like us to be?" I ask.

"You come by from time-to-time. I'm not sure what more I can ask. You've got your own life to live. I've got mine." The answer is no, but he'll never tell me that. Doesn't synch with his philosophy of raising kids.

"Do you want a grandchild?" I decide to ask the simpler questions. He's not going to understand the true situation.

"Are you pregnant?" He looks at me closer. "What's wrong with your eyes? You have your mother's eyes, but I don't see them. What did you do?"

"It's okay, Rocky. I still have them. You just can't see them anymore." I try to reassure him.

"Those aren't your mother's eyes." He's upset.

I put my hand on his shoulder. "It's okay." He looks up at me and shakes his head.

"Not okay. What happened? I count on you to have your mother's eyes, so when you come by to see me I see her in you. But I don't see her. What did you do?"

"Rocky. I was dying. I was probably going to die before you."

Rocky shakes his head. "No. You weren't dying. You're just making an excuse."

"I had to do something, so I did. And Anna Laura's eyes? Well I still have them, but you just can't see them from the outside. But I see the world as she did. And that's all that matters. Isn't it?"

Rocky looks at my eyes and shakes his head sadly. "I so looked forward to you coming by so I could see her in your eyes. Now I'll never see her again." Rocky closes his eyes and stiffens his lip.

"Nothing's changed. I'm still here."

"But she isn't." Rocky protests.

I suddenly realize for Rocky that I'd never existed. I was a proxy for his wife and my mother. Every time he saw me he only saw her. Every time he spoke to me it was as if he was reliving a conversation he had with her. Explains why I so often just ignored what he said as having no meaning for me. The ravings of some old guy who didn't care about what I did or what happened as a result. But he was treating me the same way he did his wife. She was a person with her own life that they shared. She decided what she was going to do. So whatever I decided? That was okay. Just as anything she decided? That was okay. She was an adult, even though I wasn't. It's a miracle I didn't get pregnant. Probably only because I was more interested in books than boys. The boys weren't interested in me. I was out of shape and not attractive. They were enthralled with Savannah, the perfect girl who didn't sweat.

"Okay." I close my eyes. Rocky will never understand the decision I need to make, so is there anything I need to discuss with him? He's not going to be able to help me make the right decision. All he wants is for me to show up with Anna Laura's eyes. And that means I've got to go back to my biologic body. If I do that, we will probably both pass on about the same time. Maybe he'll survive longer than I will. But that's not even on his radar screen. Then a thought hits me. "Rocky. You wouldn't want to live for a long time as an old person. But if you were twenty and you hadn't met Anna Laura yet. Think back. If it was just you. Would you want to go back and live as a twenty-year old?"

Rocky closes his eyes and thinks. "Live as I was before Anna Laura? I was a messed up kid. Live like that where I didn't love anyone and no one loved me?" Rocky shakes his head. "If you'd have asked me then I probably would have said why not? But once I experienced true love? That changed everything. I wouldn't give up a single day I had with your mother. Not one. The greatest regret of my life is that it was her who died and not me. I should have picked up Tabitha. I should have been driving the highway when the accident occurred. She would have been much better for you than I have been. She would have shown you the love you needed. Given you the advice you sought from me. But what did I know about a young girl and hormones and all that stuff? I didn't know what to say to you. I still don't. And you hate me because I failed you. I know that. It doesn't make it any easier for either of us. It's just the way it is."

I lean forward and kiss him on the top of his head. "I love you Rocky. You may not believe that, but you've always been there. For the most part, that's been more important to me than anything."

THE GHOST IN THE MACHINE

Chapter Sixty-Nine

Oriana sits with me in my office reviewing the staffing plan for the new teams. "But I expect you're going to staff it with people just like you."

I have to be careful here. She's identified A'zam's strategy on a whole lot less information than I had. "What makes you think that?"

"How long is it going to be before people like you come rolling off the assembly line? They've got to be transitioning more of you. So how long before they start showing up here?"

"What would you be willing to give up to be better at your job?" I ask to avoid a direct answer, but to show her it isn't as black and white as she thinks.

"Give up? Like for lent?"

"Forever. What about the ability to have children?"

Realizing my situation, she breathes in deeply before answering. "You can't. No ovaries."

"What about blinking as you pointed out to me?"

Oriana looks at me more closely. "Really?"

"Emotions are difficult. They're working on them, but it's primitive at the moment. I didn't even have a sense of smell until this week."

"But there's got to be an upside."

"I can do equations in my head you can't, but big deal. I can solve complex problems by researching the data and running correlations and writing algorithms. But at the end of the day being the smartest person in the room is not always the path to happiness." I respond retrospectively.

"I saw you struggle for a while. But you figured it out. Look where we are now? We're about to double the size of the team. We have more product coming out than at any time in our history. So what's the problem? The problem is expectations. Let us make more money, develop the bleeding edge products. Let us lead the way. We've earned the right to do so. We fail you, replace us. No beef with that. But we deliver, reward us. That's all we're saying."

"You don't want to talk about the fundamental gorilla in the room, do you?"

Oriana looks at me. "Transitioning like you did?"

I nod.

"What about it?" she asks although real tentative, like she really doesn't want to discuss it.

"Are you willing to?"

"I don't know." She answers honestly. "I really don't understand what it means. You've talked about the things you gain and the things you lose. But I don't know how that all stacks up into plusses and minuses."

"You live forever. But how will people perceive you? You're a superwoman amongst midgets. And the midgets are getting less and less consequential as time goes on. The midgets die and you don't. So why do you care anymore?"

"But what about your life outside of work." Oriana asks. "You could go home when we do, but you don't. You choose to stay here and work. Why is that? Why don't you go home and go to a movie or out to a bar with your friends, or go visit a relative? Why stay here? What does it get you?"

"A sense of accomplishment I don't get in my personal life." I respond. "But we shouldn't compare my situation with yours. You can be so much more than I am as an immortal."

"I don't know. It's kinda scary."

"All transitions in society are scary because you don't know what to expect.

THE GHOST IN THE MACHINE

Chapter Seventy

"Dr. Washington?" I've just answered the call in my office. "This is detective Stuckey from the city police department. Do you have a minute?"

I really don't need this now. "Sure detective. How can I be of help?"

"That knife you dropped off. It belongs to the man who died. So we now know he tried to rob you with a deadly weapon. What we don't know is why you?"

"I wish I could help you there, detective. As I told you I'd never seen the man before in my life. The only explanation I can imagine is that he was in need of his drug of choice. Happened to be in the neighborhood. Wandered into mine hoping to come across someone coming home."

"You see now, that's where we have a problem with your theory. You live in a residential neighborhood. Most robberies take place in commercial areas. He must have had a reason to be there. Must have known someone nearby. Maybe he was buying from someone who lives in that area. Or maybe he has a relative who lives there. Something had to bring him there in the first place. You've not been able to give us any indication of what that reason would be."

"Since you've explained your confusion, I understand it. But that doesn't change the fact I have no idea why he was in my neighborhood on that night or at that time. I've walked to and from work for almost ten years. I walk through there all different times of day and night depending on how late I've been working. There's no established pattern. So I really can't help you with that one."

"When do you normally go home?" The detective asks next.

"As I said, there is no normal. Could be anywhere from six or so to midnight. Usually earlier. Midnight has been a more recent situation because of the work we're doing right now."

"How much longer do you expect to be working so late?"

"I really can't give you a good estimate on that. We're adding people to our teams and it's taking a lot to get that spun up."

"Adding people. Could this gentleman have been someone who was interviewed for a job but turned down? Is it possible he was angry at you personally? Is it possible he really wanted to kill you and not rob you because he was angry you hadn't hired him?"

"Interesting theory. I'd not considered it. But no. I wasn't involved in the hiring of the new team members. In fact, none of them would have any reason to even know who I am at this point."

"And the man stuck the knife into your ribs."

"It happened quickly and was late. Like I said, I saw him carrying it."

"So why did you think he was going to rob you?"

"Why else would someone approach you late at night carrying a knife?" Keep it short.

"I don't know. Could he have been wanting you to help him cut a flower from the rose bed?"

"Was he a gardener?" I respond with the only question I can think of that will answer his question.

"He was a day laborer. Wife and kids, but no steady job."

"So no evidence of drug abuse?"

"Best we can tell, he wasn't under the influence of anything that night."

"So what's your theory? Why would a day laborer be in a residential neighborhood late at night carrying a knife and approach a woman on her way home from work?"

"That is the question, isn't it?"

"I wish I could help you detective, but we seem to be covering the same territory. I've told you all I know. I've given you the knife. So I think I've helped you all I can."

"Can you explain why a day laborer would sustain a blow to the head after trying to rob you?"

"Do you know for a fact it was after? If he'd suffered a concussion that might explain why he was in my neighborhood. Maybe he was lost. It might also explain why I was able to take the knife from him so easily."

"That's possible. We'll look into it. Any other theories for us?"

"I thought that was your job."

"You said you were from a tough part of town. But you don't talk like it. What's that all about?"

This guy isn't going to be satisfied. "I said I grew up in a tough part of town. I went on to get a doctorate in software and advanced technology."

"And your job at AppleCore?"

"Senior Vice President of Software Development." Since A'zam hasn't told me what the new title is I'll give him the one I know.

"That's a pretty important position. Must pay a lot. Why don't you have personal security like a lot of the other executives?" Is he looking for a part time job? What's the deal?

"I don't need personal security, detective." I respond sounding tired of the conversation. I am.

"On the contrary. You say our victim tried to rob you. Sounds like you need security to me."

"I don't think your observation is relevant to this conversation. Now can I go back to work or do you have other questions that are relevant to your investigation?"

"I do have a few more questions I'd like to ask. How long have you lived at this address?"

"About ten years." Minimize your answers.

"That's a long time." Not a question, don't answer. He waits and then continues. "Why were you walking home so late that night?"

"I worked late. That's been a frequent situation with the current workload. Do you have any more questions?"

"Did anyone accompany you home that evening?"

"No. I was alone. I told you that before."

"Except for our victim."

"I understand your perspective, detective, but I was the victim here. I protected myself. That's the end of the story as far as I can tell you. Beyond that you're on your own."

"Thank you Dr. Washington. We'll be in touch." Apparently I'm a suspect. But I'm sure I didn't kill this guy. I couldn't have. Takes a lot to kill someone, doesn't it?

Chapter Seventy-One

Dr. Woodall calls me at work. Asks that I meet him at the Stanford tennis courts. I think this is an unusual request, but since he doesn't want to meet until well into the evening it doesn't interfere with what I'm doing at work. So I agree. The Googlecar drops me off at 10:30 by the entrance to the courts. I look around. He's on a court well back into the corner.

"What's this all about?" I ask as I approach him. He has buckets of balls, several different rackets and a video camera set up on a tripod.

"Medical research." He responds.

"I give up? What's the long version?" He's always giving me lengthy explanations so I think he's teasing me about my impatience.

"We've been having a debate about muscle memory. We transferred your memories. That would include your memories of muscle commands you would use in athletics, for example. My team is divided into two camps. Those who think you can connect to those memories and those who don't think so."

"In this case you're readily admitting you're using me as a guinea pig to see how an immortal operates in a given situation."

"Well… yes, in this one instance."

"And I suppose the next thing you're going to tell me is you were the captain of your university tennis team."

"Well… yes, in this one instance." We both laugh.

"Okay. What do I do?"

He points to a wall at the end of the court. "Take a bucket of balls down there and try to hit them against the wall. Work on your ground strokes. Let's see how long it takes for you to get your strokes down. I'm assuming you played tennis at one point?"

I nod that I did. But don't give him the details of having played in college in my senior year. I really haven't played since then. The first few strokes are pretty poor. I vote with those who think I won't be able to map the memories. But the longer I work at it the smoother the strokes become. The control comes back too. Maybe I'm moving over to the other camp. Maybe I am mapping those memories.

After about fifteen minutes of forehands and backhands and moving easily from one to the other Dr. Woodall approaches me.

"Time for next steps. Come with me and we'll try serving into an empty court. That's why I brought so many balls."

I follow him to the baseline. I try bouncing and catching the ball a few times. Then I attempt a serve. I'm back in the first camp. I'm completely out of rhythm with the tossed ball. My swing is slow. The ball has already fallen below my waist before my swing comes through. I bend over laughing. It was so awful I can't help myself.

Dr. Woodall looks at me waiting.

"Muscle amnesia, I'm afraid." I admit.

"No problem. Take your time." Dr. Woodall returns to his camera to watch what he's recording.

Two more attempts at a serve, equally off. I'm shaking my head. But finally on the fourth try I make contact. While the ball goes into the net, I actually hit it. So my control is returning. But I can't tell if it's muscle memory, or I'm just remembering what to do. Whatever it is, I'm relearning quickly.

Two more serves. Both go in, although without much power on

them. But I wouldn't expect much power at all this time out. "You want to try a rally?" I suggest to the doctor.

"Oh, sure we could try that." He crosses over to the other side of the net.

"Here comes." I try my serve again. First one goes into the net. Second serve goes over. Dr. Woodall is easily able to return it almost directly at me. I step aside to position and swing through, connect with the ball, but put it into the net.

I return to the baseline, another serve. His easy return drops almost perfect for me to return. But I'm still gauging where to be, get my positioning and swing down, all at the same time. I try to change positioning at the last moment. That brings the face of the racket back so the return is high and short. But Dr. Woodall is easily able to get to it and tap it back over. I step back and swing through, a little faster this time. The ball leaps off my racket and drops in the far back corner.

"Nice return." Dr. Woodall praises me.

The rallying continues for about a half hour. At that point we're getting some long exchanges going. Nothing hard but the rhythm is there. The swing is smooth. I'm getting a better measure of where to be and how to step into the swing.

"Let's try a game." The doctor suggests.

I let him serve first. The service comes in, it has a little more zip on it than previous. My reflexes are quick. I'm there before the ball comes up. I swing through and place it in the back corner. Dr. Woodall slides back to swing through, again more zip on the ball. My mind is so quick I'm well ahead of the ball. I have a chance to adjust my footing and put the ball right back to him. We continue this exchange. His returns to mid court. Mine to the back corner. He then decides to come to my left side and drop it in the back corner. I move to the net with a backhand and drop it to my right away from him. He can't get to it.

"You've played more than a little."

I don't answer. Just smile at him. Over the course of this game my speed gets me into position for every return. But I double fault more than once as I try to put more zip on my serves. More go into the net than into the court. No big deal, I'm staying with him anyway.

It's his serve. I pound baseline returns into the opposite corners and take the final point. He's shaking his head as he approaches the net to shake my hand. "I think I have the answer to my question."

We walk back to pick up the equipment. He shuts down the camera and packs up.

"So which is it?" I ask.

"I vote for no. I think you were probably influenced by your game memory. But since the muscles and control systems are different I don't think it was a mapping across. So that makes me think you lose whatever muscle memory you had. But a good athlete will have game knowledge and tactical understandings that the control systems can execute. So in that case a good former athlete will learn quicker than someone who never played."

"But?" I think I hear a 'but'.

"You're incredibly fast. You to get in position well before the ball gets there no matter how hard I pound it. You had plenty of time to plan your stroke and execute it with precision."

"So what does that mean for professional athletes in an age of immortals?" I'm curious where he sees this going.

"Excellent question. We've not given that any thought at all."

"Was this fun for you?" I ask trying to gauge his interest in doing this again.

"It was fun for me to see what you can do. But was losing to you fun? No. But then I hate to lose and don't very often. I usually pick victims who will give me a good show, but don't really have a chance. Guess I misjudged what you could do."

"I played in college. So I have an idea what to do."

"So you're a ringer." Dr. Woodall laughs. I like his laugh.

THE GHOST IN THE MACHINE

Chapter Seventy-Two

We put the gear in the Googlecar and climb in. Dr. Woodall is going to drop me at my house first and then head home. Once in the car I ask, "Any more surprises?"

"I think we've caught most everything by now. But you may still find a few things that don't seem quite right. Just make a note of them when they become obvious. We'll have those ready for your next update, if you don't go back to your old body. Which reminds me, have you made your decision yet?"

I shake my head. "I'm afraid I'm going to make you wait until the end."

Dr. Woodall nods to himself. "Not a problem for me." It is, but he doesn't want to pressure me. "We're scheduling another person for that time slot in case you elect not to transition. We have a bit of a backlog. But not a problem for us or for him. We will just do an extra procedure if you go back."

"Sounds like you hope I won't." I'm trying to hear between the words.

"It's your decision." He doesn't want me to but won't say it.

"What would you do if you were me?"

"I can't comment on that. You have to be comfortable with what you decide."

"You're no help." I tease him.

"Actually on Tuesday you'll be saying exactly the opposite. 'Boy

Dr. Woodall was a big help. He made me face up to my decision and make it.' That's what I expect you'll be saying. And I expect that you will be happy with the decision you make, either way."

"So if I go back, you'll play tennis with me because you'll be able to beat me. But if I stay an immortal you won't play with me anymore." I decide to kid a bit, but I'm also looking for information as to how he will regard me afterwards.

"I will be happy to play tennis with you in either event, in the name of science, mind you." He laughs at me. Still no information as to how he really sees me.

"Talk to me about your role after Monday." I've never asked him this question.

He looks out the window of the car for a moment. "If you go back to your biologic body you'll stay in the hospital for a couple of days or until we know the transfer has been seamless. Once you're back to work I'll check up on you once a week by remote scans and telephone calls just to make sure everything is normal. That will continue for a month. Then you'll be released to your regular doctors to deal with your other conditions and general health issues. I won't see you again unless something requires my consultation."

He hesitates before he continues, probably gathering his thoughts. "If you continue, I'll be seeing you for your periodic upgrades, I'll be conversing as needed to identify and address any things that we haven't addressed. Anything that isn't part of the periodic upgrades. That will go on as long as necessary, but I would hope not more than about six months. When they become standard upgrades, which will mostly be software, they'll be done over the air. There won't be a need to come in. We'll do remote scans to make sure everything is normal. If you need a replacement for something that fails, that will be a walk in. Someone will be able to swap out the part. If I'm here I'll do it, but it could be anyone on the staff."

"No more experiments like tonight?"

"I think we're good for the moment. But if you're up to test things out for us once in a while, that would be appreciated."

"I'm open to it if it won't incapacitate me in some way."

"I'll see that it doesn't."

"I have another question for you. Why did you ever get into the Singularity project?"

Dr. Woodall looks out the window again, gathers his thoughts, then turns back to me and looks directly into my eyes. "Because I knew someday I'd be sitting here with you. The first to transition. I'm a doctor first and foremost. I've lost more than my share of patients. I wanted to find another option for those with terminal prognoses. The Singularity project seems to be one option for people with a broad range of diseases. It can help them regain a full and complete life."

"But you sold most of your slots to AppleCore. That doesn't seem to be aligned with the goals you just described."

"You're right. It may seem contradictory. But it really isn't when put into the context of medical research. Our funding is limited. You could never pay the full costs of the surgery and follow on work we've done with you. At the same time, we're constrained in our budget. We can only do so many procedures at a time or in a year. While we agreed to sell all the slots for the next year to AppleCore, the funding that provides allows us to build a complete hospital with twenty-five surgical suites. That means next year we can start performing fifty transitions a day. Without that funding it will take us at least five years to get to the same point. So you see, the agreement actually will let us serve many more terminal patients than if we didn't do that deal."

"But by doing so you've given AppleCore a huge advantage in its markets. We will be the most dominant technology force on the planet, bar none, for the foreseeable future."

Dr. Woodall shakes his head. "Not my concern. I have an obligation to serve my patients. If I have to make a deal with the devil to better serve them I have to seriously consider it."

"And you become rich in the process." I note to tell him I'm not buying his altruistic bullshit.

"I don't." He responds simply. I don't believe him.

"A'zam said he wrote you a check big enough to make you one of the richest men on the planet." I'm almost quoting A'zam.

"He gave me the check, but it all went to Southwestern Medical Center to build the new hospital."

"He said he gave you two checks. One for the first year and one for the five years after the hospital opens."

"And that goes to the clinic for the doctors and the hospital for the facilities. I only get a portion of it for the actual surgeries and follow ups I perform for AppleCore employees. So no. I won't be rich."

I don't know what to say. I've badly misjudged my doctor.

Chapter Seventy-Three: One Day

I'm walking into the office after showering, cologning and finding a particularly feminine and colorful flower print dress to wear. Of course the leather shoes, belt and purse match. I'm feeling good about how I look. I feel good about how the day is going to go. I decide to check out another rose which is growing close to Alissar and Ingrid Bergman. I select one and discover it is a Double Delight. A hybrid tea rose with a long season of bloom. The double blossoms have a rich, creamy white to pale pink center with deep, ruby edging. They have a bushy habit, growing to about 4-5 feet with a 2-3 foot spread. I expect a sweet, spicy scent. That's what I detect. I zoom in on the blossom. Then I compare it to the deep red Ingrid and the pink Alissar. I'm smelling them as well, comparing and discovering that the Double Delight is much more fragrant than the others. And then I do it again. Walk into the same man who is doing his best to avoid me. "Oh, I'm sorry." He's smiling and glances over to the roses.

"Which one were you looking at today?"

"The Double Delight." I respond and then point to it. "That one. Creamy white to pale pink center with deep, ruby edging. It's one of the more fragrant roses. That's why I like it."

"You're fragrant this morning as well. I like it, by the way."

"I'm Sage." Not going to let him get away without introducing himself this time. He must live in the area since this is the second time I've literally bumped into him.

"Even your name." He smiles. "Jackson." He holds out his hand and we shake. "I'm pleased to meet someone so knowledgeable of roses."

"You like flowers, I hope?"

"My mother grew roses. She knew everything about them. She tried to teach me, but I was never as passionate. I do remember a little."

"So, what do you do, Jackson?" I'm curious now that I have him talking.

"Right now, I'm the mayor. But when my term is up I'll return to my precision parts manufacturing and systems integration company. I'm coming home from there now. It's just down the street."

"You have a card?"

He retrieves one and hands it to me. I glance at his name, Jackson Pratt, CEO. The company name doesn't mean anything to me. I note the address. "Near AppleCore."

"One of my customers. I do low rate production parts for their new products."

I nod but don't say anything.

"I wonder, you seem to be out here early. A couple weeks ago, did you hear or see anything in the middle of the night?" he asks.

I'm guarded in my response, "About what?"

"A man sustained an injury somewhere around here and later died. My police department is still looking for leads. They think he might have fallen from a tree and landed on his head. Not sure. He was gardening for one of the home owners." He nods across the street. "Probably worked on your roses."

"They contacted me. I told them all I know." I really don't want to get into this.

"Thanks for sharing. I think they're about to close the case. Probably rule it an accidental death. Wouldn't want you to think it's dangerous here. You seem to really enjoy your walks."

"I do. And thank you for making my day more pleasant."

Jackson looks uncomfortable, like he's not sure how to end the conversation. "Well, I hope to bump into you again soon."

"Or you could invite me out sometime. I'd love to learn more about how you make your parts and what it's like to be the mayor." I hand him my card.

He reads the card, "I had no idea. Oh, I'm sorry. Just I've never seen someone as attractive as you…"

"You don't have to apologize. I've enjoyed talking about roses, and the city and precision parts manufacturing. I'd like to get to know you better too." I beam my brightest smile.

"I will." Jackson bows slightly. "Call you." He stands looking at me so I need to make the first move.

"Hope you have a great day." And I walk on to work hoping he does call.

Mindi catches me as I come in. "A'zam is waiting for you."

"Was something scheduled?" I ask. I wasn't expecting to see him this morning.

"He's in your office." I look in and see him sitting at the table, staring off into space, evidently reviewing something in his head.

I go in and, "Morning." As I close the door behind us.

A'zam disengages from his thoughts, "I need to make the announcement today."

"About?" I'm not sure exactly what he's referring to. We have so many products about to be released.

"Your promotion to President and CEO of AppleCore Products Company." This will be a subsidiary of AppleCore Corporation, of which A'zam is Chairman and CEO. A different and more important job than what we discussed.

"Thank you for your vote of confidence. I'm truly surprised, but grateful for the chance."

"I'm the one who should be grateful. If you hadn't been the first to transition I'm not sure I would have been able to do the deal with Southwestern and your doctor. You've led us into the most important opportunity we've ever had. And now it's essential we rapidly exploit our advantage. That's what I plan to do while I let you run the main company."

"We need to improve the communications between us." I point out as I sit down across the table from him.

"You're unhappy about the new software team." He guesses.

"Not unhappy. Just surprised. I'll have the responsibility to train them up and make sure they can produce what we want and need."

"I couldn't afford to distract you. What you were and are doing is unprecedented. I had to give you the resources to drive even harder. Just as you've been enabling your people, I need to do the same for you. I'm learning a lot by watching you."

"So what exactly are you going to be doing while I'm running the company?"

"I'll be finding companies we can acquire or partner with to own the complete chain that produce the immortal bodies, both hardware and software. I want to be the sole source for everything associated with immortals."

I think of Jackson's company. I remove the card he gave me and slide it across the table. "Might be someone for you to look at."

He picks up the card and looks at it. "Where did you meet him?"

"Jackson? He's the mayor."

"This is the company that built you and me."

"I had no idea." Wow. I'll make sure to bump into him again so I can learn more.

"They have a very high valuation on themselves. Trying to negotiate that down a bit. We're going to make a deal because I'm offering a portion of the purchase price in AppleCore stock. So they'll have upside if I can negotiate an exclusive supply contract with Southwestern. And I think that's likely."

"I was going to say I'm not sure there's a secret sauce to what we are." I respond. "The software seems to be the main differentiator. And I think we can bring that in house by augmenting our staff. So you need to track down who they're using and hire or acquire the right talent."

"Already have. Most of it has actually been commercial controls software or Southwestern employees on the soft and fuzzy stuff, like emotions and feelings. I know we can hire them. Southwestern will actually be happy to get more expertise behind it."

He's well down the path on executing his plan. "Let me ask a different question. Do you have the 30 day option to go back to your biologic body?"

A'zam looks at me as if I'm raising something that isn't worthy of discussing. "Yes. But there's no way I'd consider it. How could I walk away from the chance to completely change the world?"

"Have you informed Dr. Woodall of your decision?"

"No. I'm not going to do that until I'm sure there aren't going to be ill effects. But you're two weeks ahead of me and seem to be doing fine. I'm not going back."

"So what's next? Sounds like you have the immortals supply chain strategy executing."

A'zam hesitates, apparently wondering if this is the right time. He decides. "I've spun up a small team to work on proprietary software and chips for immortals that will never be sold. Chips and software for you and me. Maybe a few others. We will be the most advanced immortals on earth. We'll dominate any endeavor we want to take on. Think of it. A future where you and I can do anything we want. And we're the only ones who can."

Chapter Seventy-Four

The announcement on the re-organization was up when A'zam left my office. Mindi has a series of meetings set up for me, first with the SLT, next with the software team and then she has the afternoon open for me to meet with people who want to have one-on-ones.

So I trundle down to the SLT conference room. As I come into the room I notice my name plate is where A'zam sits and Julia's is gone. Her seat is open. Apparently A'zam is going to let me decide how I'm going to reorganize the team. "Morning everyone." Murmur of responses. I take the seat at the head of the table. "Thanks for gathering at such short notice. I know you're all very busy, but I want to give you the big picture. We'll get back together at the end of the day to see where we are."

Wallace is the first to talk. "Congratulations. You've earned this opportunity."

I hold up my hand to stop the small talk. "We need to keep this short as I'm booked all day. The first thing you need to know is A'zam is already well along on diversifying the company. That's what he is going to focus on while he's asked me to keep the wheels on the traditional business."

"What kind of diversification?" Petra asks. I'm surprised he hasn't brought her into his confidence. He's written some big checks so she has to know why. Maybe she's just playing dumb.

"We're investing in the Singularity." In looking around the room, it's clear some know what I'm talking about and some do not. "A'zam and I have transitioned into robotic bodies. Only our consciousness came over. We're the same people but have robotic bodies."

"So you're a robot?" Alix asks. Obviously surprised.

"No. I'm the same person. I just have been freed of a biologic body."

"So that's how you've been able to push your teams into new technology and tools." Wallace realizes aloud.

My description is greeted with silence from the rest. So I push on. "We will be transitioning people which will make us the most advanced company in the world. This strategy will give us a huge advantage if we execute it right."

"What about the rest of us?" Petra asks.

"You'll need to have an individual conversation with A'zam about whether you wish to transition."

"And if we elect not to?" Desirae asks. Clearly not aware of the details of what A'zam was doing, although she is now seeing the bigger picture.

"That will be between you and A'zam. I can't make any guarantees at this level. This is all so new that we haven't thought through all of the implications."

"But we will all have a choice." Desirae continues.

I nod. "I can say it's definitely getting better. Just want you to know what's going on. Let's get back together on operations at four."

I leave the Senior Leadership Team and walk down the hall to my old Software team conference room. My team leads have all gathered. They applaud as I come in and I gesture thanks, but sit down.

"This will be short. Yes, I have additional responsibilities now, but I'm not going to leave you just yet. We're in the midst of a major shift. Not a good time to introduce more confusion. So Oriana and I'll continue on as we have until everyone is comfortable. Some people may take on additional responsibilities as we go in anticipation of a change in a few weeks. But for now, no change. Just keep working with your teams so everyone is ready."

"What about the rumors about you?" Oriana asks, even though she knows the answer.

"That I'm a machine and no longer human?" I smile. I see wide eyes as people didn't expect me to phrase it quite this way. "They're partially true. I would recommend you all to read <u>The Singularity</u> by Ray Kurzweil. Then we'll talk further."

The team acts like they have already come to this conclusion about me. So I plunge on. "I'll meet with each of you to discuss it soon. Now, you should know that A'zam is working to position AppleCore to be the leader in the new Singularity market. There's a lot going on, but you'll be pleased when you learn the details of how we will be the leaders in the changes that are coming."

"Did A'zam do the same thing you did?" Jermaine asks. I'm surprised he's the one. Didn't think he paid any attention to what was going on down the hall.

"Yes." I respond but don't know what else to say about it.

"Can we discuss this with our teams?" Oriana asks, apparently remembering my request not to discuss my change. "Everyone wants to know what's going on."

"Yes. Please feel free to discuss this with your teams after you've read the book, but sit on it until tomorrow."

"Why tomorrow?" Oriana asks.

"There will be a press release. So tomorrow it will be general knowledge."

"So they did you?" Moshe asks, curious he's the one.

"Yes."

"So why are you telling us today?" Jermaine again. "It will get out now, even if we ask people not to talk about it."

"A'zam decided to announce the reorganization today and he did. So it will definitely be out there." I'm thinking he's trying to force me not to go back by offering me more than I could ever want.

"So you didn't agree with his decision on the announcement?" Moshe trying to ferret out the politics behind the scenes.

"He didn't ask me, and he didn't have to. It was his prerogative."

Chapter Seventy-Five

Oriana is the first to come see me after the meeting. Mindi and I are at her desk talking about Landon and the difficulty she continues to have getting his attention because he's always working.

"Maybe he should do what you did." She wonders aloud probably to get my reaction. "Then he can work all night when I sleep."

"There's a couple factors we should probably discuss before you make that recommendation to him." I respond as I see Oriana waiting.

"Can we chat?" Oriana has taken up using some of my expressions. I don't know whether to be flattered or not.

"Sure." She goes into my office. I follow and close the door behind me.

"I understand why you chose not to promote me, but I wish we'd had a chance to discuss it before you announced it in the meeting." She's hurt. I didn't mean to hurt her. This is all going too fast even for me.

"You're right. I'm sorry, but I walked out of the meeting with A'zam into the SLT and into that meeting. I didn't have a chance to sit and talk."

"A text message would have been sufficient." Again she's right.

"Noted. I promise to discuss things if at all possible. You'll find the higher in the organization you go the less and less you really know about what's going on. It may seem you have all this power when you get to this level. There are some things you can do that no one else can. But you have to make huge important choices with less and less real information."

"What are you thinking about me? Are you planning to promote me?"

"I moved you into the VP slot despite you being Julia's choice to replace me. And I did that because you're the right person for the job. But you weren't and still aren't ready for the next level. This is a big jump from team lead. You have to learn to manage through people to the people who are doing the work. It's a much bigger change than you expect. If I just moved you and gone off to do my new job, I would have been setting you up to fail. I don't work that way. I wasn't trying to undermine you with the team, if that's what you're thinking."

"That thought did occur to me. You didn't even ask me for a final comment today."

"We didn't have a chance to coordinate before-hand. I didn't want to put you on the spot. Sorry."

"That's twice now you've said you're sorry, but it doesn't really make me feel any better about the situation." She's telling me I've hurt her more deeply than I thought.

"Do you want me to put out the memo that you're going to be the next SVP? I can do that, but there's more to the story we need to talk about."

"I'm liking this even less." She's afraid of what I'm about to tell her.

"You're going to have to make a choice about whether to transition like I have. We haven't talked about it because it's premature. You need a lot more information than you have right now. But part of the reason I didn't promote you today is what you decide will determine whether you will be able to keep the job."

"So you're saying you don't want to promote me and then have to demote me."

I nod. "As a nation there's been a lot of discussion about income inequality. But the new world is going to have brainpower inequality. Those who transition will get the top jobs, just because they'll be able to outthink those who don't."

Oriana has a warped smile. "I used to think I was the smartest person in the room. Even smarter than you in some ways. But now, you just make me feel so inferior."

"You're not inferior. You just haven't been upgraded yet." I try to put it into perspective. "But you're already seeing what it's going to be like. Right now I'm only an order of magnitude faster than you."

"Ten times faster? I didn't realize."

"I have to slow down to have a conversation. You saw that in the lab when A'zam and I went up on the clock speed. We didn't even realize we were doing it."

"No one in the room could follow you." She remembers.

"That's why even though deserving of the job as it is currently, I'm not going to move you into it, knowing the demands are going to change dramatically. Knowing you'll fail at negotiating the change because you've decided you'd rather have kids."

"Kids?" Oriana clearly hasn't considered the consequences. "What does that have to do with my job?"

"If you transition, that's one of the things you have to give up." I inform her.

"I've not ruled out wanting to get married and have a family. My parents are always bringing that up. Can I wait, have kids and then transition when they're grown?" She's trying to understand her options.

"You can. But the problem is when we transition we become

immortal. We live forever. We're no longer biological entities. When parts get old we replace or upgrade them. We don't die. And that means once we get into a job, we don't retire. We stay in that job. So as I see it, once you're moved down, you won't be able to come back up. None of the people above you will ever leave. You have a clear shot to be the SVP of software now. That's a good place from which to ride the crest of the wave. But once you move down, you may not even be able to get a job as a coder if they all transition."

"That's a pretty bleak future." Oriana decides.

"I just want you to understand the importance of the choice. This is a much harder decision for a woman than a man. I struggle with the fact that without a hormonal system I only experience rudimentary feelings. They're mostly memories of how I used to feel in similar situations. The doctors are trying to improve the software so they're more realistic. But they have a long way to go. I know I should have more empathy, but I don't feel it. I just remember I should. Then I have to make a decision about how do I evidence that. Same thing about tension. I don't feel it because you feel tension in your muscles. I don't have any muscles. It's a very different experience."

"What about orgasms?" She's thinking about no kids does that mean no sex?

"Not ready for prime time. But I wrote the first software update. So we'll see if I did a better job than the docs."

"You haven't tried it out yet?" Oriana seems surprised. Guess she thinks I'm pretty active in that regard.

"My love life is nothing to write home about." I inform her and she seems to think about that.

"I guess if I wrote the software I'd be sleeping with anyone just to experience it." Oriana gushes.

"I did sleep with anyone with the doc's software. I wasn't going to do that again."

"Raoul?" She asks. Guess Mindi told her he'd been by. Oriana knows about Raoul from before.

"He's gone now. That's the other thing about being immortal. You've got to have a good self-concept. I feel better about how I look now than in a long time."

"You should. There are times I don't recognize you. Like when you come wearing a dress like that. You look amazing." That word again – amazing.

"You should try it. Puts me in a good mood all day when I get compliments." Oriana nods apparently considering my advice.

But then she seems to sober. "For the first time in my life I don't feel adequate to do a job I've wanted. Particularly as you've indicated the SVP is going to morph into. If I had to make the decision to transition now, I don't think I'd do it."

"That's okay. You have a few weeks to think about it and ask more questions. But only a few weeks. Then I'm going to have to do something. I won't think less of you if you decide not to. But what's weighing most on your mind?"

"Not having kids. I guess I want to experience being a mother. Being in a caring relationship with a guy. That's something I always thought I'd have someday." Oriana seems to think about my suggestion. "I don't know. It's scary and hard to know what to do."

"Think about it. As I said you have some time." As she gets up to return to work I sadly think to myself she won't do it.

THE GHOST IN THE MACHINE

Chapter Seventy-Six

I stop by Windy's studio. I called and asked if I could come by. I feel a need to close the loop with her since she's the one who went to Dallas with me.

We hug as I come into her office. "So tomorrow's the day." She notes expecting me to tell her what I've decided as we take seats in her comfortable office chairs.

"It means a lot that you've been there for me through this whole change in my life. That you'd not tell the others what was going on with me, even though they were hurt I didn't tell them until I was ready."

Windy smiles, but looks apprehensive. "So what do you think? Ready to take the next step?"

"I've run out of time, so I can't delay any further. From what Dr. Woodall said, I've pushed as far as they're comfortable trying to put me back. After today the probability of success diminishes quickly."

"How can I help with your decision?" she asks.

"The world is going to change dramatically because of what I've unleashed. And not all of it for the better. I'm having a hard time knowing where things are going at least in the short term. In some respects I'd probably be better off if I transition and die in the next few years. I won't have to live it every day."

"But you're in a unique position to influence that more than anyone else. You're the one out on the frontier. People will listen to you because you're the first."

"Less than you'd think. That's what I've come to understand. The forces that are now driving this have an agenda that will remake society, completely. You're right. I am in a unique position and will influence some things. But I won't be able to control it."

Windy shakes her head. "That's not the point. You'll be a moderating force, even if you don't control it. No one person can, no matter what you do. We live in a dynamic society. We can't go back to what it was. That one's gone. We have to live in the present and prepare for the future." Windy hesitates, gathering her thoughts. "You've never backed down from any threat. You've exploited every opportunity. That's you. And I know your illness shook your self-confidence. But you still solved the problem, in a unique way, just like everything you do. You may have a robotic body, but you're still Dr. Sage Washington."

Chapter Seventy-Seven: Decision Day

I take a long hot shower, letting the water run over me the way I used to when I was stressed. The hot water would relax me. And even though it doesn't now, the memory of relaxing in a hot shower helps me think. But in reality I don't want to think about it. My logical self has already presented the pros and cons of the decision. I've read everything I can find on immortality, on robotics, on different predictions of what the world will become. But interestingly, few venture a view of more than a hundred years. It seems that we are such an unpredictable race that we can't imagine what we will create in the future. Twenty years seems to be the norm. A few go out as far as a hundred. No one longer.

I decide it's time to get ready, so I lather up and rinse so I smell all soapy. I shampoo and use conditioner on my hair so it will smell of tropical fruit. Once I finish rinsing I turn off the shower and towel dry, wrapping the towel around my hair while I pick out clothes. A simple black dress with a texture that makes it shimmer in sunlight. I love this dress, but I almost never wear it. Like so many things in my closet. I bought it on a whim. I knew it made me look great. But it just didn't seem to be what I wanted to look like at work. That was when I was hiding from myself. I didn't want anyone to notice me for anything other than my brain and work. I didn't want the rumors that I'd slept my way to the top, even though Julia said they were out there. I made sure no one at work had any interest in me sexually. But now I don't care about any of that. I want to look good. I slip into it, straighten it and take a look in the mirror. Perfect. Shows exactly what I want people to see and no more.

Pearl necklace, shiny black leather belt, purse and shoes and I'm out the door. As I'm coming down my steps Jackson is walking by. "Good morning." I call to him.

He stops and looks at my house. "Is this where you live?" He glances around. "No roses."

"That's my next project." I tell him as I come down the steps. "So off to visit your company?"

"I am."

He turns and looks in the direction of AppleCore. "On your way in to work?"

"Not today. I have a meeting out. You'll probably be reading about it later today. But I hope it doesn't scare you off. I'd very much like to see you."

I see interest and appreciation in his eyes. But I also see he's intimidated by who I am. If he thinks I'm scary now, he'll probably freak out when he reads about me later.

"I don't scare easily." He offers. I brighten with hope.

"I'm going to hold you to that. Despite what you read, believe me that I'm just a girl who's interested in getting to know you better." I don't know what else to say.

"I will call you." He smiles tentatively.

"I'm going to hold you to that, and if you don't call me? I've got your number."

I wink at him continuing my hopeful smile. We nod and go our separate ways.

The Googlecar picks me up and drops me at the hospital. I stand there looking at the four story granite and stone building. My thirty days went by in the blink of an eye, or so it seems.

I enter through reception but don't sign in since I have to tell Dr. Woodall of my decision before they'll start me into admitting. I walk down the hall to his office. In a moment I find myself standing in front of the receptionist. I don't have to tell her who I am. She's been expecting me. Leesa comes out and takes me down to the procedure room where I've had my upgrades. She leaves me there with, "Decision day. You know when we started down this path we didn't think anyone would want to go back. But Dr. Woodall had the good sense to tell us not to think everyone will love the experience. I hope you are. Good luck, whichever way you've decided. Dr. Woodall will be right in."

I look at the artwork on the walls. Post-modernist. Didn't know he was a student of period art. Interesting pieces, but all reproductions. Wouldn't expect anything else. A knock on the door and Dr. Woodall steps in the room. No Dr. Grayson. He wants this to be just one-on-one.

He takes a quick look at me and stops. "You're stunning."

I'm pleased by his observation. "I have a question for you." I respond.

"I should have expected at least one." He reflects.

"When are you going to transition?"

He drops his gaze and then looks away. After a moment of reflection he re-engages my eyes. "As of right now, I'm not planning to."

His response catches me off guard. I'm confused. "Why?"

"I'm a doctor. I see myself as a healer. I want to help people become well, who aren't."

"Okay, but if you're an immortal you should be able to help lots of people and help them better than you can as a mortal." I push back.

"Not necessarily." He hesitates before continuing. "Because of my pioneering with immortals, other patients wouldn't want to use me. Immortal transitions will only last for just so long. Then I'll just be another engineer retrofitting parts and supervising software upgrades. That's not me."

"Then why did you ever get involved with immortals?" I ask, still working his revelation through.

"If I didn't get involved to help terminal patients have an alternative to death, someone else would have gotten involved to create a super race that will dominate the rest of us."

I'm hearing A'zam's strategy. "You don't think that will happen anyway?"

Dr. Woodall sits down on the examining table like someone who'd just fought a round of boxing. "I hope not. But the genie is out of the bottle. I can't put it back. All I can do is treat as many patients as I can, like you, who don't have real choices. And I hope that man's better nature wins out."

I know it won't. The die is cast. A'zam will have his army of elite programmers within the year. The only real question is am I going to help him realize his dream or let someone else do it? "What do you want to do with your life?"

"You're an ideal person to transition. You see where this is going. You'll position yourself to benefit from the changes. If I were to transition? I'd be one of the people cast aside by people like you. And I don't mean that in a negative sense. That's just the way I see it."

"I could ensure you'd have an important voice." Why am I trying to convince him?

He considers my assurance, and then continues. "I have no idea what mankind will be like in a hundred years. Could the people who fought World War II have any idea what life would be like today? And the change will accelerate a hundred fold. No Sage. I know what and who I am. I don't want to be something else. I want to love. I want to laugh. I want to enjoy what makes us human as long as I can."

Do I want to take this journey alone since the people I want to be with aren't coming?

"So what's your decision?" Dr. Woodall asks.

The End.

About the Author

dhtreichler toured the global garden spots as a defense contractor executive for fifteen years. His assignments covered intelligence, training and battlefield systems integrating state of the art technology to keep Americans safe. During this time he authored seven novels exploring the role of increasingly sophisticated technology in transforming our lives and how men and women establish relationships in a mediated world.

Keep up with all of dhtreichler's latest work and essays at www.dhtreichler.com.

Also by dhtreichler

Emergence

Barely Human

The Great American Cat Novel

My Life as a Frog (novella)

Succession

Life After

The Tragic Flaw

Lucifer

The End Game

I Believe in You

Rik's

The Illustrated Bearmas Reader – Ralph's Ordeals

The First Bearmas

Made in the USA
Middletown, DE
23 December 2018